DAMIANO'S LUTE

R. A. MacAvoy

BANTAM BOOKS
TORONTO • NEW YORK • LONDON • SYDNEY • AUCKLAND

DAMIANO'S LUTE

A BANTAM BOOK   0 553 17155 0

First publication in Great Britain

PRINTING HISTORY
Bantam edition published 1985
Bantam edition reprinted 1988

Bantam Books are published by Transworld Publishers Ltd.,
61–63 Uxbridge Road, Ealing, London W5 5SA,
in Australia by Transworld Publishers (Aust.) Pty. Ltd.,
15–23 Helles Avenue, Moorebank, NSW 2170, and in New
Zealand by Transworld Publishers (N.Z.) Ltd., Cnr. Moselle
and Waipareira Avenues, Henderson, Auckland.

Printed and bound in Great Britain by
Hazell Watson & Viney Limited
Member of BPCC plc
Aylesbury Bucks

DAMIANO'S LUTE

Saara turned, and her green eyes widened.

'You!' she whispered, half to herself. 'Dark boy. Damiano!' One hand, small, pink and slender, made a circling gesture.

And the lute player knew her as well: Saara of the Saami, barefoot girl who was the greatest witch in all the Italies. Damiano knew her powers as well, having both suffered them and stolen them. But now, all the strength was hers and he had none at all.

Damiano felt himself step closer to the witch, though he did not know how he did it, not having a body with which to step.

'I knew you would come at last, Dami,' said Saara softly. 'Part of your soul is waiting here.'

He reached out one doomed, immaterial hand.

'Saara,' he whispered. 'Pikku Saara. You should not be so beautiful . . .'

Also by R. A. MacAvoy

and published by Bantam Books

To my mother

*Has he tempered the viol's wood
To enforce   both the grave   and the acute?
Has he curved us the bowl of the lute?*

EZRA POUND
"Pisan Cantos"

DAMIANO'S
LUTE

Prelude

Saara's song could make a garden out of a barren mountainside, or cover a hill of flowers with snow. When she sang, it was with a power that killed men as well as healed them. She could sing the winter and the summer, weeping and dancing and sleep. She could sing the clouds in their traces and the water in the bog.

She sang (this particular morning) a mighty song, replete with clouds and boglands, barren hills and lush, summer and winter, weeping, dancing and every other sort of earthly event. She sang from dim matins to high prime. At the end of this singing her voice was ragged; she was blue in the face and she saw spots before her eyes. But Saara's power of song had for once failed her, for she had not been able to sing one doe goat into a good mood.

And this was unfortunate, for Saara neither wanted to kill nor heal, and she desired neither carpets of snow nor flowers, but only the trust of this one ungainly creature, as companion in her loneliness.

Of all creatures (except perhaps for the cat) the goat is the hardest to sing-spell, having more than its fair share of natural witchery. Further, of all the changes one can work upon a goat, contentment is the most difficult state to obtain. To make things even more trying for Saara, this particular doe was encumbered by a dead winter coat she was too out of condition to shed, and was uncomfortably pregnant besides. Her gaunt sides resembled a hide-covered boat matted with brown algae. She wanted nothing to do with company, and had to be chased from the pineslope to the hill-dome crowned with birches before allowing herself to be befriended.

1

Yet this obdurate goat was all the company springtime had delivered to Saara amid the Alpine crocus and the purple hyacinth. Saara was not about to let the beast starve herself through obstinacy, not while Saara herself so needed some kind of voice in her ears besides her own.

But this was not strictly true—that she heard no other voice but hers. There was one other: the one that echoed in her head like her own thoughts, and yet was foreign to her, a voice soft and deep in slurred Italian. A voice which asked her questions.

"Where is he gone?" it asked her and, "Is it time to go home? Can I go home now?"

Never had Saara any answers for it.

This bodiless voice had been couched within her own head for over a year, serving only to make Saara feel as discontented as it was and more howlingly alone.

To distract her from these unanswerable questions she had tried work, until now her garden was blooming as never before and all her herb-pots were full. Then she had played with the weather, making the nearby villagers miserable. Following the visit of a brave delegate from Ludica, she curtailed experimentation and attempted to lose herself in her own woods, in bird shape. But that effort was least effective of all, for what reply has a wood dove to questions a Lappish witch cannot answer?

Now, as springtime took hold of the earth, Saara found nothing in all her wild refuge to interest her but this one strayed goat.

And the goat was disappointing. After spending all morning trying to entice her, Saara could approach just close enough to feed the doe a few willow withies and some fiddleheads of the new ferns. Most of these treats the animal spat out (as though to say she was no common nanny, to eat anything that happened to be green and given).

So Saara sang the goat a new song: a song of the first day in June, with a romping kid on the hilltop (instead of kicking in the belly), crisp sun in the sky and dry feet in the grass.

Saara sang in the strange tongue of the Lapps, which was her own. It made as much sense to the doe as any other tongue. The animal stared dourly at Saara with amber eyes the size of little apples, each eye with a mysterious black box in the center.

After receiving enough song-spelling to turn all the wolves in Lappland into milk puppies, the doe condescended to recline herself in the litter of spring bloom.

Saara was already lying down, flat on her stomach, head propped on hands, mother-naked. She had braided her hair into tails when she had her morning bath. It subsequently dried that way, so now, when she freed it from its little pieces of yarn, it gave her a mass of rippling curls which shaded from red to black to gold in a cascade down her petal-pink back.

She might have been a tall peasant girl of sixteen. Her body was slim and salamander-smooth, her face was dimpled and her green eyes set slantwise. With one foot pointed casually into the pale blue sky, Saara looked as charming and ephemeral as a clear day in March.

She had looked that way for at least forty years.

"Goat," she announced, aiming at the animal a green disk of yarrow, "you should eat more. For the baby."

But the goat was still chewing a sliver of green bark she had deigned to take ten minutes before. She flopped her heavy ears and pretended she didn't understand Lappish.

"Haven't you ever been a mother before?" continued Saara. "I have. A mother has to be more careful than other people. A mother has to think ahead."

The goat made the rudest of noises, and with one cloven hind hoof she scraped off a wad of musty belly hair, along with some skin. Then she bleated again and rolled over, exposing that unkempt abdomen to the sun.

"I could sing you a song that would make you eat every leaf off every tree in the garden—or at least as high as you could reach," the woman murmured, yawning. "But then you'd explode, and that, too, would be bad for the baby." Saara, like the goat, was made lazy by the sun. She turned over and watched her blue felt dress, freshly washed and dripping, swinging from the branch of a flowering hops tree. The wind played through the hair of her head, and through her private hair as well. She chewed a blade of grass and considered.

The goat bored her, though there was a certain satisfaction in helping the beast produce a sound kid. But

Saara came from a herding people, and did not regard livestock with sentimentality.

No, it was not Saara, but the child-voiced presence within her that wanted to talk to the goat. She could isolate this presence from herself-proper and feel its warm edges. It was a bundle of visions, memories, instincts and . . . and fire. It was a shadow with dark eyes and skin: a guest in her soul. It was young, eager, a bit temperamental. . . .

And undeniably full to bursting with sentiment. It liked to talk to goats.

Its name was Damiano Delstrego—or at least the presence belonged by rights to this Damiano, who had left it with her, like some foundling at a church door, and not part of his own being.

It was wearisome that he should do this, wearisome in the extreme. Sprawled flat on the sunny lawn, Saara let her song die away. Then, for an instant, she had the urge to rush at the sad, partial spirit she harbored, dispossessing it and recovering the unity of her own soul. But if she did that, she knew that Delstrego himself, wherever the fool had wandered (west, he had said), would be half dead, instead of only divided in two.

Despite the passage of seasons and the bitterness with which Saara and the Italian had fought on this very hill one day, killing two loves together (or maybe three), Saara remembered Damiano as he had knelt in the snow before her, weeping over the body of a little dog, and so she refrained.

Besides, the dark immaterial eyes with their sad questions trusted her and depended upon her, and Saara had been a mother.

And the most important reason that Saara did not evict her strange tenant was the same reason for which she courted the attentions of this unmannerly goat. She was lonely. For the first time in twenty years and more Saara was lonely.

She flipped onto her belly again and used her hands to thrust herself off the earth, snapping her feet up under her. The goat also sprang up with a startled bleat, flailing her broomstick legs in all directions. Sunlight kissed the top of Saara's nose—already slightly burned with such kisses—and polished her shoulders.

Once upright she stood still, panting. Suddenly she flinched, though nothing but sun and soft wind had touched her. At the peak of her irritation with the voice in her head, a realization had come to her. It was Damiano himself who was making her so unaccountably lonely. It was he whom she wanted to see: this son of a bad lineage, who had ripped her soul apart, and who afterward had spared no more than ten minutes out of his affairs to come and repair the damage he had done.

Leaving her with a burden it was his own business to bear: a voice inaudible and dark eyes unseen. It was Saara's immaterial baby, and would never grow up. After a year and more its longing for Damiano had become her own.

She ought to find him, she thought, and make him take it back. Whether he would take it or not, still she would be able to see the fellow again, and to discover what he was doing. For a moment she was quite intrigued, imagining where the dark boy ("boy" she called him always in her thoughts, to remind herself that she was no girl) might have gone to, and what strange languages he might be speaking, to what strange men. And women.

She had every right to seek him out, for he was a witch born, and so one of her kind.

For a few minutes Saara played with the idea of finding Damiano, but then uncertainty rose in her mind. It whispered to her that if Damiano had a matching desire to see her, this would have been plain in the regard of those dark eyes that looked at her through the darkest hours of night. If he thought of her as often as she thought of him, then surely she would know it, holding his soul as she did. But the eyes stared without seeming to know what they saw, and the voice which accompanied the eyes never spoke her name. It seemed to Saara that all the caring in this strange bond was on her side.

And even if Damiano would welcome her...even if time had changed his unpredictable Italian mind...to search him out through all the plains and ranges of the West would be an arduous task. It could be done, certainly, by a witch as experienced and learned as she was. But though Saara was powerful, she was a woman of the northern emptiness. She was disturbed by throngs of people, and the close dirt of cities disgusted her. And at bottom she was afraid of such a journey: most of all afraid of another meeting with Guillermo Delstrego's son.

Why should she want to visit Damiano anyway—a witch born with command in his voice and a mind that might learn wisdom, who had maimed himself, throwing away wisdom and birthright together? That denial was inexplicable: an act of perversion. So what if Damiano played the lute and sang a pretty song or two? Any Lappish witch could sing, and Damiano's southern songs had no power in them (save over the heart, perhaps. Save over the heart).

He was nothing but a moonchild, twin to the hopeless presence he had left Saara to tend. There were no signs he would grow into a full man. Without a single soul, he could not.

All this Saara repeated to herself, letting the long-sought doe goat wander off among the birches. If she reasoned long enough, surely she could talk herself out of a long journey that must only have disappointment at the end of it.

But as she reflected, her criticism became something else entirely. It became a certainty as strong as presage: a certainty that Damiano as she had last seen him (a creature neither boy nor grown man, splashing carelessly over the marshy fields) was all the Damiano there was destined to be. She shuddered in the sun. Whether foresight or merely foreboding, this certainty caused her surprising pain.

Saara sat wretchedly in the grass, undecided about her journey and about her own feelings, but reflecting in how many ways men disorder the lives of women.

Chapter One

The grass showed two colors, like a riffled deck of cards. All the early marguerites bobbed in waves, up and down the hills. Each hill had an oak or two, while the wealthier elevations also possessed orchards of apple or plum—bare-branched, but with twigs swollen purple, pregnant with Easter's bloom. Brambles crawled over the fields and on to the single trodden road. Even these brambles wore a charming infant green, and their withy limbs sprawled thornless. The sky was a cool washed blue, spittled with inconsequent clouds.

This landscape was Provence in high morning during the third month of the year. Nothing ill could be said about it, except that mornings had been warmer in spring, and mornings had been a bit drier. But this springtime would doubtless produce warmer and drier mornings in its own time.

So much was of nature. As for the man-made element which completes a landscape, there was available nothing but three roofless huts by the road (each with blue light shining out through the windows, clean as an empty mind) and a trundling green wagon with two young men on the seat, pulled by a black horse.

There was one other presence in the landscape, one which was neither quite artifactual nor quite a part of nature. That was a bundle that lay hidden in the long reeds spawned of a rivulet running between two hills. The bundle consisted of four human bodies, tied together with rope and lying damply dead. They had been there for two weeks, and the thrusting horsetails had grown around them closely, forcing themselves into the linen shirtsleeve, between the wooden button and the hand-darned hole, and along the mutely gaping lips. The bodies were blackish, but since it was only March, there were few flies buzzing.

These blindly ambitious reeds stood to the west of the road, and since the wind was blowing from the east, not even the nodding horse was aware he had passed a green charnel.

This was an impressive horse: not a destrier or battle charger (that close cousin to a plow horse) but a lean, light horse built for speed and cities, built for races down graded boulevards with the vendors all up and down the course selling ypocras and squares of marchpane. It had movement, this horse, as was evident by the way it lifted up its front feet just one razor cut before its back feet overstrode them. It had elegance, as it proclaimed in its clean, glistening throatlatch, its ironic black eye and supple crest. By its lean dished head and serpentine neck-set, one could see the horse carried Arab blood. By its size of bone, and the untrustworthy set of its eye, it was part Barb. It was a tall animal, deep-chested and long of shoulder. It was a horse to produce wagers.

And it seemed not only to be bred for races, but to be in training for them, for it was thin as a twist of black iron, and its head snaked left and right with energy, snapping its poor harness of rope.

But it was not, of course, training for any such thing, for racehorses do not train by pulling wagons.

This wagon, like the knotted-together harness, did not fit the quality of the animal that pulled it. The harness was made up from bits and pieces: some of leather, some twine, some of velvet ribbon. The wagon (theoretically green) had a number of side-slats which had never been painted and were different in length and cut from one another, as well as from the green boards. Along with these went places on the vehicle's high sides and back which offered excellent visibility into the interior. The wagon was nearly empty and made a great deal of noise as its wooden wheels rolled over the earth.

The driver of this rolling drum was as black of hair and eye as his horse, and his skin was burned dark, as though the man had been in the elements all winter. This impression was furthered by his woolen tunic, which was

colored too delicate a rose to be a product of the dyer's
art. In fact, this color had been produced in the same
manner as the wearer's tan. This young man was as thin as
his horse, and he, too, possessed some degree of elegance
and movement (though not of the sort to cause men to
wager money). Like his horse, he was tall but not wide,
and like his horse he nodded. But where the animal
nodded to his own hooves' rhythm, the driver appeared to
nod asleep.

"You know he shouldn't oughta *do* that." The still
younger fellow beside the driver spoke in coarse North
Italian. This one's hair was red, knife-trimmed and carefully finger-curled. He wore a dagged jerkin of too many
colors to list. He was, if such a thing is possible, thinner
than either the horse or the driver beside him. He infused
his few words with a degree of rancor impossible for the
casual listener to understand, unless the listener first
knows that these two travelers were really close friends,
who had spent too much time in close company with one
another.

The driver of the wagon sat blinking for a moment, as
though he were translating his companion's words from a
foreign language. His eyes were fixed glassily on the
gelding's swishing croup. He was thinking in a passive and
random fashion about goats.

At last he answered. "It doesn't matter, Gaspare. The
worst he will do is unravel the ribbons, and then I can tie
them up again." The black horse chose this moment to
give a particularly doglike shake, which freed the singletree end of a length of rope and sent it snapping over his
back. At this sudden attack he bolted forward, and his
passengers skidded into the hard back of the hard wagon
seat. Hard.

"Poor Festilligambe," muttered Damiano. "He was
never meant to pull a load. And he has little enough to
please him these days, lean as he is." The dark young man
was suddenly stricken with a desire to gather leaves and
twigs for the gelding, although he knew quite well that
horses don't eat leaves and twigs.

When one's companion smarts under a weight of
self-pity, it is not a good idea to send one's condolence in
other directions. It does not promote the peace.

"Poor Festilligambe!" hiccoughed Gaspare. "Festilli-gambe? He alone among us . . ." Emotion choked the boy, and his face grew as red as his hair. "If I could live on the grass by the road, I'd have no more complaints."

Gaspare's face was singular in its parts. His nose had an aquiline height of bridge and narrowness along its length which any man of birth might have been proud to call his own. His eyes were large and soulful and his complexion was milk and (more usually) roses. His mouth was mobile.

Yet in all these features there was no harmony, but rather constant war, for the nose was too long and sharp for the shape of his face and the eyes were too big for anyone's face, and his mouth—well, since it was never without a word, a twitch or a grimace, it was very hard to say anything about Gaspare's mouth.

He was just fourteen, and he hadn't had a good dinner in far too long.

"Nebuchadnezzar did," replied the dark youth, refer-ring to the possibility of living on grass. His voice was distant, his less ambitious but more proportionate features almost slack. "Or it is said that he did. But I don't recall that he was happy eating grass."

Gaspare swelled. "I'm not happy, eating nothing!" Out of sulks he yanked a lock of hair that tumbled over his right ear. The spit curl went limp. His finger coiled it again, tighter. The boy's head looked heavy, as will a round child-face that has grown too thin over its bones. Both his leanness and the dandified clothing he affected made Gaspare appear older than he was. Consequently his tempers seemed more scandalous.

Damiano lifted one eyebrow. His form was also drawn out by fortune. In fact, he looked almost consumptive, with his face reduced to dark eyes he could hardly hold open and a red mouth that yawned. "*Hein?* My friend, I'm sorry. I would like to eat, too. But don't begrudge the horse his horseness; if he had to eat bread we'd have been carrying our goods on our backs all the way from the Piedmont."

Gaspare could say nothing to this, and so was made even unhappier.

Even in March, the warmth of noonday made wool

itchy. Young Gaspare scraped his bottom against the seat, first right, then left. He was an unusually sensitive boy, both in spirit and in skin, and since he was also an unusually poor one, his sensitivities were an affliction to him.

"Surely in such lovely countryside, we'll find a town soon," said Damiano, though the forced heartiness of his reply betrayed a lack of skill at lying. "Or perhaps an abbey, where we may be fed without having to put on a show."

"Or a rich penitent on pilgrimage," Gaspare continued for him. ". . . strewing gold coins. Or a road leading up to heaven, white as milk, with angels beside it ranked like poplar trees—angels playing flageolets and cornemuse, but the angels will be made of cake, of course, and the pipes all of breadsticks, and at the top of the road will be a piazza paved with bricks of sweet cakes, and a gate of crystallized honey.

"By the gate will stand Saint Pietro, dressed like a serving man, with a napkin over one arm and a wine cup in each hand, bowing and smiling. He will not stop us, but will thrust a cup lovingly into our hands. Then the sky will be all around us, floating with white-clothed banquet tables like so many clouds, and piled on each of them olives, puddings, pies, sweet and peppered frumenties . . ."

"I despise frumenties," murmured the driver, rousing a bit. The black gelding had maneuvered the wagon so far to the left of the road that his hooves scythed the bright and turgid grasses, and now he reached down for them in full rebellion. Damiano's eyes stayed open long enough for him to pull the reins right.

They were strange, those eyes of Damiano. They were dark and soft and heavily feathered, and in all ways what one desired and expected in a Latin eye. They were the sort of eye which is obviously created to house mysteries, and yet their only mystery was that they seemed to hide no mysteries at all, no more than the dark, soft eyes of a cow at graze. When Gaspare looked deeply into Damiano's eyes (as happened most frequently when Gaspare was angry) he sometimes had the fantasy that he was looking straight through the man and at an empty sky

behind. At those times the little hairs stood up on Gaspare's
arms.

Gaspare's own pale green eyes flashed. "Well, do not
be alarmed, musician, for I don't think you're about to be
offered frumenty. Nor olives, nor breads, nor roast pork,
nor wine, nor..."

"Do be quiet," sighed the other, his loose shoulders
slumping in exaggerated, Italian fashion. "This kind of talk
doesn't help. If you could think of something constructive
to do about it..."

Gaspare set his jaw, watching the last of the three
ruined huts pass behind the wagon and be gone. "I have
thought of something constructive. I told you, we should
eat what God has put in our path."

The weary black eyes lit with amusement. "God sent
that wether on to our road? Might He not also have sent
the shepherd to follow? In which case our skins might have
been stretched over a door alongside the sheepskin."

"We saw no shepherd," spat Gaspare.

Damiano nodded. "Ah, true. But then we killed no
sheep!" He spoke with a certain finality, as though his
words had proven a point, but there was something in his
words which said also that he did not care.

Gaspare's expressive eyes rolled. (He, too, was Italian.)
"I wasn't even talking about the sheep, musician. Nothing
to get us in trouble with the peasants. I meant hares and
rabbits. Birds. The wild boar..."

Damiano peered sidelong. "Have you ever seen a
wild boar, Gaspare?"

The redhead responded with an equivocal gesture.
"Not...close up. You?"

Damiano shook his head, sending his own black mane
flying. His hair was so long and disordered it was almost
too heavy to curl. "I don't think so. Though I'm not sure
how it would differ from a domestic boar." With one hand
he swept the hair back from his face, in a gesture that also
had the purpose (vestigial, by this time) of throwing back
the huge sleeves of a gown of fashion.

"But, my friend, how have I ever stopped you from
availing yourself of these foods? Have I hidden your knife,
perhaps, or prevented you from setting a snare? Have I by
word or deed attempted to discourage you...?"

Gaspare broke in. "I can't do it . . . when you won't."
Nothing about his colleague bothered him half so much as
Damiano's educated vocabulary and poetical syntax. These
mannerisms struck Gaspare like so many arrows, and he
never doubted that Damiano used them that way to keep
Gaspare (guttersnipe that he was) in his place. Gaspare
would certainly have used such words in that fashion, if
he'd known them. Yet at the same time the boy was as
proud of Damiano's learning as if it had been his own.

Gaspare's unspoken respect for his partner bordered
on religious reverence, and he lived under a fear that
someday Damiano would discover that. This thought was
insupportable to the haughty urchin.

Damiano, of course, had known Gaspare's real feelings since the beginning of their partnership. But that
knowledge didn't make the boy any easier to take. The
musician looked away, resting his gaze upon the purple
horizon. He didn't like quarrels. He didn't have Gaspare's
energy to spend on them. "I don't know how to set a
snare, Gaspare," he mumbled, and let the breezes of
Provence wind through his vacant mind.

The boy snorted. "But would you set one if I showed
you how? Would you pluck a lark, or clean a rabbit, or
even eat one if I cooked it for you?" He forestalled his
friend's slow headshake. "No, of course you wouldn't.
Well, that's why I can't, either—or I'll be a bloodstained
shambles-man in my own eyes. And so we'll both starve to
death."

Damiano gently corrected the horse. He yawned,
partly because of the sun through a woolen shirt, and
partly because discussions like this exhausted him. He
wished there were some way he could communicate to
Gaspare how like a blind man he felt, or perhaps like one
who could not remember his own name. Not that Damiano
was blind (only nearsighted), and not that he had forgotten
anything. But he had been a witch and now was one no
longer, and that was more than enough. Surely if the boy
understood . . .

But all he could bring himself to say was: "Please,
Gaspare. I get so tired."

His lack of response brought the flush stronger into

Gaspare's face. "We will starve, and it will be *all your fault!*" he shouted, in an effort to be as unfair as possible.

Damiano did not look at him.

Gaspare's color went from red to white with sheer rage. That he should have to follow this lifeless stick from place to place like a dog, dependent upon him for music (which was both Gaspare's living and his life), for companionship, and even for language (for Gaspare spoke nothing but Italian)... it was crushing, insupportable. Tears leaked out of Gaspare's eyes.

But tears were not Gaspare's most natural mode of expression. Convulsively he grabbed Damiano's arm and drew it to him. With a canine growl he sank his teeth into it.

Damiano stood up in the seat howling. Gaspare tasted blood but he did not let go, no more than any furious terrier, not until the wooden handle of the horsewhip came crashing down on his head and shoulders.

Damiano then threw himself down from the seat of the moving wagon, clutching his bleeding arm and dancing over the shoulder of the road. The gelding pattered to a halt and turned its elegant, snakelike head.

Above, on the high wooden seat, young Gaspare sat, red as a boiled crab, and puffing like a bellows.

Damiano stared, slack-jawed, at him. "You *bit* me!" He repeated it twice, wonderingly. "Why?"

Suddenly Gaspare was all composure, and he knew the answer to that question as he spoke it. "I wanted to see if you were still alive at all. You don't act like it, you know, except when you play the lute. I thought maybe you died last winter, during the battle of San Gabriel, and had not yet noticed.

"A man gets tired," Gaspare concluded, "of talking with the dead."

Still gaping, Damiano pulled his woolen sleeve up. "Mother of God," he whispered, staring at the neat oval of broken skin, where stripes of crimson were welling over the bronze. "You have bitten me like you were a dog! Worse, for no dog has ever bitten me." His head went from side to side in shocked, old-womanish gestures, and his eyes on the wound were very large.

Gaspare sat very tall on the wagon seat. The yellow

and green of his dagged jerkin outlined the ribs over his emotion-puffed chest. "Best work I've done in weeks," he stated. "Should have seen yourself hop."

Then he settled in the seat, like a bird shifting its weight from wings to perch. "You've been unbearable, lutenist. Absolutely unbearable for weeks. No man with a spirit could endure your company."

Receiving this additional shock, Damiano let his wounded arm drop. "Unbearable? Gaspare! I haven't even raised my voice to you. *You're* the one who has been howling and complaining since we hit the French side of the pass...."

"Exactly!" The boy thrust out one knobbed finger. "Even though it is to meet *my* sister we are traveling across France and Provence in cold, dry Lent. It is me who complains, because I am a man. And you bear with me with a saintly, condescending patience which undermines my manhood." Now Gaspare stood, declaiming from the footboard (which wobbled) of the high seat.

"To err is human. Yes! I am a human man and proud of it! To forgive...and forgive, and forgive...that is diabolic."

Suddenly the older fellow's dark face darkened, and he kicked a wheel as he muttered, "Did you have to say that—exactly that, Gaspare? Diabolic? A man can also get tired of being called a devil."

Gaspare snorted and wiped his nose on his long, tight sleeve. "No fear. You possess no such dignity. You are the unwitting—and I do mean *unwitting*—tool of wickedness, designed to lead me to damned temptation! By Saint Gabriele, Damiano, I believe you lost your head with that cursed Roman General Pardo in the town hall cellar, for you've been nothing but a ghost of a man since."

Damiano stared at Gaspare, and then stared through him. Five seconds later, for no perceivable reason, he flinched. His uninjured arm gestured about his head, dispersing unseen flies. Without a word he stepped to the side of the wagon and climbed into it through one of its large holes. A moment later he was out again, carrying a bundle with a strap and another bundle wrapped in flannel. The first he slid over his back (it made a tinkling noise) and the second he cradled with motherly care. Then

he strode off and disappeared to Gaspare's eyes, hidden by
the bulk of the wagon.

Gaspare heard the receding footsteps. He stood and
hopped from one foot to the other. Failing to see Damiano
appear around the wagon, he sprang gracefully to the dirt.

It was true. The lutenist was leaving, plodding back
up the road toward Lyons, Chamonix and the Alps. Without another word, he was leaving. By conscious effort, the
boy turned his sensation of cold desolation into his more
accustomed red anger. He caught up with Damiano in ten
athletic bounds.

"Hah!" he spat. "So you think to stick me with that
unmanageable swine of a horse? Well, it won't work. The
crows can pick his ribs for all I care!" And he executed a
perfect, single-point swivel, flung up his right arm in a
graceful, dynamic and very obscene gesture, and marched
back down the road west and south. His small, peaked face
was flaming.

Damiano, in his outrage, had forgotten Festilligambe,
and he now felt a bit foolish. His less acrobatic steps
slowed to a shuffling halt, while he heard Gaspare rummaging through the wagon. At last, when the noise had
faded, Damiano came back.

The horse, while still standing between the traces,
stared curiously over his shoulder at Damiano. He had a
marvelous flexibility in that neck, did Festilligambe. Damiano
tossed his gear back into the wagon and carefully deposited
the lute into the niche in one corner which he had built for
it. (This corner had no holes.)

Slowly and spiritlessly Damiano walked over to the
horse. He examined the knotted, makeshift harness and
the places where it had worn at the beast's coat. Festilligambe
lipped his master's hair hopefully, tearing out those strands
which became caught between his big box teeth. Damiano
didn't appear to notice.

"I shouldn't be doing this to you, fellow," he whispered,
stroking the black back free from dust. "You are no cart
horse. It's clean straw and grain for which you were born.
And fast running, with victory wine from silver cups."
Thick horse lips smacked against the young man's face,
telling him what the gelding thought about silver cups.
His near hind foot suggested they start moving again.

Having no ideas of his own, Damiano was open to such suggestion. He boosted himself up to the driver's seat and reached for the whip he had dropped after drubbing Gaspare. Carefully he pulled up his sleeve, bunching it above the elbow to allow the sun free access to the neatly punched bite on his forearm.

The horse did not wait for a signal to start.

What a misery that boy was. Squatting passively on the plank of wood, Damiano let Gaspare's offenses parade by, one by one.

There had been that housewife in Porto. She had had no business to call the boy such names, certainly, but you cannot drive through a town cracking strange women on the head and expect to get away with it. Not even when they are bigger than you. Especially not then. She had almost broken the lute over Damiano's shoulders (though he was by rights not involved in the exchange of insults, only easier to catch than Gaspare).

And in Aosta they had come near to fame, or at least a comfortable living, playing before the Marchioness d'Orvil, until Gaspare ruined things and nearly got them sent to prison with that sarabande he insisted on dancing. In front of the marquese, besides. Damiano blushed even now, wondering how he could have missed seeing all winter that the dance was obscene. Gaspare had no delicacy.

But he was touchy as a *condottiere*, where slights to his small self were concerned. And jealous. Though he never let Damiano forget the young man's inexperience with women, Gaspare's attitude was as possessive as it was mocking, and his green eyes watched Damiano's every move. Let the lute player offer one gallant word to a female of any description, whether it be a girl with the figure of a poker or a mother with a dozen children, and Gaspare purely trembled with agitation.

You'd think he was a girl himself.

And hey! Gaspare was even jealous of the horse. That was what lay behind his silly resentment of the animal. He was jealous.

Heat laid a dry hand against Damiano's face. The clouds had dissolved in the sky. The black gelding trotted now easily, ears a-prick, long head bowing left and right to an invisible audience. It was as though this trip to Provence were Festilligambe's idea, not Damiano's. Or rather not Gaspare's, Damiano corrected himself. Damiano had no pressing desire to meet Evienne and her thieving clerk of a lover in Avignon on Palm Sunday. It was Gaspare who had arranged the rendezvous and set the time. (And what a time! How they had gotten through the snows of the pass at that season was a story in itself, and not a pleasant one. It had almost done for the lute, not to mention the three living members of the party.)

Gaspare babbled endlessly about his sister, calling her harlot, slut and whore with every breath and always in tones of great pride. He had badgered Damiano into crossing the Alps two months too early, just to keep faith with this sister with whom he was sure to squabble again in the first hour.

There was nothing wrong with Evienne, really. She had a warm, ripe body dusted with freckles, a wealth of copper hair and a strong desire to please.

But when Damiano compared her to another woman of his acquaintance—a lady whose tint was not so rare or figure quite so generous—all Evienne's color and charm faded into insignificance.

Next to Saara of the Saami, all of female humanity came out second best, Damiano reflected ruefully.

And when Gaspare met Evienne again, along with her lover and pimp, Jan Karl, the boy was sure to learn more pickpocket's tricks. He was certain to wind up hanged as a thief, if he didn't die brawling.

Damiano shut off this silent arraignment of his musical partner, without even touching on Gaspare's salient vices of gluttony and greed. It was an arraignment too easy to draw up, and rather more pathetic than damning. The upset of spirits it was causing in the lutenist was making his arm throb harder.

So what if Gaspare was nothing but trash, and daily becoming worse. Who had ever said otherwise—Gaspare himself?

No. Especially not Gaspare.

And there was the truth that disarmed Damiano's argument. Gaspare expected nothing but failure from himself—failure, acrimony, wounded pride. He *knew* he was difficult to get along with, and he accepted that Damiano was not. Therefore he considered it Damiano's responsibility to get along with him, as it is the responsibility of a hale man to support a lame companion, or a sighted man to see for a blind.

And this last tirade, in which the boy had accused Damiano of exactly nothing, had been built on a bizarre foundation of humility. For by letting the lutenist know how disappointed in him Gaspare was, he also let him know how much he had expected of him.

Damiano's head drooped. Grass-broken road swept by below the cracked footboard. His fine anger dissolved with the shreds of clouds, leaving a puddle of shame.

The truth was he didn't really like Gaspare. Not wholeheartedly, except when the music gave them a half-hour's unity, or during the rare moments when they were both rested and fed. Gaspare was simply not very likable.

But the problem was Damiano didn't like anyone else wholeheartedly either, except of course one glorious angel of God. And that took no effort.

Gaspare had been right, Damiano admitted to himself. He had failed the boy. He had given him very little, on a human level, since the beginning of winter. Aside from his music, Damiano had felt he had nothing to give.

And wasn't the lute enough? Damiano rubbed his face with both hands. God knew it was work to study and play as hard as he had done for the past year. It required concentration, which was the hardest of works, as well as the best.

But no. Damiano might be a madman about his instrument, but he was not so deluded as all that. One could not pass off a *bourrée* as an act of friendship, any more than one could disguise as human warmth what was mere good manners and a dislike of conflict.

And what had he taken from Gaspare in exchange for that counterfeit friendship? Rough loyalty, praise, energy, enthusiasm. . . .

Once Damiano had had his own enthusiasm. Enthusiasm and a dog. The dog died, and then the enthusiasm, and he had had only Gaspare.

Eyes gone blind to the spirit, ears gone deaf to the natural world: it seemed to Damiano he had given as much as a man ought to be asked to give, for the sake of right. He ought to be allowed some peace now, for as long as he had left.

But how could he say that to Gaspare, who had never possessed what Damiano had now lost?

Suddenly it occurred to him to wonder which way the boy had gone. Surely he would continue to Avignon, to Evienne. Damiano raised his eyes.

A minute later and Gaspare would have been out of sight, or at least out of the lutenist's poor sight. But he was visible in the far distance ahead, a bobbing splotch of motley, jogging along faster than the horse's amble. Frowning, Damiano tossed his hair from his face. Gaspare's physical endurance inspired awe. Doubtless he would make it to the city alone, and probably he would go quicker and plumper than he would have in the lutenist's company.

Then truth stung Damiano's black eyes. Beloved or no, Gaspare was necessary to him. In a manner totally removed from the question of like or dislike, Damiano Delstrego needed Gaspare because the boy believed in him—as a lutenist, as a composer.

As a man of possibilities.

Damiano did not believe he was the best lutenist in the Italies, any more than he had believed himself to have been the most powerful witch in the Italies—when he had been a witch. After all, he had only been playing (obsessively) for a handful of years. But Gaspare did believe that, and more. Gaspare was the first and only person in Damiano's life who was convinced of Damiano's greatness.

It had been at first embarrassing, and then intoxicating, to have someone so convinced.

It had become necessary.

The world was filled with strangers. Gaspare, with all his prickliness and his ignorance (ignorant as a dog. Unreliable as a dog in heat), had become necessary to the musician.

Damiano asked the horse for more speed, snapping the whip against the singletree. Festilligambe bounded forward, honking more like a goose than a horse. Harness snapped. The wagon boomed alarmingly.

This was no good. Two miles of this speed and the mismatched wheels would come off.

Damiano cursed the wagon. He'd rather be riding. But if he was to travel with Gaspare again, he'd need the ramshackle vehicle. Perhaps he ought to catch Gaspare on horseback, and then return to the wagon.

But what had become of the boy? Damiano rose up in the seat, bracing one large-boned hand against the backboard and one ragged boot against the footrest. He jounced, clothes flapping on his starved torso like sheets on a line. His black screws of hair bounced in time with the wheels' squeal, except for one patch in the back which sleeping on branches had left matted with pinesap. He squinted in great concentration.

The road opened straight before him, swooping south and west, losing elevation as it went. Grass gave way to ill-tended fruit trees and bare stands of alder, and the wet ground was hummocked with briar and swamp maple, which twined like ivy. Less inviting countryside, was this, certainly. The clouds had returned and were multiplying, or at least swelling. In the distance appeared what might have been a village. (Or it might have been rock scree. Damiano was always tentative about things seen in the distance.)

But nowhere could he spy a lean shape of yellow and red and green, neither floating over the grass nor angrily trampling the briars. No Gaspare on the road or among the swamp maple. Not even a suspiciously bright bird shape amid the alder groves.

Damiano's curse began quite healthily, but trailed off into a sort of ineffectual misery. For seeking people missing or lost he was even less equipped than the average man. He had always before known where people were, known it literally with his eyes closed—been able to feel a distant presence like a breath against his face. But he didn't know how to *look* for a boy, using patience and reason, going up one country wagon rut and down the next. He felt that at twenty-three he was too old to learn.

As a matter of fact he felt too old for many activities, and the best life had to offer was most certainly sleep. As his mind spun in gripless circles around the problem of Gaspare, his lower lids crawled upward and his upper lids sank downward until his rebellious eyes closed themselves.

His hands, too, had snuck up one another's sleeve and hidden in the warmth.

So little was pleasant in this life, and most of what there was turned out to be a mistake. Magic was self-delusion and war just a patch of bloody snow. Even one's daily meat was the product of violent death, while love . . .

The gray stone walls, burying a nun. A gray stone grave on a hillside. A small grave in a garden without a stone.

Only music was uncorruptible, for it meant everything and nothing. In the past year Damiano had done little but play on the lute.

His present lute was his second, successor to the little instrument smashed in Lombardy and buried beside the bones of an ugly bitch dog. This lute boasted five courses and its sound carried much farther than that of his first pretty little toy. But it was shoddily made and did not ring true high on the neck, no matter how Damiano adjusted the gut fretting. In only fifteen months' play he had worn smooth valleys along the soft-wood fretboard.

But now he didn't want to play. There was no one to hear but the horse, who was tone deaf and appreciated no rhythms save his own. Besides—Damiano's hands would not come out of their hiding.

The sun winked in and out of clouds; he felt it against his face, like a memory of his missing witch-sense. His head filled with the mumbling voice which was always present if he allowed himself to listen.

Sometimes it broke into his dreams, waking him. More often, like now, it droned him to sleep. Either way, he never understood it.

And there came odd images, and thoughts. Naked women (a radiant, young naked woman: Damiano knew her name) he could understand, but why should his head be filled with concern for goats?

He let such concerns fade with the sunlight.

The horse did not know his driver was asleep. He needed neither whip nor rein to urge him to do what he liked most to do, which was to keep going. He lifted his feet, not with the exaggeration of fashion, but with racing efficiency. He nodded right and left to his invisible audience. His high, Arabic tail swept the air.

He thought about oats, and never wondered why he should do so.

Suddenly Festilligambe recognized something much better than oats. Philosophical amazement caused him to stumble, and his trot became a shuffle. A halt. He craned his long neck and regarded the crude seat of the wagon, his whinny pealing like bells.

Damiano woke up smiling, in the presence of light. His hands leaped free of his shirt and he hid his poor, inadequate eyes behind them. "Raphael," he cried. "I'm so glad to see you—or almost to see you."

Between the mortal's shut fingers leaked an uncomfortable radiance. Damiano turned his head away, but as if in effort to counteract this seeming rejection, he scooted closer to the angel on the seat. Meanwhile, the horse was doing his level best to turn around in his traces.

"I'm sorry, Dami," said the Archangel Raphael, settling in all his immateriality next to Damiano. "I don't know what to do about that."

Damiano gave a sweeping wave of his hand, accompanied by one scornful eyebrow. "Don't think about it, Seraph. It is my little problem. At least I can hear you perfectly, and that is more than most people can. Besides, I remember well what you look like." He opened his eyes, staring straight ahead.

And he sighed with relief. It was pleasant to talk to the angel again. Very pleasant, especially now when he was feeling so completely friendless. But conversation was one thing, and study another. Today Damiano was not in the mood for a lesson.

Yet Raphael was his teacher, and so Damiano felt some effort was incumbent upon him. "I've been saving a question for you, Raphael. About that *joli bransle* we were toying with last week."

"The *bransle?*" A hint of surprise rested in the angelic voice. "You want to talk about the *bransle* right now?"

"I was wondering if I ought to play those three fourth intervals in a row. Or not, you know? It's not like they were fifths, which would be too old-fashioned and dull, but still, I feel the measure would go more if I descended in the bass."

There was a moment's silence, along with a rustle like

that of a featherbed. Then the corona of radiance said,
"Dami, what are you going to do about Gaspare?"

Involuntarily, Damiano glanced over. Silver filled his
eyes, cool as starlight, chillingly cool, set off by seas of
deep blue. Damiano was falling, fearlessly falling, out into
depths of time.

There was a curtain of silence. He tore it.

And the brilliance then was white-hot and immense.
It was not infinite, but full within limits set perfect for it,
shining round and glad, and it would have been meaningless to suggest this brilliance might want to be larger or
smaller than it was, for it was glowingly content. And it
was a brilliance of sound as much as of light: wild sound,
like trumpets in harmony, yet subtle as the open chords of
a harp. It drowned Damiano. His problems dissolved.

"Dami," came the soft, cool, ordinary voice. "Dami.
Damiano! Close your eyes or I'll have to knock you off the
wagon."

Eventually the young man obeyed, dropping his head,
clutching the seatback as though fighting a formidable wind.
"I . . . I . . . ooof! Forgive me, Raphael. It leaves me a little
sick."

The angel emitted a very melodic sort of whine.
"That's terrible, Dami. What is the matter with me that I
affect you so badly?"

Through his undeniable nausea, Damiano had to laugh.
"The matter with you, old friend? Don't worry about it.
It's what I get for being neither witch nor truly simple.
And the sickness I feel happens only as I come back to
myself."

He sat upright once more, and reached out at random
to slap an immaterial shoulder. "It's good for my music,
Seraph. You have no idea how much I learn each time I
get sick looking at you."

Raphael's sigh was quite human. He plucked at
Damiano's head. "You have sap in your hair," he observed.

Damiano wiggled his fingers into the snarl. "I know.
Gaspare wanted to cut it out. That seemed a very radical
solution to the problem, so I . . ."

"Gaspare," echoed the angel. "What are you going to
do about Gaspare?"

Damiano bristled his brow. "How can I tell you? He

just ràn off not an hour ago. Maybe he'll come back. And how did you know about that anyway, Raphael? You were listening?"

Wings ruffled again. "Yes, I was." After a few seconds' silence on the human's part, Raphael added, "Shouldn't I listen?"

Damiano shrugged. "It makes me feel I have to be always on my best behavior, that's all."

This time it was the angel's turn to pause. "Best behavior? Is that like your best clothes? I'm flattered that you would want to wear it for me, Dami, but you needn't. And if you wish, I will stop listening.

"In fact"—and the angel's voice grew even softer, (softer, slower and indefinably droll)—"I ought to send you a note beforehand, each time I visit, so that you can be wearing your best behavior. And your best clothes."

Damiano snorted, smiling wryly. "I *am* wearing my best clothes. They have become indistinguishable from my worst. Like my behavior." There was something harsh in the laugh with which he followed this.

"I'm going to follow Gaspare down the road, Raphael. All the way to Avignon, if need be." His smile grew tighter as he added, "And I'll even apologize to the little weasel, when I find him.

"*That* is what I'm going to do about Gaspare. Does it make you happy, my teacher?"

Before Raphael could reply that that *did* make him happy, the conversation was interrupted by a huge crack and snap of wood, followed by a pained whinny, as the frustrated horse finally succeeded in turning around in place. The sting of the trace breaking at his right sent Festilligambe into a series of stiff-legged jumps which destroyed the last of the makeshift harness. Then, as Damiano bit his fingers in consternation, the gelding laid its long head on the footrest of the wagon and gazed up at the angel, moaning like a forge.

"There goes the wagon," cried Damiano. "So much firewood!"

"I'm sorry," said the angel (for the second time that day).

Damiano's gesture was magnanimous and very Italian. "Forget it! He's my horse. Besides—how can you be sorry

about anything when you're a perfect spirit?" He swung
down from the seat and marched forth to release the horse
from its tangles.

"I'm not perfect," replied the angel, almost hurt in
tone. "That's very bad theology. Only the Father is perfect. I am only sinless. And it is because of me this lovely
fellow has broken all his straps. Let me fix it."

Damiano stopped with two handfuls of rope. The
horse's gently swishing tail was flogging his kneecap.
"Fix . . . the harness? But you are not to become involved
in human affairs, remember?"

Raphael glided over the horse's head and hung in the
air for a moment before alighting. Damiano looked down.

"True," came the angel's voice from above, "but that is
a complex matter, my friend. If I caused the accident, then
am I not becoming more deeply involved if I neglect to
repair the damage?" The angel's voice now issued from
beside Damiano, who flinched his face away.

After a moment he asked, "Is it done yet, Raphael?"

Wings clapped together in what might have been
consternation. "Done, Dami? I have scarcely begun. There
are a lot of knots here, you know."

The young man dared a peek at one of the broken
lines, to find that the whole thing had been retied: the flax
joined to the hemp rope with a neat series of square knots,
while the leather (which had to slide) had been linked in
with a bowline.

Damiano had to laugh. "I thought you were going to
use magic."

There was a pause before Raphael answered. "I'm not
a witch, Damiano. I don't really possess much magic, but
my . . . my fingers are clever enough."

Damiano took this statement for what he thought it
was worth and, grinning, he raised his hand to scratch his
head.

"Ouch. Are they clever enough to get this mat out of
my hair, Seraph?"

Smooth fingers felt around the elf-lock. "Well, I can
certainly make some improvement, Dami. Have you got a
knife?"

The last remnants of a former vanity caused Damiano
to cringe. "You mean you'll have to cut after all?"

The angel chuckled. "Yes. The harness was one thing, but this kind of neglect is another. But I think I can do it without leaving too much of a hole."

Damiano sat perched on the wagon seat, being barbered with his shaving razor. He kept his eyes closed. Raphael did not stop when he had removed the matted patch in the back, but took this opportunity to shape the whole head according to his personal taste.

"Phew," spat the mortal. "Hair in my mouth. Gaspare won't know me, when I do find him. I haven't had my hair cut since last autumn."

"Why not?" asked the angel, as black hairs floated through his stainless radiance.

"No money," replied Damiano, but even as he spoke he knew it wasn't the truth. Gaspare badgered him weekly to let him cut his hair in the style in which he arranged his own orange locks. Damiano, who could not imagine himself looking like Gaspare, had steered clear.

"Or rather, Raphael, I am beyond caring what I look like."

"Why so?" The angel's voice seemed preoccupied.

Damiano hesitated before answering. It was not a subject that made easy conversation. "Because, Seraph, I have been told not . . . to expect . . ." His head was gently pressed forward while attention was paid to the nape of his neck. ". . . to expect to live much longer."

With absolutely no change of tone Raphael murmured, "One is told a great number of things by a great number of people. I'd be careful whom I believed."

The razor swished near Damiano's left ear. "Besides, Dami. Even if your appearance doesn't matter to you, it matters to the girls. The pretty girls: they care what you look like."

Damiano jerked around and almost looked at the angel. "What kind of thing is that for *you* to say? You—an angel of God!"

"Is there something wrong with girls, Dami? Why should you not want to please them, when I know they try so hard to look pleasing to you?"

Damiano shook a great dark cloud into the air. "Have you no . . . no regard for chastity, Archangel?"

The razor was placed carefully back in Damiano's left hand. "Chastity, yes. Ugliness, no."

Damiano growled, "Saints are often quite ugly, and filthy besides, yet I am told that God holds them in high regard." He began to pick hair from his tunic.

"I know that to be true," replied the angel equably. "But I am not the Father. And you, Damiano..."

"I know. I know." The razor was wrapped in rags and slipped into the back of the wagon. "I am no saint. But I do my best, Raphael."

The wagon was moving again. Raphael said nothing for a while, and Damiano dared not look around, but he knew the angel to be there on the seat beside him. Finally Raphael said, "God be with you along this road, Damiano." It sounded so like a farewell that Damiano replied with an "*Et cum spiritu tuo.*"

But the angel remained: unseen but almost palpably present. A mile passed, then another. Dullness took Damiano, along with a drowse that the company of his bright friend made pleasant.

The gray shape on the far hill was indeed a village, and growing closer. It had a wall. Smoke fingered the sky. There was something in the road before the village: something brown and slowly moving, like a yoke of oxen.

Perhaps it was market day, and the road was deserted only because everybody was already in town. Damiano was peering ahead for any sign of Gaspare when the angel spoke in his ear. "Keep trying," he said, and then he *was* gone.

Keep trying for what? To find Gaspare? To look at Raphael? To stay well groomed? Damiano could think of nothing else Raphael might have meant—except, of course, keep trying to stay awake.

The road was filled with fresh ruts, but no vehicles either passed or had been left beside the village's mud-plaster walls. In the distance someone was singing in an aggressive and undisciplined bass. Those were men in the road in front of the village gate; it was their coarse brown robes that caused them to resemble oxen. Over all hung a faint odor of the shambles.

The singing grew louder.

Surely this was market day, and in a good-sized

village, besides. Damiano's hands twitched on the reins, as he began to pick out his program for the afternoon.

This place would welcome nothing delicate or too subtle, certainly, and besides, much fingerwork wouldn't be heard over the noise. Country dances were the thing, and part-songs the drunks could sing along to. Too bad he hadn't a longer background in the local music; the Provençal and French music he had learned in Italy was High Art stuff and wouldn't do at all.

Damn Gaspare for running off just when his capers would come in handy.

Now the gates were clearly visible: logs of split maple hung by great square nails. They hung open. Damiano sat up in surprise to discover that the robed men in the road were engaged in whipping three other fellows who knelt in stocks set right in the open gateway.

His first reaction was typical of his time and culture. He snickered aloud, wondering how much bran these bakers had put in their bread. Then the metal tips of the cats glittered in sunlight, and he saw the blood running.

Poor sinners, he said under his breath, while the frightened and excited horse first snorted and then jammed backward, jarring the wagon and causing it to yaw. Damiano slipped down from his seat and took the reins in one hand, beneath Festilligambe's head.

The floggers wore robes, but they were not tonsured. After each blow they paused to utter a penitential prayer. The victims were nearly naked, and they did not make a sound. The monk in the middle, whose long scourge cracked like a horsewhip with every stroke, was a huge fellow, full-faced yet grim, with odd pale-blue eyes. A froth of blood spattered with each stroke. His brown-haired victim might have been dead, for he lay in the stocks with no movement.

These were felons, not cheeseparing merchants, Damiano decided. Someday Gaspare would surely come to this, if he continued on his path. The lutenist hoped his errant dancer had encountered this sight, or was perhaps watching this minute from within the town. It would do him good.

Buy why had it fallen to the Third Order of Saint Francis to execute the punishment of miscreants? Dominicans, who were called the Hounds of Christ, would be quite at home in such a role, and Jesuits even more so. But both orders were relatively dapper, and most certainly tonsured. Franciscans were the only ones who sometimes went shabby. Damiano had always felt a strong affinity for Giovanni di Bernardone (called Francesco, or Francis), who had been a musician as well as a saint. He was very disappointed to find that the Franciscans whipped people.

Even more upsetting was the fact that this display effectively blocked his entry into the village. With difficulty he maneuvered the spooky horse off the road and on to the trampled green at the foot of the wall. He yanked his bag of clothes and cookpots through a hole in the wagon wall and dropped it on the ground. Carefully he lifted out his lute and set it atop them. He slipped the gelding's black head into a halter and untied its harness. The hulk of wagon he left behind, half hoping it would be stolen.

Leading the horse, he would be able to pass between the stocks and the village wall. He hoped his passage would not offend the clerics but, really, one must be able to get in and out of a town, especially on market day.

Here the coarse singing was very loud, and shared by more than one voice. Drunken, most likely. But the sound of a silver bell, rung by the middle monk, cut through all, and as Damiano passed directly behind the burly flagellator, the man leaned forward, threw open the stocks, and tenderly lifted out his victim. The others did likewise, and the poor sufferers staggered to their feet.

Then, with a booming cry, the huge man tore off his rude and filthy robe and flung himself into the stocks, which framework shook with the impact of his weight. The other flagellators, like shadows, followed. Despite their bloody and battered condition, the former victims each picked up an iron-tipped cat and set to work with a will. Even the middle one, whom Damiano had thought half dead.

Damiano had heard of the order of flagellants (if indeed there was any "order" about it), but this was his first sight of them, and it left him feeling queasy. Surely there was bravery in their actions, and they undoubtedly canceled out a great number of sins, but still it seemed to Damiano there was more to be gained from a well-sung mass. As he passed beneath the village gate, crude and heavy as a deadfall, he met the pale eyes of the former executer, now victim. They were bright, round and electric with pain. At first the man's face held his gaze by its power to raise pity. But that power faded as the musician saw in those eyes nothing pitiful, but rather a horrible sort of ecstasy, which lit the gray face from within like living coals under a bed of ash.

And then, between one moment and the next, the penitent's face underwent a subtle alteration without seeming to change at all. Damiano stared down through the man's flesh at another face that glowed from within: a face with perfect, elegant features which were molded out of malice and fire, and which stared burning malice up at him.

It was a face Damiano had known before—a face strangely like that of Raphael, were the angel seen in a wicked dream.

It made his heart shiver and jump within him, and his knees buckled. But for his hand on the horse's lead rope he would have fallen, and it was only the strength of the gelding (who only saw the Devil when leaves blew over the road) which led Damiano by.

This was not the first time that Damiano had seen Satan face to face, but it was the first time in a year and more, and never before had Satan appeared to him unsummoned. Fear coursed like cold water through his body.

Inside, he turned the horse and looked back, only to find a perfectly normal-looking fanatic being scourged by another of the same variety. He stood confused, listening to his heart regain its proper rhythm.

The streets and stoops were littered with people, yes. But despite that, this was no market, for there were no barrows to be seen. Also, the shops were closed, unswept, some of them boarded. Drunks and singing implied a festival, yet this looked like no festival Damiano had ever seen, unless it were the third hour of night after a long day's carouse.

Along the foul street lounged men in gay velvets, sitting in the dirt next to men in rags. Women, too, mixed with them in the gutters on terms of easy familiarity. One fat woman seemed to be wearing every bit of white linen she possessed, in onion-layers over a purple woolen gown. She squatted on the stoop of a decayed shop, while above her a cart-wheel-sized wooden olive swung on chains in the wind. The door of the shop was staved in, and a pungent litter of broken olives lay scattered about the street. Her apron, too, was filled with olives.

Beside her, not touching, removed as if by time and distance, sat the undisciplined bass, singing *"gaudeamus"* as he juggled olives in his oily hands. He was not smiling, this reveler, not was the well- (or at least much-) dressed woman. Nor was anyone on the street or in the square beyond. The dry smell of wine warred with that of olives, while above both rose a reek of excrement.

And this whole assemblage of unsmiling maniacs gazed directly at Damiano. Festilligambe froze, shaking all over.

And though he had no longer any witch's staff to warn him, and would not have been able to use it if he had, Damiano sensed wrongness before him as strongly as a blind man may sense the noonday sun. He thought to back out the way he came, but the white-eyed horse stood rooted, while behind him rose the terrifying soft prayers and sharp strokes of the flagellants.

The bass voice was climbing to his feet. He approached Damiano. Indeed, the whole somber riot of them was drawing near, staring with puzzled intensity at one dark-skinned, thinnish traveler with a horse.

The singer bowed from the waist. "Welcome. Welcome to Petit Comtois, my brave one. Forgive our deshabille: we were not expecting visitors. And yet we are delighted to see you." At the end of this anouncement, the fellow forgot to close his mouth.

Damiano dropped his bag of clothes and pots. His head was swimming unpleasantly, and he didn't know whether the scene before him was as bizarre as it appeared, or whether it only seemed so to eyes which had just endured the sight of the Devil. He cleared his throat. Once, twice, three times he tried to answer. The fat woman hove up beside the first villager. She stared at the horse, and then at Damiano. She touched the mane of each.

"Hasn't he nice hair," she observed to the world in

general. Her mouth was a rosebud and her eyes were glazed like candy. Damiano stuttered harder as her fingers played through his new-trimmed locks.

At last he was able to say, "My name is Delstrego, good villagers. I am a musician, and I have come seeking after a friend."

The bass singer nodded sagely. "Good Monsieur Delstrego, welcome again. No one could please us more than a musician seeking after a friend. In Pe'Comtois you will find many friends. In Pe'Comtois we are all friends. Friends unto death." And he smiled a wise, lunatic smile.

Damiano backed away, and the horse backed with him, trampling the bag of pots. He felt a stiff, foolish smile stamp itself upon his face. He could not tear it off. Then the silver bell of the flagellants tinkled once more and Festilligambe bolted forward, dragging his master beside him. But the heavy villager grabbed the gelding's cheek-straps, and the beast went rigid with terror.

Behind them, wooden gates swung shut. The horse moaned helplessly.

At this Damiano's courage awoke. "I'll take the horse," he snapped. "He doesn't like strangers." And he pulled the villager's fingers, one by one, from the rope halter. Then he turned foursquare and confronted the town.

"What is wrong, here?" he challenged. "I can't tell whether you are all in mourning or on holiday. You are all dressed up and yet it looks like the village has been looted. Is there war? Sickness?"

He pointed over the first row of houses to where black smoke still increased. "What is burning?"

The fat woman turned to the odd-dozen villagers behind her. "He asks whether there is war," she announced. "He asks whether there is sickness. He asks what is burning in Pe'Comtois." She giggled. "He has such a sweet Italian accent."

Damiano, being only human, reacted to this with a certain amount of cold hauteur. But the male villager put up a restraining hand. "Peace, Monsieur Italian. I will show you what you want to know. I will show you what is burning. I will show you the very soul of Pe'Comtois. Follow me."

Damiano followed, between two dry stone buildings

and across another desolate street. The bizarre audience faded behind, lacking either energy or interest. At the next narrow intersection Festilligambe balked, and rather than suffer the villager's unsettling aid, Damiano left the lead rope hanging over a post, knowing no one could walk off with the animal. The truth about Festilligambe was that although he would not always obey Damiano, he would never, under any circumstances, obey anyone else.

Here the smell of dung was stronger, but it was overwhelmed by burning wood. It was houses that were burning, the white stone walls containing flame like cupped hands, while fire-tongues licked through the windows. Around the perimeter of the blazing area stood men with pails and pokers, watching the flames with proprietary interest.

"It is . . . on purpose?" asked Damiano, shifting his lute from hand to hand. "You are burning your houses on purpose?"

"In Pe'Comtois," stated the villager, "we are very rich. When we are tired of a house, then—*pfft!* Up she goes. There are always plenty to go around.

"Enough houses, gowns, linens, foodstuffs, wines—no, not enough wines, forgive me. But enough of everything else." He led the other across a court, where stood an enormous church, high-spired, windowed with glass. It was a church far too big for the village that contained it. It was a Provençal church. Together they passed in.

"And how are you so lucky, in Petit Comtois?" mumbled Damiano, his words echoing in dim stone.

With every step he grew more distrustful. Sacred ground or no, this place stank. And his ears told him it was not empty. The nave door swung open.

There, under high tiered windows of scarlet and gold, upon carved pews of oak, were strewn bodies: the dead and dying, piled neatly head to toe.

"Because there is no one left to eat, to wear clothes, to live in houses . . ." announced the singing villager, sweeping the chamber with a gesture.

"We are all dead, you see. Plague."

Chapter Two

From the right came sounds: the weak rebellion of the dying, and their terrible, whistling breath. From the left came only the echoes of the sounds, for all who reclined on the pews on that side of the church were already dead. Even as Damiano's eyes adjusted to the dim jeweled light from the stained windows, two cowled men lifted one of the passive shapes and promoted it to the left side of the aisle. No word was spoken.

"This cannot be," Damiano whispered tentatively. Then hearing his own words in his ears, he fell silent.

Festilligambe stood in the beneficent spring sun, shifting from one pair of legs to the other. It seemed to him that if he wasn't going, he ought to be eating. Or at least rolling. He tested the length of his rope. Not quite long enough. Too bad. Of course he could always pull the rope away; it was not attached to the thin wooden post in any way. But that he was not supposed to do.

For a few minutes he amused himself scratching against the painted stone wall, leaving mats of black winter coat caught on every roughness. Then he scraped his halter methodically against the windowsill. He bit off a chunk of painted plaster, and then spat it out with disgust. Festilligambe didn't know he was elegantly lean, but he knew he was hungry.

Someone was coming. The gelding pricked his fox-tiny ears and snorted. He wasn't very fond of people, except of course for Damiano. Not that anyone had ever done him any real hurt, but he was a Barb, and there it was.

It was a horse approaching. A big horse. The gelding's ears went back, because he really wasn't very fond of other

35

horses, either. He especially disliked bigger horses, who
might tend to think too much of themselves.

As it turned out, this horse wasn't really too big. He
was shorter than Festilligambe although far heavier built.
He had a human with him. That was good; it meant there
would probably be no fight, and fights were not amusing
unless the other horse was much smaller. One look in the
gray stallion's placid ram-face and Festilligambe knew this
horse would offer no difficulty. He crested his black neck
and hissed at the draft horse, for though Festilligambe was
a gelding, he knew what pride was.

Now the human was lifting his halter rope from the
post where Damiano had left it. Wouldn't he be surprised
to find that Festilligambe could not move from the place
he had been told to stay?

He never had moved, not since he had made that
agreement with Damiano in San Gabriele over a year ago,
when Damiano had promised never to spellbind him if the
horse would stay where put. He never had moved, and he
never would. Never, never, never. The elegant black set
his every muscle for the balk.

The human, however, did not try to pull. Instead he
tied the halter rope into the gray horse's harness straps.
Holding the gray's cheekstrap loosely in one hand, he
clucked to the massive animal.

The rope tightened. Festilligambe dug in with his
hooves. In two seconds he found himself flipped in the air
and landing on his left shoulder and hindquarters, his legs
still straight out before him. As he was dragged gently
along the dry road, his face was a mask of equine
bewilderment.

Plague. There must be some mistake. The plague had
vanished sixteen years ago, after destroying almost half of
Europe. Surely it was like Noah's flood, and God would
not send it again. This must be some other pestilence;
typhus or cholera. Something that would do its little
damage (great enough to the people who died of it, and to
the families of those who died of it) and fade away. Man
was heir to so many diseases.

Slowly Damiano began to pace along the great central
aisle, cradling his lute high against his chest, his breath

half choked by the stench. He peered only down the rows to his right.

This man was a farrier; Damiano could tell because he still wore his divided leather skirt. Touching his head were the bare feet of a tall woman in black lace. Her handsome face, not young, had gone green. (At first he thought it was the window light, but no, there was no green glass in any window. She was green.) Her breath whistled two notes at once. She stared stupidly at Damiano's lute, and her lips moved.

What could he do but shrug his shoulders, apologizing for his healthy presence: a lute-carrying mountebank at death's grim door? In reply she spoke one word, which he could not hear.

There was a man at Damiano's elbow. One of the religious who had ported the body from the right side to the left. A brother of Saint Francis, the musician noted.

"It was kind of you, my son, but I doubt many of them would notice."

It took Damiano a little time to understand. Then he shifted the lute from hand to hand. "Oh. Forgive me, Brother. I don't mean to disturb."

He found himself repeating his words from the village gates. "I am a musician, and have come off the road seeking after a friend."

The Franciscan nodded. He lowered his eyes and replied, "Look, then. But for your own sake, do not touch."

This misunderstanding shocked Damiano. But as he opened his mouth to tell the friar that Gaspare could not possibly lie here among the dying, having preceded Damiano down the road by only an hour, it occurred to him there was no use in it. Gaspare (if he had entered Petit Comtois at all) was subject to real danger.

And so was Damiano. Between one moment and the next he remembered Satan's words. *"Soon. Perhaps a year or two. Perhaps tonight."* And once more he touched the black bedrock of his existence, which was the fact that Satan had told him he was going to die.

His hand trembled on the neck of the lute and he chided himself, asking himself why he should be frightened now at the sight and thought of death, when he had spent the last year and more preparing himself for that inevitability. After all, was that not the reason he had avoided involvement with women? And was it not at least part of the reason he had fallen into sleeping so much, sleep being death's close kin?

But no preparation could suffice; he was not at all ready to die. There were matters unsettled—matters such as Gaspare, who was angry with him. Such as that vision of green eyes and brown braids, and the singsong voice in his head which he could not quite understand.

Saara. He wished he had said more to her.

It came to Damiano all at once that his life was not a rounded whole; it had no progression or shape. As an artist, he couldn't call complete a work which possessed neither structure nor moral—or, at least, no structure or moral evident to human eyes.

And he felt a great dissatisfaction with this method of death, perishing in hopeless and frightful stink. A man wanted to die heroically, with someone standing by to take down his final words. To sicken and die of plague, in company of a hundred others, nameless and forgotten...

"In a century you will be a man who might never have existed from a city with a forgotten name."

But it was Satan who had said that. The Father of Lies, and his one purpose had been to hurt. "I'd be careful whom I believed," Raphael had said. Damiano did not believe this prophecy because Satan had given it, but rather because he himself had accepted it. As a bargain. Yet at the same time he did not believe it at all because the archangel had also advised Damiano that no created being—including Raphael's brother Lucifer—knew the future of men. At any rate, believing or not believing, Damiano was not ready today to die.

All this passed behind his black eyes in a moment. He found himself speaking to the Franciscan. "It is the plague, Brother? Not typhus, or..."

The friar lifted his eyebrows so forcefully his scalp wrinkled above his tonsure. "Didn't you know? My poor, innocent traveler. You have come along a very bad road."

"God be with you along this road." Cursed angel. He could cut hair. He could fix harness, but he couldn't say one little word about the plague lying ahead.

Immediately Damiano reprimanded himself. He could not blame the archangel for keeping to the limits assigned him. Especially since he had broken those limits once already for Damiano, saving him from the hangman in the village of San Gabriele. Raphael was definitely not supposed to involve himself that way.

(Yet the angel still called himself sinless. Not perfect but sinless.)

Turning to go from that deadly church, Damiano thought of one more question. "Brother. Those monks I saw at the village gates. The flagellants. Are they Franciscan also?"

The friar's frown was lit crimson, blue and gold. It was formidable. "They are not monks of any sort. They are not true Christians. Pay them no attention, my brother. Fear and despair may drive men mad, and Satan enjoys our misery."

"Satan?" echoed Damiano, and he wished he knew a way to tell the friar what he had seen in the face of the flagellant at the gate. But no, the Franciscan would only think him mad. He turned to the white light of day that came through the entrance door. But he heard a call. "Lute player. Lute player."

It was the green woman in the black lace. "Play," she said. "Play for me."

The Franciscan was not around.

Damiano did not want to play, nor to remain in that house of plague for any reason, but he lowered himself gingerly onto the arm of the pew, by the feet of the unconscious farrier. Quickly he tuned.

"What do you want to hear?" he whispered to her in conspiratorial fashion.

"Play sweetly," the sick woman replied. "Quietly. I don't want to dance just now."

He played a sad Palistinelied by Walther, and then one of his own, written in midwinter, that he had called "The Horse's Lullaby." When he was done, she said no more, and only by her rough and bubbling breath did he know she was not dead.

As Damiano paced toward the vestibule a man passed him: elderly, upright, dressed like a burgher. This composed old fellow proceeded slowly up the aisle, peering down every right-hand pew. Looking for someone, Damiano decided. But then the old man paused, discovering the opening left by the body recently carried off, and he sat down, crossed himself, and lay back.

Damiano flung himself toward the light.

The air of the street was pleasant, being sullied only by smoke. "Dami Delstrego, you must stop crying," he growled to himself, blinking and blundering across the court. "You mozzarella! Someone will see you in a moment."

Was it fear or pity that clutched his windpipe? He could not tell. He had not felt so shaken since leaving the Piedmont. Since before that. Since...

He remembered the crack of his staff breaking and the terrible sense of falling, falling. He remembered Saara's glorious face, and all the rest of the world going gray.

Damiano resolved to get out of this fearsome town, if he had to inch up the stuccoed wall.

And speaking of getting out, where had he left Festilligambe?

Though Petit Comtois lay not far from the High Pass, and was in construction similar to the stone towns of Piedmont that bore Damiano, it was French enough to be confusing to him. The streets were narrow, very narrow, and they wound like ivy. The buildings were not as high as the square towers of Italy, but they tended to spread out sideways, sometimes blocking the road. And though he could read langue d'oc passably, there were no signs to be seen.

There had been an alley with a flight of stairs, where he had to leave the horse. Was this it? It was dark enough, and the burning houses were to his right, as they should be. He danced down three worn blocks of granite and on to something soft.

Staggering back, Damiano almost dropped his lute. But it was not a dead man. It was a dead rat. He went more cautiously down to the next street.

There—down at the far end of the street—that was a horse. Damiano sprinted under sunlit skies, and over a pale, packed-earth street. The beast came around the corner. It was attached to a wagon. That lumbering, round thing was not Festilligambe. It was gray, and its neck, thick as the Barbish gelding's loin, arced in a half-circle. It regarded the panting human with kindly unsurprise.

"Hah! Welcome again, Monsieur Delstrego," said an unpleasantly familiar voice from atop the wagon. The villager, who was not now singing, held the slack reins in one hand. "Do you like my stallion? He is no racehorse, certainly, but he is of the ancient Comtois line. He will pull weight all day, and when he is done with his life's work, there is no better eating!"

Damiano flinched as though the man had suggested eating his own children. "My horse! What have you done with him? You haven't..."

The villager's laughter was merry and unperturbed. He wiped his nose against his sleeve. "Oh, you Italians are excitable! Don't worry, monsieur. There is no hunger in Pe'Comtois, that we should slaughter your little pony. He is well, probably better than he has been in a while, since he is eating oats and barley. We have fodder to spare."

At this news Damiano felt more alarm than gratitude. "Oats and barley! He hasn't had anything like that since January. You will colic him. Take me to him at once!"

The wagoner only snorted. "All in good time, monsieur. I have my little duties first. I must take a little drive outside the wall, and..."

"The gate will open for you?"

The answering grin was a shade contemptuous. "Oh, they will open for me all right. Come along, musician, and entertain me on my way."

Damiano was torn between his desire to flee the stricken town and his concern for the gelding, which if permitted would certainly eat itself to disaster. But the townsman knew where Festilligambe was, and Damiano did not. He waited for no second invitation.

The wagon was so heavy it scarcely shifted under his weight. Damiano sat his lute on his lap and looked over his shoulder.

A large oilcloth covered a load of many bumps and prominences, some of which were long, and some round as a ball. One lump was quite unmistakably an elbow.

"I take my little trip from the church to the end of the common lands every day," the driver was saying. "It frees the pews, and keeps things sort of fresh, you know?

Lately, though, it's been twice a day, which is unfair, since I'm paid only by the day, not by amount of work."

Damiano said nothing. The driver inhaled deeply. "Wonderful day, today. Good clean breeze. Give us a little tune, monsieur." The townsman prodded his passenger. "It will help pass the time."

Damiano stared down at his hands, which seemed to have no feeling in them.

Gaspare prowled outside the town wall as wary as a cat. His situation boded more unhappiness than Damiano's, because, while a musician may play without a dancer to dance, people expect a dancer to have music. And he only had a word or two of this silly, spineless language. So he approached covertly, in case something useful (or unlocked) might come his way.

He heard chanting, and saw that within the gate a small troupe of religious were setting up stocks. Not liking the looks of this, he slunk off.

Attached to the plastered wall itself, on the far side of the town from the wooden gates, was another of those roofless, useless stone huts. He entered, stepping delicately over fresh ashes. He dusted a stone with his rag of handkerchief, sat on it and mulled things over.

By his strenuous trot through the fields toward the village he had put off feeling sorry over biting the lutenist. Now he could put it off no longer, and regret seeped through him.

Gaspare thought of Damiano, and he began to wiggle all over. Whenever the boy tried to think, he wiggled, because he was a dancer. As Evienne always said, his brain was in his feet.

And he could not think of Damiano Delstrego without wiggling very strenuously, for in his cynical way Gaspare stood in awe of Damiano. From the first time he had heard the fellow play, sitting on the corner of San Gabriele on market day, he had known.

Here was a new music. A music of unearthly complexity. A music that could shake kingdoms, and played all on a tiny *liuto* of four courses.

And wonder of wonders, the man who created it let Gaspare himself come along, to be part of the source and the nourishment of that art. Gaspare had never really believed his luck. How could it be that no other cunning fellow had heard Damiano before Gaspare, and taken him in tow? He was such easy prey, full of fancy ideas and nearly blind as a bat. Soft, too, and agreeable. Easily bullied. It was as though all the musician's passion was stored within the lute.

The story the fellow had told—of learning to play his instrument from the Archangel Michael, or some such— that Gaspare had taken for artistic metaphor. Damiano also claimed to be a witch, and on that first day he had accomplished a good imitation of disappearing. Gaspare could never remember if that had taken place before or after they drank the skin of wine. He rather thought it was after.

But of course Damiano never really did anything magical—except play the lute that way, of course. Gaspare had been with him now for a year, and if there were anything in the least bit sorcerous in Damiano's makeup, the boy would know.

Gaspare had been forced to realize that Damiano was a bit mad. Not dangerous, mind you—he was as gentle as a lamb, come what may—but just unbalanced.

Or maybe not mad, but just sheep-simple, for God knew he needed watching like a guileless ewe lamb. He looked like one, too: a black lamb, with all that curly hair and soft black eyes. Girl-faced, yes, but the girls them-selves didn't seem to mind that. The lutenist wouldn't look half bad, if he'd trouble to take care of himself.

Gaspare had made it his business to take care of Damiano—at least to keep him from starving. Let the fellow believe it was his quick hand on the strings, and not Gaspare's in the passing pocket, that put pennies into the bowl.

When he had gotten them to Avignon, Gaspare in-tended to unveil his musician in the courts of the Pope, saying, "See what I have brought from the wilderness. I, only I have recognized greatness in its infancy."

But it was hard to travel with a madman. Him and his angel, when he spoke wide-eyed to the air. Also him and his Devil: he claimed to have spoken with Satan as well as Gabriele (or whoever), and hinted sometimes at dark deal-

ings that made Gaspare nervous about the real source of
his proficiency upon the lute. (Gaspare, like most people,
found it much easier to believe in the Devil than in
angels.)

The most irritating thing about the musician was his
silly preoccupation with chastity. Gaspare had directed
one kind and easygoing girl after another at Damiano
Delstrego, and carefully watched the results. Each time
the player smiled, turned color and went into retreat.
Chastity!

Who cared?

Delstrego should have been born a girl.

And now it was all for nothing. Gaspare had taken a
chunk out of the fellow's arm, and no man could forgive
that.

No man with sense. A madman could, maybe. A
simpleton, perhaps. A man as soft-natured as Damiano....

Gaspare sighed, burying his sharp-nosed face in his
hands. Why did he have to have such a temper? Evienne
said it came with the red hair. He wished he could tell all
of this to his sister, though she would only yell at him.

With a single, fluid motion, Gaspare was out of the
hut and balanced on the wall. He sneaked into Petit
Comtois and beheld the plague.

"You are a cat with one kitten, monsieur," expostulat-
ed the Comtoisian. "Your little horse will come to no
harm; I promise you. I will take you to him later, when my
passengers are taken care of—you see?"

This was said as the dead wagon approached the gates
of the town. Damiano was more certain every moment
that Gaspare had had more sense than to enter a plague
town. The boy was not really sensible, but he was very
cunning.

But if Damiano left now he would have to steel
himself to go through the wooden gate again, because
Festilligambe must be found.

Preferably before grain colic killed him.

Damiano slipped to the packed earth of the random,
almost circular town square, where the crowd lounged in
their unaccustomed leisure, wearing the clothes and eating the food of the dead.

There were fewer now. Damiano counted only fourteen, as the cloddish hoof-falls faded away in the distance, along the eastern road. That was not because of plague, certainly, but the midday rest. (Even leisure must have its breaks.) Yes, there in the broken doorway of a goldsmith's (the shop was picked dry) curled a plump young mother with her infant on her lap, both asleep. The little one's mouth was open like a red rosebud. Its mother snored.

They should go home, he thought to himself, but then there occurred to him possible reasons why they did not. Damiano shrugged.

His scuffed, shapeless kit-sack lay on the earth, undisturbed. Why would anyone want to steal a wooden bowl and two raggy tunics, after all? Although his silver knife was fine, with its crystal and its phases of the moon. It was useless to him, now, as a tool of witchcraft, but still it was a fine knife. Damiano rummaged it out and stuck it into a slit in his leather belt. The rest of his gear he kicked carelessly into a corner.

He would quarter the town, calling. Festilligambe would answer, if he were not too stuffed with oats.

In truth, Damiano was a little disappointed that a mere bribe of food would tempt his horse away. He had struck a bargain with Festilligambe, once, back when his powers had given him something with which to bargain. But why should Festilligambe give him more than other horses gave their masters, when lately he'd been getting much less from Damiano? Much less food, that is.

He took a stride forward and opened his mouth to call. The next instant saw him leap stiff-legged off the ground, swallowing his words, for two plump pink arms had embraced him from behind, while a thick voice in his ear wheedled, "Aww, Monsieur Trouvere! Give us a little song."

"Madam!" he croaked, or rather squeaked, swelling his shoulders to release himself and spinning in place.

"Madam. I think, perhaps, with the troubles this town is suffering..." Here he paused to breathe, to gather his wits and to step away from the woman of many layers. "I think perhaps it is not the time for song."

She giggled and made a little moue. "Not if one has

the plague, of course. But we are the ones the plague has passed over, and for us entertainment is very necessary."

She really was not bad to look at. Her eyes were bright blue, and tilted in a manner which reminded Damiano of someone or other. Her hair, escaping from the underside of her wimple, was barley-fair. And Damiano had nothing at all against plumpness.

Yet he found this woman appalling. "Is it over, then?" he mumbled, looking around at the sunny square. "Is the plague at an end?" Under this blue heaven he could be easily convinced the plague was over, purified by spring weather alone.

She shrugged, and the many layers of linen (the top layer was real lace) puffed with air before settling once more around her. It occurred to Damiano that these Provençal people did not shrug like Italians, forthrightly. They had sly shrugs. "It has killed most all those it is going to kill," she replied, as the baby in the doorway gave a tiny, sleeping cough.

He looked into her face, and then Damiano smelled olives. His long-nursed, familiar hunger awoke like a lion, nearly driving him to his knees, while at the same instant he felt he would much rather die than eat anything he found in Petit Comtois.

"Must go," he mumbled, and he took two smart strides down the main street. Then the woman had a grasp on his left leg, and was dragging him to his knees.

"Music," she cried out. "We must have music."

An instant later a half-dozen villagers, mostly female, had added their soft, unyielding pressure to hers. Damiano sat down on the street, cursing, holding his lute away from their curious, bejeweled fingers.

Yet he was not entirely proof against this rough sort of flattery, and when someone dropped a great gold pendant with a red stone around his neck, he was not proof against that, either. With a broad, forthright and very Italian gesture, he yielded.

It was too bad Gaspare wasn't here. These mad souls would have loved Gaspare. (Like calls to like.) Yet he wouldn't wish this place on the redhead, nor on anyone. He took the pendant off and stuffed it in his belt-pouch lest it scratch the finish of the instrument, and began to play.

These people didn't need a professional dancer after all. The way that fat woman was capering was an education to watch. And the butcher jigging on one foot next to her. For a moment Damiano thought the man in the blood-stained apron was the same he had seen in the church, lying still and awaiting promotion to the left-hand side. But no. The sentence of the plague was never commuted; the only similarity between the two men was in the leather apron.

He gave them the rondel and the crude estampie, and when they were warmed up—indeed, hot was the more accurate word—he played that sarabande of Gaspare's which he had so much reason to dislike. In his single year of playing for bread, Damiano had learned to judge an audience correctly, so he wasted none of the difficult polyphonics, and nothing Raphael had taught him at all.

And if his fingers pinched the strings with a hint of contempt, and if he damped a bit harshly, well, that was all to the better, considering that Damiano's natural touch was too delicate for everyday tastes.

He lifted his eyes to see a huddle of drab brown at the edge of this graceless circle. Even the flagellants were drawn to the sound of festival, it seemed. In a moment they would be dancing.

"Mother of God," whispered Damiano to himself. "Is one fury interchangeable for another?"

Then the sound of bone against flesh broke through the music. A year ago this would have caused the young man to stop, or at least to drop a beat. But now his fingers continued their course while he glanced up to see the man in the apron laid low by the biggest of the flagellants. With a noise of childish outrage the woman of layers bounded across the dust of the square and kicked the flagellant in the middle of his horsehair and ashes.

This was not the first time Damiano had played for a dance which became a melee. His policy was to continue playing, while backing away from the ring of trouble. In this situation he found it most advisable to scrape along the row of ruined shops on the left of the main street. Following this course, he would eventually put the flagellants between him and the merry madmen (who were certain they were not going to get the plague) and seek Festilligambe in peace.

He was fingering a spirited *bransle* (what else do you play when the audience is brawling?) when a round, soft, little noise behind him caused him to turn his head.

This was the doorway of mother and baby, but mother was presently out in the sunshine, engaged in pulling someone's hair. Baby lay alone in the darkened goldsmith's shop, dressed in white christening robes, coated hands and feet with a precious, glittering dust, and coughing.

"Mother of God," groaned Damiano once again, and for a single instant he entertained the idea of taking the child with him. But in his twenty-three years Damiano had never so much as held an infant in his arms, and all he knew about their care was that he was fairly certain they could not eat grass.

Avoiding the tiny mite, he set his instrument within the shop, in the safety of a dark corner, and then he went back out to find his horse.

"Festilligambe," he called, trying to be melodious as well as penetrating. There was no answer.

His next cry was less modulated, but still he heard no reply, except from the brawl in the square. A silver tankard rolled, clanking, past his feet. He ignored it.

All these houses marched down to the street, and of those which had stables below, all were open and empty. The packed earth would hold no imprint. "Festilligambe!" bellowed Damiano. There was a scuffle of feet behind him.

It took Damiano a good two seconds to understand that the flagellants were chasing him. For one more second he stood his ground, belligerently resentful that they would try to get him involved in an argument between two breeds of lunatic. Then he sprinted.

Had he been less outraged, or had he understood the situation a bit quicker, he might have escaped, for his opponents were weakened by their mutual abuse. But four pairs of hands gripped his tunic and his feet were kicked out from under him.

"Damn the lot of you," roared the furious musician, suspended by his shirt three feet off the ground. His fist connected twice, on what felt like hard pieces of anatomy. "I've had just enough idiocy!"

Then his head was lifted from behind, by the hair. The expressionless features of the chief flagellant looked down upon him. "Corruption," the man stated. "Human flesh is corruption, and the worm is its end. You are a sinner and partake of the nature of the beast. You must be freed from your corruption." There was a tinkle as of tiny bells, as the tips of a cat jingled together.

Then Damiano was no longer furious, but frightened.

With sweat prickling all over, Gaspare backed away from the dead man he had come so close to touching. There was no doubt in his mind what had killed this fellow: those horrible round lumps like oak galls on the neck, the pus-y, discolored face and the general attitude of being left to lie where it fell...

He did not need the row of yawning doors and the desolation of the quarter to confirm his opinion. Gaspare had no trust in the world to delay his acceptance of sad reality. This was plague, just like that which had slain half the world a generation ago, and Gaspare was going back over the wall quickest.

Sinking back into the ashes of the hut where he had earlier sat in unhurried thought, Gaspare shivered all over. What an ass he was, not to have guessed why they burned the place down! He minced out through the gaping door, shaking clean one foot, then the other.

Distrustfully—hungrier than ever despite the crawling horror—he examined the road west. Rumor had it that plague, like mankind, followed the roads. And it hadn't come from above, to the east in Franche-Comté or the Chamonix Pass. Perhaps Provence already suffered the worst. Perhaps Avignon was dead, as it had been only sixteen years before. Perhaps...

Evienne.

Gaspare's heart banged his fragile chest wall like a prisoned enemy. He felt each mile that lay between his sister and himself as an unendurable deprivation: a personal insult against him and his.

An affront to pride. He flared his pinched nostrils against it.

It did not occur to him that being with Evienne would not prevent her (or him) from contracting plague. Avoiding the plague was not the issue for Gaspare. Getting through the plague to Evienne was.

Why had he let her run off with that miserable, horse-faced Dutchman, anyway? Bad enough she should be a prostitute at home in San Gabriel (among family, as it were), let alone spreading her scandal into foreign countries.

Leaving him nursemaid to a lute player who saw angels.

Damiano! Gaspare's head jerked up, and he moved away from the wall where he had been leaning. Where was that soft-eyed simpleton: lumbering the old cart back up toward the pass? Or would he have continued west? Gaspare cursed himself for not stopping to make sure. His feet led him over the cleared land which surrounded the wall of the town and into the head-high brush.

Why would Damiano go back, after all? It was he who originally wanted to see Provence, whence came the music. The lutenist had only wanted to wait until May before attempting the Alpine passes.

Well, they were over the passes. Easier to go on than back. And that meant Damiano would trot that spoiled, sullen-tempered horse straight into trouble.

Gaspare could close his eyes and see it happening: a scene complete, with Damiano yawning, the horse snapping harness right and left, the rickety wagon trundling its oblivious way past rows of grinning corpses and burned shops. His soft-shod feet gathered speed.

Looking up the road past the gate, Gaspare saw nothing. He breathed with relief. Then he noticed the familiar, derelict wagon squatting at the edge of the cleared land, its shafts angling out like the long curved tushes of a boar.

Damnation and buggery. What could be *done* with the fellow? Gaspare washed his hands in the air. It was a gesture that relieved his feelings but did not change the fact that he'd have to go in and drag Damiano out.

He went over the wall with the speed of practice, and padded nonchalantly down an empty street. Why should he skulk, when he'd broken no laws (so far) and besides, could outrun anyone he'd ever met?

The first street was without interest. So was the second.

Along the third, he heard a noise: a regular and workmanlike thumping, as of a hammer against wood. Exercising greater caution (because although he had broken no laws so far, there was no assurance he might not want to break some soon), he decreased the distance between himself and the source of the disturbance.

It was coming from a half-door set into the first floor of a square stone building no different from any of its neighbors, except that it smelled a trifle more rank.

Gaspare peeped obliquely in, to discover a horse, which was eating with its front end and kicking with its back end. It performed these actions in sequence, first chewing a bite of oats, then swallowing, then heaving up and delivering a massive blow to the oaken panels of the door. Gaspare found he could count to six during each iteration of the cycle.

The horse was Festilligambe.

Gaspare leaned negligently against the stones of the stable wall, considering what he saw.

As a picture, he liked it. Damiano would, no doubt, be quite concerned that the horse would injure himself kicking the door. The owner of the stable might legitimately be concerned as well. Gaspare, however, liked both the animal's rebelliousness and his realistic attitude. It wasn't Gaspare's door, after all. Nor his horse.

But how had the horse gotten here? Damiano hadn't a sou to pay for oats. And he wasn't likely to have sold the brute. Christ, no! The lute player would sooner part with his bollucks. And why did Festilligambe have such a grudge against dry straw and good grain? He was a perverse horse, but not that perverse.

Gaspare had a strong hunch something was wrong. He leaped lightly to the top of the door, timing his move for the moment the horse took a mouthful from the manger, and then landed lightly on the blond straw on the far side of the box from the gelding.

"Hey! Festilligambe. Idiot-face," hissed the dancer. The startled animal shrieked and spewed oats into the air.

"Shut up," rapped Gaspare, and he pointed in peremptory fashion. "So. You came into a fortune, eh, old

friend? Well, one friend's fortune is another friend's." And
reaching into the black and bitten wood manger, he filled
both his jerkin pockets (which were bigger than such
pockets had any right to be) with golden grain. Then he
filled his purse.

With enough oats, one could make frumenty. Or
flatbread. But it wasn't with the clear idea of cookery that
Gaspare loaded himself with the grain. It was only that it
was there for the taking.

When sufficiently laden, Gaspare took the gelding's
dangling halter rope and wound it securely around his
wrist. Then he led the now-docile horse to the door.
"We're going out now, nag-butt," he whispered up at the
black ear, a foot above his head. "We're going out to look
for old sheep-face Damiano. Can you find Damiano for
me, boy?"

The horse blinked down at him mildly. Gaspare untied the leathern thong that held the door. He was nervous. If the truth be told, Gaspare was afraid of horses. A
crack of light appeared as the oak door began to open.

Festilligambe hit it, chest on, roaring, and with a
display of Barbish speed and temperament, flung himself
along the empty street. They were halfway to the next
corner before Gaspare's pitiful scream hit the air.

His arm was caught in the rope. His feet never hit the
ground. There was nothing for the boy to do but grab a
handful of mane with his left hand and hang on.

Except for Delstrego Senior, no man had ever laid
punishing hands on Damiano. Or, more accurately, no man
had gotten away with it. Damiano was less prepared than
most men for the touch of the whip, and the first lick of
the tipped cat stiffened him from bucking and thrashing
into mute astonishment. The second stroke knocked him
to his elbows. On the third he cried out, or tried to.

With the fourth multifingered assault upon his back,
he gathered himself together and fled—fled in a manner
he himself did not understand—through the ragged, empty socket in the middle of his mind.

It was dark here, and green with the background of fir
trees. The grass was dotted with crocus and snowdrops,

and with gold brushes of flowering mustard. Over the flat
meadow wound a stream which expressed neither decision
nor ambition, weaving its course as random as a snail-
track.

Over and through the branchlets of the stream splashed
a doe goat, bleating unhappily, tied with a garland of grape
hyacinth. It was a brown goat, cow-hocked and very
gravid, still wearing great patches of its winter coat.

The weaver of the garland was a more delicate creature. She rubbed one bare toe against the other leg, while
she tickled the underside of her own nose with a yellow-
brown braid.

"Behave like a lady," she said to the goat, speaking
with firmness, and pointing to the fragile band of blue
flowers. "If you tear that off, I'll stuff it down your throat."

The goat stopped still, but not out of docility. It
chewed an uneasy cud, and rolled its square-pupiled eyes
at what it saw.

Saara turned also, and her own green, tilted eyes
widened. She dropped her braid.

"You!" she whispered, half to herself. "Dark boy.
Damiano!" One hand, small, pink and slender, made a
circling gesture.

And the lute player knew her as well: Saara of the
Saami, barefoot girl who was the greatest witch in the
Italies.

Damiano knew Saara's powers well, having both suffered
them and then stolen them. And now all the strength was
hers and he had none at all.

Damiano felt himself step closer to the witch (though
he himself did not know how he did it, not having a body
with which to step). The placid water passed beneath his
substanceless flesh without disturbance.

"You cannot be dead! I would know it if you were
dead," she stated, yet by her voice Saara had her doubts.
Her hand reached out toward him, as though to wipe haze
from a glass, and quietly she began to sing.

Once again Damiano was aware of having feet, and
hands. They tingled. He brushed back the coarse hair
from his face. "I don't think I am dead," he heard himself
saying. "For though I can imagine nothing more like
heaven than your garden, my lady, I have been led to

expect there will be a matter of judgment to endure before
I reach such a paradise. Assuming I am found worthy of
it."

How odd his voice sounded in his own ears: a bit thin,
perhaps, but quite composed and calm. And how confidently
he stepped through air that had more substance than he
did. Now Saara was almost close enough to touch. In three
steps, she would touch. She chanted sunlight into the
young man's eyes. He blinked. His feet sank into marshy
ground.

Then Damiano remembered. "I'm not supposed to be
here!" he announced, stepping back and into deeper water.
"This is Lombardy, and I'm in Provence. I shouldn't have
come at all!"

Saara paused, her feet resting on the tussocky grass.
Her small face tilted like that of a wary bird. "But I knew
you would come, at last, Dami. Part of your soul is waiting
here. You have only come after it—there is nothing wrong
in that." She stepped into water, and Saara, greatest witch
in the Italies, sank ankle-deep in the mud.

Floundering backward, Damiano shook his head. "No,
signora. I followed my lost powers, surely, but I did so in
my effort to escape the lash, not to mention the plague.
And in this I have done myself more harm than good."

Saara stopped in midcurrent. Her blue felt dress
darkened as it absorbed water. Her chant first slowed, and
then stopped. From behind her, the doe goat bleated
loudly.

"Plague, Damiano?" she asked quietly. "The lash?
Where are you? Where have you left your body?"

He stared down at hands like clear amber, glowing
with their own light. His breath came out soundlessly, and
he looked up at the witch again.

"Somewhere between Lyons and Avignon. In Provence,
where the music is born. And I must go back, before
I . . . I forget how."

He turned away from her, then, as though he were
about to walk down the hill, and he stared confusedly
around him.

"Saara, it's you that is holding me, isn't it? Let me go
back." His voice rose with a tinny, faraway urgency.

Her hand rested on the goat's ridged horn, while the

scruffy, decorated beast nuzzled Saara's hip. "Don't worry,
Dami. I won't hurt you. Don't I have half your soul in my
care, and by *your* wish, not my own? But before I let you
go you must tell me . . ."

"Won't hurt me! You will kill me, I think! Let me go
before it is too late." Damiano blundered forward into the
same streamlet where Saara stood. Water plashed against
his legs and hands, feeling more real by the moment.

And the slim shape in peasant embroidery, too, was
very real. As Saara stood beside him, frowning doubtfully,
disarmingly, Damiano felt that it was too late already, and
that the cord which tied him to this body was frayed
beyond repair. That Provence and life together were done
with him and he would be nothing more than a captive
elemental: a domestic spirit in the garden of the lady
Saara.

And he was glad of it.

For life was cruel and Provence dying, while Saara
was beautiful. And she, like him, had been born a witch,
with his own strange senses and stranger arts. Damiano
knew suddenly that he loved Saara, and that he had loved
her since their first meeting on this very hillside, amid the
drone of bees and the sharp fragrance of rosemary.

And as once before he had risked a rival's blade for a
chaste and unpracticed kiss in the witch's garden, so now
he stood calf-deep in the spring thaw of the mountains,
and he reached out one doomed, immaterial hand.

"Saara," he whispered. "Pikku Saara. You should not
be so beautiful!"

Saara laughed, hearing the Fennish word in the Italian
mouth. She looked into Damiano's black eyes. Then her
little nostrils twitched, and the laughter was cut off. She
examined his amber visage with a cold, scientific thor-
oughness. She raised a hand, but did not touch.

"You were right!" she stated. "You should not be here.
It is very bad for you."

Then Saara clapped her hands, or she made as though
to clap her hands. But Damiano heard no sound, for his
whole world went out like a candle.

Where the hell the beast was going Gaspare had no
idea. The boy forced his eyes open, lest the spiteful horse

scrape him off on a wall. If it tried that, Gaspare promised himself, then he would make his hands let go. Right now he could not quite manage the feat, for his fingers were welded into the black mane and the halter rope, which he should never, never have wound around his arm.

Festilligambe swung around a corner and Gaspare's heel plowed dust. Fear itself drove him to mount to the horse's back.

"I swear, you pig-head, you pig-heart, pig-collops, pig . . . pig of a pig! I swear I'll wear your hide someday soon, and if you dump me it will be today, I swear by Saint Gabriele and by Maria, the Mother of Christ, I'll eat your eyes and tongue roasted on a skewer and sell your bladder for a fool's toy. I swear . . ."

With a constant stream of such encouragements in his flattened ear, Festilligambe bolted past the basilica, where the odor of death was only a bit less terrifying than that of the burning houses on the street beyond. Each of his yellowing teeth was exposed to the wind. His nostrils were round as drainpipes, and gorged purple. His eyes were ringed, not with white, but red. He ran with his belly to the ground, carving the dry, packed road with his hooves. He went rough. He cornered viciously. He went from sun into darkness, leaping a flight of alley stairs and landing in sun again on the next street.

He made straight for the square of Petit Comtois where the wooden gates stood solidly shut. Gaspare's scream was soundless but heartfelt.

There in the road lay a woman's shirt of linen, and beyond it another of lace, stained olive green. Gaspare flashed by them too quickly for curiosity. Still farther toward the gate he passed a plump and fair-haired woman dragging along a monk by his long, untonsured hair. Both were bellowing; it all seemed perfectly natural to the panicked Gaspare.

The wooden gate loomed, solid, oak-barred and five feet tall. The horse had no sense—he would brain himself against the palings, and Gaspare as well. It was time to let go.

Gaspare told his fingers it was time to let go. He tried again. He shrieked at them, but from fingers they had become gnarled tree roots wound in the black earth of the gelding's mane.

A circle of brown-robed friars stood before the gate. Evidently Festilligambe intended to smash into them on his way to oblivion. Gaspare held to the selfish and forlorn hope they would cushion the impact.

But neither the collision with the religious nor that with the maple palings happened, first because the brown robes scattered like so many dun doves of the wood, and second because Festilligambe ceased his mad pounding between one step and the next, and Gaspare's convulsive grip dissolved. He went over the horse's head and landed rolling. Twice he rolled free, escaping harm with the elasticity of youth and training, but on the third roll he came up against flesh. His warding hand slipped against skin slick with blood, on the lean, whip-scored back of a man whose head and arms were tied up in a shirt.

All the bumps and knobs of that back were vaguely familiar, and in the leather belt that circled it was stuck a tiny, intricately-worked knife which was very familiar.

"Pig's head of an ass!" ejaculated Gaspare, as he plucked free the knife and cut the shirt apart.

Damiano's eyes were wide and staring. "Gaspare?" he asked, his usually rather deep voice cracking. "Gaspare— is this still Franche-Comté? Or . . . Lombardy, or . . . ?"

Fury warred with a strange ache in Gaspare's heart. He took the shaggy black head (no, not shaggy any longer, but trimmed somehow) in the hands that had so lately been locked in the gelding's mane, and he shook Damiano's head roughly back and forth. "You damned, swiving sheep-faced lunatic," he shrilled, and then he bent the unresisting head down and, still more roughly, kissed the top of it.

Damiano, meanwhile, was staring nearsightedly through the four black pillars that arched above him, at a huddle of wary, pointing townsmen, both of the robed and the bejeweled variety. He squinted, but they were too far for him to make out the expressions on their faces. He brought his own, soiled left hand up to his face and flexed it, looking puzzled.

Gaspare also looked at the whip-wielders, and his excellent vision gave him cause for alarm. "Get up, Damiano, before they regroup and come back to you. And once

we're five miles from this foul-stinking bed of misery you
can explain to me just what..." and as he tried to rise
Gaspare's head hit something. He ducked once more,
swiveled his head, and discovered why the townspeople
were pointing.

Gaspare collapsed once more on top of Damiano, the
air whistling out of his throat. For above them stood a
half-ton of rigid outrage, iron-legged, hissing, with a tail
stiff as a terrier's. The gelding's head coiled left and right
as though the beast were a dragon, and it dripped white
froth onto Gaspare's upturned face.

"Call him off!" shrieked the sufferer. "Dear Jesu, call
him off and I will sin no more!"

Damiano, too, looked up, but either trust or poor
vision saved him from Gaspare's terror. "Festilligambe!"
Awkwardly, like an old man, he climbed to his feet. Dirt
grayed his hair and caked to the ooze on his naked back.
He leaned one arm over the sweaty, trembling withers.
"Hey. I went looking for you. But you found me instead!"

The gelding nickered, but its defiance did not weak-
en. It stamped one hind foot. Gaspare moaned.

The lute player peered down at Gaspare (squirming
full length on the ground between the black hooves) as
though he could not remember how the boy had gotten
there. He reached down one hand and yanked him up.
"Stand up. You shouldn't play games with an animal this
size," he chided.

Then he added, "We've got to get out of this town,
Gaspare. They're all mad here. You can never tell what
they're going to do next."

"Mad?" Gaspare rolled his gooseberry eyes. "Oh,
certainly, yes. I've noticed it myself. Well then, we should
certainly get out of here, shouldn't we, Damiano? In fact,"
and the boy pointed surreptitiously to the wall by the gate,
"why don't we just run over there and slip over that wall?
I'll help you up and you pull me up behind, heh?"

Damiano frowned hugely and touched his still-bleeding
shoulder blades. "Don't be silly, Gaspare. We can't take a
horse over the wall. Nor a lute.

"I'll go get my lute now," he finished, and Damiano
calmly stepped across the square toward the yawning black
doorway of a shop. Gaspare watched him go, and he

watched the tall shape, black as vengeance, stalk behind him, black tail slashing like a blade that would love to cut. The gelding's muzzle hung just above Damiano's shoulder, unnoticed. Damiano seemed to be quietly talking to himself.

It was very lonely, standing in the middle of the square, without even a vicious horse for protection. Gaspare shifted from one foot to the other and raised his chin high into the air. No one came near, for all eyes followed the wounded musician and his strange protector as he vanished into the dark shop and reappeared, bearing his sheepskin-wrapped instrument.

Damiano was frowning. "There was a baby in there before," he said to Gaspare, "but it's gone, now. I certainly hope it was its mother that came back for it. So much despair around, you know." Then he raised his left eyebrow very high, and regarded Gaspare with more rationality than he had yet shown, saying, "It is the plague that has hit here. You knew that, didn't you?"

Gaspare sighed hugely. "Yes, musician. I was aware of that, and that is another very good reason for... for hastening our departure, maybe?"

Damiano swung onto the horse's back. His mouth gaped with the pain of his flayed back. He leaned down and reached a hand toward Gaspare. "Get up in front," he commanded the boy.

Gaspare backed. "No, thank you. I have already ridden that horse once today."

"Get up," said Damiano with some temper, and he snagged Gaspare's unwilling hand. "I don't want to lose you again, before I even have a chance to tell you about the strange thing that happened, or a chance to apologize, as I promised Raphael I would."

"Apologize?" Gaspare was so astounded he allowed himself to be pulled up in front of his friend on the steaming black back. "You, apologize, after I bit you?"

Damiano was not listening. "I think if we just ride confidently up to the gate, that huge fellow in the robe— he's not a real monk, you know—may just open up for us. Or at least not interfere with *our* opening it.

"What is important," he added, sententiously, "is always to appear to know what you are about, and most especially when others are uncertain. That is a fourth part of magic and the half of all medicine. It is most important of all in military matters, such as . . ." And Damiano gave a gentle kick (a nudge, really) to the gelding's sides.

The beast reared, turned on its haunches, and spurted along the street directly away from the gate. Then it spun again, nearly toppling both its riders, scrabbled its hindquarters under it, and flew directly for the wooden fence.

A woman screamed. So did Gaspare. Damiano looked merely irritated as he clutched the mane, the lute, and a hysterical passenger. "He's going to kill me after all!" wailed Gaspare. Once more the townspeople fled.

But Festilligambe did not hit the gate. Instead, eight feet from the oak-bound, maple palings, he gathered himself under and leaped.

The ground fell away. Weight fell away. Festilligambe nicked one black hoof against the top of the gate and he grunted an equine profanity. When his forefoot touched down, his rider was ready—ready enough to have Gaspare secured against falling, and to soften the thump of his own descent on the horse's back with his knees. Together Damiano and Gaspare lurched against the gelding's neck as it came up, pitching them back into position.

The horse came down galloping, and galloping they disappeared along the Alpine highway.

It was dark before they dared sneak back for the wagon.

Chapter Three

The countryside south and west of Petit Comtois was even gentler and more temperate than that which they had left behind them. What was more heartening, there were scattered almond orchards and fields of green lavender.

But the almonds were in bloom, not fruit, and what use to a hungry man was lavender, sweet-smelling though it was?

After Gaspare stole the clutch of some peasant's goose, nearly having his finger broken and finding in the end the eggs were useless, being ready to hatch, well, it seemed the least said between them, soonest mended. Along the road they met no one, save the occasional meandering and always dry cow.

It was unusually warm for the month of March, or at least it seemed so to Damiano. But then neither he nor Gaspare had ever experienced any but the Alpine spring. The present temperature was a saving grace to him, on this, the third day since his whipping in Petit Comtois, for he could bear no touch upon his scabbing back. He lay upon his stomach in the booming belly of the wagon, his woolen shirt folded under him and swaddled around his sides.

He was husking oats, by hand, one by one. Boiled oats had been their diet ever since leaving the town. They had discovered that oats took a long time to boil. This little double handful was the last from Gaspare's purse.

Damiano's face bore a look of pained concentration. Each ovoid seedlet went into the bowl of his lute for safekeeping, since no simple cup would maintain them through the roll and pitch of the wagon.

The husks went all over. Many pale flakes had found their way into his hair and eyebrows.

"I feel so guilty, doing this," he mumbled, his voice coming strained because of the angle of his neck.

Gaspare was driving, which is to say he sat in the driver's seat, his hands clenched doggedly upon the tattered reins. But the lines hung from hand to surcingle, and from surcingle to bit in great, looping swags which swung left and right with the horse's steps. Festilligambe was trotting decorously down the road solely because that was what he felt like doing.

"Guilty?" echoed the boy. "You feel guilty husking oats? By the Virgin and every saint, Damiano, do the little grains cry out as you break them?"

Damiano sighed and rested his chin on the boards for a moment. The muscles of his back hurt. He was also lightheaded from lack of nourishment, and his temper was on edge. He therefore collected himself before answering,

"No, of course not, Gaspare. I meant I feel that Festilligambe is expecting us to give the stuff to him."

Gaspare's florid face grew pinker and his mouth worked. But he bit off whatever he'd first intended to say, and said only, "The creature would be better off with wealthier owners."

Damiano did not reply, though it was on his tongue to remind the boy that Festilligambe did not have owners but *an* owner.

Emboldened by this silence, Gaspare spoke the corollary to his statement, which was that the owners would be a lot wealthier if they sold the horse.

Damiano rested his face on the backs of his hands and resisted a temptation to escape from this unpleasantness into the familiar vacancies of his mind.

"Gaspare," he began, "please try to understand. That horse likes me."

"Likes you, maybe, but doesn't listen to you a pig's fart. And he doesn't like nobody else in this world. Especially me."

Damiano glanced up, for he heard a tone of real hurt in his companion's voice. "Oh, he likes you all right, Gaspare. He likes you better than he likes anyone else except me.

"And in the beginning..." and Damiano's thoughts went back over a year in time, to the sheep pastures above Partestrada, where he had first seen the black gelding in the string of Carla Denezzi's brother. The horse had been flourishing then.

So had Damiano. He had worn soft boots, white linen and a full cloak of weasel skins.

Painful and distant came the memory to Damiano that he had once been respectable. He had sat at table with the parish priest. Once, he had spoken with Petrarch.

He had had a house. And a city.

Now that was over, and he was that pitiful creature—an Italian in exile. According to his bargain with the Devil, he must not return home. According to the Devil's bargain with him, he was now living the tag ends of his days.

For a moment's intense, ashen melancholy, brought on perhaps by starvation, Damiano was sorry the plague had spared him. But then that moment passed, and he remembered what he had.

He had an angel. An archangel, who had shared with him as much as mortal may share with spirit—which is to say, music. And he had a horse—a temperamental horse, but a fine one—and a still more temperamental distinguished colleague.

He watched a roadside row of plums pass by the wagon, just entering into their pale bloom. The tended landscape was sweeter than anything he had ever seen in Italy, and the soft air was gauzy. The sight and the smell and the warmth together sank Damiano into a diffuse and pleasurable stupor in which he could almost forget the stiffening lacerations that crisscrossed his back.

An angel and a horse and a friend (of sorts). And of course a lute, too. That was important, even though it wasn't much of a lute. Together, Gaspare, angel, horse and lute made a total for which it was worth losing a bit of respectability.

Especially while the weather remained so fine. Respectability was much less important in good weather.

Oddly enough, thought the sleepy musician, in some ways Raphael was the least respectable of his companions. It was talking to the angel, after all, that caused people to edge away from him. Were it not for Raphael, Gaspare would have no cause to think Damiano a madman.

All these reflections took the time of one long sigh and a shift of weight from left elbow to right. Damiano continued his interrupted sentence. "And in the beginning, the horse liked me least of all men.

"But, Gaspare, I want you to listen to the strange thing that happened to me when I was being whipped in Petit Comtois."

Gaspare's laugh was not kindly. "I can think of many possible strange things. . . ."

The half-naked man ignored this interruption. "I sort of blacked out. But not really, for I found myself standing somewhere else. In Lombardy, I was, in a place I have been once before, though I never talked about it to you. A beautiful garden."

The ironic light died behind the boy's eyes. "That happens," he admitted. "When a man is in pain, or sick.

When I was five and had the spots I had such a fever Evienne says I thought she was Saint Lucia, though why Saint Lucia, I have no idea. . . ."

Damiano raised his chin again and frowned fiercely at Gaspare. "I spoke, not with Saint Lucia, but with a woman I know. A very beautiful woman. . . ."

"A beautiful one? Sounds less and less real all the time."

"And she was surprised to see me standing next to her. I was like a spirit, for my body was left in Petit Comtois. We both agreed I should not have come there, and she sent me back."

One rusty eyebrow shot up. "She sent you back? Isn't that the way with beautiful women? But you should learn persistence, musician. Otherwise there will never be any little black-haired, sheep-eyed babies running around."

Damiano pushed himself off the floor of the wagon. It seemed the heat of his own irritation was lifting him.

"This woman I speak of is a great lady, Gaspare. The most powerful witch in the Italies, if not in all of Europe. You must learn to think before you speak of people, or you will never grow *old* enough for there to be any little red-haired, pointy-nosed babies running around.

"And surely by now you know me enough to take seriously what . . ."

Gaspare's small brow beetled enormously. The reins dropped from his hands and lay on the footboard of the seat. "Do you think I'm not old enough already, lute player? I'll have you know that I may only be fourteen, but some fourteen-year-olds are men already, while some twenty-three-year-olds . . ."

Damiano would not be sidetracked. Not even by this subject. Especially not by this subject. ". . . to take seriously what I say on the subject of powers unseen. I was trained from birth to feel and manipulate these powers, by a father who was no mean witch himself. . . ."

Gaspare's eyes dropped with queasy self-consciousness. He plucked up the reins.

"And on top of his training, and my natural predisposition to magic, I have added a thorough course of study in the works of the great Hermes Trismagistus, along with the additions and commentaries of Mary the Jewess. If I, out of all mankind, tell you I have visited Lombardy in immaterial form, then me you can believe!"

Gaspare set his long jaw. Rough-mannered as he was, he had always avoided this particular confrontation with Damiano. Now it seemed inevitable. He pulled on the reins with a long, exaggerated "Hoa." Festilligambe stopped out of sheer surprise.

"Damiano. My dear, close friend," he sighed. "You have no magical powers."

Damiano blinked. "Of course not. Not since last year. I gave them all away."

Gaspare's regard was steady and pitying. The horse shook his glistening, sweaty mane under the sun and opened his nostrils hugely.

"You gave them away."

Damiano blundered stiffly onto the seat beside him. "Yes. But I still had them when I first met you in San Gabriel. Don't you remember? I disappeared in front of you and scared you half to death."

Gaspare was affronted. "I don't remember being scared half to death by you. You had a trick or two, I grant. You could make it seem your bitch-dog talked. That was fine, and I'm really sorry you lost that dog. I like dogs. Much better than horses."

Damiano pulled his hair in consternation, while he bit down on his large lower lip. "Gaspare! What are you saying? I'm always talking about how I was a witch, and how my staff worked, and about Raphael, whom I summoned—or rather requested audience of—and so learned to play the lute. I know you don't believe everything I say, but if you don't believe that I was a witch, then you must think I should be locked away in a cellar!"

Gaspare glanced up and away again. He brushed a stray fly from his colleague's back. "Not at all, Damiano. But I think that it is important to you to feel special."

"Eh?" The dark, curly head jerked up, and the black eyes opened round.

"It is important to every man to feel special," continued Gaspare moderately. "But what you don't realize is that you *are* special. You are singular. You are the finest lute player—oh, God's bollucks, the finest *musician*—we have seen in all our travels. I doubt there is another here or back in Italy as original and progressive as yourself. Being a magus or a wizard fades to nothing next to that. You need not wish to be a sorcerer. You need not ever think about it again."

"I was not a magus, or wizard, or sorcerer. Just a witch." And he stared and stared at Gaspare. "But what you are saying is simply that you do not believe me."

"I do not believe you," replied Gaspare quietly.

Damiano snorted. He folded his large hands together and his eyes wandered over the gentle Provençal horizon, where stood small cots and ricks, and ponds of water floating with ducks. Five seconds of silence grew into ten. Into twenty.

"I feel very strange right now," Damiano announced.

Gaspare shot him one wary, concerned glance. "Perhaps that is how it feels to come to your senses," he suggested, trying to say it as inoffensively as possible.

But Damiano spared only one distracted glance. He stood up on the footboard, and then climbed on the seat itself, holding to the wagon eave for support. Both Gaspare and Festilligambe looked up at him standing above them.

"No, Gaspare. I mean I feel magic. Even now. There is power in the air above us." He waved hugely at the empty sky.

"Oh, Christ!" groaned Gaspare. "I have done it!" He hid his face in his hands. "He is beyond recovery."

And now Damiano was pointing. "Look! Look, Gaspare. It is coming. Can't you see?"

The boy peeked. "I see a little bird," he said in a flat voice. "A little bird bobbing and flapping, like little birds do."

"She is looking for us," the other insisted. "She is looking for me, I think." Now he gesticulated with both hands, nearly overbalancing on the flimsy seat.

The horse snorted. Unobtrusively Gaspare sidled to the edge of the seat. The little bird (it was a dun-gray dove, with a ring around its neck) passed overhead, banked in the air and circled the wagon.

Gaspare glared from the dove to Damiano. The action was too perfect. He suspected this whole scene was a trick arranged especially for him, but for the life of him, he couldn't think how it had been done. As the bird circled again, Gaspare began to feel silly. He watched the dove descend to the dust of the road, where the horse sniffed it and uttered a very wise, deep nicker.

And then, while Damiano clambered down from the wagon seat, capering with what enthusiasm his striped back would permit, and as Gaspare's vision swam, the dun dove turned into a very beautiful—not lady, certainly, not with that blue felt dress which showed feet and ankles and more besides—a most exquisitely beautiful brown-braided, barefoot peasant maiden.

She put one hand upon the horse's shoulder, perhaps with the apprehension that her sudden appearance might have upset the beast. But Festilligambe might have been accustomed to transforming people since foalhood. His left ear twisted around but his right ear did not feel it was worth the effort. His head neither inclined nor flinched away. He inched away from her touch with only his usual diffidence.

She looked at the horse and the wagon and she looked at Gaspare (and at that moment the boy knew that this one *was* a great lady after all, even barefoot and in felt, so he swallowed firmly and bit down upon his unruly tongue) and then she looked through him and finally she allowed herself to look upon the young man standing in front of her.

"Where is this plague?" she said, speaking Italian with a strange, broad, bouncing accent. "Neither of you has such sickness in you." Her small face showed concern, along with a certain shade of accusation, but as she frowned at Damiano, the tiny hairs that escaped her braids caught the sun. "Your only trouble is that you don't eat right."

Damiano was looking at the gleaming bronze hairs instead of at the frown, while he himself was smiling so that he thought perhaps he would not be able to talk. "You—you came all the way from Lombardy, Saara. To see me? Because of my strange visit to you? Gaspare here was just telling me that you were a fever dream, like the time he had the spots and saw his sister as Saint Lucia."

Then, before his bubbling triviality might have time to irritate Saara, he added, "Yes, my lady, there is plague behind us, and if we have escaped it I am only too glad. And the flogging I mentioned, which caused me to flee to you—that was real, too, though nowhere so terrible as the plague. But I did not think you would trouble yourself so. . . ."

Saara the Fenwoman put her hand on Damiano's bare arm, intending to turn him around. As they touched she saw some shade of feeling in the movement of his eye and she said, "Don't worry, Dami." Her frown dissolved. "Now that we are both present in body, it is no longer dangerous for me to touch you."

Damiano's eyes opened wide. He scratched his own bare shoulder, and from his confusion he rescued some element of gallantry. "No longer dangerous? My sweet lady, it is because of our bodies that danger enters into it." But as he spoke, pride turned his mangled back away from her.

"It is nothing worth looking at," he declared. "No more than bramble scratches. Forget I ever spoke of it. I took off my shirt because the day was warm."

Damiano met Saara's eyes slowly, for he was not a good liar, and he found in them a swirling, green-brown angry fire at this silliness of his.

As around Saara (and around the power of Saara) all things had unexpected color and focus, so even her anger took on brightness. Though once Damiano might have met, or at least understood this light of anger, now he could not even look at her. For she was the greatest and most assuredly the most beautiful witch in the Italies, while he had not even the fire with which he had been born.

So he was silenced and his eyes slid away. And as Saara saw this, her anger faded into something like pity, or like hurt, and upon that emotion yet another sort of anger fed.

"You fool! What under all the winds have you been doing to yourself? Don't you know that plague is death, and not all the magic that is in the earth can overcome it? And this . . ." as she spun him about and pointed to the scabbing weals, "how did you let *this* happen? Do you forget who you are? You! You who were once strong enough to carry half of my soul away with you, and then wise enough to bring it back!

"I know you, witch, for I carry around a dark child

you have abandoned, and all it does is whisper your name! You cannot lose your self-respect without bringing shame to me. And if you should die, witch—Damiano—if you should die of plague in a far country, then what am I to do with that little shadow?"

Self-possession returned to Damiano between one moment and the next. His head snapped up and he rested his own large hand upon hers. "When I die, Saara, then you must release anything of mine that you hold. A dead man should be dead."

Saara blinked: catlike, green, but uncertain. "Not 'when,' but 'if,' Dami. You are not sick, remember, but only underfed." And in a whisper she added, "And I am much older than you."

In that instant their positions were reversed, for the young man stood with quiet assurance, while Saara stepped back a pace, slipping her hand from his.

"And I ask again . . ." She raised both her arms in a world-embracing gesture. "Damiano, in a land filled with food, why have you starved yourself?"

During the prior conversation, Gaspare had sat on the wagon seat as motionless as the whipstock, while magic and talk of magic turned his head around, and while talk of dark children turned his ideas of Damiano on their heads.

But at this last question Damiano himself turned from Saara to Gaspare, and what he saw in that pinched, ruddy face caused him to break out laughing.

The boy took this as a sort of permission, and his own strong need pulled him from the wagon seat to the presence of the terrible, angry, beautiful barefoot lady, where he knelt and clasped his hands about her knees.

"Oh, signorina bellissima! He will never admit it, being too stiff-necked and mad besides, but he is starving to death in truth, and I am also. And if you are as great a lady as your appearance declares you, you will have pity on us and give us a little something. If you have no silver, then bread will do. Enchanted bread is very good, I have heard. Or enchanted roast pork, or even enchanted boiled greens. . . ."

Saara had been aware of Gaspare on the wagon seat, just as she had been aware of Festilligambe between the traces, but when the boy fell at her feet, and clasped her embroidered dress she gaped from his red face to Damiano's dark one.

"Who?" she asked.

Gaspare's gesture began at Damiano and ended theatrically, slapping his own breast. "I'm his dancer," he announced. "And if he has lost a little of his looks, signora, do not exclude him from your graces. Some of his decay is age, of course, as he is all of three and twenty, but most of it is only hardship, curable with a little kindness."

His gooseberry green eyes stared wildly into her green ones as he stage-whispered, "I beg you only to remember the dark child!" Then, seeing in the elven face no perceptible sign of softening (indeed, Saara's expression was frozen by complete incomprehension), Gaspare added, "But if after all these entreaties, it still seems the fellow is beyond saving, it is perhaps worth noting that I am only fourteen at present, so my best years are certainly before me."

Saara shifted within Gaspare's unslackening knee-clasp. She looked up once more at Damiano, who was so trapped between anger at Gaspare, sympathy with the boy and a general desire to laugh at the picture he made, that his face had gone nearly as red as the redhead's.

"Why do you need a dancer?" Saara inquired of him.

He cleared his throat. "Gaspare. Let the lady go now," he commanded.

Obediently Gaspare released. Then in a reaction toward dignity the boy stood upright, brushing himself off.

Damiano brushed one hand through his hair as he continued, "I need a dancer, Saara, because I am a musician. I play. He dances. People pay us—when they feel like it.

"That is also why we are starving." He laughed at his own words, not because they were very funny, but because he found it easy to laugh around Saara.

"I don't mean because we're bad, so no one wants to hear or see us. I don't think we're bad, either of us."

"We're certainly not," interjected Gaspare with a great deal of confidence.

"But no one in Franche-Comté knows us yet, and we don't even know where and when the markets are, so . . . it is not easy."

Saara continued to stare, and though Damiano believed, or wanted to believe, that he knew the woman well, he could not read her expression. From somewhere within him a spark of defiance rose. "So why should I apologize?" He shrugged. "Being hungry isn't a sin."

The woman started, in abrupt, birdlike fashion. "Ruggerio would talk like that; he would say, 'If I want to sleep till midday, so what? It isn't a sin.' Or in the summer he would say, 'When you walk around without your clothes like that, Saara, you are sin waiting to happen.'

"Someday I must learn what a sin is," she concluded.

Gaspare's guffaw at the mention of walking around without clothes was rather overdone. But then he thought that line expected a guffaw, and was rather annoyed that Damiano had missed his cue.

Because he did not like to be reminded of the Roman he had killed, Damiano remained sober. "I myself am never certain, my lady. But I have found that harm done to another person is usually a sin, while harm done to myself usually is not."

Saara took her left braid in her right hand, and her right braid in her left, and she yanked on them both. Thoughtfully she regarded the sweet hills of grass and trees.

Behind them rose a height of vines, their leaves just breaking, waxy green against the chalky soil. Down ahead the road looped around water, and the rough calls of ducks rose in the air. Set back from both pond and highway was a house: a rural mansion, limed white and possessing at least four rooms. To the right of the road spread pastureland, dotted with sheep. As though apprehending her notice, a sheepdog began to bark.

The witch stood motionless, her lips twitching slightly. Gaspare opened his mouth to speak, but Damiano elbowed him neatly, for he knew what Saara was doing. "There." She pointed. "Three people are in that house. There is a whole new lamb hanging over a smoke-fire. Also a barrel half filled with sleeping roots: turnips, maybe. And in the oven, pot pies are baking now; I think even the simple nose could smell them."

Gaspare emitted a strengthless whine and leaned against Damiano, who could scarcely support him. Saara, with the forced patience of a mother with very slow children, spoke slowly and distinctly.

"You go down there and clap at their door, and tell them that you are hungry and have nothing to eat."

A dozen expressions chased themselves across Gaspare's features.

He whispered, "And you will enchant them into feeding us, O great and beautiful lady?"

Saara's smile was scornful. "Of course not. I will do nothing. They will give you food because it is what they ought to do, and they will be glad to do it."

The boy deflated, and even Damiano looked a trifle wan. "I'm sorry, Saara," he said. "But they will not. These are the civilized peasants of France, and they will give away nothing for free."

She looked at him sidelong, but the honesty of his regard was convincing. "But how do they expect to live themselves, when their sleds are empty, if they do not feed the unfortunate now?"

"They rely on providence and their own management to prevent that from ever happening," he replied, and Gaspare chimed in with, "They are hard, the people of France. Very hard!"

Saara sought advice from the black, disinterested eyes of the horse, and failing there, from her naked toes. She nibbled delicately at the end of one braid. Finally she raised her chin and nodded.

Her face was stern. "I believe what you tell me, Damiano, though I cannot see how a land can work so. Things are more just in the land of the Lapps...." Her words fell away, as though her memories had changed in midsentence. "Well, no mind. If they will not feed you, you must take what you need. It is only fair."

Gaspare jumped up and down in place. "Hah. That's what I've been telling him since November last!"

Damiano did not respond to the boy. "Saara," he said instead, "if we are caught stealing we could be hanged, or could have our hands chopped off. Without a hand I will not be able to play the lute."

Saara sputtered, and her pink feet danced over the road. "Is that all it would matter to you? That you would not be able to play the lute? Well, Damiano, I will try to see you do not get caught. What more can I say?"

Pain added an extra glitter to Damiano's eyes, for he had donned his woolen shirt. The three thieves strolled casually along the dry and empty road, with Saara's witch-sense keeping watch. Damiano walked stiffly, and the Fenwoman kept to his side, so that left Gaspare to lead the foraging party.

As was only appropriate.

Stepping her sun-browned feet in the dust next to Damiano, Saara was touched with meaning, with an importance of line, of color, of gesture that was almost deadly to him. It was nothing she did, for she did nothing but patter along childlike on his right side. It was not the beauty of her face or form, for though her skin was infant-fine, her green eyes were tilted like those of a fox, and were foxlike sly, and of her figure, though Damiano felt that he knew quite a lot about it, still all he had ever seen was the shapeless, felt dress.

But the sun became glory, when it burnished her hair. And the road of dirt became adventure, because reaching out Damiano could touch her. And this hot March afternoon marked the clear end of something, and the beginning of something else.

Yet under the heat of his face and behind the smiling mouth Damiano was not happy, for his feelings knew too much of yearning and not enough of rest. If this was love, it was not the same passion he would have said he felt for Carla Denezzi, now behind convent walls at Bard.

This was no blessed or consoling feeling. He thought perhaps he wanted to strike Saara, to hit her across her petal-pink lips and knock her down. But of course he would not be able to strike her; if he lifted his fist she would turn and look at him and he would be the one to fall.

Or perhaps he wanted only to shout at her, to tear her heavy dress off, to shock her in any way possible.

Why? Was it because he wanted her, and desire made him feel like a fool?

Then Saara turned her glance from the gray ducks of the pond to Damiano. In an instant he felt his mind had

been read, and flinched with guilt, but what Saara said
was, "Why 'sheep-face,' Dami? Why did he call you
sheep-face?"

Relief was exquisite, and the silly question settled his
mind as little else could have done. "Because he thinks I
look like a sheep," he answered her, and then he yielded
to the temptation of adding, "Can you see a resemblance?"

Saara's eye went dry and analytical. Damiano swallowed.

"I see what he means. It is the nose, mostly. It is
broad down the middle and almost turns under. And the
eyes, also."

"I see," said Damiano, as stoutly as he could.

"I myself have been told I look like a fox about the
face," she added, but Damiano interrupted with an angry
hiss.

"Not at all!" he cried, with all the more heat because
he had been thinking exactly that—that Saara looked like a
fox. "There is no resemblance! Your face is as fine as ivory
and roses, and you move like a bird in the air. Fox
indeed!"

She skittered two feet away, amusement written all
over her fox-face. "So. Is that the way I was supposed to
answer you? 'There is no resemblance!' Well, I can look
like roses and a fox, too, I imagine, and you, Damiano
Delstrego, are a vain young man, just like...".

"Don't say 'like Ruggerio,'" he pleaded. "I am not a
duelist like him, and he was a Roman besides."

"I was not going to say that," she replied, subdued
suddenly. "But never mind. I think you are a handsome
boy, Damiano. Handsome and more besides. And you can
be all that and still look a little like a sheep." The part in
her hair (straight, but slightly off-center) came just under
Damiano's eye level. As he looked down upon it suddenly
his roiled emotions clarified and he did what he wanted to
do, which was to kiss that warm, bronze-brown head.

"I love you, Saara," he whispered, regardless of Gaspare,
trotting on ahead. "I know all men have to love you, so
that is nothing special to you, and I know further that I am
last of all who should speak to you of love, but I do love
you.

"I hear you in my mind a thousand miles away, and
your image floats to me through pain and darkness, like a

golden lamp. I have nothing to give—not even time—but still I love you."

Saara stepped back and her gaze was not soft but shrewd. "You don't love me, Damiano, though I might wish you did. You hear your other part; your broken self is calling to be whole."

Damiano heard her. He answered nothing, though his mouth formed words. He shivered. By the pure Mother of God, he whispered to himself alone, she's right, or at least partly right.

Of course Saara was important, her every gesture imbued with meaning. *Her* every gesture was flavored by *his* every gesture, and her eyes gave back his own familiar fire. How could he not have seen? He had become simple indeed to stand next to his own spirit and not feel it.

He was ashamed.

He was ashamed, but he raised his head. "You know what I do not, Saara. Probably you know me better than I know myself, anymore. But still I love you."

They had stopped together, just beyond the duckpond. Together they stood under the sun, amid the buzzing of the season's first dragonflies. And Saara's smile was most maliciously sly. "All right, my pretty, sheep-face Damiano. So if you do love me what do we do about it?"

But if they had forgotten the purpose and urgency of their mission, Gaspare had not. He danced back, his feet impatient and demanding. "First you dawdle," he hissed. "And then you stop entirely. I'd like to know how you expect to win your bread that way. Are you still bothered that our purpose is not holy enough, Damiano?"

The older fellow glared, but he was really glad of the interruption. A greater interruption followed, as the sound of unhurried footsteps scuffed up the road toward them, their maker hidden by the last hillock between the pond and the house.

With instinctive smoothness Gaspare's face became casual and innocent—far more respectable than its usual habit. He bent down and snatched up one of his cloth-booted feet, and examined the many rents in the material with proprietary interest. He also pointed to his foot, looking up at Damiano so that the approaching household-er would see a tableau that raised no suspicious questions.

But to the ruin of his plans, Damiano's barefoot lady began to sing. Perfectly loudly she caroled, and tunefully, too. But her eyes were closed, and the words were quite mad.

> *"Damiano, Gaspare, me.*
> *There is nothing here to see.*
> *Damiano, Gaspare, me.*
> *There is nothing here to see."*

The fine hairs on Gaspare's arms prickled. He stared wildly at Damiano, but his friend's dark face wore a peculiar expression of listening, colored by satisfaction. His face shifted from Saara to the person approaching as that one rounded the hillock.

It was a girl of perhaps sixteen years, her smooth hair hanging loosely over her shoulders. Her dress was pale homespun. She swung a flat basket, looking as bored as a sixteen-year-old girl may look, when out to gather eggs.

> *"Nothing but sky above your head,*
> *Nothing but dirt on which you tread,*
> *Damiano, Gaspare, me.*
> *There is nothing here to see."*

The girl passed them by and she did not look toward them at all.

Damiano was grinning broadly. "It has been a long time," he whispered in his throat, and then to Gaspare, "I don't know how she finds the rhyme so quick."

But Saara paid him no mind. Still singing, she jerked on Gaspare's sleeve and signaled them both to follow. Feet of pinkish-brown leaped from the dust of the road to the grass bank, and hopped tussock to tussock into the wet. Gaspare and Damiano imitated her steps, Damiano with less agility, for despite adventure and an epiphany of the heart, his back still hurt.

"Damiano, Gaspare, me
There is nothing here to see.
Hear no sound of splashing legs,
Nor ducks' squeal as we steal their eggs.
Nothing but sky above your head
And slimy ooze through which you tread.
Damiano, Gaspare, me . . ."

"It is getting longer," said Damiano for Gaspare's ear only. "And she changes it a little as she goes. It's a wonder she can remember!"

Gaspare leaped over a freshet and helped his friend after. His spare face was transfigured, and his prominent eyes stood out. "Is this magic?" he hissed back. "Real magic? The goosegirl cannot see us?"

Damiano nodded. "But that is not to say she cannot hear us talk." But even he could not resist adding, "Well, what do you think of magic—real magic?"

The boy made an owl face. "It is silly! And in terrible taste. But if it works, it's wonderful, of course."

"Of course. All wonderful things are silly, and most are in abysmal taste."

Saara, with unerring instinct, took four eggs from three squalling, sitting ducks, and then would search no more. Instead she slipped the eggs down the neckline of her embroidered dress, causing Damiano and Gaspare to wonder what held them there. Saara left the goosegirl rummaging through the nests, cursing the nips on her ankles, and she led her small parade over the grass and to the house.

"There is nothing here to see,
Nothing moves but wind in tree."

They entered the farmyard, which was marked out by being slightly boggier and more laden with manure than the surrounding grass. A shortish, stocky horse of the Comtois breed stood grazing not fifty feet from the white house wall. The calloused scars of the ox-yoke covered his shoulders.

Damiano spared a moment's disapproval. "A horse shouldn't plow in a yoke. There are perfectly decent horse harnesses. Or better yet, they should get an ox for plowing."

Both Gaspare and Saara shot him glances of irritation. She took him by the wrist and put a finger to her mouth, all the while singing her simple, repetitive song.

> "Damiano, Gaspare, me,
> There is no one here to see.
> Nothing stirs upon the planking,
> Form is missing, voice is lacking."

"Ouch!" whispered Damiano, and Gaspare (who in all matters of art was sensitive) cringed his shoulders. Saara spared one offended sniff and then pulled them in behind her. Into the house.

It was dim within, and the stones were damp. Yet in this, the largest room of the house, two cook-fires gave their smoky warmth, and the odor of lamb and pastry was overpowering.

In the middle of the room, where the black rafters rose highest, a long table had been set, with benches at either side. On one side sat a man: burly, bearded, short, liberally daubed with mud. He reclined on one elbow, while he played with the last corner of the hard piece of flatbread that had been his dinner trencher. On the far side of the table sat a mug, surrounded by crumbs: remnants of the goosegirl's meal. A tall woman, thinner than either husband or daughter, was tending the fire beneath the iron oven-pot, which was raised on fieldstone to the height of her waist.

"It don' draw none," she declared in a patois of langue d'oc and langue d'oil even Damiano could scarcely follow. "It needs you to build it again."

The man turned to his wife with the slowness of seasons revolving. "You want I should build something, the time to say that is winter, not when the ground is open."

"In winter you say you can't work stone because the ground is froze," she replied, but without rancor. Indeed, this entire interchange had been conducted with a boredom on both sides equal to that shown by the girl at the duckpond.

Saara took Gaspare by the shoulders and set him down on the far end of the bench from the householder. Damiano she motioned to the bench on the far side of the table. Both young men sat in a paralysis of fear, to find themselves in such close and protracted contact with the people they were robbing. Gaspare's pale green eyes glowed almost white.

Now Saara's song changed, fading into the back of her throat, and the odd words Damiano could pick up were not Italian. She moved with practiced efficiency through the smoky kitchen, carving a quarter of lamb and cutting black bread with a knife as long as a boar spear and thin from much sharpening. Both the meat and the bread she wrapped in a scrap of dirty linen which lay by the pot-stove. This bag she dropped on the table in front of Gaspare, but as the boy goggled at it between terror and fascination, his mouth wet and working, she shoved it across the boards to Damiano, thinking perhaps that he would be the more trustworthy keeper. Then she went from the kitchen into a darker room behind it. Damiano heard her digging in sand.

The goosegirl returned, her wood-shod feet making a great racket on the floor. Gaspare started in panic, but Damiano leaned painfully across the table and put his restraining hand upon the boy's bony shoulder.

"I can't believe," the girl announced, setting her basket between the intruders. "Only two eggs."

Her father grunted heavily. "Not right, this season. There should be a half-dozen, at least, with all the ducks we kept over winter. It must be the foxes again. I'll set the dog on them."

This last suggestion infused Damiano with a warm glow—a ridiculous warm glow, as though he had been personally praised. A fox it had been in truth: a lovely, sly, green-eyed fox, and he heard her now in the pantry, stuffing things into a sack.

Magic or simple, whole or sundered, let no man say he did not love Saara the witch. And for a moment, in the middle of peril, with one hand on the racing pulse of Gaspare and his nose full of the smell of food, Damiano convinced himself that this was his own house he sat in, at his own kitchen table, with his own Saara singing from happiness in the next room.

Of course if it were his, the house would be light and dry, the walls fresh-limed, and the floor painted tile. If it were his, there would be rows of books, and one would be able to look out the window and see the clean mountains. And the beasts in the stable would be full-fed and glossy, with never a scar.

And this vision of bucolic contentment raised in him such a dizzying desire that he choked on it, and Gaspare looked up, his own fear turned to concern. Damiano frowned hugely, to show he was all right.

The peasant rose then, moving ponderously for his moderate size, and the goosegirl took his place by the table, staring. No word passed between her and her mother.

One year ago, or fifteen months, perhaps, Damiano reflected, he had lusted after immortal greatness. He had wanted the name of Delstrego to be linked with that of Hermes, the alchemist, and with Dante, the patriot. His only quandary had been whether to achieve his greatness through literature, music or natural philosophy.

And he had accomplished something.

For one night he had led an army (much against its will). On one winter's day he had bested the greatest witch in the Italies in single combat (and there she was in the pantry, singing). He had won a peace for the city to which he had bargained away his rights, forever.

And now, in the spring of his twenty-fourth year, Damiano could imagine no greater happiness than to live an unexceptional life within four rooms by a duckpond, in the company of a woman—a rose-faced, fox-faced woman—who went barefoot through the cold.

Viciously he informed himself that he could not have that form of happiness, nor any other that came upon the earth, for along with his rights to Partestrada, he had bargained away all rights to the future.

Damiano was standing by the table when Saara came singing from the pantry.

Sunlight hit them like a blow; even Saara blinked

against it. Damiano gave Gaspare the bag and took from Saara the rough sack she had slung over one shoulder. The witch trotted them up the road the goosegirl had taken.

Without warning, a dog—the forgotten sheepdog, the dog that was to be set on foxes—exploded from a ditch at their feet. It was a heavy creature, almost the size of one of its own wooly charges, headed like a mastiff and bobtailed. Gaspare shrieked but clutched his parcel to him.

Damiano leaped forth. He stood between the animal and Gaspare, raised one arm and shouted, "Go! Go home!" in his most commanding bass.

The beast slavered, crouched down and sprang for Damiano's throat.

It was a sharp stone the size of a man's fist, and it caught the dog exactly over its left eye. Its charge went crooked and it landed on its outsized jaw. It peered at Saara—author of the stone—with a single working eye which was the size of that of a pig. With its little tail tucked down against its rump, the sheepdog backed sullenly away.

Damiano was full of admiration. "Not a beat!" he exclaimed, hefting his sack once more. "You missed not a beat while you jumped sideways, bent down, found the stone and tossed it!"

Saara returned his glance without enthusiasm. Her face was slick with sweat. Yet still the sure line of melody passed her lips, endless as a Breton ballad. She led them back to the wagon.

Out of green brush and long grasses Damiano hacked a nest for Saara. He bathed her face with water from Gaspare's leather drinking bottle, and dried it on his single change of shirt.

"You must keep watch," she said weakly. "I won't know if someone comes near. I'm too tired."

"I know," replied Damiano, as he sat beside her, his head resting on one propped knee, his hand smoothing her braid. "Who should know better than I, how weary song-spelling becomes? In fact, when the girl came in, I half expected the spell would fray."

Eyes closed, Saara shook her head. "No. But if I had been singing in Italian it might have. What inspired me to try that, I don't know. I do not much speak the tongue, let alone sing in it!"

She looked up at him. "I guess that was for you, Dami. So you could know how it is I work."

"I know already." Damiano smiled. "You sang all the snows of winter upon me, along with a very large pine tree."

Then Saara looked away again. "Is Gaspare keeping watch?"

"He is keeping watch and eating," came the reply from above her head. The redhead sat cross-legged upon a spit of rock, with a trencher of black bread on his lap, piled with lamb. "He is very alert, and can do both at once," the boy added.

Saara's face shifted from Gaspare to Damiano. "You," she said. "You should be eating, too."

He shrugged. "I'll wait for you."

Saara pulled a soft pouch on a string from around her neck, and from it came four perfect, white eggs. She caught Damiano's eye. "I bet you were wondering," she whispered slyly.

She divided the remaining bread and lamb into two piles, giving the greater share to Damiano. He, in turn, piled the meat back onto her trencher. "I can't eat it," he admitted, shamefaced. "Not since I was a cow once."

Saara stared. "I have been a cow before. I have been a lamb, for that matter, and yet I have no trouble."

Damiano looked past her, and past the clearing off the road where the horse was tethered, to the light of the westering sun. "Ah, but were you ever a cow that someone butchered, my lady?"

She shook her head forcefully. "No, my dear, I was not." And she scooped the shredded lamb on her fingers. "How about eggs, Damiano?" And then she giggled. "Unless you have been an egg that someone has cracked. . . ."

Damiano's heavy eyebrows rose. "You are sounding more and more like Gaspare, Saara. No. I can eat eggs, as long as they do not have slimy unborn ducklings inside."

"Oh, no," replied Saara. She held up an egg, pierced it with an experienced fingernail, and drained it raw. "These are fresh this morning."

"Nobody can eat old eggs," vouched Gaspare, rattling

down from the spur of rock. "But even old sheep-face can eat fresh ones." He took an egg, snipped it against the edge of one ragged tooth, and followed Saara's example.

Glowing green eyes looked into his pale ones. "Don't call him sheep-face too much," she said to Gaspare.

Chapter Four

The sun was sinking and the travelers' fire lit the hummocked rock walls of their tiny dell. As always, Festilligambe's ardor for fire had to be restrained, lest the gelding burn off his mane and tail. Gaspare was almost as bad; having no warming fat upon his body, he huddled so close to the flames he would occasionally singe his nose and knees.

It had been surprisingly easy to fill up their bellies. Strange that a hunger built for months at a time should disappear within two meals. Damiano sat cross-legged, practicing left-hand changes upon his lute and wishing he could lean back against something. Satiation demanded rest, but he refused to lie flat on his stomach like an infant with Saara watching.

At night it was bad enough—in the wagon with her gentle breathing on one side and Gaspare's adenoidal rasp on the other. And Gaspare so pointedly turned his head away. (Gaspare had explained that his instinct was to withdraw into the wood and leave Damiano alone with the lady with whom he seemed to share such a disturbing past, but that there were not sufficient blankets to spare, and on cold ground he would never last till morning. And Damiano had replied, of course, that it didn't matter at all where Gaspare slept.)

"Whose fief is this through which we're driving?" he asked casually, just to be saying something.

Gaspare grunted. "Dunno. There's nothing important between Lyons and Avignon. It may be the riots have swept the area already, and no one greater than a monsignore has a head on his shoulders. . . ."

Damiano shook his head. "The riots were in the north, in France, and their year is ended, anyway. Gaspare, you are just trying to frighten the lady."

"What is a riot?" asked Saara, sounding not at all frightened.

"It doesn't matter. They are all in the north of France," replied Damiano, a touch too sharply.

And he chastised himself for it. It was bad enough to move like an old man in winter, and to know one looked like a beggar (save for the hair), but now he was becoming surly as well.

"Is it like the plague?" she pressed them.

Gaspare, making some connection in his brain evident only to himself, gave a nasty laugh. "Not at all," replied Damiano.

But the witch wasn't ready to let the subject drop. "About the plague. You must be very careful, for if you should catch it, I cannot help you."

Damiano glanced at her sidelong and sighed. "I know, my lady. My father read to me at least a dozen collected cures for the plague, and at the end of each one he said 'That is very fine, except that it doesn't work.' I grew up knowing that there is no cure in grammerie for the pest."

Saara reacted to this mention of Delstrego Senior by staring at the fire. "Yet a strong witch," she qualified, "will not catch the plague."

Heavy black eyebrows lifted. "That I didn't know. So you, Saara, are in no danger?"

"Neither would you be," she added casually, "if you were undivided."

Damiano dropped his eyes to the lute.

Those green eyes rose a vanity in him, and more than vanity, a desire to impress. He switched from exercises to a newly learned piece in the sharp, Spanish mode, only to find his fingers unexpectedly clumsy.

Resting the instrument on his lap, he flexed both hands together. "I'm tight all over," he mumbled to the world at large. "I need a lesson."

Saara was lying flat on her back, at a four-foot remove from the fire. She needed far less heat than the two

Italians, and in the wagon at night used no more than a corner of Damiano's woolen blanket. As he spoke she was playing with a feather, a white down feather, which she was sailing right and left with puffs of air. Languorously she turned onto one hip.

"A lesson?"

"From his angel," came a voice from the crackle of the fire, and Gaspare withdrew a red face beaded with sweat. "Damiano takes lute lessons from an angel whom one cannot see or hear."

"One—meaning Gaspare of San Gabriele—cannot," answered Damiano mildly. "And I will not inflict upon Gaspare Raphael's invisible presence." Scissoring his legs, he rose in place, and with the lute in one hand, walked to the edge of the circle.

"My lady Saara," he began, suddenly formal. Suddenly uncertain. "If you have any desire to meet my teacher . . . he is a wonderful person. An archangel he is, with great spreading wings—but very easy company."

Saara's interest was quick. Amusement made her eyes slant further. She popped to her feet, stroking her chin with a bronze braid. She accompanied him out of the circle of light.

There was a lot of moon showing tonight. Perhaps it was full. Once, Damiano would have known the hour and minute of the moon's fullness. Once, it would have affected him. Perhaps it still affected him, but he was no longer aware of it.

He was thinking he should not have invited Saara. Introducing Raphael had never been a great success, since other people could not see him. (Or since nobody else could see him except Macchiata, who had been a dog and therefore did not count. And now the horse, who counted even less, being without speech.) Saara was a fine witch, certainly, but Damiano wasn't quite sure that being a witch was enough. And if she was able to see the angel, Damiano knew that he himself would wind up showing off in his lesson instead of working.

Here—on this bright dome of stone, with its glitter of glass in the granite rock. This would make a good setting for an angel, if the wind were not too high. Being in all things an artist, Damiano liked to set Raphael like a jewel against his surroundings.

He sat himself down, noting that moonlight hadn't warmed the rocks. Saara folded herself a few feet away from him. He cleared his throat.

"Seraph?" he called into the shining night. He spoke as another student might call "Professor?" down rows of musty bookshelves. "If you have the time..."

This was meaningless, as he knew. Raphael always had the time, if he chose to come. In fact, he probably had an assortment of times to choose from. But Damiano had never been able to reconcile angelic dimensionality with human courtesy, and he was, after all, human. So he called, "If you have the time..."

And Raphael appeared above them, descending light as milkweed. Damiano felt him and looked away.

He gazed instead at Saara, who had no difficulty with the angel's form. She stared at Raphael brightly and bird-wisely, but without reverence. Without, in fact, a great deal of courtesy. In an instant Damiano was regretting the introduction of two powers, neither of which he could control.

"Good evening," he began politely, letting the angel's radiance leak into his closed eyes.

"Yes, isn't it?" replied Raphael, and his voice held such a rich and living equanimity that the mortal relaxed a bit. Surely the Archangel Raphael was too great to be offended at a certain lack of respect out of Saara. He had never demanded respect out of Macchiata, and in some ways a pagan was much like a dog.

"Very good. Air and earth are singing together," continued the angel. "And if you are quiet you can hear them."

Saara was smiling with that secret, superior amusement of hers.

"I was rather hoping for a lute lesson," he replied to Raphael, wishing he could see whether *he* was watching Saara.

"That needn't break the peace," was the answer, and then, unexpectedly, Raphael added, "God's blessing on you, Saara Saami."

She showed the composure of a small, grinning pagan

idol as she replied, "So you are what these Italians call an angel, Chief of Eagles. How curious."

The dark musician glanced wonderingly at Saara. "You know him already?"

"Every Lappish child knows the eagle-spirits of the high air. There are four of them."

"Once there were five," added the archangel.

Damiano, in his confusion, made the mistake of glancing at Raphael directly.

When the dizziness passed, Saara was speaking, an edge of sharpness in her voice. "So why don't you take care of him, then?"

Raphael's answer was slow in coming. "I don't know how to do that, Saara. Do you?"

Damiano focused with effort on the witch's face, which was a little too faraway for his eye's comfort, especially when he was already woozy. What he saw gave no comfort, for Saara's fox-face was to the fore. Not only was she lacking reverence, she did not appear even friendly toward Raphael. "I have a certain earthy wit," she was saying. "Mother wit. I know, for instance, that he cannot continue in the way he is."

"Mortals by their nature cannot continue in the way they are. What matters, I am told, is the direction in which they change." Raphael's words were slow and reflective; Damiano could barely hear them.

But they gained clarity as the angel added, "Be careful, Saara."

To Damiano's pained astonishment, the witch laughed outright. "That advice I will take," she crowed. "I will be very careful." She leaped to her feet, shook dust from her heavy dress and padded off the moonlit dome.

Damiano did not know what to say—whether he should apologize for Saara, explain her background or merely ask what had transpired while he had been hors de combat.

But Raphael spoke first, and he spoke very calmly. "On what did you want to work tonight, Damiano?"

The young man took a moment to collect himself. His fingers drummed on the thin wood belly of the lute. "I'm all tight again, Seraph."

Raphael waited the perfect moment before he replied, "Yes. I can imagine."

Gaspare was still haunting the fire. When he saw Saara approach alone he settled back and squinted at her cannily, as though there were a sly understanding between green-eyed people. "Is there an angel?" he inquired.

With a lift of her chin she repelled this familiarity. "Yes, there is an angel," she replied. "A great spirit of the air. Did you think Damiano was lying to you?"

Gaspare shrugged. "No, lady. I just thought he was mad." He snickered ruefully. "You have to admit, when a fellow talks about being a magician and then never *does* anything magical, it's easy to doubt."

Then Gaspare's interest drifted in a different direction. He poked the fire with a stick. "This angel, Lady Saara. Does he play the lute like old sheep—like Damiano? I mean, is that where he got that style of his?"

Saara stood above the blossom of flame, and to Gaspare's amazement, she thoughtfully began to braid the fire, as she would her brown hair. "I . . . don't know, Gaspare. I didn't stay to listen."

When Damiano awoke, the wind was blowing against (and through) the wagon side. Already the sun was well risen. Saara sat at the open foot of the vehicle, combing her hair with her fingers. Her feet swung in the tree-dappled light.

Damiano's back was taut and stiff, as it always was upon waking, and his neck muscles were sore from the lack of variety in his sleeping position, but he could tell he would feel much better today.

He was wearing his rough mountain trousers. He did not usually wear them to sleep, but with a woman so close . . . His first touch of the morning air caused him to reach for his shirt.

He blundered about, probing and peering, until he had covered most of the wagon. The lute protested hollowly as he banged it with one knee.

Saara observed him idly. Finally she scooted back into the depths of the wagon. "Gaspare has it," she announced. "He was feeling very cold this morning. He has no blood."

"Then what is it that makes his face so red?" mumbled Damiano, and he sat back on his haunches, wrapping the wretched blanket around him and over his head. His face he rubbed between his knees, grunting.

"He's got my shirt? Well, what about me; is my flesh less sensitive, or am I any bloodier? And where is he, anyway?"

Saara regarded him with the superiority the quick riser feels for the poor brute who wakes up slowly. "He is out setting rabbit snares. He said he would rather do it while you were sleeping. And since the grass is so good here, we thought we'd rest the day. So you can stay in the blanket."

"Deprived of all dignity," muttered Damiano, and he slid to the ground and stalked away, robed and cowled like a monk, to perform his morning offices in privacy.

Breakfast was mashed turnips, and a cup of the goat's milk that Saara had acquired without fuss or explanation. Damiano was not really in a bad mood, but he did not know how to behave around Saara, having grown up without mother or sisters.

One could not remain gallant and lyrical for three days unbroken.

"Speaking of dignity, my lady," he began, and then reconsidered his angle of approach. "Or rather, I am curious to know why you did not . . . like . . . Raphael very much."

Saara's eyes grew almost round with surprise. "Not like him? But I do like him, Dami. As much as I have liked any spirit I don't know very well. Why do you think I don't like him?"

Damiano folded his large hands around his knees. "You did not seem trustful, Saara. And then you walked away from him."

Her child-soft mouth tightened. "Should I stay to chat with him, like two women at a well? Him? It is the custom in the North that spirits keep to spirits and people keep to people. And as for trust: you, Damiano, are much too trustful."

Damiano's hands clenched over his knees. He made a rude noise. "If there is one sort of . . . of person, spirit or flesh, whom you can trust, it is an angel of God! And

speaking of that, why did you call him Chief of Eagles?
Raphael is his name."

Very carefully, Saara crossed her feet on her lap. Her
face showed no expression, yet the air in the old wagon
was charged.

"I know his name as he knows mine. I call him Chief
of Eagles because that is what we call him. After all, he is
a white eagle in form, isn't he?"

"No," replied Damiano, nonplussed. "Of course not.
I used to see him quite clearly, and he is a man—a
beautiful man with wings."

"An eagle," she contradicted. "With human face and
hands."

Damiano recoiled from the idea. "Monstrous! Why
would he look like that when the angel form is higher and
more beautiful, and he himself is by nature high and
beautiful?"

She snickered. "Evidently you think the body of a
man is more beautiful than that of an eagle. There are two
ways of thinking about that. And as for being higher, well,
you cannot dispute that an eagle is much higher than a
man. Most of the time."

His forehead creased with puzzlement as Saara continued. "And I say again you trust too easy, Damiano.
Even if this Chief—this Raphael—is all you say, as true as
the Creator (and with the way you defend this spirit,
young one, it is too bad you cannot marry him), still you
place your trust in other strange places."

"In Gaspare? It is not so much I trust him as..."

She shook her head till the braids flew. "No, Dami. In
me. Why should you trust Saara, after all? I hate—hated
your father. You killed my lover. I killed your little dog.
We have torn at each other worse than wolves. Yet you
place your soul in my hands and go off, like leaving a baby
at grandmother's."

Damiano hung his head. "But there is no more to it
than that, Saara. Also, we know each other as well as any
brother and sister, for I have walked in your mind, and
you in mine. You know I never hated you, and... I would
like to think you have forgiven me.

"When I broke my staff and gave you my power, I
thought it would be a useful servant to you."

"It is a charge," she amended. "A burden."

"It has not made you stronger? When I held your power I was terribly strong, I felt, and could do almost anything I could think of."

Then Saara stared out the open back of the wagon, and her face was cold, distant and unreadable. "Oh, I am strong now, all right. Damiano—remember how your father told you I was the greatest witch in all the Italies? Well now, holding your fire with my own, I am without doubt the greatest witch in all of Europe.

"And if I wanted, I could go home." She made a small noise in her throat. "I could go home to the North, where all are witches, and make a tribe around me. My power would stand as a wall of protection against winter and all the lesser enemies. I would be great, and the men of the fens would fight each other for my notice. They would pile skins at my feet: milk-colored skins of the reindeer, soft as butter. They would chant a new kalevala to me."

Her glance shifted back to Damiano. "The thought makes me sick."

Damiano was so sun-darkened that when pity drew his face darker, he seemed to fade into the shadows. "I understand. Last year, my own strength made me so sick I had to be rid of it."

Saara drew closer. "But it is not last year now, Dami. It is this year. Will you take it back, your power? Your broken soul?"

"No."

His answer was abrupt, almost involuntary. Saara snapped her head back, and bit down on one knuckle in frustration.

"Let me explain, Saara. It is partly the lute, you see."

"The lute?"

"Yes. When I was a witch, then being *that* came first. It had to. A witch must be true to his senses first, before anything else.

"But an artist—a musician especially—he must be *that* first, and there is not much left over." Damiano spoke very earnestly, fearing it was impossible to communicate what he meant. "And music is far more important than magic.

"That, at least, is what I believe."

"You are muddled, Damiano," Saara answered him,

but not with anger. "They are not two things, music and magic. Unless you want to say my small songs are not magical. Or not musical." And she smiled at this last.

"Neither one, little nightingale." And with these words the prickle and tension between them dissolved and was gone. In the dim and fusty warmth of the wagon they heard one another breathing. On impulse, Damiano took her hand.

She let her fingers rest on his. "So," she whispered, "there is an old question unanswered. If you love me, Damiano, what are you going to do about it?"

It was not a large gap between them: two feet at most. Damiano reached across and placed both hands on either side of her waist. He pulled her to him, so that she sat between his knees, both of them facing the green world at the foot of the wagon. The blanket, which had fallen back as he stretched forward, he arranged once more, wrapping them both in.

He laid his chin on her shoulder. "Saara. I also said I had nothing to give."

"Not even time, you said. Does that mean your practicing the lute leaves you no..."

"No." He chuckled and softly kissed her at the nape of the neck. "I'm not such a madman. But I have struck a bargain with the Devil. Do your people know the Devil— the most evil spirit?"

She nodded, and her hair tickled his nose. Saara was very warm to hold, and Damiano grinned to think that had he been a little bolder, he might have given his blanket to Gaspare.

"Yes. We know many wicked ones, like the bringer of famine, and the ice-devil, and others whose tricks do harm. But the worst of the devils is the one called the Liar. Any man who deals with him we call a fool."

Damiano's grin went hard-edged. "It is the same all over. Father of Lies. Yet I struck a bargain with him, and I am no liar and—usually—no fool."

Saara twisted in an effort to see his face, but Damiano held her tightly. It ws easier to say certain things while staring out at the grazing horse. "It was after we fought, you and I, and I felt full of ashes. I traded him my future

for the sake of my city. It is to have peace for fifty years,
and I may not return to it.

"And I am to die," he said. "Very soon, now, for he
said the situation could not permit my living more than
two years more, and that was over a year ago."

And now he could not hold the woman, who writhed
snakelike around and fixed him a look of astonished accusation. "What? Are you about to walk up to his door and
say, 'Throw me in your caldrons of mud and sulfur?'"

He, in turn, stared at her shoulder. "No, certainly not.
He said it was not he who was going to . . . to kill me at all,
but circumstance."

"And you agreed to this?"

"Yes, of course. Saara—that was the smallest of my
concerns. He also said Partestrada itself would shrivel and
die unless fed on the blood of violence, as is Milan. I am
an Italian, my lady, and my city means to me what a
mother would mean to another man. That was why I came
to you, rather than accept the evil one's judgment."

"And I said to you 'go away.' I sent a man to whip you
away." Beneath his hands, her shoulders hardened like
steel.

"No matter, Saara. He did not succeed. Anyway, all
my efforts turned bad; neither my city nor I am meant for
greatness. We will be forgotten," he said, but without
bitterness, and he rested his head against hers. "But we
will not be murderers: neither Partestrada nor myself
anymore."

Now he turned her face to his by force. "Saara, don't
start crying. I was not trying to make you unhappy."

But the witch was not precisely crying. She was tight
and trembling under his hands, but full of rebellion,
rather than sorrow. "What is it?" she asked herself
aloud. "That every man I touch . . . even as much as
touch . . ." Her gaze was wet and angry.

"Why couldn't I have met you thirty years ago?" Saara
took Damiano in a hug that squeezed the wind out of him.
"Thirty years ago, when I was as foolish as you are."

"Thirty years ago I wasn't yet born," he replied,
hugging back. "And I'm heartily sorry for being so tardy.
Hey, dry up now. Don't be a mozzarella, like me, crying

for every little thing," he chided, rubbing a large, square finger over her reddening eyes.

And Saara's leaking tears did cease, between one moment and the next. "You're a fool to give up, Damiano. The Liar does not keep faith with men, and does not expect any better in return."

"I still want the bargain, Saara. It is a good bargain." He scratched his head furiously, as his eyebrows beetled over a scowl. "It is just—just that this year and a half has been a very long coda for a very short song."

The Fenwoman's face was stern, but filled with an odd fire, neither cold not hot, but wild like the green lights of the north. "Damiano—witch—I say to you you are a fool, but you are not as easily killed as you think. Take yourself back to yourself. The Liar cannot hurt you."

Damiano closed his eyes, bathing in her fierce radiance. "He cannot hurt *you*, my lady. That I'll grant!" His hands held her closer, and his knees pressed against her.

There was a moment's silence, and Saara leaned back her head. Their mouths were very close. "What if I were to say," she whispered, "that all I want of you is to couple together, and let the future go hang?"

His reaction was something between a snort and a chuckle. "I would say, Saara Fenwoman, that you should learn a more elegant vocabulary. But if you thought I intended to let you go now..."

He was wearing only one piece of clothing. So was she. Soon the blanket covered them both.

"You feel so warm to me," murmured Damiano in her ear. "That must mean I feel cold to you."

"No, Damiano. Don't worry." Her reply was even softer.

And then he giggled. "What if Gaspare returns now?"

Playfully she pinched his ear. "You sound like a young girl behind the shed!"

He ran his hands down the length of the woman's body. His mouth was dry, and his throat full of pounding. With her hot flesh against his, he seemed to be embracing the summer earth itself, lying prone upon it, dissolving into it.

And it seemed he was touching himself as well, for there was a familiar fire, the floating strength he remembered as a birthright. He heard the mole scrabbling in the earth beneath the wagon. All the planets, too, reached out and spoke to him, with the voice of a long, black flute.

And of course he *was* touching himself—touching that part of him he had exiled, and exiled with reason. Fire sprang through his hands into his head and heart, flame as blinding as the punishments of hell.

He snatched himself away. "Saara!" he screamed, still half-choked with passion. "What are you doing to me? You . . . you . . ."

Saara lay wide-eyed and panting on the blanket. Naked, she shone like a sword in the black cavern. No words came out of her, but only a grunt of animal surprise.

Damiano shrank from her to the wall of the wagon. He was shaking. He shook his head as though flies were buzzing, and his eyes were staring mad. "You knew what would happen. You tricked me."

He hugged himself tightly until the shivering slowed. "It's gone again," he whispered at last. "I have only just escaped."

Saara was grabbing her dress. "So have I. Only just. Goodbye, Damiano."

Gaspare came whistling back at noon. He found Damiano still in the wagon, blanket-wrapped. "Eh! Why didn't you put on the white shirt?"

"There is no warmth in it," replied Damiano, and indeed, he seemed to need more than the warmth of wool, for he was shivering and blue. His eyes wandered hungrily in the dark.

"Where's Saara?" asked the boy, plumping himself down on the boards beside his friend. His jerkin pockets were hugely distended.

"Gone," said Damiano shortly. "Flown away." His eyes, seeking somewhere to rest, fixed on Gaspare's pocket, from which protruded a brown, dead hare's foot, its black claws spread like spokes of iron.

Chapter Five

It was the blackest time of the night, and it was raining. Gaspare lay huddled under every blanket of their mutual possession, listening to Damiano practice the lute. First the fellow spent a half-hour practicing every scale in common usage, taking it through various times and rhythms.

These ought to have been simple exercises, boring to the player and listener, but Damiano's playing tonight held such a brooding intensity that Gaspare listened in a sort of tranced horror, as though to a madman who whispered to himself while the rest of the world slept. Just as the boy began to fear for the lutenist's mind, ornament appeared in these repetitive exercises, as though squeezed by effort out of the structure. Finally, after almost two hours had passed and gray light was beginning to leak in through the cracks of the poor wagon wall, he exploded into melody.

Gaspare said nothing. Who was he to criticize the pursuit of excellence, especially in one whom he considered rather his own creation? So what if the sounds were not restful? Gaspare, too, was an artist and he understood.

Besides, he was a little afraid to talk to Damiano anymore. Especially when the musician had the lute in his lap.

He let the covers slip from his head, only to discover that the air outside was not cold. The lute player saw the movement. He stared at Gaspare with wide black eyes.

"Good morning," the boy was emboldened to say.

A moment's silence followed, and Damiano sighed heavily. It seemed by his face and by the strain of his breathing that he was approaching Gaspare from a distance, laboring to get close enough to exchange words. Finally he said, "Today I want to try that castle we saw off to the east. They may be interested in entertainment, even though it is Lent. There is certain to be a village with inns nearby."

Gaspare squirmed uneasily, exposing one shrimp-pink foot and a portion of his rib cage to the air. "I . . . would like to get to Avignon as quickly as possible. There are only two weeks—I think—until Easter."

The dark, drugged gaze didn't waver. "Three, by my count. We are very close to the Rhone, I think. In the village we can find out whether we are on the right road. And I thought you had objections to being hungry."

Gaspare wanted to shout that Damiano's argument was a cheat, that they both knew full well that the musician wanted to play because he wanted to play, not because he was worried about his own hunger or Gaspare's. There was little Damiano did anymore besides play the lute, in a music which grew more fluid and yet more passionate every day. When he spoke, it was usually either to himself or to his angel; Gaspare rarely knew which for sure, and never asked.

All the strings of the battered lute were fraying.

"I'm up," said the boy apologetically, as though it had been a case of his lateness instead of Damiano's inability to sleep. He slipped out into the rain to void his bladder.

Damiano did not like to see the daylight well up, for it intruded upon a world he had created for himself alone, and which he had filled with order. When he played the lute he was not a witch grown blind, deaf and witless. When he played the lute he was not a man who had thrown away life and love. When he played the lute he was all the musician he could be, and let the rest of the world burn. Now that the sun was rising, he would have to go back to being maimed.

His fingers hit the lute neck harder and plucked with more force. The lute whined and a wild overtone sang out of the treble. As if in answer, the horse called out to him.

Indeed rioting peasants had not swept the local land-holders (nor any other fief of Provence). The Comte de Plessis sat in his fortress as had three hundred years of his ancestors, bestowing law and breaking it. Requiring entertainment, one hoped.

Damiano did not know how Gaspare arranged for him to play before the comte. Damiano himself, were he a seneschal of some great nobleman, would find it difficult to take seriously a ragamuffin like Gaspare.

But Damiano did not appreciate how Gaspare changed when acting on Damiano's behalf: how the honor and responsibility of the position of artist's agent turned the disreputable boy into a man of character. Or in other words, how confident Gaspare was as a salesman that his goods were the best. Damiano only knew that Gaspare had a gift for getting jobs.

The ancient wagon creaked up through the village that the castle had spawned and into the nobleman's demesne. It was a few hours before sunset and the two companions held ready expectations of being offered a cooked dinner before playing their part in the comte's grander meal. And there was always the chance that Festilligambe might take some share in the oats of the fortress destriers.

Gaspare, who never had to be shown the way more than once, led Damiano through a field of adhesive mud, along a wall of pearl-gray buttresses and into the kitchen quarters, where the seneschal had his offices.

He was a sandy man of no great size, taut of skin and sharp-faced, as Gaspare himself might be in twenty years. He glanced at the boy with recognition but no great welcome, and when he saw Damiano his ragged eyebrows shot up.

"This is the lute player?" The man's voice was as tense as his appearance. "He can't go before people like that."

Gaspare bristled. Damiano merely stared.

"He looks like a lout."

Gaspare's right arm went up in an Italian gesture of devastating scorn which was quite wasted on the Provençal. "This is the finest musician you have ever had in your establishment, and the finest you will ever have!"

"Certainly the shabbiest," added the seneschal in an undertone, but Damiano's opaque black eyes had locked on his own, and the tawny official fell silent.

Damiano took a step forward. His square, spatulate hand rested on the tabletop. When he spoke it was in good langue d'oc, and very quiet. "Shabby clothing makes an outfit with an empty purse. Employment can alter both together. We have traveled all the way from the borders of the Italian Alps in a bad season, and our appearance only reflects that. My friend Gaspare's purse has a few oats sticking to the lining, so he is less shabby than I, for my purse is completely..."

And he slapped the small leather bag on his belt, only to discover that his words were false; there was something in the bag after all. Something hard-edged and tiny.

Between two words, regardless of the others in the room, Damiano sat himself on the carved oak table. He pulled the pouch from his belt and upended it onto his open palm. A small twinkle of gold slipped out of the leather, dotted with bright blood.

"Ah, yes," he murmered to himself. "I had forgotten this, which was given to me in Petit Comtois—to induce me to play."

Gaspare, standing behind, could not see what Damiano was holding. But it was understood between them that their visit to that town of the pest was not to be mentioned in public, lest the reputation of the place had spread to discolor their own. So he cleared his throat, and when he saw the face of the seneschal fall open like a book of blank pages, he feared his lunatic charge had ruined their hopes.

Then "That...is a ruby?" asked the tawny man.

Damiano shrugged. "I believe it is. Once I could have told you with more certainty, for the ruby and the topaz are the stones my family is accustomed to wear on their person. But of late my...eyes are not what they were, and this could be some other stone of similar coloring but other virtue. For all stones have their virtue, you know, and the most precious is not always the most useful."

The seneschal took this lecture meekly enough, his eyes resting in a kindly manner upon the jewel which dangled by its golden chain from Damiano's fingers. Then, gazing at the dark man with new appraisal, he cleared his throat.

"I think, monsieur," he said at last, "that you are not too different in size from myself, and I may be able to find an outfit to suit."

"You forgot?" whispered Gaspare once more, as Damiano

slipped the shirt of black brocade over his linen. "You simply forgot you had been given a ruby?"

His colleague regarded him as if from a great distance. "It was a day crowded with events, Gaspare," he replied, and Gaspare shivered at something in the sound of Damiano's words. The musician adjusted his somber velvet sash. Lace shone at his collar and cuffs, white as teeth against his sun-darkened skin. "Besides, I can't wear it or I'll scratch the top of the lute."

"I wasn't thinking of your wearing..." began the boy, and then fell unaccustomedly silent.

He *was* afraid of Damiano, now. This was no more the gentle simpleton he had shepherded from San Gabriele to Provence, whose greatest fault had been absence of mind, (along with an unreasonable concern for the proprieties). This fellow had a face like Damiano's but it was a face carved in stone.

It occurred to Gaspare that he had traveled with this man for exactly a twelvemonth, and had never known him at all.

Damiano now was staring out the arrow-slit window, drumming finger-patterns on the stone: three beats with the left hand, five with the right. He carried the rich brocades as though he'd worn nothing else in his life. That was encouraging, but could this black presence be trusted to play tonight before important people? Gaspare bit his lip.

He might break out in tears—the old Damiano had been known to do that (always for reasons that made no sense to Gaspare, like seeing that kid with a worm in his eye in Chamonix, or finding in ruins a church he had read about once in a book).

But no, this Damiano was dry as sand. He wouldn't cry.

He might kill someone, however. Squinting critically at the lean figure (hard as an English mercenary, the phrase went), Gaspare imagined him with those big square hands around some pasty throat. He might easily kill someone and get them both hanged, the boy reflected, but this Damiano wouldn't cry.

It was all that witch's fault: the silly peasant girl with her dirty feet and her terrible, magical rhyme. Clearly she'd been infatuated with Damiano, and something she'd said or done had caused this alteration in the lute player. Strange—for she had seemed easy enough. Not the sort of woman to keep her lover on the other side of a door.

And Gaspare had thought that, for once, old sheep-face wouldn't refuse an honest offer. In fact, Gaspare would have laid florins on his chances of coming back that last sunny day to find them both under one blanket.

What had gone wrong, to make her depart in a puff of whatever?

Suddenly he found a new perspective on the problem. He asked a question.

Damiano raised his distracted head. "Physical problem? What kind of problem, Gaspare? I don't understand."

This was going to be more difficult than Gaspare had thought. "A . . . lack of compatibility, perhaps? A difference in size, or in expectation?"

Damiano frowned tightly, and one of his hands ceased its drumming. "I don't know what you're talking about. Start again."

Gaspare took a deep breath and leaned back into the leather chair so kindly provided by de Plessis. "You . . . seemed to be getting along very well with the pretty little witch, and then . . . and then you weren't."

"She is the Lady Saara," replied Damiano, with hooded eyes and obvious restraint, as though correcting a stranger. "And no. There was no physical problem."

All this while Damiano's right hand had continued beating its rapid five-beat rhythm. Now his left hand rejoined it, tapping in threes, sharp as a fast horse running. "There is no problem," he repeated. "Except that I have to practice now."

"Practice what?" asked Gaspare, for the lute lay swaddled on a table in the corner.

"This," came the laconic reply.

Gaspare listened, trying to imagine how one would dance to such a rhythm. "What is it?"

"I don't know," said Damiano. "Yet."

There were fourteen people sitting at the high table with the Comte de Plessis and thirty-five at the long table just below the dais. They began with a soup of dried

mullet and onions, followed by various roast birds decked
in feathers that had never been theirs in life. The sweet-
bread was saffron, and the wine was amaranth purple. A
tall honey cake, studded with raisins, had been built into
the exact image of the Fortress Plessis; the diners demolished
it without superstitious scruple.

More souls than sat under torchlight broke their
trenchers in the shadow, on crude slatted benches at the
far end of the hall. These did not eat of saffron or amaranth, nor did they pick raisins out of their honey cake, for
they had no cake. But they did eat.

Gaspare sat in the shelter of an arras, one leg propped
before him and one leg folded. He was neither hiding nor
was he precisely there to be seen. His eye was on Damiano,
who tuned his lute on a stool behind the main table, and
whose garment shone like black damask under the light of
torches.

The musician spoke no word, and his face wore the
expression of inviolability it always assumed when playing
the lute.

Gaspare had given up expecting the player to make
amusing patter. Damiano almost never spoke when playing,
and when he did it was in a whisper that could not be
heard five feet away. But it was better that he should be
quiet than to speak at the wrong time.

Before this fearsome Comte de Plessis, for example.
The landholder's right arm was the size of Gaspare's thigh,
and his blue eyes were leaden. A puckered scar pierced
the man's mouth, giving him a perpetual snarl, and he ate
with great concentration. Better be discreet before a man
of this kidney. Discreet and conservative.

The process of tuning took a bit longer than necessary,
Gaspare thought. But then Damiano never would hurry
his tuning or apologize for it, and the lute's rather brittle
wooden tuning pegs were crotchety. Laughter was heard
to rise at the high table, but it did not issue from the
comte, whose mouth was full. A rather beefy-faced bald
man in soiled white was gesturing at a dark woman in
yellow. He pointed with a bird's leg, scaly foot still attached. he chewed with his mouth open.

The dark woman was young, demure, clean-faced,

quick-eyed. She divided her attention between the coarse
gentleman and the figure in black behind the dais.

The musician's fingers brushed the open strings with
harplike effect, while his left hand twitched over the
tuners. After a while the left hand hovered, not touching,
while the right hand began to dance. Tuning became
music imperceptibly.

Damiano did not use a plectrum on the lute, because
in the beginning he had not known he was supposed to use
one, and later because he did not see the use of the quill.
He struck the strings with his nails, playing as many lines
as he had fingers, all together. "Devil's music" had said old
Marco of Partestrada, and in that opinion he had not been
alone. But Damiano's teacher had been the Archangel
Raphael.

Now the lutenist was playing in earnest, his left hand
spread spiderlike over the wide black neck, his curled right
seeming not to move at all over the strings. Gaspare
recognized it, and was relieved. This was an ancient piece,
just right for Provence, and if Gaspare could remember
correctly, by Ventadorn. Damiano played a great deal of
Ventadorn; it was popular.

But then the musician inclined forward, rounding
over the instrument until his wiry black hair fell over the
lute face. He rested his cheek against the wooden neck
and swayed from side to side with the beat of the music.

This was not so good. Better not to call attention to
oneself in that way. Gaspare watched, wondering if anyone
besides himself thought Damiano was looking a trifle mad.
The simple Provençal tune, too, was changing. It took on a
strange new form under Damiano's fingers, salted with
sweet, knotted ornamentation in Hibernian style. Out of
nowhere was added a bass line from Moorish Spain.

Gaspare looked into Damiano's black eyes then, and
he knew that this night would not be safe: not safe at all.

Where was the troubador's tune? Had the fellow slid
into a new piece without stopping? No, for there was the
melody again, or a piece of it. But, great Saint Gabriele,
what time was this? Three-time? Five?

It was five over three, and it went on and on, under
the melody and over it, changing the love song of Bernard
de Ventadorn into something lunging and bizarre. For a

moment—one cowardly moment only—Gaspare considered sneaking out alone.

But the ancient tune did not die under this treatment; it lived and grew, thrown from treble to mid to bass as a juggler throws a ball.

The player's mouth was open, but no sound could be heard. His head nodded left and right with his music, and he baby-rocked the lute.

He has forgotten we are here, thought Gaspare. He has forgotten the comte.

He has forgotten me.

He is finally unmanageable, decided the boy. Mad beyond concealment. He looked around to see whether by unlucky circumstance any of these doltish noblemen were paying attention to the music.

No. Only the woman in yellow, who watched calm-faced, with eyes Gaspare did not trust.

And then between one moment and the next Gaspare did not care whether Damiano was mad beyond concealment. For the rhythm caught up with his fears and outpaced them, and one particular turn upon the melody took him by the throat.

He was standing; he didn't know how that had come to pass. He was standing between two folds of musty tapestry, gold-chased. He saw Damiano's head nod with the driving beat, moving up and down like that of a horse in the traces. The musician's lips were pulled back from his teeth.

What was he playing now? This was not Ventadorn, or anything Provençal. And it was not Italian, not with that bass, and the great arcing sixths of the melody. Christ! Had he ever complained that Delstrego did not have enough bass?

But what was it? Gaspare had never heard this piece, though tiny licks of melody (tiny, delicate, curled like cats' tongues) were familiar.

And then the boy realized he had heard the piece without knowing it, incomplete and embryonic, through the booming of rain in the darkness. It was Damiano's own music.

The redhead smiled a smile that made him seem old. "This," hissed Gaspare to himself, "this is my reward for

sitting up all the night while he makes noise. For keeping
food in his belly, and keeping his pennies safe in his
pocket.

"He was created to make this music," continued
Gaspare, speaking quite audibly to no one at all. "He was
made to play, but it is I, I myself who nursed him to it. It
is I who made this moment possible."

And wind pulled the arras into billows and splashed
the red torchlight over the floor. It turned Damiano's black
brocade into embers, deep burning, and struck stars from
his black hair. It blew a thick river of music over the dais
of the high table and through the cold, dark hall where the
bread was also dark. The servants lifted their heads to
listen.

And even at the comte's table, conversation had died.
The warrior in soiled white still leaned toward the woman
in yellow, but his head was craned back and his flat gray
eyes stared at the table.

And she stared at the musician directly now, as light
played games with her yellow-brown eyes. Her small
nostrils flared and two spots of color stood on her cheeks.

"So," whispered Gaspare at her from twenty feet
away, his motley making him invisible among the brilliant
threads of the hanging, "so you think you understand, do
you? You think perhaps this music is for you, pretty lady
with red cheeks?"

Then he snorted. "Well, it is not for you. Nor for you,
Plessis, who has finally condescended to stop chewing and
listen. You have not the brain nor the training to understand Delstrego. Nor have you suffered enough to pay for
the music you hear.

"No, nobles of Provence, or of Italy or China, for that
matter. His music and this moment are mine."

And silently Gaspare stepped out of the folds of the
arras and stood beside Damiano, quiet as a young tree,
and as straight from pride.

Damiano raged within his music, but could not escape. Sweet Mother of God, that the planets should arc
above him and he not see them. That the mouse should
squeak in the stone and he not hear. That a horse who
served him should speak and be not understood. And that

men—and women—should walk by and leave him as
numb to them as a dead man.

He *had* died last year in Lombardy, breaking his staff
on the stones of a grave. He had died and felt not the pain
of it until now.

If only Saara had let him be, dead or alive, but free
from pain.

I feel my blindness, he sang, using no words. I am
deaf, I am numb. There is nothing in my life left.

Nothing but this, replied the lute.

The Comte de Plessis had a brow that might have
been dug with a plow. His right hand was full of cake.
Raisins dropped through his fingers. He brooded at Damiano.
An ancient in gray doeskin addressed him; he shrugged
the man away like a fly.

A peg had slipped. Damiano was tuning. The comte
extended an arm as wide and hairy as the haunch of one of
his own hounds. "You," grunted the comte. "Where are
you from? Where did you learn all that?"

Gaspare's stomach tightened like dry leather. Genius
was a very fragile fire, as compared with feudal arrogance.
Genius can be guttered by a stupid man's blow.

Damiano stood respectfully enough, despite his drunk-
en eyes. "I am from the Piedmont, my lord," he replied,
with a three-point bow. "And the music . . . is from no one
place."

De Plessis settled back on his ebonpoint stool, which
creaked beneath his weight. He cast his eyes over the
assembly at the high table, which waited in silence for
what he might say.

"Good," is what finally came out of that misshapen
mouth. "Good enough for Avignon. He ought to go to
Avignon."

"That is the tack we must take," repeated Gaspare,
bouncing ahead, his shoe heels not touching the ground.
"No more playing for loutish dances. It is not the size of
your audience but its quality that will make you famous."

Damiano was leading Festilligambe by a handful of
mane. The horse's ears were back; he had been very
nervous for the last few days—since Saara left, to be exact.

The lutenist leaned against the brute's black shoulder, for he was tired. "Ah," he replied. "Is that so, Gaspare? Well, I have always thought it more pleasant to play before wealthy people than poor, and before the educated rather than the ignorant. But the problem has always been that there are so many of the poor and ignorant and so few of the educated and wealthy."

The redhead dismissed this observation with a head-shake, as together they passed through the jaws of the portcullis. The echo of hoof-falls rang in the dry ravine beneath the castle bridge. "Yes, but now we have the ruby. We can afford to wait."

Behind Damiano's weary eyes a curtain was almost drawn away. Almost, but not quite. They flickered, and he put his hand to his leather pocket as he replied, "If it is a ruby."

"It is genuine; the seneschal recognized that right away. It is your good luck—or, no, your rightful reward after what I heard tonight. We must sell it in Avignon and buy more suitable clothes."

"Clothes?" Once again Damiano was clothed in his tunic of inappropriate blush pink. "A better lute is what I need. I have to keep hopping over those terrible frets in the middle."

The boy raised an admonishing finger, which shone like a white worm as they passed a cottage window lit with oil light. "A lute will come, Damiano, but right now respectable clothes are more important. Listen to your manager."

Amusement lightened the black eyes for a moment. "My manager? I thought you were my dancer."

Gaspare snorted. "The music you are playing now can't be danced to, sheep-face."

"Enough of that." Damiano's whisper was metallic. The horse shied suddenly, almost pulling its mane from Damiano's clutching fingers. "My name is Damiano."

The boy came to a shivering halt. It flashed upon him like lightning that having gotten the musician to Avignon, to the feet of power and acclaim, it might be felt he was no longer necessary. In fact, to one who silenced the high table of the castle of Plessis, and who sparked the massive Comte de Plessis himself to say "Good enough for Avignon" (much too good, if the hulk really knew it . . .) and who had in his pocket a gold-set ruby, what use was Gaspare at all?

The black tail of the horse swished ahead of him. Damiano's pale pink shirt was melting into the darkness. Gaspare folded his arms in front of him, hugging himself. They felt like steel bands around his ribs.

Damiano slowed the horse. He turned, his white teeth visible under starlight. "What are you waiting for . . . manager?" he inquired.

"I have it in writing. I asked him to give it to me in writing." Gaspare tapped his bony breast. "It is here."

Damiano sat at the back of the wagon, cleaning his teeth with a bit of chewed stick. Sometimes he didn't shave, or comb his hair for days on end, but about his teeth he was fastidious. "Who—the comte? You were crazy enough to ask the Comte de Plessis for a recommendation. In writing?"

Gaspare sprang from the earth onto the floor of the wagon, landing in a front roll. "I was. I did. Why not, after all, if he liked you? And he did."

Damiano spat out flecks of wood. "I am rather surprised the man can write."

Gaspare pulled a rather furtive smile. "He can't. He got his daughter to do it. Do you remember her? She wore daffdowndilly yellow."

Damiano nodded. "I thought perhaps she understood a little of what I was doing. At least she paid attention."

Gaspare peered studiously out into the night, where the only sound was that of equine jaws grinding. "She . . . has an interest. I was told to tell you she will probably be hawking tomorrow, with her ladies."

Damiano stared. "Why should I know that? Do you mean she wants . . ." The question dissolved in a noise of contempt.

"We are going into Avignon tomorrow," he said finally. "Easter is coming very fast. We don't have time for play."

Gaspare delivered an oddly formal punch on the arm. "Delstrego," he said. "Delstrego, you are going to be receiving a lot of attention: this kind and other kinds. Isn't that what you've wanted? Isn't it the game for which you've come to Provence?"

Somewhere out among the invisible leaves an owl hooted. Damiano cringed from the sound, and bit down savagely on the knuckle of his left thumb. "I want a game that is worth the price I've paid," he muttered, but only to himself.

Chapter Six

They came within sight of the Rhone River, which had in times past carved out the sweet and fruitful valley through which they had driven half the length of Provence. Now the road bent toward the river, kissed it, and followed it into the white city of Avignon. Gaspare and Damiano passed beneath rusty gates and into a checkerboard of limed shops and limestone cobbled streets.

Under the vernal sun Avignon wore a smiling face.

Gaspare trotted tiptoe ahead. Festilligambe stepped heavily behind. Damiano walked in the middle, one hand upon a shoulder of each. Gaspare was more difficult to manage.

"Perhaps we'll find her right away," yodeled the boy, skirting a public well and three men carrying an alabaster urn. "Just sitting on a corner, talking to some new gossip. Or cadging sweets; Evienne has no shame where sweets are concerned."

Frantically Damiano prodded the black gelding out of the stonemasters' way. "I didn't know she had shame of any kind," he mumbled, and then added in a louder voice, "Well, it's more likely we'll meet her on the streets than in the Papal Palace. But if I know Jan Karl at all, he will see us before we see him. He likes so much to be on top of things."

Gaspare didn't hear him, for the boy's nervous feet

had carried on ahead along the row of close-set stucco buildings.

The street was very narrow. Very narrow. A stream of pedestrians flowed about him and threatened constantly to clot about the horse. Avignon made a Piedmontese feel smothered.

And Damiano could not make the confused gelding hurry.

He could not see Gaspare anymore; he gave up trying. With a sigh, he put his weight against the high chalked wall of an enclosed garden. Festilligambe, in turn, tried to put his weight upon Damiano.

"Don't do that," muttered Damiano, jabbing the beast with a thumbnail.

And then he said "Hush!" and raised his head.

Festilligambe, who had been making no noise at all, pricked his ears also.

They heard music, not loud but close enough to ring clear: a flow as complex as water broken on rocks. It shimmered from many strings together, like an entire concert of lutes—if lutes had been strung in metal.

For half a minute longer Damiano listened, motionless with the rigidity of a pointing dog. Finally, with a word to the gelding to stay, he leaped upward and boosted himself onto the wall.

It was a small garden, planted with tubs of rosemary and fennel. Three anemic olive trees fluttered their silver, sword-shaped leaves, while the cool smell of thyme warred with Avignon's odor of almonds and human feces.

In the far corner of the garden, under a vine-woven trellis, sat a man playing on a harp strung with brass. It was from him the broad splashing music had come. But even as Damiano spied him, the player paused to examine his left hand, which was clawed like the talon of a bird. With a fragment of pumice stone he buffed his middle finger, muttering.

"Hello," called Damiano, letting himself slide onto a walkway of stones. The harper glanced up and his handsome fair face expressed his disturbance at finding a stranger where no stranger should be.

Damiano noticed, and he grimaced an apology. But though Damiano had manners better than the average,

certain things were more important to him than manners.
"I'm sorry, monsieur, but I had to come right over. It is
because of your bass line."

"Because of my what?" The harper was about fifty
years old. His flaxen hair had been made frizzy by lime,
and a line of stubble made clear that his high forehead had
known the assistance of a razor. His eyebrows were black
(whether by nature or art) and his eyes blue. He was
impeccably groomed and clean shaven, and dressed in a
house robe of full Provençal cut. But his gentlemanly
appearance made his talonlike nails even more noticeable.

"Forgive my langue d'oc. It is awkward, I know," said
Damiano with no sincerity. "I said because of your bass
line, monsieur. That which you do with your right hand, at
the bottom of the instrument. I could not help but notice
that you pull your hand off smoothly, so that the notes
come off almost together. They sound together, in fact."

The older man listened without apparent comprehension. Damiano tried again. "Perhaps you think of it as
ornament—what you are doing. But I hear it as polyphony. A polyphony of many lines."

Still the harper's heavy-browed, snub-nosed face
remained blank. What am I doing here? Why do I care?
thought Damiano, and answered himself: There is something to be learned here.

He added, "And polyphony is what I am doing on the
lute, you see. It is a technique I have had to invent
myself, for I have never heard anyone (save for my teacher) try to put so many lines on one instrument."

The harper took a deliberate breath. "And this is why
you climbed the wall into my garden, breaking the law,
and getting yourself covered with chalk?" He regarded his
visitor with less wariness and more humor. "Because of my
right hand?

"Well, lad," the older man said didactically, "that is
neither called polyphony nor ornamentation. It is merely
the style of the clàrseach: ascending and descending strikes
of the right hand, using fourths and fifths. It has always
been the style of the clàrseach. It is not the style of the
lute."

Damiano shrugged. "Never yet," he said. "But my
teacher . . ."

"Why not let the lute be the lute, and if you want to sound like a harp, play one?" The sharp talons curved, and the harper flurried up and down his strings.

Damiano smiled, crouching down before the harper with his chin resting on his knee. He had not come hundreds of miles through snow and sun to hear somebody tell him "it's done that way because it's always been done that way." Nor was he impressed by pyrotechnics: he possessed a number of impressive effects himself. But the sound was pleasant and the man made a striking picture. When it was quiet again Damiano sought to say something appreciative. "You make me understand why it is common to paint angels with a harp."

But the fellow was either tired of this particular compliment or didn't take it as a compliment at all. "'Tisn't angels who play the clàrseach, young man. It's Irishmen."

"Oh?" Damiano lifted his head. "You are an Irishman?"

The man had mobile nostrils and a wide mouth. The first flared, while the second tightened.

He curled his barbed hands before him and squared his broad shoulders. With a round gesture he pointed from the heavy harp with its ranks of gleaming strings to himself.

"What—do I look or sound Provençal to you?"

Damiano showed his teeth politely. "I cannot say, since I myself have just arrived in Provence. And never have I met..."

Unwillingly he let himself be interrupted by a grunt and a scuffle from the other side of the wall. He sprang up. "Forgive me, monsieur. I have left both my horse and my lute."

He attacked the wall once more, growing twice as chalky as before. There below him was Festilligambe, as Damiano knew he would be, still bearing his lumpy pack of belongings, the neck of the lute protruding behind. The horse wore also a crude rope halter, however: wore it with very poor grace, and against the fat man pulling and the fatter man with the switch behind, he had set his obstinate will.

Since the ground seemed fully occupied, Damiano slid down onto the horse's withers, first giving the beast a warning whistle. Both fat men gaped.

"This is my horse, messieurs," announced Damiano, and since the two were both too loud and too clumsy to be thieves, he smiled at them. "Is it that he is where he should not be?"

The fat man in front (he was wearing a dirty apron) had difficulty with this sentence; perhaps Damiano's langue d'oc did have its faults. Finally he replied, "But the animal wears no restraint, monsieur. It was our idea he had run away."

Damiano slipped to the cobbled road. He removed the contrivance from Festilligambe's head. "No, not at all. It is only that he does not like ropes, so I don't use any."

The man in the back had hitherto stood silent, brushing the ground with his weed-switch as though it were a broom. Now he said, "Monsieur. You were visiting the Master MacFhiodhbhuidhe?"

Damiano tried to fit this collection of sounds into his mouth. "MacFhiod . . . the harper. Yes, I guess I was."

The fellow (this one was dressed in serge d'Nîmes. He did not wear an apron) pointed with his switch at the head of the lute. "You are perhaps also a musician by trade? An Italian musician, if my ears do not deceive me?"

Damiano began to brush himself off. It was a fruitless effort, which was just as well, for a coating of chalk concealed much of his clothing's decay. "I am a musician, certainly, monsieur. And that I am Italian cannot be concealed. Why do you ask? Have you need of an Italian musician?" he asked, and he laughed at this conceit.

"Yes, I have," replied the fatter fat man, astounding Damiano completely.

"I thought I would never find you," stormed Gaspare, throwing himself on to the far end of the bench where Damiano sat. The musician had a green glass cup of wine sitting before him and he wore a tunic of wine-red, chased with gold. He was in the best humor he had been in for weeks. He brushed white bread crumbs from his front.

"Find me, Gaspare? I am not a hundred feet from where you left me, running off as you did, like some goat in the mountains. Indeed, it was you who were lost, and I feared Avignon had eaten you."

The boy stared from Damiano's face to the street before the very pleasant inn-yard where they sat. He did not seem to know or care where he was.

"You did not find her," stated his friend.

"No." Gaspare was hot—flushed. Possibly he had been crying.

Damiano's shrug communicated a certain sympathy. "Did you really expect to? This is a city of many thousands of people, and our appointment is not yet for a week or more. According to the innkeeper here, my account is correct and next Sunday is Palm Sunday."

Then Gaspare's green eyes drew out like the stalked eyes of snails. "Innkeeper? Damiano! What are you wearing? And eating? What *is* all this?"

On impulse Damiano reached out and ruffled Gaspare's carefully managed hair. "This, my dear manager, is human comfort. I have been to see a jeweler—also a harper, but that is a less relevant story. The jeweler and I had an interesting conversation about the hybrid nature of electrum, as well as a mild disagreement as to whether amethyst or adamantine is the stone more pure. He gave me thieves' prices for the ruby, I think, but where could I have gotten better?"

Gaspare blinked about him, then, and Damiano placed the green glass cup in the boy's unresisting hand. Gaspare downed it and stared again at his friend. There was something pinched, thwarted and ancient in the boy's face that stung Damiano's own eyes and tightened his middle.

"You shouldn't have shopped without me," Gaspare declared, growing a bit belligerent from confusion. "I would have advised you to buy black. You look more impressive in black."

Damiano pulled a lopsided smile and reached across the table to deposit the last heel of the loaf in Gaspare's lap. "I'm black enough in other ways, my friend," he murmured. "But whether the name be for fame or shame, I am still Delstrego—the only Delstrego left—and our colors are crimson and gold."

Gaspare felt his role as manager slipping away from him. He bolted the bread and more wine. "But you should not have spent this kind of money before even trying to find work."

"I have found work," answered Damiano gently.

Two years ago Damiano might have scorned an inn room like this one: slate-floored, poorly lit, smelling of piss. His father, with whom Damiano first went to Torino and Milano, would not have stayed a minute, and it would have been bad for the innkeeper who had shown him such quarters.

But two years can make a difference. In two years a baby can talk. In two years a dead man can turn to earth.

Damiano sat by one of the long slit windows, tuning the lute.

The sun was up, slapping long bars of yellow light against the ground between buildings. The air was changing so fast it was hardly worth the bother to tune, but then Damiano was hardly aware he was doing it.

The other six inhabitants of the room had vacated for the day, including Gaspare. Certainly there was no reason to lie huddled on straw upon stone and within walls of the same: not when it was actually warmer out-of-doors. But Damiano had slept poorly and was without ambition for the moment.

It had been an owl. Somewhere in Avignon an owl had hunted, calling half the night, and for some reason Damiano could not hear an owl without remembering all he had lost. And this morning it was still there for him: a distant knowledge that the heavens were circling in their complex rhythms without his consent or understanding. That wolves conversed and ghosts walked, but not for him.

And locked into this grief—to his greater misery—was a memory of his lips against skin in the cold of night, and the smell of clean flesh under blankets.

Out the window he could see a vertical slice of the city, where the white stucco housefronts stood identical, shoulder to shoulder. On the ground floor of this inn—Heather Inn, it was called—Festilligambe had been stabled, in a large, square box with two goats and a Sicilian donkey. Damiano hoped the horse was enjoying himself. Perhaps he was sleeping late.

Without warning Damiano's melancholy became unendurable. He rose from the upended box he was sitting on, as though he would fling himself out the door, down the stairs and into the crowded street below. His heart pounded. Mastering himself, he sat down again to think.

Perhaps he should visit the horse—make sure he had food and water. But the groom would think he was crazy, for he had seen the buckets filled already this morning. Neither would Festilligambe understand such a visit, for although he liked his master he was not a sentimental horse.

Where was Gaspare anyway? Out looking for his sister, certainly, though he had not said as much to Damiano. Gaspare's need to find Evienne had grown into a pitiful thing, and Damiano was a little afraid of what would happen if she failed to show up at their long-planned appointment.

This last worry was too much. The musician needed someone to talk to. Someone reliable.

He put the scuffed bottom end of his lute down upon the tops of his boots and laced his fingers together around the neck. With his eyes closed and his forehead resting against the tuning box he cleared his throat and spoke to the empty air.

"Raphael . . . Seraph. If you have the time . . ."

By the sound and by a faint flutter of shadows behind his eyelids Damiano could have sworn that Raphael had come in through the far window. It was an illusion that made the man chuckle, for he had the sophistication to know that heaven was not in the sky above Avignon, or any other worldly place.

"Good morning, Dami," said Raphael, in a voice like the sweet after-ring of a bell. "How do you like Avignon?"

"So far it has been very generous with me," answered Damiano, in an effort to be just. "But still, I am not in a very good mood today."

"You are lonely," replied Raphael without pause.

Damiano squirmed, trying to keep his eyes fixed on

the stripes along the back of the lute. It was unsettling and a bit demeaning to be read so easily. "How did you know?"

There was a shrug of wings: a noise like heavy-falling snow. "Because there is no one here. And you have just come to a city that is strange to you. From what I have learned about men . . ."

An idea came to Damiano. "Do you know Avignon well, Seraph?"

"No."

The man had not expected this answer. He lifted his eyes from the lute. "You do not? But it is the Papal city."

Raphael's wings were bowed forward in the confines of the room. The first pinions touched together on the floor almost at Damiano's feet. "I don't know the Pope, either. I have never been to Avignon before," the angel said.

"Not even with messages?"

Again that feathery shrug. "I am not a messenger by calling."

Still, Damiano's idea must be spoken. "I . . . had wondered if perhaps you knew where Gaspare's sister, Evienne, was staying. We are supposed to meet her, you see, and the boy is very nervous."

Raphael's pale hair was heavy as the mane of a horse, and like a horse's mane it fell where it would. His midnight eyes gazed out from a frame of light. "I know where Evienne is," he admitted.

Damiano straightened with the news. "You do? Well, where is she?"

It was the angel who dropped his eyes. "I would rather you didn't ask me, Dami. I think there are other ways you could find out."

The mortal sat again. "Of course, Raphael. Of course. I am embarrassed. I . . . asked without thought, forgetting that you are not supposed to involve yourself . . ."

And then this small understanding was lost within a larger. "Raphael!" cried Damiano. "Raphael, Seraph, Teacher! I am seeing you—really seeing you. And I am not sick!"

The angel's grand, opalescent wings rose up like flowers opening, till their tips lodged in the corners of the room. His look of joy was as full as Damiano's. But it was mixed with something less definable.

"I am glad, Damiano," he said. "It was never my desire to make you sick."

Placing the instrument hurriedly down to one side (for he treated the lute with the care necessary to something upon which his living depended, and not the care deserved by a tool one loves), Damiano crouched down at Raphael's feet. He squeezed one alabaster hand. He slapped a samite knee. He fished a bright wingtip from the air and held it between his hands, as though to restrain Raphael from flying untimely away. "Hah! Raphael, my dear master . . ."

"Not master," said the angel, and Damiano nearly lost the wing.

"Teacher, then. You are a vision to rest my eyes. And it has been so long. . . . I thought my sight would not be so rewarded on this side of death's door." Behind his grin Damiano's quick mind raced.

"You know, Raphael, I think I know how it is I can see you again. It is because of Saara, and the trick she played on me."

"Ah? So it seems to you that it's you who have changed?" asked Raphael, and there was a shade of diffidence in his question.

"What else?" Damiano pushed closer to the angel, until he was almost sitting in Raphael's lap. I am clumsy as a dog, next to him, he thought. Like Macchiata, I wag my tail so hard I knock things over. But I don't care.

Aloud he said, "Of course the change is in me. You are an immortal spirit—how can you alter?"

The fair, chiseled face grew serious for a moment. "Not alter? Dami, even if that were true for me, standing out of time and place, once I had set foot upon the earth of Provence or the Piedmont, and spoken with you, who alter so dramatically every moment of your life, and touched you, too . . . how can I not change?"

Now Damiano let the great pinion slide through his fingers. "I don't want you to change, Raphael. And for me—me to be changing you? That doesn't sound good." Again he cleared his throat and scooted a few inches across the stone floor, away from the simple, gleaming robe. "I don't want to be a bad influence on you, Seraph."

Raphael laughed. His laughter was never like bells, or sunshine, or running water. Raphael laughed like anyone else. "Don't worry about it, Dami." His lapis eye glanced down at the lute in the corner.

"Did you want to play something for me?"

Without taking his eyes from the angel, Damiano scooped up his instrument. "I have a dozen things I could play for you." His voice took on a note of warning as he added, "They are not like your pieces...."

"I wouldn't want to listen if they were," answered Raphael dryly.

Of course, contact with the stone flagging had put the crotchety lute out of tune again. As he worked it back, Damiano had a sudden idea, brought on by the splendor of the moment. "Hey, Raphael. Do you think we could... I mean, would you be willing to play with me? I mean, not as a lesson, but for fun?

"It has been a long time that I've wanted to do that," he added plaintively. "And I think my playing has improved lately."

Raphael's left eyebrow rose. His right wing twitched like the tail of a thoughtful cat. "I did not bring my instrument," he demurred, but his fingers drummed his knee as though hungry for work.

"Your lute? Or harp, viella, viol, recorder? My dear teacher, what is it you play when you are not giving lute lessons?" demanded Damiano, and in asking that question (which had bothered him the better part of two years), the young man felt he had crossed a sort of Rubicon.

Raphael opened his mouth to answer, but then his flaxen brow drew down and he turned his head, listening. There were trotting steps in the passage. Raphael extended his hand and shook Damiano gently by the shoulder. "Later," he whispered. "We have all the time in the world to play. Right now the boy is unhappy."

White wings and white gown flashed upward, fading into the rising light of day.

Gaspare burst the crude door open. His face was red and white in blotches. "She isn't anywhere," he growled. He kicked his bedroll and cursed. "Not in the taverns and not in the churches. She's not washing, nor praying nor eating nor drinking nor whoring. Not anywhere."

An Italian musician, the innkeeper had said. How ironic that seemed to Damiano, whose journey to Provence was largely a pilgrimage for the sake of its music. After a bit of questioning, Damiano became certain that it was not any essential Italianate quality that the man desired in an entertainer, but only that he be an exotic, like the Irishman. Damiano was confident he could give the fellow something he hadn't heard before.

This was no poor establishment, the inn across the street from Monsieur MacFhiodhbhuidhe's house. Had it possessed sleeping rooms, Damiano and Gaspare would never have been able to afford the use of them. But it was only called an inn for lack of any better word to call it, being a place where wine was served by the glass and little tarts on salvers of pewter. Originally, before the Papacy moved from Rome, it had been the house of the Bishop of Avignon, and still, of an evening, functionaries of the court of Innocent VI filtered through the guarded gates of the Papal Palace and lounged about in the great top-floor assembly room, eating, drinking, gossiping and ignoring the music. The Bishop's Inn maintained a pastry kitchen and offered a large selection of wines, both local and imported. In fact, it was almost a café, in a country in which coffee had not yet been discovered.

Damiano considered this perhaps the most civilized establishment he had ever seen, and he was glad to be employed in it. He was also nervous. He was—barring the pink-cheeked serving girls—the youngest person in the music room, too. That made him even more nervous.

He sat in the shadow of the pillared colonnade at one side of the room. Above his head a small window let in the twilight and the rooftop breezes of the city. Vine tendrils sharpened one another not far from his ear. He toyed with a spice bun he had been allowed to buy for half-price.

These old men, and churchmen, too. If ever there was an audience before which he ought to play conservatively, this was it. Could he? Touching the top of his lute (damned instrument: poorly made, badly fretted. No hope for it), he knew he could not.

For he was the tool of his music. As once his will had
passed like braided winds through the length of his black
staff, so now the music which sounded on his lute seemed
to come through him from another source. If he tried to
play for prudence—if he tried to play as he had played a
year and a half ago, he would only play badly.

Gaspare sidled in. Now Damiano was not the youngest
man in the room. "Almost ready, the fat man says," hissed
the redhead. His drooping finger curls were oiled glossily.
He wore a bright green velvet mantle which pulled his
shoulders back and pressed against his neck. Having just
bought the garment today, Gaspare was immensely vain
about it and would not take it off, even though torchlight
and the heat of many bodies had made the chamber stuffy.

"Don't call Monsieur Coutelan that to his face," chided Damiano, and he fished in his pocket for the piece of
soft leather which would keep the bowl of the lute from
slipping on his lap.

Gaspare ignored him. "You know, Delstrego, there is
a guild in Avignon. A guild of musicians."

The dark man grunted, lost in tuning. "A guild is a
good thing. We should join it."

Gaspare danced a nervous step. "I told Coutelan you
were a member already."

"Then we will certainly have to join," said Damiano,
and he walked toward the torchlight.

He did what he could, in the beginning. He played
the dances of home, which bored him, and he emphasized
the treble at the expense of the bass. He played no piece
that the average man of Provence might be expected to
feel he had desecrated. He did not sing.

Yet, for all that, it was not anyone's usual music, not
even in Avignon, where the New Music had been born,
for Damiano's polyphony went from two lines to three to
four, and sometimes dissolved into a splash of tone in
which no separate lines could be discerned at all. He
pulled his strings with his left hand till they whined like
the viol. And he brushed his strings with his right hand till
they rang like a harp.

And after ten minutes, when he realized that none of
this plump, balding, oily-eyed crowd was listening, he

gave up trying to please them. Instead he did as he had done very often in the past year, when the audience was drunk, argumentative or merely absent. He played for Gaspare.

In a way, this was fortunate. In a way, this made him happy, for with Gaspare there was nothing he could not do without being understood; the boy knew his idiom as no one else could, and could not be satisfied by anything other than the best Damiano could do. Damiano played for Gaspare as one old friend might converse with another: fluently and without theatrics. In his self-satisfaction he began to sing a nonsense descant above the melody, adding sweeping arpeggios to the accompaniment.

"Let the lute be the lute"? Why, this *was* the lute, and anything it did well belonged to it by right. Damiano smiled to himself. He liked what he was doing and how he was doing it. It didn't matter if the audience was not listening.

But it had grown very quiet out there. Perhaps they *were* listening, now. Even the comte had started to listen, after Damiano had quite given up on him. Damiano glanced up without breaking rhythm.

He could see five ornate little tables, each with a small group of men—only men, of course—seated around it. Beyond that distance his eyes couldn't focus.

And these small groups were silent, and their attention fixed not on Damiano, but on a half-dozen well-dressed fellows who stood between the musician and the audience, leaning on brutal-looking wooden clubs.

Damiano blinked at six faces set like stone into bad intention. It took him another few seconds to realize that their hostility was focused on him. Then he was aware that Gaspare was standing behind him.

All his confused brain could do was to repeat to itself, "At least it was never much of a lute. At least it is no great loss." He was just finishing the refrain of a Hobokentanz. He began it again, and he spoke to the men who he knew were about to attack him.

"If you are all planning to hit me together, I don't think there is much I can do about it, messieurs. However, I would like you to know that I have no idea what I have done to offend you." And then he kept playing.

One man, a tall, narrow-chested fellow wearing a dagged jerkin of red, hefted his thorn stick. The others followed. "Mother of God," whispered Damiano, "this is terrible." He felt Gaspare behind him, shaking like an angry dog.

Then a blond head swam out of the red torchlight into Damiano's shortsighted vision. It belonged to the harper of the impossible name whom Damiano had accosted the day before. The Irishman put out a hand on each side and the ruffians froze.

And so Damiano played on. He played thinking that this might be the end for him—that he might never play another song—and so he played to please himself. He freed the base line. He feathered the strings (let the harper glare). He sang to his lute like a mother with a sleepless baby.

And he finished the piece without being knocked on the head.

There was silence. The ruffians had gone; the harper stood alone. Damiano rested his lute on his boots as the harper approached, stepping with great dignity in his Provençal robe.

"So that is what you meant," he began, with his odd, shushing, boneless Irish accent, "by all that babble about bass lines and polyphony and my right hand."

The younger man nodded, half smiling. "Yes. That is what I meant. Does it seem . . . terrible to you? An offense against the nature of the lute, perhaps?"

The blond man pulled up a chair. "No. It does not. But then I am not particularly sensitive to offenses against the nature of the lute, especially when they seem to flatter the harp." He shot Damiano a sharply pointed magnificent glare. "Oh, my philosophy is unchanged, young man. It is always better to treat an instrument as what it is. But I cannot criticize your music. Because it works. It obviously works. And when music works, philosophies cannot touch it.

"Now I am going to get a honey and walnut roll from these people, along with a glass of something, and then I shall come back to listen once more."

Damiano was so caught between confusion and gratitude that his face grew hot. But as MacFhiodhbhuidhe rose again, the harper paused to say, "Oh, by the way, monsieur, you cannot play the lute in Avignon without belonging to the guild."

"Eh? Is that why the . . . gentlemen were upset with me? Well, I didn't know it was an obligation, and now I most certainly shall join."

Two black eyebrows arched up and the harper's smile was wry. "It isn't so easy. Men have waited ten years to be accepted into the Guild of Avignon. And unless you have a sponsor, it is very expensive."

Damiano heard a cry and a stamp of disappointment from Gaspare behind him. He himself stared down at the parquet floor, wondering, "What next? What next?"

"But I wouldn't worry about it tonight," continued MacFhiodhbhuidhe, as his eyes roved the hall, seeking the attention of a maid. "I myself happen to be the Mayor of the Guild of Musicians at Avignon."

One more surprise would leave him numb, thought Damiano. "And . . . you . . . would consider sponsoring me, Monsieur MacFhoid . . MacFhioda . . ."

With a contemptuous wave of his taloned hand the harper swept away both Damiano's incipient gratitude and the problem of his name. "I said don't think about it tonight." The maid appeared then, with a wooden tray upon which were piled seven varieties of heart's delight.

As Damiano tuned, preparatory to playing again, the harper downed the last of his honey walnut roll in a long draft of wine infused with violets. He wiped his mouth with the back of his hand. (Like a cat, the harper kept his hand soft and round, the claws hidden within.) "You know, Monsieur Delstrego," he said conversationally, "it is part of the duties of the Mayor of the Guild to lead the disciplinary companies."

It took a moment for Damiano to digest this. "You mean . . ."

"Yes. To beat the pulp out of any intruder who dares to play an instrument for money within the limits of Avignon." And MacFhiodhbhuidhe chuckled mildly to himself, took out his block of pumice, and began to file his nails.

Damiano and Gaspare grinned uncomfortably at each other.

Chapter Seven

Last summer, during the excited farewells spoken by Gaspare and Evienne and the more composed ones of Damiano and Jan Karl, Gaspare had arranged to meet his sister again at the door to the Papal Palace in Avignon on Palm Sunday. Jan had said there was such an edifice as the Pope's Door, and the rest had believed. From that ten months' distance it had seemed that to slice through time with an accuracy of one day was feat enough.

Now Damiano wished heartily that they had stipulated the meeting more exactly, both in time and space. The Pope's Door probably meant the main door into the Papal enclosure, but one could not be sure.

Gaspare and his friend had set down stools, courtesy of their employer, near the station of the right-hand pikeman at the gate. This pikeman was a tow-headed northerner, very tall and quite amiable. He was glad for their company because Damiano had brought his lute.

Of course they had come at dawn, because dawn was part of Palm Sunday. Damiano had left this station of waiting long enough to attend mass, but otherwise the two of them sat like toads on a log, as hour followed hour.

It was not hard on Damiano, for this day was mild, and coincided with one of his periodic spells of lethargy, brought on perhaps by daily performance and practice. And it was quite gratifying to find how many out of the Sunday crowd already knew or recognized him, stopping for conversation and compliments.

"Already you're making a name for yourself," whispered

his youthful manager. "Not seven days into Avignon and people of the better sort recognize you."

Damiano grunted sheepishly as the most recent well-wisher departed: a fellow whose embroidered tabard signified that he served a cardinal. "I was born with a name, just like everybody else. And by what criteria do you judge that these are people of the better sort, other than by the fact that they recognize me?"

Gaspare did not answer. His repartee was not at its best, today. He was not happy: torn between an expectation too strong for comfort and a fear that fed upon that expectation. His face was sweaty and his hair (despite much attention) lank. He could not sit still—not for a moment—but neither would he let himself stir from his post of waiting. The result was an itching agony.

Damiano did not wonder at the boy's distress. If he had had family of any sort (he thought) he would cling to them like glue. Had Damiano a sister, he would have used any means, whether force of persuasion or force of arms, to prevent her fluttering off to a foreign country with a scapegrace conniver like Jan Karł.

Had Damiano a sister, of course, she would never have had to start selling herself on street corners. His fingers ceased to move on the strings as he became lost in reverie on the subject of his nonexistent sister.

Life would have been different, certainly. This sister (without doubt she would have been younger than he. He could not imagine an older sister, bullying him and calling him a dirty boy . . .) would have been the natural playmate of Carla Denezzi. Damiano would have then had far more occasions to meet with the lovely Carla, for whom he still had a sweet and somewhat painful regard. Perhaps he would have proposed marriage to Carla in better times. Perhaps she would have accepted.

How strange that would have been! He would by now be a different person entirely. Certainly a man with a wife could not have left the Piedmont for Lombardy, seeking the greatest witch in the Italies, nor subsequently wandered down into Avignon and sat in the sun by the Pope's Door, to pass the time of day politely with a cardinal's functionary.

Would he have ever met Raphael, had he had a sister?

Damiano was beginning to regret the existence of this

imaginary sibling. She would be a girl of problems. If she
had proven a witch, as was likely, she would have had a
difficult time finding suitors. No simple man wanted to
marry a witch, and even the sighted were just as happy
with a simple wife. (And it was not too much easier for the
male witches, for no father wanted to give his daughter to
a man who might, in fit of irritation, turn her into a snake.
Guillermo Delstrego had had to search all the way to
France to find a suitable helpmate. Of course Delstrego
Senior had had problems of visage and temperament as
well as livelihood. Damiano was always grateful that he
had taken after his mother in all ways but one.)

By the crowded calendar of saints, what if Damiano's
sister had looked like her father? Oh, it was much, much
better that the girl had never been born.

Reverie and sunlight together filled his head with
sweet, amber adhesive honey. He could not think anymore. There was no need to think anymore. His right
hand nestled into the strings over the soundhole. His left
hand fell away from the lute's neck.

Damiano had no idea how long he had been asleep
when either the shadow on his face or the rough voice
woke him up. He opened his eyes and started in terror, for
it was the tall, narrow-chested guildsman who had come so
near to assaulting him ("beating the pulp out" of him, to
quote) on his first day at work.

This time the fellow had no club, but he looked
angrier than ever. His langue d'oc was far too rapid for
Damiano to follow, so the Italian made the universal
I-do-not-understand-you gesture with both hands. The
response to this was a grimace of disgust, and then the
fellow began again, more slowly.

"It is bad enough that you crash into the city of
Avignon, and I am forced to watch you receive what better
men than you have waited years to have. This is shameful,
and if we had a Provençal for the Mayor of our Guild, as
we should, this would not happen.

"But you are not content with one of the most honor-
able and lucrative positions in the city; you must also ruin
the livelihoods of poor men by playing them off the street.
I must assume, monsieur—and your misshapen nose con-
firms me—that you are some Jew whose lust is for money,

and who strides through Avignon with the idea that the
protection of the King, the Pope and the Mayor is
everything..."

Since it is not pleasant to have someone yelling abuse
six inches from one's face, Damiano squirmed in his seat,
and turned his head to the side. There were so many
recriminations in the man's tirade that he could not keep
track of them, let alone answer.

And this last, accusing him of being Jewish, was only
confusing. In Partestrada there had been no Jews dwelling, but only old Jacob benJacob, who was Swiss as well as
Jewish, and who came through once every three-month,
selling, among other things, thread. It was from him that
Damiano had purchased his first little lute. No one had
suggested to him that Jacob was rich.

In Torino there was a Jewish quarter, certainly, and it
was also from a Jew that he had purchased the gold-
embossed volume of Aquinas which he had given to Carla.
This had struck him as odd at the time, since if the man
was Jewish he by definition could not be a Christian, and
so what was he doing with a book of theology?

But for the most part, Damiano had never thought
about the Jews for good or evil.

But his nose, now. He *had* thought about his nose,
having at least the average share of vanity. And he had just
been congratulating himself at having escaped the physi-
ognomy of Guillermo Delstrego. This was disheartening.

Gazing resolutely across the avenue which was never
for a moment empty, and where the Sunday garb of the
strollers gave only the slightest nod toward Lenten re-
pentance, he spoke. "Monsieur Guildsmember, you do me
wrong. I am not trying to steal the brass sous of the street
musicians (although I must say I would not regret them,
being not as well paid as you think). I am only practicing,
for I must play this evening. You notice no bowl?"

The fellow did not look down, except to spit. "Worse.
Who is going to pay for music, if you give it to them for
free?"

Damiano's fingers drummed on the spruce face of the
lute. He was losing his patience. And where was Gaspare,
anyway? Wasn't it a manager's job to keep him from this
kind of disturbance?

He searched the street as he replied in his slow, careful langue d'oc, "Monsieur, I do believe it is you who are the mercenary one, for I was sitting here quite content to play for myself, in quiet practice to which no one, as far as I can tell, was listening. And in further answer to you, no, I am not Jewish, though it was necessary for me to learn to read Hebrew as a child, along with a small nibbling of Greek. But in fact, I have just come from mass, and with the communion in mind I hesitate to trade insults on . . ."

The words froze on Damiano's tongue and his tongue itself clove to the roof of his mouth. For as he stared across the busy street where butchers and bishops came and went, one passerby stopped to stare back at him with the face and hair of Raphael.

Damiano's expression flashed through stages of confusion, welcome and again confusion. The pedestrian stood stock-still. He was dressed in an elegance of gray and scarlet. If only he were closer.

Damiano stood, squinting, and shoved past the belligerent musician. "I . . . I . . . I mean, that is . . ."

And the ruddy, arrogant face came into focus. Satan smiled at Damiano, flourished and bowed, and then disappeared behind a wicker cage on poles filled with chickens and carried by two boys. This utensil swayed by as ponderously as the sedan chair of some dowager, and when the squawking affair had passed, so had the apparition.

Damiano swallowed. "That was . . . someone I know," he whispered, feeling both frightened and foolish. The guildsman then grabbed Damiano by the arm and spun him around. The lute banged alarmingly against the wall.

"You will not ignore me, you black-faced peasant!" the fellow bellowed, and swung his bony fist at Damiano's face.

He ducked, but even before the fist passed above his head the gleaming length of a sharpened halberd sliced the air between them. The guildsman blinked at it, his arm still cocked for the blow. Damiano followed the wood and iron length back to its wielder, the gate guard both musicians had forgotten was there.

"Enough," growled the guard. "No fighting around

the Papal Palace. Haven't you any respect for the Holy
Father?"

The guildsman evidently did have respect, either for
the Holy Father or for the instruments of war, for he
backed off, cringing and snarling together, like a dog.

"Hah!" grunted the guard, once he and Damiano
were alone. "That was one of the few amusing moments of
my day." His weathered blue eyes twinkled down at
Damiano, who had sunk strengthless back onto his stool.
"That and your pretty playing, of course. Don't mind that
fellow. I know him: he's usually here, with a hurdy-gurdy
out of tune, playing the same five songs. He's got at least a
dozen children, and his wife leaves them with him while
she takes in laundry. Quite a racket, they make."

Damiano smiled his gratitude, as he reflected to
himself—they protect me. The strangest people protect
me: guardsmen, Irishmen, horses. Dogs. Why? And then
he thought, The Devil. He is in Avignon. What does that
portend?

Gaspare returned in late afternoon, looking worse
than ever. Damiano put down the lute. "Where did you
go?" he asked, offering the boy some of the bread and
dates he had paid a child to buy for him.

Gaspare wanted nothing. "Around. To every other
gate into the enclosure. And then to each of the outer
gates."

"All around the city?"

The boy threw himself upon the ground against the
stucco wall, regardless of his exquisite new mantle. "I
thought . . . I thought perhaps we had the place wrong. I
wanted to see if they were waiting elsewhere. They weren't."

Damiano said nothing, for there was nothing he could
say, except that he had seen Satan on the streets of
Avignon. And that was not something Gaspare would want
to hear right now. So he spent another hour improvising
quietly on the treble strings, and when it could no longer
be avoided, he said, "I'll have to go now. I have to work."

Gaspare glanced up at the setting sun and flinched as
though he had just received a blow. His arms, nothing but
skin, bones and twisted tendon, were wrapped around his
knees and he buried his head between them.

Damiano bit down on his lip. Poor child: his sleeves did not come within three inches of his wrists, so fast he had grown in the past winter. Damiano for a moment had the feelings of a father. He put the lute behind his stool and considered what he might say or do to help.

But Gaspare was beyond easy consolation. He rocked stiffly back and forth, his dusty boots soiling the velvet of the cloak. "Perhaps she never reached Avignon," he said in a strangled voice. "Perhaps she has been dead the greater part of a year!"

Damiano grunted. "We have no reason to . . ."

"She is dead! I feel it. I have felt it for a long time!" Now Gaspare raised his head, and, yes, as Damiano suspected, the boy was weeping, reddening his protuberant gooseberry eyes. His nose was as pinched as an old man's, and indeed, Gaspare looked very aged right now, aged and in despair. "She was all I had. All I had. No father, no mother, no name of our own, and she was only a dirty slut, but she was all I had! And now she is dead and I have nothing!"

It was on the tip of Damiano's tongue to say that Gaspare still had him, but that seemed such a conceited thing to say.

Evidently the guard had some Italian, for bending at the waist and pushing his steel helmet back from his forehead, he whispered in Damiano's ear, "What a shame. How did she die?"

"We don't know that she *did* die," hissed the lutenist back. "She simply did not show up for an appointment."

Raphael knew where Evienne was. Damiano was tempted to tell Gaspare as much, to allay his fears. But how could he reveal that, without being therefore obliged to ask the angel for more specific information, which the musician did not want to do. Besides—was Raphael's knowledge a comforting thought after all? The fact that Raphael knew where the girl was did not mean necessarily that she was alive. For all Damiano knew, angels were on close terms with the dead. He remembered the little ghost of Macchiata, half hidden by Raphael's robe, and he decided not to mention Raphael's words to Gaspare.

Damiano crouched down in front of the boy and with both hands forced Gaspare to look at him. "You are being very unreasonable, Gaspare. Think whom we are dealing with. Evienne has no more sense than a kitten—I doubt she even knows how to read a calendar, and Jan . . . well, Jan Karl would not get out of bed to save his mother's life. Not if the bed were comfortable.

"Evienne is not dead; we have merely been stood up."

Sadly Gaspare shook his head, but there were no more hysterics. Damiano left him to keep faith during the last daylight, under the small blue eyes of the interested guard. He ran the whole way back to the Bishop's Inn.

Damiano knew that Coutelan, the innkeeper, did not know what he was saying when he said Damiano had a genius; probably the man didn't know the difference between a genius of the lute and a genie in a lamp. Coutelan only repeated and magnified anything the Irishman said. Mac Whatever, who lived next door and had invested a certain amount of money in the operation of the inn, was his authority.

Which was why Damiano had gotten this job in the first place. It was because he had been seen by the innkeeper exiting the harper's garden in that unorthodox manner. And because he had an accent.

But though Damiano repeated these things to himself, he was still human, and praise could make him drunk. Especially after a long winter and hungry spring. And tonight he had gotten a good dose of it, for MacFhiodhbhuidhe had walked in leading a good ten other men, all musicians, and he had called Damiano his "glorious exception to the rules." The young man had also been bought three glasses of violet wine, which was the harper's favorite but not Damiano's and consequently he had a fire in his middle and a bad taste in his mouth.

In spite of this, as he wrapped the lute in its baby blanket and strode out into the street toward his poor accommodations, Damiano was singing to himself.

That owl on the wall there, making noise every night. Bothersome as a tomcat: it was a wonder somebody didn't kill the creature with a brick. And what did it find to eat in the stone and stucco city of Avignon?

Damiano, who was not the man to flip a brick at any animal, snapped his fingers and clucked to the bird as he went by. It followed his motion with a head that turned ridiculously far around. Its eyes were two orange full moons, mirroring the one in the sky. He went through the quiet, leather-hinged door.

And then Damiano remembered Gaspare and the sister who hadn't shown up. Queasy pity hit him, making his stomach worse. At least, he hoped, the boy had been able to sleep. Reaching the Heather Inn, he tiptoed down the hall and into the room they shared with four other men. One of them was snoring.

On Gaspare's pallet the clean straw glistened under the spear of moonlight admitted by the street-facing window. His blankets were lumped beside. There was no Gaspare.

Damiano cursed under his breath. By his own pallet he left the lute, still swaddled, and his lean legs took him out of the room and out of the inn in five strides.

Guilt that has been stored gathers interest, and Damiano was feeling very guilty at leaving Gaspare to wait. He loped the moon-washed, empty streets, stepping silently through long training—his father's training. He imagined Gaspare squatting there by the Papal Palace all evening, as the sun went down and the friendly guard was relieved by another, and the shops closed and the hawkers shut up and slowly all the avenue became still.

While Damiano, who did not really care if Evienne missed the appointment, save for Gaspare's sake, and who did not care for Jan Karl at all, had been playing to a room full of gentlemen, receiving heady praise and sweet wine. Shades of hell, that was a sorry thing, and most especially since Damiano's genius had always been Gaspare's faith, much more than Damiano's, and so the confirmation and the praise rightly belonged to Gaspare.

Above his head Damiano saw the silver white body of the owl float by on noiseless wings. He watched it swoop down upon a roof. Just before it struck it emitted a sharp, predatory cry. It did not reappear.

But then Damiano thought of another explanation for Gaspare's tardiness. Perhaps Evienne *had* come after all, and taken the boy with her to wherever she lived (preferably apart from the Dutchman). That made sense. And of course they would come back for Damiano, sooner or later, after the first flush of reunion was past.

With this conviction, Damiano's feet slowed to a more comfortable pace. He sighed deeply, feeling some great crisis had been only just averted. He strolled as far as the Pope's Door, to see whether they'd left any message.

There was the high, Gothic-arched gate, with a glistening sentry at either side, behind an avenue that the full moon made look decently clean. And there, like a bundle of rags beside the right-hand pikeman, was the huddled shape Damiano had decided would not be there. And because he had decided this halfway between the inn and the Pope's Door, Damiano was not prepared for the sight.

"Mother of God!" he whispered to the moonlight. "He *is* there. What on earth am I to do about this?" And he came to a stop, still a hundred feet away from the pathetic thing in the green velvet mantle. "What on earth *can* I do?"

And worldly fame turned to ashes in Damiano's soul. He turned on his heel and ran away, down the first, random crooked street he came to, fleeing because he could not meet the boy he had no way to help.

But had he no way? Raphael had said he knew where Evienne was, and would tell him at need. But he had also said there were other ways he could find out. There were, of course. If he were a witch he could find the girl, just as a hound could find her, given time enough.

If he were a witch.

Well, for God's sake, why not?

Because of his music? Hell and damn. What did it matter if he was the smoothest and most intellectual lutenist in all Provence and Italy? Was it important that ten men with reputations came to judge him as though he were a prize cow, while they ate pastries and talked musical philosophy? (While inside he nursed a slight contempt, knowing he was better than they.) Someday, then, he could be five and forty years old, and sit judging the young whose reputation is still to be made, secretly afraid that they might be better than he. Afraid they might be nursing a slight contempt.

Damiano then remembered the little tunes Raphael

delighted to play: children's pieces without ornament or
heterophony, and how the angel's head bent over Damiano's
instrument, lost in simple melody, far beyond self.

Tears stung his eyes, and his stomach hurt like sin.

For what reason, besides devotion to the lute, had he
refused his powers, when pressed by Saara? He had told
her he was afraid his magic would hurt people.

It *had* hurt people. He'd killed at least fifty men with
a force of terror one winter's day in the Alps. Perhaps he
also saved that many, or five times that many, by
circumventing a battle between Savoy and the *condottiere*
General Pardo. But one was never sure about saving men,
while killing them was incontrovertible.

And Gaspare was hurting already: hurting in a way
that only magic could help. And of all the people in the
world, Gaspare had most claim on him.

So all his reasons, musical and magical, were empty.
In fact, what did it matter whether it was wise or foolish,
saintly or sinful, for him to deny his witchhood?

What did Damiano matter at all? He had mattered
too much to himself in the past year. Gaspare—loyal and
uneducated, without philosophy, lost in the sea of his own
sorrow—mattered. He had to be helped.

His feet raced on for another half-block, almost of
their own accord. He passed a man who was casually
pissing out of a ground-floor window. The white owl circled overhead, silent as any of the planets. When he
finally stopped he realized that this decision carried him
no closer toward a solution to Gaspare's problem.

For Saara held Damiano's witch-soul within her own,
and Saara had said goodbye to him. Not *arrivederci*, or *au
revoir*, or any other of the thousand ways to say she would
see him later. She had been angry and had said goodbye.
By now she was in Lombardy.

She could not be expected to come to him again.

The weariness of the long day descended on Damiano
then, and he leaned upon the nearest wall for support. It
was a dirty wall, stucco and timber like all the rest in
Avignon. There was a bestial roar and a thud. The wall
itself trembled and Damiano snatched back his hand.

Bandog. Mastiff. He backed away and for the first
time looked about him at the sagging, dilapidated row-

houses, and the cobbles mired with human filth. He had not previously seen this side of life in the Papal city. He found himself standing in the exact middle of the street, scanning the shadows for movement. He feared thieves.

What a difference in fortune a week can make, he thought. I might have been lurking in the shadows myself. Slowly he turned on his heel and departed the way he had come, accompanied by the barking of the mastiff and the silent white owl.

He must try. Though Saara might refuse him, though she would certainly laugh at the way he was denying all his carefully thought-out reasons for remaining simple, still he must make the effort.

If he could remember how.

There—that silver strip against the hill with the river beyond—that was the wall of the enclosure. There stood the pikemen. There sat Gaspare, beneath his weight of fear. It was try now or never.

Damiano came to an ancient grapevine trained into an espalier. The wood was heavy, the burgeoning leaves few. The dirt of the city had half killed it and age was completing the rest of the task, but it was yet alive, and its leaves rustled as he laid his face against its trellised surface. He took comfort from the strength of wood as he tried to remember.

It was difficult—difficult and painful as well, for he no longer trusted the torn vacancies of his mind where he had slept away a year. He clung in fear to the smell of furry grape leaves, to the rough brush of bark, to the sound of the hooting owl. He could not let go.

Damiano began to sweat with effort. It seemed he had lost the art of withdrawing which had protected him since losing his powers, and which had once taken him to Lombardy, to the garden of the witch.

Would he need someone with a cat-o'-nine-tails, to whip him into remembering? "Saara," he whispered, and he closed his eyes. "Saara."

But in his mind's eye he saw not the winterless, stream-broken garden. Not the goat with flowers around her rusty neck. Not the fairy shape in a blue dress enbroidered with stars. He saw the human woman's form: naked, hot against him.

"Yes," she whispered to him. "Yes, Damiano. I am here."

He heard clearly but he saw nothing except the red darkness behind his closed eyes. He opened them to find Saara standing before him on the cobbled street of Avignon.

He felt as he had sometimes in the past when riding— when Festilligambe came to a sudden stop and he almost did not. The world lurched, and he put out his hand to brace himself. But there was nothing to hold on to except Saara, so he took her firmly by the wrist.

Her eyes narrowed at his astonishment. "What is wrong, Dami? You called me, didn't you? You are still calling me; I can hear it."

As he straightened he dropped her wrist. "You are here. You are not in Lombardy."

And as she said nothing in reply, he added, "Why?"

There was no expression in the witch's face as she answered, "I don't know if I could have gone far, Damiano. Not after ... last week. My strength is half yours—more than half yours, I think—and it wars against me. But anyway I did not want to go, for I was afraid for you."

"For me?" he echoed. "You feared I might do myself harm?"

She shrugged an Italian shrug. (Had she learned it from Ruggerio the Roman? From Damiano's father?) "I have pain, young one. Like I was having a baby and the head would not come out. For you it cannot be any better."

He said nothing.

"Why did you do it, Damiano?" she continued. "To throw me away like that. In my long life I have never been treated so."

Damiano's eyebrows disappeared underneath his hair. "I—why did I ... ? Saara, it was a dirty trick you played me, leading me to think you wanted ..." He took a deep breath. "I don't think I want to talk about it," he said.

The Fenwoman had taken a step backward, and her stomach tightened with a miserable understanding. "You thought I wanted you only to be rid of the burden I am carrying? That is dreadful. It is not true. I will carry it until I die rather than have you believe that."

"No," answered Damiano in a voice that sounded foreign to himself. "No. I need it back now." And as Saara stared, openmouthed, he added, "I need to be a witch again. Tonight."

The moonlight (and only the moonlight) streaked Saara's hair with gray. She stood in an oddly formal pose, her hands cupping her elbows and her bare feet gripping the cobbles.

"You do? Tonight?"

He nodded. "It is not my need but Gaspare's. His sister is missing, and I need full sight to find her for him."

One of the woman's hands crawled toward a hanging braid. White fingers clawed into the hair, tangling it. Saara glanced from the foul street to the eaves of the crowding buildings. She did not look at Damiano. From far away, the bark of the bandog could still be heard. "It would be easier if I found the girl," she suggested.

Damiano shook his head and, leaning against the ancient grapevine, he slid down till he sat on his heels. "I thought of that, Saara," he admitted. "I also asked Raphael's help, when I first knew there was going to be a problem. But he told me to look elsewhere before asking him to do what he should not do—and since then I have had to think about what I am asking of everyone."

Saara squatted beside him, her toes splayed out before her like those of a frog. "More thinking, Dami? You think too much, I think."

Though her words were friendly, he ignored them. "I need witchcraft, or at least 'sight,' to find Evienne before Gaspare throws himself in the Rhone, or sickens with grief. If I use your skills just because I don't want the responsibility, then I have done the deed and yet tried to evade the price, don't you see? And we both know that does not work, in witchcraft or in life."

Still she did not meet his eyes.

"Saara. What is it? Don't you want me to take back that . . . that illegitimate baby that confused Gaspare so much?"

This pulled a smile from her, and a quick green glance that made it hard for Damiano to swallow. "No," she replied. "Now that the moment comes, I do not. A person gets used to being the way she is."

Then she reached toward him, a flame of concentration on her face. "Here, Damiano. Take my hand. Quickly."

He obeyed, but his black eyes darted up and down the cobblestones. "Here? In the middle of the street?"

Saara giggled. She seemed herself again. "All *that* is not necessary, Dami. Nice, but not necessary." She squeezed his hand roughly and leaned forward, placing her other palm against the young man's forehead. "Only remember," she whispered.

Saara's touch was warm; that itself was easily remembered. And with that warmth came other memories from beneath the blankets in the old wagon: the mouse in the woodwork, the mole beneath the grass, the planets circling (each with its name, each with its song), the lake of fire which somehow came not out of hell. The corona that lit each living thing from within, and arcing green flame of its extinction. The touch of human presence, like a feather against his face.

Hermes Trismegistus, Albertus Magnus, the broken black staff, taller than his body, banded with silver, crowned with red and gold, through which once (as though it were a great flute) he'd played the wind of his will.

Once, only two years ago, he'd played that music better than he played the lute.

Damiano remembered, completely and without violence to body or mind, all he was born to be.

His blood was singing like a chorus. He felt the hard, rounded stones beneath him, and recognized that they had been pulled from the Rhone. He heard the bandog, and a hundred other hounds crying, droning, quarreling or snoring through the city of Avignon. He heard that segment of the human population which was awake at this hour; they sounded much like the dogs.

As a man orients himself in time by glass or sundial, he felt (with his tongue against the roof of his mouth) for the hour by the position of the heavens.

And in the next street he heard the sorrow-clogged breathing of Gaspare, who had fallen asleep against the Holy Father's wall.

Damiano opened his eyes and was forced to squint against the glare of the moonlight off white walls. Saara's face, too, appeared bleached and colorless. The fingers of her left hand, which had held his, hung limply.

"You are weary," he whispered, and he helped her to her feet.

"Of course I am. Not you?" Saara disengaged herself from his arms. She inspected Damiano minutely and impersonally: head, hands and booted feet. "You are not tired, nor sick?" With a proprietary shove she turned him completely around.

He submitted to these attentions with the docility of a child. "I feel," he announced, "as though I will never be weary again. Nor sick."

Saara smiled wanly. One of her braids was completely undone and hung in waves, like falling water. She looked pale and thin and, despite her height, frail. Damiano could see a pulse pounding in the hollow at the base of her neck. "Good. Then it has been worth all the mice and rats."

"All the what?"

Saara seemed to feed off Damiano's confusion. The sly smile returned to her mouth, and color to her cheeks. "Mice and rats. I had to eat something in Avignon, you know. Since, as you say, these people will not feed a stranger."

Damiano felt obscurely guilty, as well as revolted. "Mice and rats? Surely, Saara, if you had let me know..."

Saara giggled then, lifted one leg cranelike, and (since her braid was pulled apart) nibbled on one twisted lock of hair. "It is not so bad, if you are an owl."

"An owl? You are the bird that has been ruining my sleep since I have been in Avignon?" Her grin spread to Damiano's face. He snatched Saara off her feet, knocking the breath out of her as he spun her around. "Not a fox and an owl, too? Saara. You should be nothing but my little dove!" Her bare heel knocked against the gnarled trunk of the vine. With an apology Damiano put her down.

Forcefully she pulled away. "It is good you feel so strong, fellow. But you must be careful; you don't know what you are doing, now. You are like a baby."

"A baby?" Even moonlight could not steal the warmth from Damiano's olive countenance. As Saara spoke he closed the gap she had made between them and embraced her again. He kissed her on the cheek, the chin, the side of her neck. Her skin tingled his lips and tasted like wine. "How a baby? I have been a witch all my life, minus only one year and a little bit, and the whole time has been spent in study. I studied," he declared fervently, "until my brains began to curdle."

Then Saara sighed, and the irritation in that single sound chastened Damiano completely. He took a step backward and let her continue. "You were a witch whose magic was locked within a stick. You lost both magic and stick. Now you have had the magic back for two minutes, and already you have both bruised my foot and made me angry."

"I'm sorry," he said, and through the glow of his exaltation remorse did seem to be working. "I was just a little drunk with . . . being able to see and hear. I will be a gentleman from now on."

Saara muttered something he was not meant to hear. It might have been "Too bad." Then she spoke aloud.

"You will be all right, Damiano. Come with me and I will teach you to sing-spell. You will be very good at it, I am sure, having made so much music of the simple kind."

He broke out in surprised laughter. "Simple? My music—simple? Well, each to his own opinion, my lady." But his antic mood softened again. "Saara, Saara, I will most willingly come under your tutelage. (There is at least one lesson between us still incomplete.) But till Good Friday my time belongs to Bernard Coutelan and the Bishop's Inn. I must remain a baby that long."

"Then until Friday I must eat mice and rats," interjected the Fenwoman, and for a moment her eyes went round, bright, orange and moonlike. Damiano sputtered with laughter.

"No, my lady. Return to the Heather Inn with me and eat like a burgher, if not a queen."

Saara made a prim little grimace. "That place? I have sat in their courtyard every night, watching men and women make their beds in straw a reindeer would not touch. The fleas, mice and bedbugs have an easier life than the people."

Damiano shrugged. "That is an inn. I have been in much worse."

Saara wound her fingers in Damiano's coarse hair. She

drew him to her for one more slow, thoughtful kiss. "I would rather eat rats than have them run over me.

"Friday," she added. Then with an odd, almost angry look upon her face, Saara shrank into a white pillow of feathers, orange-eyed. This flew onto Damiano's shoulder, where the outsized talons pricked his skin. Then she hooted maliciously into his ear and rose into the sky on soft, shrouded wings.

Chapter Eight

When Gaspare was awakened, his first thought was that the deep, commanding voice belonged to the Holy Father's pikeman, or some troublesome soldier whose job it was to keep poor souls from cluttering the streets of Avignon. But the hand that reached down to take his was lean, calloused and very familiar, and when Gaspare raised his head...

"By Saint Gabriele, Damiano," the redhead hissed, "the moon in your eyes made me half frightened of you!" Then as the boy locked his knees in the upright position and freed his hand from the lutenist's grip, he remembered why he had fallen asleep at the Pope's Door.

"Oh, Christ, sheep-face. She never came. I will never see my whore of a sister again."

Damiano let the nickname pass. His wide drunken eyes stared from Gaspare to the swarthy face of the night gate guard, and across the wide avenue to where hundreds of black holes in pale walls revealed the sounds and smells of human sleep. His left hand was twitching like a small animal. Once more he snagged Gaspare.

"If Evienne and Jan are in Avignon, we will find them tonight," said Damiano with sweeping confidence. "Come, little dear," he added. "Start walking."

Gaspare's offense at being addressed as "little dear" was drowned completely in his amazement at the rest of

Damiano's behavior. He found himself dragged along the wide street, his eyes still grainy from sleep, his long mantle flapping behind.

If the Damiano of the past year had been unaccountable...if the Damiano of the past few weeks had been enough to make Gaspare tread warily...this new Damiano was an Act of God. He strode through the empty streets like the conqueror Alexander, his black eyes flashing, his rather large nose turned arrogant by the force of authority in the shaggy head. Though the night was chill, and Gaspare suffered despite his velvet cloak, the hand that held his was warm—warm like beach sand in the sun.

At the first corner, an abrupt change of direction nearly popped the boy's arm from its socket. "What are we doing?" he yelled in protest. Half a dozen dogs were set off by the noise. "How are we going to find her this way? I have been up and down these streets every day for a week; she's not to be found."

Damiano looked back over his shoulder. "If she's not here, Gaspare, then we won't find her. Otherwise we will."

"How?" demanded the boy, pulling free with great effort.

Damiano smiled mildly enough, though his eyes were still dangerous. "I will feel her presence. I am a witch again, Gaspare. I will know."

Gaspare felt a sinking in his heart, though he would have thought it impossible for him to get any lower. "Oh, no, Damiano. Not that again."

The dark eyes flickered with irritation and Damiano raised his hand. For a moment Gaspare believed he was going to hit him, but then from Damiano's outspread fingers five points of flame sprang up.

Gaspare staggered back.

"Not a Hand of Glory," whispered Damiano. "But my own." He laughed at the boy's goggle eyes and general air of amazement, but as he did so the tame, domestic fire in his hand leaped upward like the flame of a torch dipped in oil. He shook it out.

"Needs practice," he muttered, slightly shamefaced, and then cleared his throat. "So you see, Gaspare..."

"Don't hurt me," the redhead blurted, stepping still farther back.

As the flame had gone out from Damiano's hand, so now it went out from his face. With almost a look of suffering, the witch replied, "Hurt you, Gaspare? No. All of this is particularly to avoid your hurt. And I am only the same fellow you befriended in the market of San Gabriele, who knew how to disappear, but not how to make a broken florin. But enough time for talk after we find Evienne." Without putting his hand upon the plainly frightened boy, he turned again and strode off down a side street, his lips parted, his face to the wind like that of a hound.

The city of Avignon existed because of the Rhone. Both the secular city and the city which was the Papal Palace crowded the water's edge. But while the stone and stucco of the ecclesiastical center sat on a prominence from which garbage was piped into a river that was not even seen, the burghers built their jumbled houses in intimate contact with the mud. Damiano saw parts of the city that night which he might never have seen otherwise: not though he had lived in Avignon for years. And had he been a simple man, he could not have seen what he saw at all.

The houses of Avignon were not jammed with residents, despite the way they crowded together on the occluded streets. Some of them had no more than a single sleeper breathing within. Yet it was not a city of the rich, to be sure. Poverty had its own odor, and it was stronger and less mistakable than any expensive perfume. Damiano smelled poverty and rotting fish on the mud flats of the city.

"There are three men sleeping under that boat," he observed to Gaspare as they hurried by a small neighborhood wharf.

"Men?" repeated Gaspare. "Not Evienne." He stopped to stare.

Damiano frowned. "Not Evienne. I just thought it worth mentioning. There are also people sleeping beneath the stilts of these waterside houses. What they do when the river runs high I don't know."

Damiano tilted his face to the sky and stood silent for

a moment, as though he were reading something. Then he looked behind him, to where Gaspare still wandered on the dried mud by the boat dock. The boy had his arms out stiffly before him. "Gaspare," he called quietly, "what are you doing?"

Gaspare was startled, hearing his guide so far away. "Heh! Damiano. I can't find you. I can't find anything."

The witch covered the ground between them in three strides. "What's the matter, Gaspare? The moon is full. Are you night-blind?"

The boy caught his arm and stared with goblin eyes. "Night-blind? I don't know. What does it matter? Lately I have taken to sleeping at night, you know." The arm beneath his pulled him away from the river once more.

"Damiano, where are you taking us?"

"Everywhere."

"It will be easier for me to find Jan Karl." murmured Damiano, talking for Gaspare's sake. "I have this little knife in my belt, with which I cut off two of his fingers. Did he ever tell you about that?"

"Yes" was the short reply. Gaspare was stumbling and out of patience. Then he remembered more.

"He told a weird story. He said you got him drunk and then cut his fingers off in some kind of magic rite."

"They were infected," replied Damiano with some reproach in his words. "Gangrenous. Did he not tell you that?"

"No."

Damiano sighed. "He was grateful at the time. I would not have done it for fun, I assure you, and especially would not have sacrificed all my supply of wine to play an ugly trick on a Dutchman. Didn't he ever mention his night in the snow?"

"Certainly. He was benighted in the Alps in November and nearly froze."

Damiano smiled grimly. It was on his tongue to explain to Gaspare how Jan Karl's two roving companions had tried to kill Damiano, and but for the fierce (and loquacious) bitch Macchiata would have succeeded. It was Damiano's dog that had driven the thieves out into the Alpine winter and thereby frozen Jan's fingers.

It was a wonder the Dutchman hadn't found some way to turn that story on its head and present it to Gaspare as an example of Damiano's perfidy and his own innocence. Damiano was liking him less and less as time went on.

And for that reason he did not speak. Why impress upon the distracted boy that his sister was off with a lout of such repulsive character, now that it was too late for Gaspare to do anything but worry?

They ran on together: Gaspare through empty streets, Damiano buffeted by the presence of thousands. Fifty thousand had Avignon before the great pest. At least half had died. Now the city had begun to swell toward its former size.

Damiano fingered his little knife as he jogged along. He sang wordlessly under his breath, both his own tunes and those he was picking up daily from MacFhiodhbhuidhe. Meanwhile, through his mind was running a different sort of melody: a tune which, like the music of Raphael, could find no expression in the hands or voice of man. Just now he was not trying to express the music in his mind; it was expressing him.

Never grow weary. Nor sick. He felt like a scrap of paper in the draft of a chimney, flaming and floating, weightless.

But Gaspare was wheezing like a wind-broken horse. The boy had started at a disadvantage, under a debility of sorrow. Now, as they watched a lone man in white—a baker—trudge toward his work with lantern in hand, Gaspare was near spent.

He pulled down on his friend's arm. He sat in the street, miring his mantle further, and without words he shook his head.

Damiano put one hand on the boy's head, which was sweaty. He did not attempt persuasion. Instead he said, "You'll cool down fast. Take my overshirt."

Gaspare peered up incredulously as Damiano yanked the red-and-gold tunic over his head. "You didn't like it when I took your shirt before," he panted. "And why should I have both overshirt and mantle and leave you in your linen?" Yet he took the tunic from Damiano, who paced in circles, toying with the sliver of silver and crystal in his hand.

"Because you are going to be cold and I am not," the witch replied. "Not tonight." Damiano whined—again like a hound. "I keep thinking about that no-good. I feel we are close."

"Don't call my sister a no-good," growled Gaspare sullenly. He was not offended enough to get up.

Damiano smiled with all his teeth. "Why not? You call her much worse. But I was not referring to little Evienne, of course, but to Jan Karl. It is as though I can hear him talking in my mind. Or snoring, maybe."

Gaspare peered around him. "Well, my dear old sneep—uh, Damiano, I don't know what you see or hear, and I myself can hardly see my hand before my face, but I have a funny feeling we're back where we started, having covered Avignon with a layer of shoe leather."

Damiano glanced at the open mouth of the Pope's Door without surprise. "That's exactly what we have done, though to be sure we haven't covered but half the city. We've been by this spot four times, and do you know it is always here that I begin to simmer inside about the Dutchman. I think we'll find him on the other side of that wall."

Gaspare glowered from Damiano to the gate and back again. Exhaustion gave birth to scorn. "Maybe Jan's been elected Pope, eh?"

Damiano was too intent to rise to the bait. "He started out as a cleric, Gaspare, right here in Avignon. Do not forget that. Though he may be a thief and a procurer in other lands, behind those walls he will be remembered as student and lector of the church." Damiano sighed. "I've wasted time. We should have started looking in the Papal Palace."

The boy scooted around on his behind until he also was peering through the darkness toward the looming white hill of the Pope. "Great," he grunted. "We'll just walk up to the pikeman there and announce that we must enter in order to search for a prostitute and a pimp." Then he turned on Damiano a glare that was hard with disappointment. "Shall I go first or would you like that honor?"

Damiano was chewing on his lip. "That method might

have had a chance while the big blond was at the gate, although even then... Now, I think, we shall have to resort to skill."

"Over the wall?" suggested Gaspare with a glimmer of professional interest.

Damiano chuckled in his throat, and there was behind that laugh a feral arrogance that Gaspare did not associate with the lutenist. "No, Gaspare. A different sort of skill."

He crouched down next to the boy. "Don't you remember the ducks' eggs and the peasant's house south of Lyons? How Saara took us in and out unnoticed?"

"Saara isn't here," said Gaspare unnecessarily.

Damiano pulled him to his feet. "We don't need the lady. Invisibility used to be a specialty of my own, remember, and I don't feel that I've lost any of my ability. Watch."

And Damiano sorted himself out for the effort. Within his head, behind closed eyes, he allowed the world of stone and night air to penetrate, so that his body would be no obstruction: not to air, sound or moonlight. It was a pleasant discipline while in process, and only tended to weary him afterward.

Out of habit he reached for something—for his staff, which was a focus for his power and his intent. His hands touched only Gaspare.

He jerked back. God knows what would happen, either to the boy or to the spell, if he tried to use a human being like the wooden length of a staff. He had no staff and would simply have to do without.

The spell was familiar, and he certainly hadn't lost any of his ability. He felt the scattered moonlight, heavy as mist, penetrate the borders of his body. Shape fell away. And thought.

Very pleasant.

There was commotion and someone flailing about in the street. Gaspare was shouting his name in a whisper. "Damiano! Damiano! Where have you gone?"

The boy crashed right into him and took him by the shoulders. "You stupid sheep-face! Where by the sufferings of hell have you been for a quarter-hour?"

Damiano cleared his throat. He could not rouse an

anger to match Gaspare's. "Ho. Nowhere, I guess." he
scratched his head with both hands.

"You know, Gaspare, not to be—I mean, to be *not*,
you know, is not bad at all. I don't mean not to be born, of
course, but rather...Never mind." Damiano shook his
head forcefully to clear out the moonlight, and returned to
the work at hand.

"Well. I'll have to make some changes in the way I do
things, I see. I need a tool. If I can't use a staff, like a
respectable magician, I'll do like Saara."

Gaspare frowned dubiously. "Are you going to make
up bad verse now?"

Damiano turned his head and struck a belligerent
attitude toward the gleaming hill of the Pope. "I am," he
declared.

> *"We pass beneath the arched gate.*
> *Unperceived. No blade will strike..."*

They were right under the door, with the black iron
portcullis raised above their heads. Damiano stopped to
stare and his concentration faltered. (Strike. What rhymes
with strike? Dike, like, pike...)

> *"And leaning is the sentry's pike*
> *Against the wall. The hour is late."*

If they were challenged, thought Gaspare, they would
simply plead innocence. For there they were parading
openly through an open gate, with guards at either hand.
It was not like being caught climbing a wall. If they were
challenged...

They were not challenged.

> *"So quiet are the cobbled streets*
> *Where the Holy Father sleeps,*
> *Or his prayer vigil keeps*
> *That..."*

Streets. What rhymes with streets? Sheets (terrible). Sweets. (Worse. Oh, God!) Beats?

"That one can hear his slow heartbeats."

The doorway loomed deep in shadow. Damiano plunged in, dragging Gaspare behind him. Once concealed, he began to blow like a winded horse. "That," he wheezed, "was awful. Hideous."

Gaspare's hand made an equivocal gesture, unseen even by the witch in the dark of the overhang. "Oh, I don't know. I think it was much better than Saara's. The ABBA rhyme has more subtlety than . . ."

Damiano snorted. "I'm not working in a foreign language. But it was terrible, nonetheless. I thought I would be found standing there under the portcullis, mouth open, knees knocking, and all for lack of a rhyme. There's got to be another way to work it."

This was what people meant all over Europe, when they spoke the word "Avignon." It was a single building and an entire city as well: the Holy Father's city. Damiano and Gaspare passed sedately down its passages, expecting to be impressed.

First glance was a little disappointing, for the nearest hall was a rather musty library of no great size.

"I've seen better," murmured Gaspare. Being illiterate, he wasted no time staring at the books.

"Oh? Where?" replied his friend absently. "In San Gabriele?" But even his interest faded when he discovered that the library specialized in canonical law.

The chambers beyond were plain but serviceable. Damiano fingered his little knife as he went. Jan Karl was not too near.

"I don't think, after all, that we entered by the main gate," he remarked to Gaspare after a minute. "For these seem to be little-used offices. Perhaps it was we who missed the rendezvous."

"Nope. I ran circles around the building," grunted Gaspare. "She wasn't anywhere."

Turning a corner, they came upon a region where the passages were broader and admitted more moonlight.

"How straight the walls are," murmured Damiano. "Look at them. It is hard to believe this whole enclosure is only one enormous building."

"That doesn't give me any trouble," replied Gaspare, whose ignorance of engineering principles made him blasé. "But what gets me is that there's no smell of shit anywhere."

"I've read that there are tubes in the rooms and one can piss into them and it travels all the way down to the Rhone," commented the lutenist. "Very civilized."

"Oh, I dunno. Must make the river stink. Is that any better?"

Damiano could not answer this question. He did not try, actually, for he had found a door with light behind it, and very carefully he was opening it.

Here was a courtyard, larger than many large houses, and soon the pair of intruders stood beside a massive pile of stone carved with bulge-headed dolphins, spouting thin streams of water into the velvet sky. Damiano's hand rested on his little knife and his lips moved soundlessly.

Gaspare put his hand on his friend's arm, for the moon was setting and the dolphins' faces bore a monstrous cast. "What is it, Damiano?"

"I . . . I am annoyed. Really annoyed," was the reply. "Though I can't think why. And therefore I think Jan Karl is near." He pointed toward a high, brass-doored entryway on the far side of the court. "Through there, in fact."

Gaspare followed the dim finger. He trembled appreciably. "There? That is where the Holy Father lives, I am told."

"Ah?" Damiano lifted his eyes to the bulk of the building. The palace appeared heavy, squat, ungainly from within. He felt the presence of humanity beating against his face like the heat of a hearth. Which of these sleeping souls was the Holy Father himself? No way to tell. "Well, it could very well be," he assented. "Good for Heer Karl. I always knew he had it in him. Of course it may be he is merely robbing the rooms of his superiors. Let's go find him."

Closing his eyes, he prepared the beginning of his song.

"Through the palace now we tread . . ."

And then he stopped. "No," announced Damiano to the darkened dolphin court. "No more of that."

He began to improvise a lullaby: wordless, full of ornament and with a tune that wandered. He sang high in his nose, almost at a whisper, like a mother with a baby who was already asleep. Gaspare strained his ears to hear.

Damiano took Gaspare by the hand. He touched the brass door and found it unlocked. Together they entered.

Here the windows were shuttered against the night air. Into unbroken blackness Damiano introduced fire: a tame blaze which he held in his hands and stroked. The walls danced and then revealed themselves to the intruders' eyes.

Perhaps this was the Holy Father's wing of the palace, but evidently he didn't reside on the ground floor, for there were no hangings or rugs, though the hall was of marble. Thoughtfully Damiano latched the door behind them. "No use inviting thieves," he whispered, and then gestured up the large staircase which stood before them. "He's up there."

"You are so sure?" hissed Gaspare, clinging very closely to the taller man.

"I am," replied Damiano lightly, and led him up the steps.

The palace made no sense to Gaspare, but then he was at a disadvantage, being largely in the dark and quite terrified besides. He followed Damiano from one cold length of passage to the next, his normally quick feet made clumsy by the hour. He watched the tiny tendrils of flame wrap themselves around his friend's fingers; Damiano's face was lit satanically from below.

But it did not look satanic. That was Gaspare's sole comfort. His good friend looked both cheerful and interested, and darted from passage to passage with the confidence of a man who has finished a long strange journey and reached neighborhoods he knows very well.

And Damiano sang as they went: sang, hummed and even whistled a snatch of his tune which bounced from wall to wall of the huge, frescoed chamber they were passing through. Gaspare yawned, though whether it was Damiano's lullaby or his own long sad day making him sleepy he could not tell.

"I would like very much to see the Pope," said the musician to Gaspare, standing beneath a dome of blue and gold. He extended his arms, allowing the flame to crawl up both to the elbow, the better to examine the architecture. "Wouldn't you?"

"Not under these c-c-circumstances," replied Gaspare, whose teeth chattered despite the wool and velvet. "Can't we hurry, please?"

Lowering his eyes from the painted grandeur, Damiano obediently strode on.

The black wood doors were plain along this wall: like what one imagined of the rooms of vowed religious. But still by their spacing the doors said that these were not poor quarters inside, and the wall itself was inset with parquetry. Damiano stopped and leaned against the stone, sighing.

"We're lost?" quavered Gaspare, drawing his cloak around him.

"No," whispered the witch. "We're not lost. He's found. Jan Karl. He's within."

His was an unfortunate head for a tonsure, being pointed slightly off-center. That head and the drawn, ascetic face below it were all that was visible of Karl, poking out of a roll of soft blankets on a bed with sheets.

"Nice situation," mouthed Gaspare to Damiano, who was singing and therefore could not reply. The witch fed his pet flame to a candle, then shook his hand out. He knelt tenderly down beside the sleeper.

Oddly enough, it was when Damiano stopped his singing that Jan Karl awoke, to see figures standing over him by the light of his own devotional candle. Before he could open his mouth Damiano had clamped a hand on it.

"Early for matins, I know," he whispered cheerily into the man's ear. "But after all, it is Holy Week."

Jan gurgled, and when Damiano brought the candle close to his own dark face (the flame touched the skin) and to Gaspare's (he was more careful) the Dutchman seemed in no way reassured. His deep-set blue eyes shifted warily and his swaddled form thrashed about.

"No fear, Jan," crooned Damiano. He removed his

hand. "It was only that I did not want you to wake your saintly neighbors in your surprise at seeing us."

Gaspare was standing behind Damiano. He pushed forward. "Where's my sister?" he demanded. "Why weren't you at the Pope's Door, like you said you would be?"

Karl sat up, dragging his blankets with him against the night chill of the stone walls. "Gaspare," he began in his wretched Italian. "And Delstrego, of course. I did not forget our appointment. No, not at all. But there is a story behind that . . ."

"Evienne!" spat the boy. "Tell me now. Is she alive or dead?"

Karl raised his hands to his head in a gesture of horror which turned into an admonition for Gaspare to be quiet. "She is alive, of course, and may Christ preserve her in health."

"Where? Where is she?" pressed the boy with unabated volume. Jan Karl turned to Damiano as the more sensible member of the pair. "We cannot talk here," he said. "Let us meet someplace later."

Damiano smiled beatifically. "I'm afraid later may lead to another story, Jan. Let us go someplace else and talk now."

The blond head (bald in the middle) shook from side to side. "No. Impossible. I'd never get out of this building unnoticed."

The dark musician rolled a little ball of blue fire between his hands. He squatted convivially next to Karl and showed the trick to him. "Oh, yes, you will," he whispered. "You'll be surprised at how easy it is."

And again he began to sing.

They sat like three rooks on the stone step of the dolphin fountain, under cover of the plash of water. Jan Karl was in the middle, with Gaspare and Damiano crowding him close on each side. Both Gaspare and Karl, wrapped in wool, shivered in the predawn chill. Damiano, who shone like a ghost in his white linen undershirt, felt not the cold at all.

"You have to understand," repeated the Dutchman for the third time, "it has been a year. Things change in a year."

"Things change in a day—in a minute," replied Damiano. "Gaspare cannot forget it has been a year since you left with his sister."

"Where is she?" One of Gaspare's bony hands flexed painfully on Karl's thigh, causing the cleric to wince. "In a single word, you can say it."

Karl stared peevishly at the boy. "At Cardinal Rocault's great house. There. I've given you five words. Are you any the wiser?"

"Explain," suggested Damiano, and he dealt Karl a comradely blow upon the shoulder, using a hand from which fire only lightly flickered.

Jan turned on him between fear and anger. "Delstrego, you have it in you to be a real bully, do you know that?"

Damiano only smiled.

"This child's poor sinful sister has had the spiritual elevation of finding a place in the household of a very important man, in the cardinal. I rejoice in her good fortune."

Though Jan was speaking Italian, not French, it took Gaspare a few seconds to translate. "In the household of a cardinal? What is she doing for this cardinal—scrubbing pots?"

The Dutchman tried vainly to hide his smile. "I think her position is more delicate than that." He smirked.

Damiano blinked at Karl as earnestly as a dog. "Cardinals are all very old men, are they not, Jan?"

The grin on the Dutchman's wide mouth grew and grew, but it didn't change his blue stone eyes. "Some are, some are not. Cardinal Rocault, for instance . . ."

"Yes. It is about him I ask."

"He is not an old man at all. But very learned." The Dutchman's smile went out. "And powerful."

Gaspare took some time digesting this information. "My sister," he began at last, "has attained to high position?"

"High position?" Jan considered. "You could say so. A position under the cardinal, anyway."

Once more, he cringed away from the witch's licking flames.

"I have some authority," he stated, his face expressionless, though his eyes sought back and forth to see what effect his words had. "I translate when necessary from the

Dutch and German. I manage the Holy Father's ordinary dinners occasionally. I have been able to find work for . . . friends."

"My sister's work," grumbled Gaspare, feeling that the conversation was departing from its proper channels. "Did you find *that* for her?"

The Dutchman opened his cold-sea eyes very wide and innocent. "I did, though I did not know the trouble it would cause."

Damiano broke in. "You mean, you did not know that the cardinal would become enamored of Evienne?"

Jan's long face grew wry. "I didn't know that the cardinal would become enamored of the Papacy. That is the problem between Evienne and myself. And—that is why I had to miss our appointment today.

"Yesterday, rather," he corrected himself, gazing with obvious forbearance at the black heavens.

There was puzzled silence from his two listeners. Jan pulled the foot of Gaspare's mantle over his knees and elaborated further. "Cardinal Rocault, you ought to know, expects the Holy Father to die at any time. He is an old man, and not very sound, and Rocault helped elect him, judging that Innocent would live just long enough for his own campaign to come to fruition.

"Well, how long has it been? Six years? Six years of Innocent VI, and the old fellow is in better health than when he started. All the world knows that Rocault is getting impatient."

Damiano's eyes were more earnestly doglike than before. "Are you saying, Jan, that Cardinal Rocault has designs upon the life of the Holy Father?"

Karl recoiled against a stone dolphin. "I did not say that, did I?"

"But it seemed to be your meaning."

"Seeming and meaning are free, Delstrego," pronounced the Dutchman. "Saying can cost you your head. If you are to live in Avignon, you must remember that.

"But to return to the subject. When first I returned to Avignon, the party of Rocault had not come into open confrontation with Innocent, and I used my position on the household staff to introduce Gaspare's sister . . ."

"Your lover..." interjected Damiano, just to keep things clear.

"Evienne of San Gabriele," countered the Dutchman, "to the cardinal's steward. It was a happy circumstance, at least for a few months. But now there is a great deal of tension between the cardinal's staff and those of us already here in the palace.

"I am watched," Jan Karl announced. "Always watched."

Damiano was not impressed. "So what does it matter, then, if you are seen with us? I, for one, am not of any Papal party. I am not even a thief."

Because of his wide mouth and the length of his jaw, Jan Karl's grin seemed to cut his face in half. "It is true, Delstrego, that your language does not give a bad impression, and your manner is haughty enough. But you and Gaspare are both so raw to Avignon that you may compromise me any time you open your mouths."

The open earnestness died from Damiano's face. "It is true," he whispered. "I can think of very little truthfully to say which would not compromise you, Jan."

Jan stood. "I can have you thrust out of here on the point of a pikestaff, Delstrego."

"I can send you to hell at the point of a pitchfork," answered the witch, as fire of three colors bloomed in his outstretched hand.

"Please," hissed the boy Gaspare, whom both the others seemed to have forgotten. "Please do not argue with him, Damiano. He has yet to tell us how to find Evienne."

But this exchange of unpleasantries had the contrary effect of cheering Jan Karl considerably. His lean shoulders wiggled under the wrap of bedding and he chuckled at the dark and glowering Italian. "I will tell you how to find her, Gaspare. The rest is your problem.

"But Damiano—I just remembered. Do you still play the lute a little, like you did last winter? If so, maybe I have a job for you. Private dinner, on Easter Saturday. For the Pope and the terrible cardinal together."

Damiano felt the blood drain from his face. "To play? For the Holy Father?"

"And Cardinal Rocault. It is to be quite an occasion.

Keep your eyes and ears open and you might learn
something. Which you must relate to me, of course."

Damiano said nothing. He was breathing hard.

"Are you afraid, Delstrego?"

Gaspare spoke up. "Of course he is not! He is merely
planning what he should play."

Chapter Nine

Damiano woke because the lute was gouging his skin.
He wormed his hand in between the neck of the instrument and his cheek to feel a rectangular gridmark of
strings and frets. He felt alert and ready for the day,
though he had slept only a few hours.

Last night (this morning really) he had known ten
minutes' panic that his change of state had destroyed his
ability to play. But that had been only nerves, as well as a
confusion of sensations to which his past year as a simple
man had left him unaccustomed. And since the other
occupants of the inn-chamber were already waking for the
day, he had been able to practice until sleep took him.

Gaspare was still asleep. Of course—yesterday had
been harder on him than on Damiano. Deliciously, Damiano
stretched his feet out over the yellow straw and yawned,
feeling more at home within himself than he had for long
months. He could not think why he had allowed himself to
remain immersed in melancholy all that time, when life
was really quite enjoyable.

Tomorrow he was going to play before the Holy
Father. That was enough to make one nervous. But it
would quickly be over, and why should he think Innocent
would be listening anyway, with Cardinal Rocault across
the table from him?

More important to Damiano's practical concerns, he
had five days more at the Bishop's Inn. Five days of
playing in the corner of the high gallery, being alternately

praised and ignored, while smiling respectfully at both
Coutelan and MacFhiodhbhuidhe, (who spent more time
in the inn than the innkeeper). And on the last day maybe
he would say to them, "Messieurs, your interests are very
limited. I myself am going off into the countryside, to
make my music with a lovely white dove."

No. He would say nothing of the kind, for he would
want to come back. Besides, he should be nice to the
Irishman, for he intended to ask him to take over at the
inn for him tomorrow.

And also, such proud words could prove false, for
Saara might not come in the shape of a dove at all. She
might be retaining the form of an owl.

Or she might be a woman. Most likely she would be a
woman.

Suddenly Damiano was very nervous: more nervous
about Saara than about the Pope. He threw back the
blanket. It was quite warm out.

Had he crawled off among the vines with a wine-
stained Alusto grape crusher at the age of fourteen, like
other boys, his heart would not now be assaulting his lungs
in this manner. Had he not panicked under the covers
with Saara herself, a few days ago, he would have no more
reason to be nervous.

Damiano pulled on his clothes, all the while telling
himself that a man ought either to fornicate like a dog as
soon as he was able or keep his chastity for life.

Half-measures just made a body awkward.

Yet he felt unshakably committed to the impending
effort at sin, and even his attack of nerves could do no
more than spice his expectation. He trotted down the
corridor and stepped into the sun.

Along the white cobbled street strolled Damiano,
accompanied by the Archangel Raphael. Early afternoon
sunshine liquefied the air around them, and the cries of
hawkers (for Avignon was a huge market that never closed)
echoed against the limed stucco, meaningless and orna-
mental as birdsong.

The mortal felt very privileged that Raphael had
decided to come along, for as once before the angel had
said, he was no great walker. He could no more walk

without moving his wings than a Latin—Damiano, for instance—could talk without moving his hands. The great shimmering sails arced up and out, or down, or rolled together behind or in front, or pointed like great fingers to the sky. And it seemed an effort of concentration for the angel to put his foot to earth and keep it there.

Yet his progress was not clumsy but terpsichoric, and Damiano regarded the seeming fragility of his companion with great fondness. Whenever there was no one else within hearing, he spoke. "Seraph, your feet are not really touching the ground, are they? I mean—you are barefoot, and these cobblestones are dirty."

In a very human gesture, Raphael brought his right foot up along his left shin and held up the sole for inspection. It was dirty. At Damiano's air of apology his eyes flickered with amusement.

"Would you apologize for the entire world, Damiano? Did you create it, that you should feel responsible?" Raphael walked on.

There was something infinitely touching about the appearance of Raphael today, reflected Damiano. Of course this was the first time in a year and more he'd been able to see—to really *see* the angel. Perhaps memory had made him more intimidating than he really was.

But look now: save for his galleon-sail wings, he was no taller than a man. No taller than Damiano. And he seemed to be made of spider-silk, so delicate were his face and hands. Damiano felt obliged to step between the angel and a passing merchant sailor whose entertainments had known no Lent.

"You know, Raphael," whispered Damiano, ducking under his left wing, "four years ago, when I was young, you frightened me a little. It seemed you were like a . . . great cloud in the sky, which could produce lightnings if I wasn't careful."

The tip of that wing curled over Damiano's head like a great question mark. "And now I don't seem that way?"

Damiano shrugged and smiled. "No. I don't mean to offend you, but no, you do not seem so dangerous."

Both wings touched together along their forward edges, from just above Raphael's head to their tips many feet in the air. (They barely cleared an overhanging third floor.)

For a moment Raphael made a picture of formal symmetry, like one of the row of angels behind the altar of Saint Catherine's Church in Partestrada, far away.

"You certainly do not offend, Dami. I have never desired to frighten anyone. If I do no longer, then that alone has made it all worth it."

Damiano stood stock-still, even after a woman with babe in arms slammed into him from behind, cursing.

"That alone has made it worth it." It had been said in the same tone in which Saara had said, "Then it has been worth all the rats and mice." Damiano felt uneasy. He cleared his throat.

"But, Seraph, this change has been in me, not in you."

Raphael shook his head—a gesture Damiano had never seen from his teacher before. He replied, "No, Dami. I know it becomes hard to tell, when people, like boats moving across the water, have no reference point. But I know I am not what I was."

"Then what are you?" blurted Damiano, regardless of the press of people on both sides of him, who were carefully not touching the madman. "Is it something I have done?"

For the sake of other pedestrians, Raphael nudged Damiano forward. For a minute he did not speak.

The angel's midnight-blue eyes roved from face to face with a probing interest, but he found none who looked back at him. He maneuvered his charge onto a less crowded street.

"What I am, my friend, is one of the Father's musicians. Or perhaps one of his pieces of music: it is not an easy distinction. And like any music—put into time—I go through change. It is not against my will."

Damiano stood between disreputable housefronts, where wooden shutters still sealed the windows on this balmy and seductively breezy day. Before him an ancient grape twisted out of a hole in the cobbles. He was only a few feet from the spot where he had met Saara the owl.

But his thoughts were on Raphael, and he considered the angel's last statement. "Then, outside of time . . . you would not appear to change?"

The fine-etched golden brow drew down. "Damiano,

you are not making sense," the angel said, and raising
both wings behind him he continued his careful parade.

Damiano did not feel like making sense today, but he
did feel like talking. After the passage of a laundress, a
red-tabarded member of the Guild of Sign Painters and
two louts of undiscernible occupation, he began again.

"You were right, Seraph. I was not meant to be a
saint."

The angel turned in a baroque curl of feather. "I was
right? I, Damiano? Did I ever say you were not meant to
be a saint?"

The mortal thought back. "Well, almost. When I said
that God loved dirty, sloppy-looking saints, you answered
that you were not God and..."

Now the great wings pulled down and back, like those
of a teased hawk, and Raphael's perfect nose grew a trifle
sharp. "That I was not the Father. And that was all I said. I
certainly didn't mean to put a limit upon your aspirations,
Damiano."

"Oh." Damiano found himself staring at a misshapen
alley corner which was decorated with plush blue mildew
and yellow mold. He scratched the day's worth of beard on
his chin. "Oh. Well, I don't even aspire to being a saint,
Raphael. You see I plan... to ..."

The wings lifted slowly, as though raised by ropes.
"Yes. Yes. You plan to... what?"

"To... uh... marry Saara the Fenwoman."

In truth, the word marriage had never occurred to
Damiano until this moment. But what else could he tell an
archangel: that he planned to copulate like a dog?

Besides, why shouldn't he marry Saara? She was
lovely and amusing, and had talents which could do his
own career no harm at all.

Because she had been his father's lover, replied a
whisper within his own head. Wasn't that enough reason?

But Raphael was speaking. "That is a very important
decision, Dami," said the angel slowly. "But what has it to
do with becoming a saint? Or with not becoming a saint?"
As he spoke he very carefully preened his flight primaries
with both hands.

Damiano watched the process. Surely Raphael's were
not real, physical wings for their feathers to become

disarranged. It must be that he needed something to do with his hands. The angel seemed to be nervous, in fact, for he shifted from foot to foot and his dark-sky eyes were wandering.

"Marriage," Damiano began, "is the mediocre way, not the path of perfection. Very few saints have been married, I believe, although many were wicked and licentious until God showed them their error."

It must have been that Raphael was not really listening, or else he would not have replied, "Well, why not begin by being wicked and licentious, then, Dami?"

The mortal grunted in disbelief which changed to confusion as Raphael turned as though oblivious of him and passed into the alleyway of mold and mildew.

Damiano followed, out of the sunshine and into damp, odorous shadow, and as the chill patted his face, there came a cough out of the alley: a cough rich, phlegmy and spineless.

Never before had he understood the expression "his blood ran cold," but now the witch had to retreat for a last breath of sunny air before following the glimmer of samite into the murk.

The coughing continued, horrid as that of the dying farrier in the church of Petit Comtois, and Raphael was leaving him behind. Damiano bounded forward, fixing his eyes on the clean form once more before it rounded a corner.

Here was sun again, for they had come out on another street. The taint of decay vanished, to be replaced by an odor of wet ashes, as though some nearby housewife had scrubbed an entire winter's dirt out of the kitchen hearth.

Raphael stood talking to someone; his wings were spread sideways and Damiano could not see through them.

Wonderment, spiked with jealousy, bent Damiano around the cloudy wing. Who could the angel be talking to, when no one except Damiano (and Saara, of course, and assorted domestic beasts) could see him?

He was talking to his own image, which sat at a small round table, dressed in gray and scarlet, toying with a bowlful of grapes.

It took no time at all for Damiano to recognize Satan. The witch's first impulse was to duck back behind Raphael's

sheltering wing. But that panic faded in a moment and a
more belligerent reaction took its place. Damiano stood
upright. He strode forward out of the shelter of the angel's
wingspan and stood between Raphael and his brother.

And was ignored by both.

Satan had plucked a purplish orb from his bowl of
dainties, and was rolling it from hand to hand. (Somehow
Damiano's stomach was bothered to realize that the grapelike
things in the bowl really were grapes.) He was saying:

". . . really don't look very well, my dear brother. I
might almost think your decisions had gone awry, except of
course, for knowing that you do not *make* decisions, but
rather float on the Divine Will." The Devil's voice was
urbane and well modulated, expressing just the right
shade of sympathy touched by the diffidence due before an
estranged member of one's family.

"I am rather pleased by the way I look," answered
Raphael, and Damiano felt a fierce pride in the fact that
the angel's voice (though not overly subtle in modulation
at the moment) was more beautiful than Satan's. "It was
just today I heard pleasant things about my appearance."

Satan let his deep-set blue eyes slide from Raphael to
the young man at his side. Looking at Damiano, Satan
very deliberately coughed. "If one travels widely enough,"
observed the Devil, "one will eventually find someone to
verify one's prejudices.

"But then, Raphael, you have always had an antic
taste in companions." Satan leaned back and peeled a
grape with his thumbnail. "How is the fat bitch-dog? Have
you tired of shepherding about that meaningless little
shade?"

A lump grew in Damiano's throat, and nothing except
the hand of Raphael on his shoulder kept him from
assaulting the Devil barehanded. "She is well, Morning
Star. Happier than you are."

Satan's guarded face did not change expression, but
Damiano heard the faint sound of ashes falling, light as
snow. Then the Devil glanced toward Damiano. He shifted
on his three-legged stool and propped one elegant boot
insouciantly against the table. Satan had a small foot—
almost too small—and the toe of his black suede boot
curled up as though there were nothing within it.

"But you, Signor Delstrego. It has been a good long time since I have spoken with you."

"A year and three months," said the witch from behind clenched teeth.

"Ah? You keep a close record. But then, you are a careful worker in all things. I suppose then . . ." Satan let the worried pulp of the grape slide from his fingers to the dust beneath the table, "that you have kept your affairs in order. No debts outstanding, no good works undone, nothing to make your . . . passing an inconvenience to the people around you?"

A swarm of flies was circling Damiano. He heard them. And Satan and his repulsive bowl of grapes seemed to be retreating from him, down the length of a black tunnel.

How had I forgotten, he railed at himself. Here I am talking about marriage, when I am only going to die.

Were it not for Raphael behind him, surely he would fall on his face now. Perhaps he would be dead already.

And Satan was coughing again.

"Begone, miserable sufferer, and come not near this man!" It was Raphael's golden voice that Damiano heard. But gold, like any other metal, may be sharpened to an edge.

The angel had stepped forward, his pinions stretched taut in a great circle that brushed the wall of stucco. His face was lit from within by a white fire of anger. Yet he was only as tall as a man, and his wings were made of feathers, not fire. As Satan slouched to his feet, laughing, Damiano became painfully aware of these facts.

"Come not near him?" the Devil mimicked, his scraped-ashen voice no longer bothering to be subtle. "But my dear nest-mate, it is my right and privilege to come near him. You, on the other hand, are overstepping badly. One look at you and it becomes obvious."

Damiano also looked at Raphael, and his empty heart filled again, this time with a protective fury. He crowded between Satan and the angel, and with a single, unsubtle, inelegant kick, he upended the little round table. Grapes bounced over the strangely empty street. "Worm!" he bellowed. "Twisted snake!" he roared. "I am finished with your lies. Finished for good!"

He spat dryly, like a cat, in Satan's direction. "If you have the power to kill me, then do it. Otherwise, get out of here. You smell bad!"

The Devil stood, letting the three-cornered stool fall behind him, and as he faced Damiano he swelled and quivered like the snake he had been named. His face turned wine-red and his eyes went white. "Piece of mud!" he hissed, with a mouth full of teeth like needles. "Ordure! Worm, you called me? Well, you are food for worms, you walking bladder of blood and scum: bizarre travesty of spirit, created for the amusement of a jaded God..."

All resemblance to Raphael was gone now, for hate had given Lucifer a goat's face. Damiano glanced from one to the other and was glad.

Though it was getting quite hot in this corner of Avignon. Satan had dropped his human form entirely for one red and boneless and loathsome. The leather of the little stool smoldered. The table burst into flame. The smell of ashes was overpowering, and joining it now came the reek of sulfur, like an alchemical experiment gone out of control.

He can do no more than kill me, whispered Damiano to himself. He cannot hurt me more than that. He can do no more than kill me.

And as the Devil threatened and Damiano defied, Raphael withdrew a step and stood motionless and intent, like a man watching the play of actors in a drama.

The witch sheathed himself in a close coat of blue flame as he spoke aloud. "I have fire of my own, Satanas. Not as hot as yours perhaps, but less offensive to the nose."

The red flames licked out, touching the blue, spreading against it, attempting to envelop it. Where the fires touched, they created a purple glow which reflected in lights of pearl from Raphael's peacefully furled wings. And though the red was the larger and the noisier flame, where it touched Damiano's aura it grew quieter, and its color changed.

Damiano himself stood with eyes closed and hands over his face. He only looked up when the snap of withdrawing energy told him the contest—if it had been such—was over.

Satan had regained his composure in a marvelous fashion, and neither his tight jerkin nor his odd-shaped boots were soiled. "Delstrego," he said conversationally, "are you aware you carried the plague in your pocket from the north?"

Damiano stared. "I did not. We were all clean. Saara said so."

"Saara? And who is that?"

"Someone you don't know," was Damiano's growled answer.

Satan let this pass. "In your pocket." Satan smiled sweetly. "You had it in your leather pocket all those miles."

And then he was gone.

Raphael's wings slowly settled. He turned toward Damiano and his eyes were as mild as they had ever been. "Once," he began, his voice distant, "there were four of us: Michael, Gabriel, Uriel and myself, who stood together against him and his followers. We were the instruments of his downfall, as he does not forget."

The angel shuddered then, not out of fear, but as a bird will shudder its plumage into place. "Also the instruments of his own desire, since to be cast off from peace was what he most wanted."

Damiano felt himself returning from that silent fury to his human nature again. It was like climbing out of a hole. He bent and touched the charred table which lay on its side in the road. Its flames went out. "Yet you called him 'miserable sufferer,' Seraph. Why? Do you pity him?"

One angelic eyebrow shot up while the other pulled down. "Pity Lucifer? No—should I? Remember, Damiano, he is not locked into being what he is. It is a matter of his own choosing, always."

The stool he treated like the table. The leather seat had burned clean through. Together the two pieces of furniture made a sorry little picture beside the fire-discolored wall. "His own choosing? Of course. Yet one can be locked into his own choosing. As a mortal man, I understand that. When I act my worst, I know I am sinning, and that thought makes me wickeder than ever. I can pity the Devil."

The mortal blinked nearsightedly from the wreckage to the street beyond. Now, with Satan removed from the

scene, he recognized it as one of the shabby streets which
led down to the mud of the Rhone. "Though if I had the
power I would smash him flatter than a cutlet."

The Archangel Raphael gazed deeply at the unaware
Damiano, then clapped the mortal from behind with an
enthusiastic wing. "Dami, Dami! You have a power of
philosophy beyond the merely angelic. Perhaps you have
hit on the reason for man being what he is."

Damiano was tired. He remembered he had to play
for the Holy Father, and that he had not yet asked
MacFhiodhbhuidhe to substitute for him. "Reason? I did
not know we *had* a reason for being, Seraph. To understand the Devil?"

"To forgive him. It is more than I can do."

Slowly the man found the ability to think again, and
he thought about what had just happened. "What . . . what
he said, Raphael. About me. Was any of that true, do you
know?"

"About your dying? I do not know the future, Damiano,
and I don't think he can know any more than I. At any
rate, he certainly backed off . . ."

Damiano shook his head till the black curls flew. "No.
With that concern I am through. Whether I live or die is
no one's business—and least of all my own. I meant about
the plague."

"Why should that be straight, when all else he says is
twisted?" Raphael put his hand once more on his friend's
shoulder and drew him in.

"Well, you see, by coincidence I *did* carry something
in my pocket from Petit Comtois to Avignon. It was a ruby
pendant that some madwoman gave me."

The angel reflected. "Is it rubies, then, that carry the
pest through the world?"

Damiano shrugged. "Who knows? It comes without
warning and leaves when it is ready to leave. But I saw, or
thought I saw, Satan's face on a man in the plague town."

"Ah! Then he would be expected to know that you had
a pendant. Dami . . . he is a very clever fool, my brother
Lucifer. He would make you believe your own nose was
your enemy, if he could. Besides. Is there plague in
Avignon?"

Damiano gazed up and down. There were people on

the street: a good dozen. Masons, laborers, clerics, mothers, gentlefolk. Where had they been before? He sighed in confusion. "Not to my knowledge."

Damiano brushed nonexistent dust from his clothes. "Raphael, I am supposed to play before the Holy Father tonight."

"Good for you," replied the angel. "Give him something he has not heard before."

"I am suddenly terrified of it. Please come with me."

Raphael laughed. "I will. I would be interested to see the man."

Chapter Ten

This was just more of the same, said Damiano to himself. Placed here in the corner in insufficient light, playing to a drone of conversation, he might as well be back at the Bishop's Inn. At least in that high gallery, he wasn't half hidden from his audience by an armoire.

Audience? He knew better than that, too. The Cardinal Rocault had not looked his way once, and as for Innocent himself, though he was facing the musician directly, and though he occasionally let his eyes rest upon Damiano's quick-moving hands, it was obvious that his attention was taken by his demanding dinner guest.

Yet Damiano did have listeners. The table servants flashed him quite human glances, and Gaspare (who was in no good mood, having spent all the previous day and part of this afternoon haunting the house of this same ambitious cardinal, hoping for a sight of his sister) was offering his support. The boy, who was wholly hidden from the view of the diners along a passage at the other side of the chamber, stared at him with an intensity designed (by sheer effort of will) to prevent Damiano from making a mistake.

And Raphael had come, too. The angel sat within touching distance of Damiano, curled sideways around a heavy-backed chair. He listened as though he had never heard his protégé play before.

To Damiano's slight disappointment, it seemed the Holy Father was as oblivious of an angel's presence as was the great mass of humanity. Of course the Pope was not a witch, but surely some preternatural authority ought to have been vested with his office along with the spiritual. Enough, at least, to recognize an angel when one plumped himself down in your dining room.

At least the acoustics were better here than in the Bishop's Inn. The voice of the lute neither echoed nor faded within the intimate, muraled chamber, for there were just enough hangings to keep the sound clean. It was as though the room had been built with his art in mind.

"Give him something he has not heard before," Raphael had said, so that is what Damiano did. Scorning the ballades of Provence and the boring (to Damiano) folksongs of his native Alps, Damiano played what he had composed himself: music so new it was hardly born yet, wild in both time and harmony, colored slightly (almost against Damiano's will) with the ornate ornamentation he was picking up from MacFhiodhbhuidhe.

He had no intention of listening to the dialogue of the Pope and the cardinal, though Jan Karl had arranged his concert with that end in mind. He had no desire to get mixed in with politics he could not be expected to understand, and besides, if he were playing at his best, he would have no attention free.

But the conversation impinged upon his attention, because of its subject.

"They tell me three hundred, in Lyons. Mostly children, of course," the cardinal was saying. He was a big man, black-eyed, brown-haired, who looked good in the color red. Damiano had a long stare at the back of his head.

"Of course," echoed Innocent, who appeared much older, but not appreciably frail. The Pope's nose was raptorial, his eyes fine. "These days the plague prefers youth. I have it on good authority that is because those who were subject to it of my generation died in '50.

"But it comes back every year, or every other year,

somewhere in Europe. Last year it was Spain and Poland. This year it is France. Next year Italy, perhaps."

Damiano's fingers kept playing while his mind reeled. Plague again. He could not escape it. He had a fervent, irrational desire that people would shut up about plague in front of him, for he had been through too much lately.

"All very well to take the long view, Your Holiness," interrupted Rocault smoothly. "But people expect you to do something about it."

Innocent's elderly-eagle eyes flickered from the cardinal to the lute on the other side of the room. The old man seemed to have no problem seeing at a distance. "Ah? Well, I am, my son. I am praying daily, and offering the mass.

"Or did you—forgive me, did the people—have in mind something different? Something more like a bull?"

"That is what I had in mind," replied Rocault dryly. He followed Innocent's eyes and regarded the musician with no very friendly stare. For a moment he said no more.

What was Damiano to do? He had been told to play for the Holy Father, and he would continue until that one told him to stop. Surely Cardinal Rocault was not distracted by the sound of a single lute in the corner.

Perhaps he merely did not appreciate the New Music.

"A bull, certainly, Your Holiness, would let the people of France know they are in your prayers. And the best sort would be a bull rescinding your predecessor's protection of the local Jews."

Jews again. Jews and the plague. Damiano wished momentarily that he were back in the north of Italy, in Partestrada, sans plague and with only one Jew to speak of.

Innocent chuckled, and tapped his silver knife on his golden plate. "Hah, Rocault, my old friend. Here we have gotten half through our dinner without your mentioning this *bête noire* of yours: protection of the Jews. I had even begun to hope you had left it behind.

"You know I think it is silly; Clement's very reasonable exposition of why the Jews cannot have caused the plague did not prevent the burning of the ghettos, nor the murder or exile of thousands. If I should publish a statement turning Clement's logic on its head, would that make the behavior of the populace any different?"

Damiano snarled a finger and returned his attention perforce to his playing.

There was a sound of thunder above their heads; the good weather was at an end. Raphael leaned—no, slouched—against the chair back, one elbow propped on the finial of cherubs carved from oak. With his calm, interested visage and generally passive attitude, he might have been any intelligent listener at the Bishop's Inn, with a seed cake and a cup of violet wine on the table before him.

There was a piece Damiano had written only the previous week, which reminded him of Raphael. (It fell short, the lutenist thought, but then of course it would.) Though it was not part of his professional repertoire, he played it now for the angel.

"There is everyday truth, and then there is a metatruth, Your Holiness. And while in actual fact the plague may not be due to the Jews poisoning the water supplies, the higher truth is that all our misery upon the earth is due to the wickedness that murdered our Saviour . . ."

"I thought," murmured Innocent, seemingly inattentive to the cardinal's words, "that our misery was due to the sin of Adam, expressed anew in every man, and that the sufferings of our Lord were our happy redemption." The Pope cleared his throat, laid down his knife and gestured for his chair to be moved to the other side of the table, closer to the music.

"After all, Rocault, it *is* Eastertide, you know, and we generally try to adopt an attitude of thankfulness."

When the old man finally spoke to him, Damiano had gone so far from attention to the conversation that a lackey had to nudge him on the shoulder.

"Lutenist." Innocent stood immediately in front of him. Damiano rose hurriedly.

But the Pope sat, knowing a chair would appear to receive him, and he gestured the same for Damiano. "You sound like an entire consort of lutes, here in your corner. Along with a harp or two, and at least one tambour."

Damiano mumbled his thanks, and then, to his astonishment, Innocent VI reached out, asking if he might see the lute.

The Holy Father played a few quiet scales. He smiled. Back by the dinner table, Cardinal Rocault was not smiling.

"It sounds very different when I try to play," observed the old man.

"I did not know, Your Holiness," began Damiano (and his voice humiliated him by cracking on the word "Holiness"), "that you played the lute."

"A little. When I have time. I play enough to wonder why you, who get such a variety of sounds out of your instrument, don't play more at the far end of the neck."

"The lute is not true up there," replied Damiano.

Innocent chuckled to himself. "Not true. Nor metatrue?" And his glance at the young man sharpened and held a covert amusement. "Are you Jewish, young man? You could be, by the look of you. Sitting here and listening to all this talk, it would be very frightening for you if you were Jewish. You would not easily forget, nor keep secret what you heard, if you were Jewish."

"I am not," said Damiano in turn. "I am Piedmontese, and this nose I got from my Italian father. It is very frightening to hear anyway, but I don't understand enough to repeat it. Nor do I know many people in Avignon to whom I could repeat anything."

The Pope smiled sweetly at him and smothered a yawn. "No matter, my son. I am not about to issue proclamations this season, and the whole world is permitted to know that." His Holiness stood, and his chair was toted back to the table.

As the old man turned to follow it, Raphael rose from his place and stood beside him. His fair face was only inches from the Pope's ear. "Claude," called Raphael softly. "Claude Rabier!" And then he whispered in the Pope's ear.

Innocent grimaced and blinked, rubbing one age-stained hand over his eyes, but he did not pause.

The angel watched him go. White wings drooped down to the carpet.

"He couldn't hear you?" whispered Damiano.

"I don't know if he heard me or not," replied the angel.

"... you forget the usuric taxes, Rocault. Your cardinal's vestments were purchased out of Jewish..."

Damiano felt easier at heart. Not that he was about to confuse the astute Innocent with Saint Francesco, but now he had a certain faith in the man as well as the office. The old Pope was not about to be ground under heel by Cardinal Rocault.

Damiano was more and more certain that he did not like Rocault, who was making life more difficult for everybody, from the Holy Father to Gaspare.

And therefore for Damiano.

The food was cleared away. Was the music supposed to be cleared away as well? Damiano looked about for some sort of signal from one of the lackeys. Discovering none, he continued playing.

Rocault had a plan which he insisted on describing to His Holiness. It involved the disestablishment of all lending institutions except those beneficiary associations belonging to the guilds and (of course) the church itself.

Innocent listened with what appeared to be little attention, occasionally murmuring phrases on the order of "killing the goose which lays the golden eggs."

From strain and general weariness, Damiano had created a small headache. When the lackey who had handled the Pope's chair returned with a bundle in his arms, his eyes could not at first make out what the thing was. When by its shape it proved to be a lute, he was filled with mixed feelings.

Did the Holy Father want to play for him? Or with him? That could be interesting. Or dangerous for Damiano, since it was a direct insult to the cardinal, who plainly wanted to talk. It could also prove embarrassing, since the Pope was the successor to Saint Pietro, but music was still music, and about it Damiano could not lie.

He kept his head down toward his strings but out of the corner of his eye Damiano watched Innocent open a case of gilded leather and pull out an instrument.

Mother of God, what an instrument. As Innocent carried it from the dining table over to Damiano's corner, the lutenist could no longer pretend to be uninterested.

The lute was larger than Damiano's, but by the way the old man hefted it, very light. Its back was of many woods and its soundboard bleached white. The neck of it was black ebony, inlaid with gold wire, and the pierced cover of the soundhole was a parchment lace as fine as cheesecloth. The tuning head of the lute bent sharply back from the neck, the better for the musician to play in ensemble.

Damiano was stricken with base jealousy: that a man who played "when he found the time" should have such an instrument, when Damiano, who ate and breathed the lute, was forced to carry a box poorly joined and false at the top of the neck...

But he shoved himself roughly back into line. How could he object to the most important man on earth owning a pretty lute? Besides, it was probably made for show and possessed a voice like a crow's.

Innocent sat himself down between Damiano and the angel, who was also regarding the lute with interest. Perhaps the lutenist's conflict of feeling had not passed entirely unnoticed, for the first thing the Pope said was "People give me things." And he shrugged.

"Lutes, among the rest." With a touch of a quill to each string, the Holy Father checked his tuning. He seemed to know what he was doing. Then he took Damiano's lute by the neck and made an exchange.

"I want to hear that piece with the bass like a harp again. On this."

Damiano said nothing. When he touched the top course with his fingernail, the lute thrilled weightlessly on his lap. He played an aeolian scale, to get used to the spacing, and then a myxlodean. He found he was holding his breath.

The instrument had a soul. Before five measures of the song had passed Damiano had forgiven it its excessive prettiness, and with the final sprinkle of notes he forgave it for not being his. He extended it to its owner.

Innocent VI shook his head. "I like this one better," he stated. "It is such a poor lute, and when I look at it I can remember to what heights you took an instrument which showed so little promise. When I consider my own soul, I would like to remember that. And besides, I, who am a halting musician, can play this instrument without feeling unworthy of it."

"But neither am I worthy of this," blurted Damiano. And he believed it, without for a moment discounting his own abilities. For it seemed to him that the only sort of musician who ought to have such a lute was an old man who had played all his life, on the good instruments and the bad, and who had surmounted his obstacles and learned all that life was going to teach him.

Damiano saw himself, on the other hand, as a beginner. A beginner who was already better at his art than most masters, but a beginner nonetheless. He tried to give the lute back.

Innocent would not take it, and neither did the old man smile as he said, "That's not for you to say, lad. But it wouldn't matter anyway. An instrument like this—one cares for it for a while and then passes it on. As I do, to you. I was not its first owner, and perhaps you will not be its last. Something told me it was time to pass it on." Innocent shrugged. "If you meet a man who is more worthy, or who has the greater need..."

The old man fixed Damiano with a fierce hazel eye. "Is it a trade, musician?"

"You... Your Holiness," stuttered Damiano, and he tipped his chair over as he rose to bow.

"Gabriele!" exploded Gaspare, as soon as they were out of the private quarters. "What a present! And from the Pope himself! You should have gotten him to sign it."

Damiano glanced up from the case of gilded leather. "Sign it? Don't be an ass, Gaspare. Sign it where? The signature of God himself is on this lute; it is perfect."

He looked over his shoulder. "What do you think of it, Raphael? Isn't it perfect?"

Gaspare giggled at the sight of Damiano conversing with empty air.

Raphael was smiling. He marched with wings straight out behind him, for the passageway was low and narrow. Because of this posture, he resembled a man fighting gale winds. "It's a lovely lute, and as soon as you let me play it I'll tell you more," he answered. "But I doubt I'll have much to criticize.

"I'm glad he thought to give it to you," added the angel, with more than a hint of complacency.

They descended to the clean cobbled streets and the guard watched them walk away. Damiano sang in the rain all the way back to the inn.

"Do I look so old to you that I can't carry my clàrseach by myself?" bristled MacFhiodhbhuidhe, stooping to place one hand beneath the base of the soundbox, while the other hand rested on the serpent-curve of the string arm. Grunting, he hefted the weight of black wood.

The harper's instrument was garnished with a great deal of silver and crystal. It was splendid, certainly, but to Damiano's Italian eye it lacked grace. It looked heavy— not like MacFhiodhbhuidhe's music, which was almost frivolously light.

"It's lighter than you would think," the harper said, almost as though he had read Damiano's thoughts. "It's carved out of willow. The box is hollowed from a single piece of wood: like an old log boat!" MacFhiodhbhuidhe chuckled.

"But here, boy. You can carry my stool," he added grandly, handing the item to Gaspare, who had not been the one to volunteer his help.

The big Irishman, like Damiano himself, was in a glorious mood. "I haven't enjoyed myself this much in years. And it has been years since I played like this, in public, for whoever wanted to stop and listen. For the most part, I have my patrons."

He stood at the door of the inn, peering out on to the wet pavement, scowling against the chance it might still be sprinkling. Finally he decided to chance it, and strode out to the street. Damiano and Gaspare tagged behind.

"Your patrons, Monsieur Harper?" piped Gaspare (when he should have kept his mouth shut). "Is the Holy Father one of your patrons? Have *you* played for the Pope, like Damiano?"

Nothing in Damiano's witchcraft had ever taught him how to drop through solid stone, or else he might have vanished from view then and there, out of sheer embarrassment. He gave the boy a shake and a barely suppressed hiss. But MacFhiodhbhuidhe only stopped in the middle of the road and peered down at Gaspare. A chase of cloud and moon flashed his image larger than life, and his long, carefully frizzed yellow hair bushed out like a halo. "Many times, child, have I played for His Holiness. Every good musician in Avignon has been heard by the Pope, whose interest in music is active.

"Of course," continued the harper, "not every good musician has been given an instrument by the Pope. Your friend has a right to be proud."

"I'm not proud," mumbled Damiano, following Mac-Fhiodhbhuidhe through the gate of his pretty little garden and into his pretty little house. "I'm only astounded. And besides, he said he did it because of a song that sounded like a harp."

The Irishman's elderly serving woman came with a candle in each hand, and lit them in.

In the middle of the harper's front room stood a cabinet, lined with woolens, floored with absorbent sand. In this cabinet the clàrseach lived. As MacFhiodhbhuidhe placed it upright in its stand, he sighed. "Everyone is attracted to novelty. But I'm sure His Holiness had more reason than that.

"But the clàrseach, you know: it is different from all the other instruments." The burly man gave a tolerant glance over his shoulder, knowing he would not be understood. "Looking at that great, weighty thing of wood and brass and silver, would you believe that there is nothing holding it together but its strings?

"That is the case, however. A clàrseach is three pieces of wood, fitted with pegs and holes. The box is female, the bow male, and the arm, half and half." His bushy black brows drew together in good humor.

"We Irish are very fond of threes. We pretend to have invented the Trinity."

Damiano, though he enjoyed the occasional intellectual exposition, was more interested in the instrument than the philosophy behind it. He bent around the wider man, examining the harp's joints. "Do you ever take it apart?"

MacFhiodhbhuidhe sat back and allowed him to touch. "On the long trip from Galway to Quimper and through Brittany and the valley and south...there it traveled wrapped like a bundle of fagots. That was an odd trip, my friends, and a fortunate one for me, because I took it in the year of the Death."

Damiano flinched unnoticed.

"Yes, I left Ireland before the plague struck, and entered Provence when its fury was spent here, consequently I never encountered the disease at all. Spared by grace, I have always said.

"But to return to the clàrseach: it is better for an instrument, as it is better for a man, to remain taut—fit for work." He thumped his round and sizable chest.

"As long as I live, these three pieces will remain in one."

"Why did you want to hang around talking to *him?*" whined Gaspare, querulously dancing from one foot to the other.

Damiano, who paced the shining streets with his thumbs in his belt, turned on him. "Why did I . . . ? Why did *you* have to be so unforgivably rude? Asking him if he, who has been my greatest benefactor in Avignon, had ever had good fortune to equal mine . . ."

Gaspare lowered his head like a spindly goat. "What does he matter, lutenist? His music is of the past, and so is he. You have a better ear and better hands than he; he is privileged to help you."

Damiano hunched his shoulders. "God preserve me from friends like you," he growled. But within him was some part, not wholly submergible, which agreed with Gaspare's analysis, and was buoyed up by the redhead's cruel words. He recognized this in himself, and it made him more angry than ever.

Gaspare hung back, silent for a moment, while both of them paced determinedly down the main north-south avenue toward the Rhone.

Finally he spoke again, lugubriously. "What do you expect out of me, Damiano? I'm not your angel, you know. I am only a man, and I must say what I feel. Besides, it's not three hours ago that some churl of Rocault's assaulted me, merely because I asked him whether my sister was being kept within.

"This business is wearing upon me. I can't count

when last I slept a night through, what with worrying
about Evienne."

Damiano recognized the truth of this. Though it was
not a complete truth, since Gaspare spent his nights very
quietly, for a person who wasn't sleeping. "Well, we're
doing something about that right now, aren't we?"

Gaspare trotted up beside Damiano. He nodded.
"Yes, musician, we are. We are going to get ourselves
killed, to be exact, and have our heads stuck on pikes over
the cardinal's wall."

Damiano grimaced. "Why do you talk like that, Gaspare?
This was your idea, remember? And we are attempting
nothing we did not do easily within the Papal Palace
itself."

"Certainly. But bad-talking is good luck. It is an old
thieves' custom."

"I am not a thief," insisted Damiano once again:
obdurately, but with less conviction than he would have
shown a few weeks previously.

The night before last the moon had been full, but
tonight's fast-scudding clouds stole its brilliance. And it
was late; soon the night orb would set, leaving darkness
even Damiano would find thick.

Yet he couldn't ask Gaspare to wait longer, and he
himself was eager to try his abilities on the task for which
he had reclaimed them.

"Quite a wind," mumbled the boy, who in the interest
of stealth had worn neither his richest nor warmest clothing.

Damiano agreed, feeling his feet skid on muddy
stones. "I hope the cardinal's roof doesn't leak," he added.
"A wet reunion would be a pity."

He glanced ahead, along the low riverfront road. His
vision, imperfect in daylight, was sharp enough now to
catch the pattern of light on the ruffled surface of the
Rhone, and the movement of restless gulls that clustered
under the house eaves. There was the outline of a bridge
half spanning the river. Broken, or incomplete. Vaguely
Damiano wondered who had built it, who had broken it
and why it wasn't repaired. "I see the house, I think. At
least I see a building larger than all else by the wharves."

"That's it," replied Gaspare. "It has peach trees flattened

against the west wall—they are in bloom—and vines covering the south."

"I see the espalier. It looks like it is shielding the house from the wind with a fence of flowers."

Avignon was no city of gardens, but with the immense thrift of Gallic peoples everywhere, foodstuffs were grown there wherever a square foot of soil stood undisturbed, against any white wall that caught the sun. The mansion of Cardinal Rocault rose high and proudly enough, but pots of kitchen herbs dangled out the first-story windows, and from the small enclosure came a sleepy quarrel of chickens. Damiano also smelled rabbits through the sweetness of the blooming trees.

"It's no Papal Palace," pronounced Gaspare, with the easy criticism of the man who has nothing. "I can see why the good cardinal is envious of the Pope."

Damiano crept up to the wall which fronted the river road. Seven little peach trees, no taller than the second-story windows, had been pruned and trained into shapes as flat as heraldry. The sight and smell of them made him drunk; he rubbed his face against pink-white blossoms. "I myself," he whispered, "have a certain envy of Cardinal Rocault, for I would sooner own this pretty house than inhabit the Pope's warrens."

But a snort and sniff from within silenced him. Damiano held up a warning hand to Gaspare and began one of his oldest magics: one learned neither from Saara nor Guillermo Delstrego, but particular to Damiano himself. With images of hearthrugs and bowls of hot porridge he seduced the cardinal's bandog. With a bodiless scratch in places no dog could reach, he turned the creature from its duty.

Even Gaspare, who was watching his friend curiously, not understanding, heard the scrape of heavy dog claws at the other side of the wall. He hissed and bounced back into the road. "It's the watchdog, Damiano."

Damiano had begun to sing. "Shut up, Gaspare," he crooned melodiously, "or I'll throw you to him."

The studded gate was locked by a mechanism more complex than any the intruders had seen before, but it opened itself at the witch's cheery adjuration.

They entered, and Damiano was almost knocked flat by a gigantic course-hound which dropped its front feet onto the witch's shoulders and demanded the promised caress. Standing head to head with Damiano, the beast was only halfway upright.

Gaspare cursed weakly as Damiano produced the tickles and scratches. "What *is* it?"

"A war-dog," caroled Damiano, catching his balance and placing the huge feet on the ground. "From the islands. Scotian or Caledonian. Described by Cambrensis. I have seen pictures of such as this."

Gaspare understood none of this, not knowing that Scotia was Ireland or Caledonia, Scotland. And never having read Giraldus Cambrensis, being unable to read. But he saw his old friend take liberty after liberty with the gray and shaggy pony-sized creature.

"Not much of a warrior, for a war-dog, is it?" said the boy critically, as the dog bowed its forequarters till its muzzle touched earth, then set off in a lolloping gallop around them.

"We won't get into that," replied Damiano, and he led Gaspare (and the affectionate dog) past the coops and the hutches, through the truck garden and into the back door. "He probably has another face to show to strangers."

Damiano was enjoying himself again. One of the unhappiest aspects of being a simple man had been his loss of special understanding with the animals around him, dogs especially. The memory of the sheepdog's attack at the farm south of Petit Comtois rankled no end, for he had been used to believing that the beasts saw in him something wonderful: something the narrow eyes of men could not. That day he had to come to grips with the truth that it was no moral excellence that gentled the predatory canine, but mere witchly trickery.

Now, once more he could forget that humbling verity, and others of like nature.

Never be weary or sick . . .

Inside the back door a fat man was sleeping, for all the world like another watchdog. Damiano had to croon with great concentration to wedge the door open without awakening the sleeper. The witch and his two companions then crept by, the great hound wagging furiously at finding himself in the house.

"Watch his tail," whispered Damiano, too late, for

Gaspare winced and grabbed at his stinging thigh. They found themselves in a looming, sooty kitchen, lit by the orange embers of a fire so large that no single night of inattention could kill it. It smelled still of the evening's roast veal.

Gaspare grimaced, still rubbing his smarting leg. The hound's tail had the lash of a bullwhip. It occurred to Gaspare as he hopped by the fireside, that between the Holy Father and Evienne, Damiano's dinner (and his own) had been forgotten.

Damiano, meanwhile, had scooted himself onto the great plank table which filled the center of the kitchen. There he sat, his hands laced around one knee, casually humming to himself. His eyes were closed.

Gaspare prodded his musician with a gentle finger, but pulled back in alarm when the war hound put back its rough ears and growled.

"Uh, Damiano. No time for daydreaming. Don't fall asleep."

Black eyes flashed open, filled with firelight. The lullaby was cut off. "I am not likely to fall asleep in the middle of events, Gaspare. The Damiano who did that sort of thing is gone, and I don't think he'll return. But I am having difficulty finding Evienne."

"Oh, no! She is taken. She is dead." The great dog lifted his head from an intensive search for scraps on the floor, and Damiano darted a glance out the hallway, where the round-bellied sculleryman slept.

"No fear, Gaspare. It is only that there are many sleepers within here, and it has been a long time since I have seen your sister. I never knew her very well."

"You alone out of all the world," grumbled Gaspare. Then he whispered, "She is taller than me, being five years older. She is bigger in the hips than in the bosom, though plenty big in both. She has a lot of temper, and of course, red hair like mine."

The witch's face lit. "Red hair! Now there is something real on which to focus. Gaspare, come here."

Gaspare approached, strangely unwilling. "Why? What is it you . . ."

Damiano grabbed the boy's carefully curled hairdo in both hands. Gaspare smothered a squeal of protest, and

the bandog put its long head between them to see what
was going on.

"Aha." Damiano chuckled. "No more difficulty." Releasing Gaspare's rumpled head, he swung his legs off the
table. "Follow your general, troops."

Evienne of San Gabriele put her small nose to the
linen sachet and whuffled. The trouble with all sachets and
pomanders was that after a while you didn't smell them
anymore, and then you didn't know whether the fragrance
was gone, or whether your nose simply had grown used to
it. Then you added some rose oil or orris root, and
someone would come in—someone like Herbert, in a bad
temper—and shout that the sweetness was making him
gag.

But that was his own fault, for if she were allowed a
promenade every day, or even to do her own shopping,
then she would be able to tell when the room smelled too
sweet.

Better than smelling like a pisspot, anyway.

Evienne turned on her back (it was more comfortable
for her to sleep on her back) and sighed. Herbert was so
difficult: not letting her wear red, even if it matched her
hair, and keeping her indoors nine days out of ten, without
even a girl companion.

What good were baubles and silk, if you didn't have
another girl to show them off to?

And he made her the butt of jokes—funny dry jokes
in private, when there was no one to laugh. Just because
she was not educated, not a real lady. In that way he was
like Jan, but of course with Jan you always knew where
you were. Jan needed her. (Had needed her? No. Still.)
The cardinal was a different matter.

She wrapped her arms around her body, over her
ample and growing abdomen. *This* might give her a certain hold on Herbert. Maybe.

Of course men could be so cruel. And what if the
baby had yellow hair? No one of the cardinal's family (she
had ascertained) had yellow hair.

But because Evienne had a naturally sanguine temperament as well as blood-colored hair, this worry could

not depress her for long. She still had three months during which the cardinal would surely not boot her out.

But Jan—if she started thinking about Jan, then she'd be crying all night. For Jan had not come to see her in two months, and the last time was only to steal away certain of the jewelry she'd been given by Herbert. He was going to copy it in glass, in case Herbert wanted it back someday. He'd never even come back with the copies.

Had he been torn apart by Couchicou, the dog? The hound had almost gotten him once before, he'd said. But surely she would have heard about that. Had he taken ill, then? There was no one she could ask.

Or was that stinking tomcat already back in Italy, accompanied by another, younger, less pregnant woman?

Evienne's fists balled into the pillow. Her jagged nail caught a thread. Herbert was telling her all the time to stop biting her nails.

She sobbed. Why was she doing this—caged in a chamber of goosedown and brocade, if not for Jan's sake?

Evienne thought she heard singing. Because the sound was more pleasant than her thoughts, she listened. It was a lullaby, soft and sweetly sung. Not a woman's voice.

Who in the cardinal's house could be singing a lullaby in black night? The closer she listened, holding her breath, the more she thought she could recognize the voice. Now it was a trifle louder.

Without warning, Evienne fell asleep.

At the very top of the winding stair Damiano stopped. His lips were parted and he sniffed the air pensively, adding a staccato character to his melody. He turned right down a low-ceilinged narrow hall, dragging the night-blind Gaspare behind him. "Close," he murmured.

Suddenly the witch stiffened. His song died in his throat and he seemed to convulse under Gaspare's grip. "My God, Damiano," the boy whispered almost without sound. "What...?"

"I...I..." Damiano said no more, but grabbed a double handful of his shirt and buried his face in it. Three times he sneezed, each time more convulsively than the last, until Gaspare felt the sweat break out on his friend's forearm.

Then Damiano lifted his head, taking a slow, deep breath. "Orris rood," he pronounced phlegmily. "Terribly strog. It has cofused my sedses."

Gaspare himself sniffed, and then nodded. "Evienne. My sister all the way. Now *you* follow *me*."

The young thief led Damiano along the black and dismal hall, his less sensitive nose working stertorously. Damiano wiped his eyes (and nose) on the hem of his overshirt.

The source of the floral bouquet was a small wooden door with a simple lock on it. Damiano did not need his nose to encourage the mechanism to work itself.

He shoved behind Gaspare into a room in which sweet smells had taken on a fetid aspect.

It was small, hardly wider than the height of an average man, and scarcely longer than it was wide. Its single window was inadequate and firmly shuttered. A rug carpeted the floor, while other hangings of similar nature lined the walls till it was all as furry and as stiflingly close as a cocoon. Save for a closet of white oak huddled in one corner between folds of heavy wool, the place was occupied solely by bed: a soft and formless bag of white linen stuffed with feathers (Damiano's nose was tingling again) lying on the floor like a very fat dog.

And on that bed, half unblanketed, with her left shoulder and left breast wholly exposed to the night air, lay Evienne of San Gabriele, Gaspare's sister.

Gaspare had not moved. After a moment Damiano remembered that his friend was simple and could not see in the night. The witch lit a dim blue fire-pet in his right hand and stroked it with his left.

"Evienne!" hissed Gaspare, and he stalked closer. The boy's first action, motivated either by shame or by a strange sort of fraternal caring, was to adjust Evienne's blanket under her chin.

Damiano stepped backward and sideways as far as he was able, which is to say, two steps. He felt woolly fibers against the back of his neck and had to stifle a sneeze, crushing his domestic flame in the process. He lit another and watched the scene before him.

He had forgotten how pretty a girl Evienne was, with her heavy auburn hair, pink cheeks and infant-round limbs.

Had she always possessed such a delicate complexion, and such amplitude? Damiano regarded Evienne intently while Gaspare did the same at close range.

The young woman had stirred after the moment of Damiano's sneeze, but as he began his song again (this time almost without sound, like a man who hums while adding a column of figures) her slumbers grew quiet once more.

"Shall I let her wake, Gaspare?"

The boy nodded. "Her, but not everybody else in the house, hey?"

"You ask a lot," replied the witch tunefully, but stepping over to the bed he placed his nonfiery hand upon Evienne's.

Gaspare had his hand ready to muffle his sister if she should wake up screaming, but it was not necessary. Evienne was not the sort of girl to react in that way to the presence of a man in her bedchamber.

"Herb . . . ?" she moaned, then opened her eyes and looked blearily at Damiano, who seemed to be cupping a votive candle in his hands, and so possessed the only spot of light in the room. "Who?"

Damiano simply pointed at Gaspare.

Recognition came slowly, but the subsequent embrace was bone-cracking. The boy escaped his sister's arms long enough to deliver a savage tweak to her pretty pink cheek.

"Hah!" he growled, with what seemed perfectly un-mixed fury. "Here you are, wrapped in perfume thick as a cloud of summer dust, lolling on goosedown, speckled— positively speckled—with priceless gems, with no thought of your poor brother walking every street in Avignon, thinking you were dead."

Evienne opened her eyes very wide and sat up straighter, thoughtless of the effect this action had upon her modesty. "That isn't fair, Gaspare! For one thing, I'm not wearing a single gem, and for another . . ."

Her angrily suppressed voice trailed off then, and Evienne's green eyes wandered from Gaspare to the linen sachet on the pillow by her head. She inhaled in a great, unladylike snort. "Does it really smell strong in here?"

"Nearly choked him," attested Gaspare, pointing with his thumb in the direction of Damiano.

Evienne saw a dark young man, looking impossibly tall and slim in the light of the strange bright candle in his hands. His hair cast black river-shadows against the ceiling. Damiano looked back at the half-naked woman, hoping his expression displayed a suitable insouciance.

Evienne thought he looked a bit cruel. "Who... who is he?" she mumbled to her brother.

Gaspare glanced from one to the other in surprise. "That's Damiano, my lutenist, Evienne. You remember him." Once more he tended her blanket.

It was hopeless, for Evienne sat completely forward, peering closely at Damiano. "Oh, yes. I do remember. Funny you two should still be together. Jan always said he didn't see why."

Damiano had tried hard to keep his eyes on Evienne's face, but with her last comment he relaxed the effort.

She was a very pretty girl, only a trifle big in the belly. Just a trifle.

"There are a lot of things," he whispered, still keeping the tune of his lullaby, "that Dutchman cannot see, I think."

Her loyalty to Jan Karl did not extend to the point of defending him against slights of so vague a character. Especially now, when she was feeling his absence as a slight against her.

At the sound of Damiano's voice she lifted her head and remembered. "The singing I heard tonight. That was you!"

He nodded. "Damiano's a witch," said Gaspare, as though that explained something.

The girl paid no attention. "And... and you still look like that," she added, decisively. "Who'd have thought it?"

Damiano could think of nothing to say in reply to this. He wanted to believe it had been a compliment but was not at all sure.

Gaspare shook his sister by her peach-blossom shoulder. "Enough of what he looks like. I want to know why you missed our rendezvous."

Evienne gave him a disparaging glance. "Because there is a lock on the door, of course. I can't go anywhere anymore. Herbert gets so jealous." She was momentarily startled as a monstrous gray head thrust itself under her

hand. "Couchicou. You're not supposed to be in the house
at night."

"He followed us in," explained Damiano.

"Not much of a watchdog," grunted Gaspare, as he
watched the animal fawn over Evienne.

Who giggled weakly. "Couchicou almost tore Jan to
pieces that last time he came to visit. Didn't Jan warn you
about Couchicou when he met you?"

At this mention of Evienne's lover, Damiano reacted
automatically. He reached out and gave the bandog a
hearty, approving slap. "Jan did not show up at the Pope's
Door either, Evienne."

She caught her breath in unfeigned alarm. "He is
dead, then. It is as I feared."

The witch shook his head. "How you are like your
brother! No, the Dutchman is not dead; he only decided
that it was not politic to fulfill his promise to us."

Evienne's concern hardened into resentment. She
snatched a gorgeous emerald robe from its lodging under
the covers at the foot of her bed. It was very wrinkled.
She thrust her arms through the holes and struggled
out of the bed with a certain lack of grace. "Politics,
again. Jan never shuts up about politics. What does
'politics' have to do with him and you—or with him and
me, for that matter?"

"Wasn't it politics that got you this nice little cubby
with the cardinal?" asked her brother. Gaspare was not
disillusioned on the subject of Jan Karl; like all cynical
people, he trusted implicitly anyone who acted even more
cynically. He turned from a hands-on examination of the
contents of her dresser table to finger the padded Oriental
silks of her garment.

Evienne gazed around her at the crowded little chamber. For a moment it appeared she was going to cry, but
instead she raised her arms a few inches and flapped them
at her sides, penguinlike. Then she raised her eyes to
Damiano, who had withdrawn to the corner of the room
and sat sprawled on the rolled bottom of a tapestry which
was much too long for the wall on which it hung. His black
curly head was bent forward as he examined the bright
thing in his hands. Softly, sweetly, he was singing to
himself.

Evienne shuffled forward till her hair shone like sunset. "What . . . ? What have you got there? Is it a candle? You'll burn yourself if you're not careful."

"No, he won't," replied her brother in a voice of authority. "I told you Damiano's a witch now. He's got the rest of the house sleeping with that song of his, and that's why no one's come banging on the door to see what the noise is." As Evienne continued to stare at Damiano's hands (warmly translucent, lit from within), Gaspare took the opportunity to drop into his jerkin pocket one green glass flacon, stained with dried perfume, and a pair of silver earrings.

The girl knelt rather cumbersomely beside Damiano and attempted to pry his hands apart.

He shook his head and pulled away from her. "No, Evienne. It *will* burn. Just sit still and watch." And he opened his hands together, palms up.

It was a little blue hedgehog with flickering, yellow-tipped spines. It ran from his hand heel to his fingertips and then back again, before dissolving.

He shook his head. "It's too difficult to do two magics at once," he sang aloud. "If I'm putting the house to sleep, that's about all I can handle."

Evienne's green eyes were wide as an eight-week kitten's. "How pretty!" she giggled, without any hint of fear.

"Come with us," Damiano said on impulse. "Rocault is no lord, that he can keep you prisoned this way. Neither are you bound to this house like a peasant to his patch of ground."

Evienne sat back heavily and hugged herself. "Come with you? Where?"

Gaspare had turned and was staring at Damiano with as much confusion as Evienne.

"To the Bishop's Inn, for now. Later—when the baby is closer—then we can find you a little house somewhere. We're not so poor as we once were."

Gaspare mouthed the word "baby." Then he exploded. "Baby! Baby. By Saint Gabriele, woman, don't tell me you are pregnant!" The boy gave such a perfect imitation of a brother whose honor is outraged that both Damiano and his sister sat silent for the next few moments.

"Hush," hissed the witch, pointing meaningfully toward the door. "There are limits, Gaspare, to what a spell can do for you."

"Yes," answered Evienne sullenly. "I am pregnant, Gaspare. Is that any of your business, I'd like to know?"

"How'd it happen?" demanded Gaspare, in unreflecting rage.

Damiano beheld his friend's behavior with rising irritation. The only creature more volatile and irrational than Gaspare of San Gabriele was Gaspare when in the presence of his sister.

"Are you going to challenge the Cardinal Rocault to a duel, perhaps?" The question slid away from song and ended in a tone of disgust.

Evienne decided to ignore her brother. "It is because of the baby I must stay. If it's Herbert's, you see—well, I know him enough to say that he'll take care of it very well. And take care of me also."

"And if it's not?" growled Gaspare, as his limber fingers snaked a choker of blue beads into his pocket, to lie beside the earrings.

She shrugged. "Then it's Jan's."

Gaspare mock-spat into the corner. "Tell me how you were such a fool as to get pregnant. You never did before."

"I didn't have any girlfriends in Avignon," she said simply. "What was I to do? Besides, Gaspare, I want this baby. If it is the cardinal's, then it will be my fortune. If it is Jan's..." Her face softened, till Evienne appeared about five years old. "I really love Jan. Even when he does awful things, like not coming to see me for seven weeks together. I feel sorry for him, I think. He can be so bad."

Into Damiano's mind came the words of Raphael. "Perhaps the purpose of man is to forgive the Devil." He smiled sadly at the pretty, pregnant girl.

When had he stopped singing? He couldn't even remember. But he was very tired. It had been such a day. And the cloying, close air. And the muffling drapes of woolen. Damiano yawned. He ceased to follow what Gaspare and his sister were saying. He gave his fire to an oil lamp on the dresser.

It was Gaspare who first heard the footsteps. "*Hisht!* Damiano!" the boy whispered sibilantly. "Someone's coming."

Damiano came bolt upright out of a dream in which Saara the Fenwoman had red hair and dog's feet. His heart lurched.

Gaspare was gesturing like a mad consort conductor. "Sing. Sing!" In another moment the boy had given up on his friend, and seemed to fling himself out of the third-story window. Evienne was standing with both hands on her mouth, her green eyes circled by white. Couchicou, on the other hand, sat with his nose pressed expectantly against the door, his whip-tail banging.

Damiano could not remember the lullaby he had used to quiet the house before. He could not remember any lullaby. Any song. His hands lusted vainly for a staff.

"It's Herbert," the girl said, in a teeny-tiny voice.

Damiano, too, went out the window.

"Evienne—what's that dog doing in here?" demanded a voice which Damiano, who was hanging by his fingers from the window ledge, recognized as Rocault's.

"He has been here ever since I got back from dinner," Evienne replied. She lied with professional skill. "I have been too afraid to have him removed. He might get angry and bite me!"

Male laughter, half contemptuous, half amused, and the sound of a door opening and shutting again.

"What the hell happened to you?" snapped Gaspare in Damiano's ear. The two hung side by side, like banners— or pots of kitchen herbs—from the window.

"I fell asleep," whispered Damiano in reply. His hands were slowly slipping from the angled wooden sill. He regripped with his right, causing his left to lose what it had gained.

He was developing a bad case of splinters in his fingers, and that worried him almost as much as the fact that there was thirty feet of air between himself and the ground. Of course the peach trees were immediately below. They would break his fall before bouncing him out to the pavement of the river road. Perhaps he would survive the fall. It was unlikely, but not impossible that both of them would survive.

He stared down into the illusory softness of the blossoming trees. From here he could smell them again.

And out of nothing swam the memory of a sprawling rosemary bush that at the Fenwoman's command had snarled his feet in its twining embrace. He heard again the drone of bees and Saara's clear voice singing words he couldn't understand.

Then, he hadn't been able to understand. Now—

Well, why not? Though Damiano's special skills were with animals, and his sympathies did not extend to the vegetable kingdom (he ate carrots with gusto), still he would make the effort.

"I'm going to drop," announced Gaspare, "into the peach trees. I'll try to grab the branches to break my fall."

"No." Damiano fixed him with a desperate glance. "Wait just another minute." Then his face went blank with his interior effort.

"Wait for what," hissed Gaspare. "Sunrise? My hands are slipping now!"

But even as he did lose his grip, something hard touched the sole of Gaspare's foot. He fell no more than two feet and then crashed forward, bumping his long nose against the wall itself. Slowly Gaspare rose again, his legs tangled in a wildly expanding growth of blooming peach.

Damiano let the green wood embrace him. He sighed. He blinked unhappily at his wounded hands. "Damn!" he whispered. "Right in the tip of the first fretting finger." He stuck the damaged digit into his mouth.

Meanwhile, Gaspare was kissing the peach boughs with great passion with a face to which the sweat of fear had stuck bruised petals. He swung to the ground, nimble as a monkey.

Damiano followed, favoring his left hand.

Once on the pavement (still shiny with rain) he turned back to his handiwork, scratching his head with his right hand. He had no idea how to properly terminate such a spell.

But Damiano was nothing if not mannerly. "Thank you, peach trees," he called out to the growth. And within five seconds the trees had sucked back into themselves their unnatural extension.

Gaspare swore in awe.

"Everyone is taken care of," sighed Damiano, slumping

against Gaspare's shoulder. "Gaspare, Evienne, Jan, the Holy Father, the Devil: everyone.

"Now it's Dami's turn. He's going to bed." And he leaned on Gaspare all the way home.

Chapter Eleven

It was an awkward and lumpy bundle of blankets, clothing, cheese, dried pears and bread. Inside it, like the golden yolk within an egg, was hidden an exquisite lute. Wine went in a separate bag; that also for the lute's sake. "It will hold, anyway," grunted Damiano. "With all that rope, it will hold."

The constraining rope went from end to end of the bundle. Damiano slung it bandolier-style, groaned, took it off, padded the rope with a rag and tried it again.

"Better. And then, of course, the horse will carry it easier than I."

He had decided to meet Saara in the open, out of the city. The Fenwoman, after all, didn't like cities, and among the trees and grass there would be more of what his euphemistic mind liked to think of as opportunities. He had no doubt that Saara would be able to find him.

"You look like a fool," stated Gaspare, although the boy had not turned from his position in front of the window, staring at the dark street below. "It does your reputation no good to be seen like that."

Damiano glared. He foresaw this night's mood being ruined by another of Gaspare's seizures of temperament. "Well, if that's all that's worrying you, the moon is half-past full and I doubt anyone will be able to see me at all."

"Another reason to wait until morning."

"Why? I can see well enough by half a moon. Saara can see excellently at all times. We are witches, remember."

"Heathen," said Gaspare in the same dry, suppressed tone.

The lutenist, who had a temperament of his own, was straining to be away. Yet it would be a shame to leave Gaspare on that word. He stalked over to the boy and spun him around by the shoulder.

"What is this, Gaspare? Don't I deserve a rest, after all that has happened in the past month? You, too—you're always complaining how hard it is to live with a madman.

"That is, when you're not telling me I am not a man at all because I have no mistress. Well, now I have a mistress, and I'm on my way to meet her."

The boy stood with his hands in his jerkin pockets, one hip cocked—an attitude that mimicked carelessness very unconvincingly.

"Go, if you're going already. We'll talk about it if you come back."

"If?" cried Damiano. "If?" A curse issued from the far end of the room, where an early sleeper had had his first rest broken by the noise. With one accord Damiano and Gaspare stepped out of the room and down the corridor.

"If? Mother of God, Gaspare. Do you believe I'm running out on you?" The heavy bundle banged along the narrow hall.

Gaspare cleared his throat and spat. "I believe nothing. It's much safer that way."

Once under starlight, Damiano desired urgently to bolt and run. His mind rebelled at the thought of one more depressing wrangle with the redhead. But he took a deep breath and began again.

"Two weeks at the most, I will be gone. The room is paid up and you have enough money for food till I get back—if you don't spend it on clothes."

"This is not good for your career, you know, musician," said the redhead distantly, peering into the darkness toward the city gate. "In two weeks Avignon can forget. You can't expect to find a job waiting vacant when you come back." Then he looked straight at Damiano. "How can I reach you if I need you?"

Damiano stared back. "Why should you need me?"

Gaspare ignored this. "I am your manager. I must be able to reach you. If you turn into a dove and flap off to Lombardy with that woman..."

The dark man leaned back against the white wall,

where his hair made a shadowed halo. "Ah. So that's it. I'm
not turning into a dove, Gaspare. I feel little enough
human sometimes as I am. And a long journey is not the
purpose for which I am . . ."

Cursing the limitations of the simple man, who would
not be able to locate a friend hidden in the countryside
outside the city, who indeed couldn't even find his sister
when she was hidden behind a plaster wall, Damiano
stood and cogitated. An idea came: not a good idea, for it
interfered with his plans a bit, but one that might pacify
the boy.

"I will leave Festilligambe with you," he said. "Since
he is a horse and not a man, he will have some notion of
where I am. If you have to find me, just get on him and
give him his head."

In the middle of Damiano's explanation, Gaspare had
begun to shake his head. The movement gained both
speed and power, until at the end it shook the boy's entire
frame. "Oh, no, I won't. The last time I tried something
similar . . ."

"He found me right away, as I remember."

Gaspare snorted. "And almost killed us both. I wouldn't
touch that beast with anything but a butcher's blade."

That was enough. Damiano's patience snapped like a
lute string, and he turned on his heel.

Already, as Damiano disappeared into the darkness,
Gaspare was beginning to regret the violence of his words.
He was reassured to notice that Damiano left the horse
anyway.

Each rustle was a mystery, and more a mystery as the
witch's ears put a name to it. That rhythmic pinging was
this week's rain, still dripping in a pipe somewhere. It
rang in his head like the music of the spheres. That tiny
interrogative shriek was a bat, chasing insects by the light
of a pedestrian's swinging lantern. The lantern itself hung
by a cord from the man's wrist, and creaked of rust and
leather. The man's breathing, too, creaked. He was ancient.

A second squeaking joined the first, but from below.
This was not a bat, but a rat, making sad complaint about
some rattish problem or other. While passing the next
block Damiano heard a louder sound: a thumping, also

rhythmic, from behind an upstairs wall, accompanied by a duet of heavy breathing. Though recognizable, like the call of a bat or rat, this sound seemed to Damiano the very essence of mystery. He stopped still, listening. His hand tightened on the rope of his bundle.

Finally he reached the North Gate of Avignon, where he had entered the city less than two weeks ago. As he passed under he gave a silent prayer of gratitude.

What a clear sky, and what good fortune that three days' rain should have cleared when it did. Even the mud underfoot had been half dried by today's ambitious sun. Damiano nearly tripped over the broad flat road, then, as he remembered that Saara was a weather witch. Could she have worked this change for his sake? Or her own? For both, really. . . . The thought made him blush. He looked about him.

Twenty years ago Avignon had been threatening to burst her gates. The fields beside the road were dotted with small stone huts and large stucco houses, some roofless or without doors, either unfinished or subsequently cannibalized for materials.

All were abandoned now, for who else but a barbarian would live outside of Avignon when there was plenty of room within? They shone like ghosts, rain-washed, moon-lit, surrounded by the susurrating new grass.

Two miles from Avignon, Damiano left the road, high-stepping over the soft earth, to look into one of the most imposing of the skeletons. (After all, why hurry when you don't really know where you are going?) This dwelling was in better shape than most; because it was so far from the city gate, no one had yet stolen its roof of tile. It possessed three large rooms through which the wind blew at fancy.

He entered. The stucco walls still stood, though cracked and sea-blue with mildew. The roof did not appear to leak much. Damiano placed his bundle carefully in the driest available corner and leaned out a front window.

No fortress, this, but the house of an ambitious peasant. The windows were square—indefensible, perhaps, but more pleasant for viewing the road. The rooms were big enough that a large family would not bump elbows too often, and the largest of them—the stable—had a loft which still appeared serviceable. Damiano scrambled up and peered down. Then he dropped to the floor and peered up.

He liked this house. He wondered if it were still owned by a man who had plans for it one day, and that was why it had not been pillaged like so many others. It was not too far for a man to live in and work in Avignon—if he had a horse.

Owned or not, the building was still occupied—by a nest of black snakes, many of whom were spending the evening within, their whip-bodies lumpily satiated. Damiano went over to talk with them.

"Boy, boy, solitary boy." The song approached without noise of footsteps. The hair on Damiano's neck rose. Three snakes lifted sleek heads and listened with their tongues.

"Your playmates are the beasts of the fields."

Outside the window where Damiano had lately leaned stood a shining girl, her loose hair whipping back from her face. Her dress was sprinkled with stars, and her eyes bleached silver by the colorless light of the moon.

"Saara," whispered Damiano, thickly. The snakes all slithered away.

He came to the window, and gently he caught her wild hair in his hand.

"In what way am I solitary, Pikku Saara? And how am I a boy?" He kissed her.

Saara stared vaguely at the rough beams of the ceiling above the loft. "The sun is beautiful today. It would be warmer out there than in here."

Damiano lay beside her, his head comfortably wedged between Saara's neck and her pink shoulder, his knees clasped around hers. He felt perhaps he should be examining himself this morning, assaying both the state of his witchery and the state of his soul, to see what the loss of virginity had cost him. But that seemed such a dreary enterprise. Much more interesting to examine Saara's hair. "That one," he observed, "is coppery-red, almost as red as Gaspare's. And it is straight. But the one next to it is dark, and it has more curl to it."

She giggled, for his breath tickled her ear. "Probably it's your hair."

He grunted. "So it is. But this other one is not—my hair is never so fine—and it, too, is dark. And all around and between you have lemon-pale hairs, and ones of rabbit brown. . . ."

"Don't tell me about the gray ones," Saara murmured, and she cuddled in closer, making her own investigation of his neck.

"Eh?" Damiano gave a scornful snort. "You have no gray hairs. Don't be silly."

One wisp of hair fell across the woman's face. She regarded it cross-eyed. "Not yet, maybe. But it will come. We all grow old, Damiano." She squirmed in his grasp until she could reach his own shaggy head. He bent to allow her fingers in his hair. "What are you looking for, fleas?"

"Whatever," she murmured in reply. "You don't have any gray hairs, which does not surprise me. Nor fleas, either."

"I tell them to go away."

"But your hair, Dami! So thick. If it didn't go in circles, I would think it belonged to a horse."

He smiled and kissed the base of her throat. His head slid lower. "I thought I was a sheep," he said, his words muffled between her breasts.

"You are a thousand creatures," whispered Saara, and then nothing else was said for a quarter of an hour.

"Did I tell you Gaspare's sister is going to have a baby?"

Half his words were lost within a yawn. Saara made him repeat them.

"I have never seen Gaspare's sister, Dami, but my good wishes to her nonetheless."

"It is either the child of a cardinal or a thief," added Damiano, grinning up at his mistress, who was slipping her nakedness into her blue embroidered dress.

(He would dress her in silk satin, and in cloth-of-gold, and buy green velvet ribbons to wind in her hair. She would be the crown of Avignon.

But would Avignon accept a crown that did not wear shoes? There would be no use in buying Saara shoes.)

Her glance held a child's slyness. "Which would be better? I don't know what a cardinal is, but a thief I understand." Saara shrugged an Italian shrug. "If the child is strong and handsome, that is what matters." With practiced hands she braided her hair.

Damiano had a wonderful thought—a thought that made him feel both young and old, which turned him both to stone and to jelly. "Saara. Perhaps we will have a baby?"

Her green eyes darted to Damiano and her mouth opened. "Why—are you worried about that, Damiano? You need not be."

"I would love it," he said, and he laid his head in her lap, mussing his hair back and forth against her belly. "Nothing could be better."

The northern woman turned her head away in some confusion. "But I thought, Dami, you did not...believe...in your own future."

He raised his head to hers and there was fire behind his black eyes. "I was a fool," he stated. "But since then I have met the Devil and called him a liar to his face. I am free of his words, Saara."

She said nothing, but continued with her braiding. After a moment his mood softened again and once more Damiano yawned. He let his feet dangle from the edge of the loft and swung them back and forth.

"What a fool I have been, Saara: wrongheaded and self-centered and backward, as well. Everything I did around you was always the wrong thing."

Saara primmed her mouth in superior fashion, but then spoiled the effect by giggling. "It couldn't have been too much the wrong thing, Damiano, or we would not be here now, yes?"

"But Ruggerio..."

She put a slim hand on his lips. "Dami! I will bury my dead if you will bury yours."

He kissed the hand and said no more.

"Besides," she continued, "it would be a miserable sort of young man who did not act like a fool now and then."

Saara slid from the high shelf with no more fear than a

bird, and landed almost without noise. "Come out, Damiano, and show me what you know about magic."

They lay down in meadow flowers, side by side. "Eh!" Damiano protested. "We are going to get wet if we stretch out on this hill."

Saara laced her hands behind her neck. "So?"

Damiano went up on one elbow. From here he could see the red tile roof of the empty house he had already begun to regard as his, and the reddish ribbon of the road beyond, which his dim eyes could see was busy with people. Easter pilgrimage, most certainly. "All my clothes are new."

She played his rich overshirt between her fingers. "Take them off, then."

"If you will."

She gave him a canny glance and giggled.

They lay down naked in meadow flowers, side by side.

"Now, little witch-man," began Saara, "make for me a cloud."

Damiano only stared at her.

"Come now, Dami. You have all the earth and all the sky to work with. Make one little cloud."

He shook his head. "Show me."

The pretty girl yawned. Idly she knotted her braids together under her chin. "It's easy. First you sing your water out of the earth; there is a lot of it sitting there today."

Saara began to sing, not in Italian (thank God) nor in langue d'oc, but in her own far northern language. "DAH dah DAH dah DAH dah DAH dah" went the rhythm of her verse. It did not seem to have a rhyme scheme, but the sounds of her speech were so limited, and so harsh in his Latin-tuned ears, that he could not really tell.

Damiano flipped over to watch her as he listened. In only a few moments he felt a chill against his damp back, while the hair on his head was gently pulled away from the scalp. He scratched his head.

All around the two witches the air wavered, like that above a boiling pot. The grass on the hillock was complaining in a slow hish and hush as it gave up its glut of moisture.

Damiano opened his mouth to exclaim, and immediately his tongue and palate went dry and powdery. He swallowed and blinked sandy eyes.

Saara's own eyes were closed, and her hands folded on her breast. But her pink, rosebud lips were not dry, and a glistening drop balanced on her chin.

"Then, when you have the water in the air..." With the cessation of Saara's droning song, the electric pull in the atmosphere vanished. A wet heaviness settled over Damiano's shoulders, as fog shut their wild hillock away from the world. "....you must send it high into the sky, where it belongs."

It was the same insistent, repetitive melody as before, but sung at least an octave higher. Damiano smiled to watch her, for the Fenwoman singing high in her nose sounded and looked about twelve years old.

Now her green eyes were open, gazing vacantly at the misted sky. Damiano noted a large spot of golden-brown in her right eye, which he thought quite charming. Water beaded on the wisps of hair in front of her ears, water that sparkled like adamant when the sun reclaimed the sky.

Once again Saara yawned. "There." She pointed straight above them. "See my cloud."

Damiano's bare back fell upon the chilled, sodden grass. He repressed an unmanly shudder. In the blue heavens from horizon to horizon there rode only one cloud: tiny, fleecy, slightly translucent.

And directly overhead.

He commended her. "It is very pretty. The whitest cloud I have ever seen. But for a little while I thought it was going to take my teeth with it."

"Keep your mouth closed when someone is making clouds, Dami. I should have told you that. All Lappish children learn very early."

Damiano regarded the shapeless wonder in the sky at some length, chewing on a stem of sorrel. "Is there nothing to clouds but water?"

"What should there be?" asked Saara. "Fish?"

"Some binding element," he replied, frowning with thought. "Something to make steam adhere to itself—for you know that the steam from a kettle doesn't make a cloud in your kitchen. It merely dissipates and runs down your walls."

Saara giggled. When she turned on her side her right breast hung above the left one, almost (but not quite) touching.

Damiano found this fascinating. He ran a trilobed sorrel leaf between her breasts. Not quite touching. He had to ask Saara to repeat what she had been saying.

"I said the sky is all the binding element you need. Take water high enough and it will be a cloud. And now it's your turn. I will try to translate the song for you and . . ."

"No," replied Damiano, not raising his head from his interesting task. "I don't use words in spells anymore."

The Fenwoman's eyes opened very wide. She snatched the sorrel leaf from his fingers. "That tickles. Well, what *do* you use?"

"Just . . . song," replied her lover, giving only half his attention to his words. "One melody or another. Or three at once. It doesn't seem to matter." Deprived of the sorrel leaf, he tried using his nose.

Saara scuffed away over the squeaking grass. "That can be very dangerous, Dami. If you have no shape to put your meaning in, you can lose control."

He smiled. Snickered. "I do lose control, Saara. I am losing control right now." He dived after her and bit her gently on the softest part of the belly.

There is no soft part of the belly of a great white bear. Damiano recoiled, skidding down the grass on the slope of the hillock.

"Weren't you the one who trusted yourself so little you kept your magic locked in a stick, like it was a criminal?" asked the bear.

Damiano, who lay naked with his feet pointing down the hill, face on a level with the bear's paws, realized that each of those black-clawed feet was about the size of his own head. He answered the bear very politely.

"I always clothe my spells in shape, Saara. My music has a lot of structure—Raphael has made sure of that. And anyway I find I cannot make up words on the spur of the moment, or even remember ones I knew before. With tunes I have more facility."

The huge, deadly animal sat on its haunches and scratched its side with one front foot in very human fashion. "That is only a matter of practice. First you learn the basic songs by heart, and then you change them as you need to. There is really very little you make up new."

"Then, with all due respect, Madame Bear, I would rather continue my own way. After all, I cannot have the advantage of a Lappish childhood, and my personal methods, though unorthodox..."

The bear rocked back and forth. "You use too many big words," it whined in a deep bass. "And you talk too fast to understand."

"I'm sorry," said the human contritely. "But what other weapons have I against a beast of your majesty?"

"Make a cloud, Dami," begged Saara. "Any way you want to, just get on with it."

Send his song into the earth? No, it was more that his song was the only part of him which remained above as Damiano probed through the soil after water.

Once before he had descended beneath the earth's wrinkled skin: that time after fire. This was a more gentle journey—gentle and permeated with a coolness which could not chill the spirit as it chilled the body. He had to wander far to find water that Saara had missed. He sank down into rock (rock is no barrier to the spirit) and out beneath the rough, silver grass. Here was a river running sunless between two beds of stone, deep underground. There lay a pool where the water had not trembled its surface since the birth of Christ. Everywhere in the deep soil was water bound to stone, bound to rotten wood, or filling the feathery lace within the bones of the dead.

"You are taking a long time, Dami," came the voice from everywhere. It pulled him regretfully from a search which was becoming a goal in itself.

Shape. His magic needed shape, if he was to control it, instead of the other way around. He sang (in his head) a song of marvelous symmetry, in which the two lines of music followed one another at a distance of two bars, like horses in tandem. Then he added a third line, which took round part with the first, while the second line went into a contrasting rhythm. He was no longer pretending to sing. He played in his mind and spirit a lute, and then (dissatisfied with its five courses of sound) an entire consort of instruments.

He called the waters from the ground and led them into the air.

Saara was right. The thin, high atmosphere imposed cloud form on the rising moisture. The problem was structure, of course. He was to be in control, not the vagrant breezes or the roiling weight of water itself. He dictated structure upon his creation.

"Damiano," spoke Saara again. "Is that what a cloud is supposed to look like?" Her words held no criticism, but a vague uncertainty.

He opened his eyes and beheld the enormous, stark-white lenslike formation which covered a third of the visible sky. It was ovoid, regular and pierced in the middle, making a perfect setting for the noonday sun.

"Ah?" He repressed a smile of pride at this, his maiden effort. "What did you ask for? A spell with shape to it will create a cloud with a shape."

In the loft of an abandoned house two miles north of Avignon, there was no light by which ordinary eyes might have seen. But neither the black snakes who curled together beneath the loft or the witches who curled together upon it had ordinary eyes.

It was in the middle of a black hour of the morning before the dawn of Easter Sunday. It was the hour of the soldiers' amazement: the hour of the rolling of the stone.

And Damiano, though he was not thinking of stones, or of soldiers, was all amazed. His mind was lit with a mystery—not the Paschal Mystery—which set him glowing.

"What joy is this," he whispered, half coherently, to his mistress, ". . . that dissolves my body and soul together, so that I lose my name and my voice . . . and though I give all away I am richer in my heart. Though this is called debauchery—though it is called sin—never have I felt more holy nor more hale."

Saara chuckled gently, in part because she did not understand Damiano's words, and in part because she did.

"I did not know I could be so happy," murmured her lover, his lips brushing lightly over smooth blushing skin, ". . . not on this earth. In fact I had been told that happiness was not meant for us; a close friend assured me that misery was our lot, and I . . . I believed her.

"But had I known—had I known before what it would be, to lie with you, Saara of Saami, I would have died years since, with the impatience of waiting."

Saara lay curled against the wall. In her long hair was tangled the stems of clover and mustard and vetch: sweet weeds the witches had plucked together, along with bundles of spring grass, to make a fresh bed upon the rough wooden platform. She cradled Damiano's head on her breast and gazed down at that tousled head with a wondering care.

"It was only yesterday you said to me that you were not alone, Dami. Not a solitary nor a boy, you said."

A smile pulled his mouth wide. With a single motion he rolled from Saara's lap and rolled her on top of him. "I am contradicting myself, bellissima. Nonetheless . . ." and Damiano paused, sniffing left and right. He drew Saara's head to his and buried his nose in her hair.

"Your hair smells a little of pond water, Saara. That's what we get for playing the part of frogs."

"Better than what we might have smelled like by now, my dear," she giggled. "It is my practice to bathe every day, even when I have to break the ice to do it."

Damiano snorted. "You have strange tastes, beloved. Rose water and a steaming ewer—that I understand, but to immerse one's body . . ."

He combed the offending tress with his fingers. "No more breaking ice, Saara. No more cold beds shared with a pregnant goat." Then his musing smile faded.

"Saara. Your life has been so sad. You have loved proud men, violent men, vainglorious men. I may be a madman—Gaspare tells me so often enough—but at least I can be gentle about it. I will live to make you happy."

The forearms which locked about Saara's breast were very hard and strong, laced with the muscles and tendons used on the lute. Damiano's upper arms and shoulders were less well developed. His body, except for the face and hands, was the greenish olive of dark skin which has not seen the sun. He nuzzled the nape of her neck, rocking all the while from side to side.

Saara was rosy all over, though her shoulders, her

nose and the upper surface of her nipples were dusted
with bronze from the previous summer. Her eyes were
closed, as she relaxed into Damiano's slow, rocking embrace. She leaned back and bit his ear gently, whispering
something which made him chuckle as he replied:

"I spoke the truth. I have not been solitary. I have
even had creatures I could love, and who would love me
in return: not women, it is true, but dogs and angels at
least.

"And none of that is wasted. Oh, no, I would be a
churl to say it is wasted. . . ." Releasing Saara, he propped
himself up on one elbow and sniffed to clear his nostrils of
the intrusive dust of the mustard flower. Half mockingly,
Saara rubbed his nose with a wisp of grass. He sneezed.
She stuck the white globe blossoms of clover into his black
hair.

"But this, beloved. To lie here sleepless on rough-
hewn boards all the night of the most sacred day of the
year, while you tease and abuse me this way—biting me,
hitting me with sticks—with no regard for my dignity, my
manhood, my comfort . . ." He turned his face slightly, for
Saara was now kissing his neck with a predatory passion,
and biting a bit harder, ". . . for this I was created. Ah,
woman! My queen. My paradise. My great good friend."

For some while now the Fenwoman had not been
listening to anything her lover said. Italian was difficult
enough, for her, and impassioned Italian of a poetical cast,
uttered with a strong Piedmontese accent and half smothered
by blankets—that was beyond her. By Damiano's tone of
voice she gained enough understanding to make her happy, and in turn she endeavored with a forthright Nordic
sort of enthusiasm to transcend her own limited vocabulary. But his last sentence she understood, and it made her
laugh.

"Ho! Damiano. I have been called a queen before, by
Ruggerio (although he did not really mean it, since he did
not usually do what I wanted him to do). And I have been
called a friend. But never have I been a friend and a
queen together. I think you will have to chose one or the
other."

His response was a huge, mauling hug. "No! No, I
can't chose. I am Delstrego the madman—just ask Gaspare

if it's not true that I'm mad—and I have to have impossible things. You are to be my queen and my heaven, and my friend to love and play games with, and my teacher and my singer and . . ."

His touch quieted into something feather light as he concluded ". . . and maybe the mother of my troublesome children, heh?"

Having the eyes of sight and the eyes of love and the black eyes of a man, still Damiano could not see the look of pain that lashed over Saara's face. She hid her eyes against his shoulder.

He could not see her face, but he could feel her stiffen. "What is it, beloved, what have I said?"

Fear dripped cold in Saara, like blood from a stabbing wound. She thought, He will not want me when he knows. He has youth, time. . . . He has the world, and I am only the first of many. . . .

And though Saara dreaded the truth, she was not tempted to lie. "I can't have your children, Damiano. The children I had are dead: they are all I will have."

The silence that followed was terrible. Then Damiano said, "I am sorry I spoke, beloved. I didn't think. But it is no matter. If we can't have a child ourselves, we will merely buy one."

"Buy one?" Saara nearly hiccuped in surprise.

"Certainly. Of course, such a child would almost certainly be simple: not a witch. If that would disappoint you too much, then we will have dogs instead."

"Dogs?" she echoed.

"Or horses. Or the big, flat-footed deer your people raise. The important thing, bellissima," and Damiano gave her hand an urgent little squeeze, "is to be surrounded with life, don't you think? Creatures that are young and growing, that look to the future."

Saara smiled in spite of herself, and the cold wound in her heart warmed unexpectedly, as though it might possibly heal someday. "With only you around, Dami, I feel . . . overwhelmed by life!"

She snuggled into the bed of greenery.

By the taste in the air it would be dawn soon. Damiano (in spite of never feeling more "hale" in his life) felt it would not be a bad idea to sleep Easter away. Sinful, of course, to miss the mass, and especially for such carnal purposes. But sin was man's nature, he had been told, and Damiano had a lot of carnal sinning to do if he was to catch up to the human norm.

Besides, he could not really believe there was sin in anything touched by Saara.

"... has taken my fancy," he was saying. "It is a well-built house, with a good view and at least a rod of flat land on all sides of it. We could do worse than to settle here, at least for a while."

"Mnnh?" Saara was more than half asleep.

"I will go into Avignon to play—for I must play for people, or I will decline—and of course we will use the city as our market, but here we will have both ease and privacy."

"Have what?"

"Oh, we will live very well, Saara, you and I. Between the money I can make from my lute, and that which can be charged for purifying wells and assessing metals (always assuming there is no guild restriction in that area) we can live very respectably."

Damiano felt an impulse to remind Saara that he had begun as a respectable fellow, and of good family. But as he remembered Saara's position as the outraged mistress of his father (which now seemed so poor a reason not to love) he decided that the thing was better left unsaid. Instead he added, "Or we will live respectably once we are married, of course."

He felt her stir in his arms, and her long hair glimmered in a beam of the first light of Easter. "Married? You want to marry me, Damiano? How . . . cute."

"What do you mean—cute?" Damiano was stung. "I offer you a lifetime's protection and devotion and you call it cute."

Saara's eyes were limned clear and colorless in that single intrusive beam. Her lips remained in shadow. "It *is* cute, Damiano. Ruggerio always said that marriage was not courtly, while your father called it the death of love. Jekkinan . . ."

"Shut up about all these other men," snapped Damiano,

hot in the face. "Especially my father. If I were not a very mild man, you would drive me to hit you with such talk."

Saara took a deep breath. "Then we would have another battle on our hands, wouldn't we, dear one? The walls of Avignon would shake, I think, if we went to war again. But you must let me finish. My people know no courts, so they don't care if a thing is courtly. I did not cease loving Jekkinan because I married him.

"I think it would be very sweet to marry you, Damiano. It is only that I did not know the men of Italy ever wanted to marry. And also, I don't know what you would do with a wife like me, all stubborn and full of teeth."

She showed him her small white teeth then, and he pretended to be cowed by them. Then he craned his head over the edge of the bed. "What is that?" he whispered.

Saara listened also, with senses honed by wilderness. "A horse," she answered.

Damiano twisted onto his stomach. "*My* horse," he corrected her, full of curiosity. "I know because he comes down especially heavy in front. He has never had proper training."

He ought to get down from the loft. He ought to wait for Festilligambe by the road: the poor brute wasn't full-sighted, after all, but just a beast with a beast's instinct knowledge. But a strange reluctance to move paralyzed Damiano. He lay poised at the edge of the loft, half out of the blanket, listening to the urgent pa-rump, pa-rump of galloping hooves. Saara put one comforting hand between his shoulder blades. She kissed him on his unshaven cheek.

The horse needed no fuller sight than he had. His hooves left the road at the spot Damiano had, that previous Friday. They plashed heedlessly through puddles and scrabbled over slopes of wet grass. The two in the loft heard a squeal of protest that did not come out of the throat of a horse.

"Hmph. Gaspare. He is stiff as a stick, on horseback," snickered Damiano, but still he did not move.

The horse approached the door at a trot and then stopped. Damiano heard great equine sniffs of nervousness, as the beast passed under the lintel.

"Where the hell are you going, you filth, you sow?" cried the horse's rider between gritted teeth. "I can't see my hand in front of my face in here."

The tall horse stood immediately below the loft. It nickered to its master, who dropped a hand down to the rubbery nose. The horse sniffed the bed of greenery and settled back onto his haunches to reach for it.

Gaspare cursed, grabbing handfuls of mane.

"Up here," whispered Damiano. "We're up here in the loft. Don't let the horse eat this grass—it isn't fresh.

"What's wrong, Gaspare?" he added, though Damiano's tone itself denied that there could be anything wrong anywhere on this dawning Easter Sunday in Provence.

Gaspare choked twice before he could speak.

"Plague, Damiano. The plague has struck Avignon. People are dead on the streets.

"And Evienne—she's gone. She's been stolen."

Chapter Twelve

The walk back to Avignon in the Easter sunshine had not so much the character of an awakening from a good dream as a descent into nightmare. Damiano and Saara hurried south, following Gaspare, whose preoccupied steps tended to weave across the broad, rutted road.

Damiano's belief in Gaspare's words was fragile, for his own personal happiness was strong enough to force the misery of others out of his mind.

But plague. Happiness could not conquer that. Nor love, nor witchery.

I would stop time, he thought. If I could, I would stop time before we reach the city. Before I have to see them die again.

But as Damiano could not stop time, he walked on.

Behind the three paced a winded, halterless horse, whose own progress went by fits and starts: fits of grazing interrupted by explosions of catching up to the humans.

The breeze came down from the north, pressing Damiano's shirt against his back and whipping Saara's dress against her calves till her skin reddened. It was fresh but not cold, its Alpine origins having been softened by hundreds of miles of Provençal indolence.

Traffic upon the road for the most part was heading straight into the wind, as a parade of souls issued from Avignon, dressed not for Easter but for a long journey. Their horses and oxen were burdened and their small children cried. None of those who fled the city spoke to Damiano's company, and he had nothing to say to them.

So the procession he had thought was going into Avignon for Easter was actually going out of it, escaping disease. Yet Avignon was a big city, and these few dozen people hardly constituted an exodus of fear. Perhaps conditions within were not so bad. His memory also told him exactly how stable Gaspare's emotions were and how far his word could be trusted.

Saara stepped beside Damiano, saying nothing, her face unreadably thoughtful.

But there would have been no room for her to open her mouth, had she so desired. Sharp-faced, shaky-voiced, young Gaspare held the floor.

"It was only the day after you left the rumor came, that a man had died all black and swollen. Whether it was the plague that did for him, though, no one knew.

"I myself could have told them," continued the boy with a vicious slap to his own chest, "having seen more of the world than these sheep of Avignon.

"But no one asked me. Besides—who wants to get so near the pest as to diagnose it? Anyway, old Coutelan shut up the inn. No more soirees for the cardinals. Our own hovel, too. No pillow where Gaspare of San Gabriele may rest his head."

"Is it only a rumor, then?" broke in Damiano. "Before you said there were people dead on the streets."

"I said . . . I said"—the boy lost his tongue for a moment in his excitement—"it was a rumor on the day after you left. The day following that it was no more necessary to ask what sickness was making a fellow retch and wheeze and pop out in aching boils.

"Now the vendors are gone from the streets and the shops are boarded. No one goes anywhere except the man with an ox and an open cart. It is just like Pe'Comtois. Chhhaah!" Gaspare spat in the street.

His reedy voice had held a peculiar horrified satisfaction as he cataloged the plight of Avignon. His exophthalmic eyes glinted.

"But Evienne," asked Damiano, trying to put concern behind his words. "How does this affect your sister? Have you reason to believe . . ."

Gaspare's odd cockiness collapsed like wet paper. "I have no reason to believe anything good. I went to see her and . . ."

"How? How could you find your way into the cardinal's house without me?"

Gaspare curled his lip. "How do you think, sheep-face? A sop for the dog and rope with a hook of applewood. The old, reliable methods. But Evienne is gone, and her dresses and blankets with her. They left nothing behind worth taking away."

Saara spoke for the first time. "This is your sister who is going to have a baby?"

"Yes, the slut. They say the cardinal is in conference in the Papal Palace, and I don't know if that means he is in chains or he has old Innocent in chains, but I can't believe he took my sister with him."

Gaspare snorted and his long nose twitched. "Evienne is not the proper stuff for the Papal Palace."

Damiano's head lifted. The soft wind tunneled through his hair. "I hear bells now," he admitted. "Surely they would not ring the Paschal carillon if the city were infested?"

Saara, who could not follow Gaspare's rapid speech, had been listening to the peal for some time. "No, Dami. There is no joy there. I think those are black bells. They ring because people are dead."

Now the wind shifted and the note came clear. It was a slow, tedious, effortful tolling, and as he listened to it Damiano's last armor fell away from him. He tasted fear on the wind, along with something worse.

Avignon was now a dome of white rising up the hill from the Rhone, scarcely farther from them than an arrow's good flight. The city swam in the morning light, but approaching along the pale pink and busy roadway was the oxcart Gaspare had only just described, driven by a thick and brutish man whose shape Damiano found familiar.

The three people stepped out of the wheels' path, while Festilligambe shied onto the road's shoulder. A great bronze-burnished ox nodded its head solemnly as it passed them, as though to say "Yes, yes. This is the awful truth."

The driver of the cart tugged his beast to a stop before them. As he peered down from beneath the brim of a rough straw hat he sighed hugely.

Damiano was relieved to discover that the man wore neither the features of the Devil nor the mad cart driver of Petit Comtois. Because it was Damiano who regarded the driver so closely, it was to Damiano that the man spoke.

"Turn back, young gentles," he said earnestly. "There is no purpose so urgent it should take you into Avignon today."

Damiano's eyes slid back to the tall solid wood wheels, doweled to their axle, and to the high wooden slats that sided the wagon. "You are certain it is the plague, then?"

At the word "plague," the driver pulled off his woven hat and held it in his hand. "It was fifty dead yesterday, good monsieur. Today there will be a hundred, I am certain.

"Turn back," he repeated, his gaze on Saara's fair face. "For this plague is merciless and it seeks out the young." With those words the driver lashed his ox into movement.

Gaspare, who had stood silent during this interchange, staring with dread at the uncommunicative slats of the wagon, now ran after the man. "Hello, hello! Tell me, have you seen a redhead?" he asked in halting langue d'oc.

The driver mauled his beast to a stop again. "Seen what?"

"A girl with red hair, very pretty," shouted the boy, and as the driver blinked without comprehension Gaspare added, "with a biggish belly. Pregnant."

After a moment the man shook his head. "Going your way on the road there has been no one but you. Or did you mean leaving the city?"

Gaspare grimaced. "I didn't mean on the road. I meant..." And then, without another word, he turned on his heel and dashed the fifty yards back to where his friends were waiting. They asked no questions.

The gate stood open. When Damiano expressed some surprise at this, Gaspare only shrugged. "Why not? It's too late to keep the plague out now."

"But to keep it from spreading..."

"Is it the business of Avignon to watch out for Lyons?" replied the cynical fourteen-year-old. He made to step under the arch of stucco.

Damiano, stepping behind, felt a cold, premonitory sweat. He grabbed at the boy's jerkin. "Wait a moment, Gaspare. I think it would be better if you returned and waited for us at our house."

"Your... house?" Gaspare's lank hair had fallen inside the collar of his shirt. Frowning hugely at Damiano, he pulled it out. "Where do you have a house?"

Saara interrupted. "You are thinking he should not go into the city, Dami? You are right. He is simple, and it would be very dangerous for him."

Gaspare turned from one to the other, insult darkening his uneven complexion. "Simple? From you, sheep-face, that is laughable."

Damiano refused to be offended. "You don't understand, Gaspare. We are witches."

"So you keep telling me...."

"And if we are careful, we will not get the plague. You, however..."

Two white patches appeared amid the crimson mottling on Gaspare's face. "Everyone gets the plague. Even Jews get the plague; remember the Pope saying so?"

"Wait for us in the clean air and sunlight, boy," suggested Saara, using what was to her the most pressing argument against Avignon (or indeed any city). "We will bring your sister out to you."

Gaspare glared his scorn upon both of them and entered Avignon.

There was no crowd upon the streets, no press of bodies in the cobbled court before the Bishop's Inn and no one at all sitting at the inn-yard tables, which had been turned upon their ends and now stood ranked against the ground-floor wall.

"This," reflected Damiano aloud, "is not like Petit Comtois, where all was madness and buffoonery. This resembles more my own city, Partestrada, on a fast day with the shops all closed. It doesn't look like plague at all."

"Nonetheless," grunted Gaspare stolidly.

Saara stepped lightly over the cobbles. Her toes grabbed and curled, like those of a stalking bird. One slim arm settled on Damiano's shoulder. "Don't be fooled, dear one. This place has evil in it," she said.

And Damiano could feel that. Despite his words, he could feel trouble in the air, and fear in the smell of the bodies hidden by walls all around him.

How odd, to stand in the middle of a disaster which could not touch one. I am a witch again, he thought. I have a power of flame so strong the plague cannot enter in. My lady, too. We could stroll together among piled bodies and suffer no hurt.

And in spite of this knowledge (or perhaps because of it) Damiano felt a surge of hopelessness, almost like despair. He turned to Saara. "We have to help these people, beloved," he whispered, out of Gaspare's hearing.

Her eyes were windows over the sea. "We can't. Years ago, don't you think I tried? In Lombardy, when I felt sickness in the village below, I came down to them. I sang till I became so weak I might have sickened myself. Not one lived who had caught the plague. Not one.

"This plague has jaws like a trap, and those who fall into it, die in it."

"What are you saying to him?" Gaspare whined shrilly, stepping between them and hopping from one foot to the other. "Is it about Evienne? Can you tell me where she is?"

Saara looked down upon him from a height of years. "You should leave this place, boy. You cannot help your sister by dying."

Gaspare cursed. He swore before them both that he would never leave the trail of his sister until she was found: not for food, nor drink nor rest, and especially not for safety's sake. He kicked the pavement and called Saara crude names in Piedmontese argot. She listened with the calmness of a person who understands so little of a language she cannot be offended in it.

The black horse, who was also out of temper because there was no grass in Avignon, and because he had to step so very carefully over each round cobble, brushed by the irritatingly noisy boy on a search for some growth of green among the stones. Festilligambe found what he sought behind a small garden gate, which swung open at the touch of his nose.

"That's MacFhiodhbhuidhe's gate," murmured Damiano, cutting into Gaspare's tantrum. "He doesn't leave it open." And the dark witch followed the horse through.

The little garden was empty. With some difficulty Damiano shooed the gelding away from a pot of herbs and back into the road. He closed the gate on the animal and then crossed again toward the courtyard door.

Open also. Damiano stepped in, and although his senses told him there was no one within, he called out his presence.

The harper's house was dim and tidy. Downstairs nothing moved. Damiano took the steep, uneven stairs two at a time. MacFhiodhbhuidhe's bedstraw was swept into a corner and his bedclothes were folded. Gleaming balls of brass wire lay in a smug sunny row on a bookshelf. There was no sign of MacFhiodhbhuidhe or of the ancient who did for him. The young witch clattered down the stairs again.

This house gave an impression of age. It seemed all the heavy furniture, neat-dusted and smelling of beeswax, had stood in place unmoved for a long time. Like the harper's music, which probably hadn't suffered alteration since he left his Leinster academy. Damiano once more felt his spasm of irritation at MacFhiodhbhuidhe, tempered by the knowledge that the man was kind. On

impulse he crossed the downstairs room. He stopped
before the low cabinet to peep again at the exotic Irish harp.

After a minute, he picked up what he found and
carried it to the door.

There, in the sunlight, stood Saara and Gaspare, with
the horse. Gaspare was looking sulky. So was the horse.
Saara had one hand wrapped in the black mane, and she
had evidently been bestowing a few home-truths upon
both of them.

Damiano came out blinking against the white light. In
his arms he cradled three lengths of black wood, wrapped
in a twist of brass wires. "It has been taken apart," he
announced. "The harp. He said . . . he said to me . . ."

"That he would never take it apart again," added
Gaspare.

"Not . . . while he lived to play it."

"He was your friend?" Saara asked gently.

They had been walking with great purpose toward the
river for some minutes before he answered her. "I guess
so. He was very good to me. I did nothing for him."

Gaspare giggled awkwardly. "What were you supposed to do? He had money and position. You didn't. And
we only knew him for a few weeks."

Saara watched Damiano rub his eyes with his shirtsleeve. He noticed. "Pay no attention to that," he barked
at her. "I do it all the time. It means nothing—no more
than a sneeze." Then, in an excess of frustrated feeling, he
drew back his fist as though he would slam it into the
nearest wall.

But as he was a musician and that wall was made of
stone, he thought better of the action and hit his fist into
his opposite palm. "Curse it all to hell!" he shouted, and
then stared wildly from one friend's face to the other.

"Wait for me here," he commanded. "There's something I must find out." He darted down a side street.
There followed a disgruntled whinny, and the tall horse
followed his master at a trot, a small pot of blooming
violets hanging from his mouth.

"He is mad, our Damiano," said Gaspare complacently.

*   *   *

The door was locked from within, the hanging sign was missing, and the windowless face of the jeweler's shop gave no clue to what lay within. Yet Damiano's senses told him that there was someone alive in the shop or above it. He pounded on the door repeatedly.

Finally a voice cried out from a slot window above his head. "Closed! Go away."

Damiano backed into the street. "Ormerin, let me in. It's Delstrego."

"Who?"

"The man with the ruby pendant." There was no answer, and Damiano added, "I swear by all the saints, man, that I am not sick of the plague. In fact I am probably the safest man in all Avignon to let in your door."

After a moment's reflection, the jeweler called out, "What do you want, Italian? Do you want to buy your ruby back?"

"You still have it, then?"

The jeweler cleared his throat. Damiano could see one small brown eye and half a mouth at the burglar-proof window. Ormerin was watching Damiano's horse as the beast tried its black nose into all the ground floor windows on the street. "It's not the sort of thing one sells every week or two. I haven't even shown it yet."

"Ah?" Damiano nodded his head forcefully, as though this bit of information was important. "And your family, Monsieur Ormerin. Your wife and little ones. Are they well?"

Ormerin, who was small and smooth-faced, regarded Damiano with his other eye. "So far, and may God maintain us."

"That is all I wanted to know," replied Damiano, and he ran away again. Festilligambe followed reluctantly.

Damiano returned breathing hard. He had twisted his foot slightly on a stone and walked gingerly. "He hides his lies in a shell of the truth," he gasped. "Like a worm in a hazelnut. You think you have learned to ignore him, and then you find he has struck you in another level of deceit."

Saara stared at her lover without comprehension. She bent down and took his ankle in both her hands. After a few moments the pain departed. "What are you talking about, Dami?" she asked at last.

"The Devil. He told me I was responsible for the plague in Avignon."

Gaspare's gooseberry eyes rolled. He put one arm at the small of Damiano's back and marched him forward. "When was all this?" asked the boy indulgently.

"Last week," replied Damiano, testing his leg.

"Last week there was no plague in Avignon."

The sprain was gone entirely. At the end of the street the Rhone sparkled, its surface shattered by the breeze. "That was what made him so convincing. He said the sickness came in my ruby, which I sold. But the jeweler is well, along with his family. I think if the ruby *were* a plague stone, they'd have been the first . . ."

Saara's child-pure features expressed anger. "You said you had thrown it away, Dami. You said you believed nothing that he said. . . ."

"No more do I," he replied shortly, and ran his hand over Saara's sleek braided head.

"You did not bring the plague to Avignon." She pulled away from his touch. "It came on a bat, I think."

"A bat?" Gaspare snickered. "A ruby is easier to believe."

"A bat or a rat." She shrugged. "Something with a squeak. Or that's what the earth tells me."

The peach trees were past their best bloom, which is to say that tiny green leaves peeped and pried among the pink petals. The three stopped beside the house, while Festilligambe trotted down to investigate the river.

"Sing us in, my lady," whispered Damiano. "Let's see whether Evienne is missing, or whether Gaspare merely missed her."

The boy cursed under his breath, but made no objection as the Fenwoman opened her mouth in a wailing, foreign chant. Damiano sprang the lock with a word.

Cardinal Rocault's pleasant villa was in considerable disarray. There was broken crockery in the garden, and the chickens were loose. Lying disconsolately across the front stoop was Couchicou, the wolfhound. Damiano stroked him, exempting him from Saara's spell. His tail, heavy as a man's wrist, beat the stone stair.

In the kitchen sat three of the cardinal's servants: two

women and the man whom Gaspare and Damiano had met earlier guarding the kitchen door dog-fashion. They were eating the cardinal's cheese and drinking the cardinal's wine. The older of the two women sat on the fat man's lap. They consumed their illicit pleasures determinedly, but none was smiling.

Saara, Gaspare and Damiano passed by with no more regard than they would have displayed passing a public fresco. The dog tarried at the table.

Gaspare was quite correct. Evienne was missing, along with her tapestries and her feather bed. A glance into her armoire revealed that her clothes had likewise accompanied her. In fact, the tiny cubby above the peach trees held nothing which would interest a thief—even a poor thief like Evienne's brother. Damiano's senses told him further that the girl was nowhere in the house.

"Gone," he stated. "But not run away by herself, unless she did so atop a loaded cart."

"It is as I said," insisted Gaspare, searching futilely once more through the empty drawers. "She has been stolen."

Damiano made an equivocal gesture. "Stolen? Say rather taken to a place of safety by her protector, the cardinal."

"Whatever, still we must find her." Gaspare shoved home a drawer with emphasis.

Damiano sighed. "Again?" Saara looked from one to the other.

"Surely that will not be so difficult?" she asked brightly.

"But it's Easter," replied her lover. "Easter Sunday itself. And there are more pressing problems in Avignon than a sister who keeps moving about. And also"—he gave an enormous, jaw-distending yawn—"I'm so sleepy."

He walked into Jan Karl's office alone and shut the door behind him. The blond cleric didn't see him at first, as the table at which he sat with quill and ink faced away from the door, and he was very busy writing a list of names. Damiano gazed calmly at Jan Karl's bald crown until the man turned around.

"Delstrego! What..." And Jan's glance darted quickly from his visitor to the paper under his hand and then back again. He covered his script with blotting sand and swiveled his stool around.

"What brings you back here, today of all days?"

"Today of all days?" repeated Damiano very politely. He pulled the only other chair in the room over to the table and he sat himself down in it, lifting his feet up onto the table. His heavy, black mountain boots were pointed at Jan Karl like a threat. "Why is today special, aside from the fact that it is Easter?"

The Dutchman scraped his chair sideways, so that Damiano's feet were no longer pointed at him. He ran a hand through his border of silky yellow hair and his long face drew longer. His mouth made a small moue and he raised his blue eyes to the ceiling. "Do you see these authorizations?" he began. "They bear the Holy Father's own seal. Today I woke up as a lector of the church. An hour after dawn I became a deacon. Just before you walked in I was informed that I was about to be ordained a priest and—by the way, Delstrego, it was a great good thing you didn't take but two of my fingers back there in that wretched hamlet in Lombardy. A man without fingers cannot offer the mass—and as I was saying, I am also made officer of the palace refectory. Before this day is out, I could be a cardinal."

Damiano nodded in calm good humor. "Or you could be dead. Life is full of surprises, especially when there is plague in the city."

Karl's face froze and he gripped the short arms of his stool. "The plague is part of the reason for my advancement, certainly. The court has known many losses in the last few days, especially from among the lower ranks."

These two men who faced one another without friendship were built in quite similar fashion: tall, lean and not too broad of shoulder. It is hard to explain, then, why the Dutchman, Jan Karl, gave the impression of having been stepped on by something large at some time in the past, and of expecting to be imminently stepped on again, while Damiano gave a very different impression. The dark Italian slouched by the window, imperturbable, with eyes of black stone, looking (had he only known it) like the Roman General Pardo, when he interviewed young Damiano himself in Partestrada.

"But it is not only that, of course," continued Jan, as he poured more sand over his parchment. "It is also the discovery of Rocault's plots."

Damiano watched the Dutchman empty his sandpot. The effort seemed less directed toward drying the ink than concealing the substance of his writing. Damiano considered telling Jan not to bother: that he could never read script across the width of a table, but Jan's last sentence stopped him.

"Discovery? Of Cardinal Rocault?"

"Inevitable," replied the blond with a superior shrug. "Considering how the man was overstepping himself. It was in the kitchen, you know. That is how the post of officer of the refectory has so suddenly become open.

"Oh, there are many new opportunities in the hierarchy now, Delstrego." Jan gave a little giggle. "It is so good to be in the right place at the right time for once."

Damiano rubbed his left hand over two days' growth of beard, making a noise like a pumice stone at work. "Hmmph! I see. The kitchen, was it?" Then he was silent.

Jan, too, had run out of things to say, and stared at Damiano, whom he suddenly seemed to remember was not exactly his friend.

"I, too, once wanted to become a priest," mumbled Damiano, giving the impression of a man deep in thought. "Of course I discovered that a born witch cannot be ordained, no more than a man who is missing his thumb or first two fingers." He scraped his stubble again and peered vaguely at Jan from under a thicket of black curls. He yawned. "And anyway it's just as well, considering what I've been and what I've done."

Then his head was raised an inch and once again the eyes were made of slate. "It's too bad Evienne couldn't also be in the right place at the right time, isn't it?"

"E-Evienne?" Jan Karl stuttered as though the very sound of the name were strange to him. "What has she to do with my ordination?"

"With your ordination? Nothing, I imagine. But with the discovery of Cardinal Rocault's plot . . ."

Jan snorted. "She had nothing to do with that. She hasn't the brain for politics."

Damiano nodded assent. "I agree completely. She has

nothing to do with any plot against the Holy Father. So why has she vanished, my dear Jan? Who has stolen her, and where did they take her? Her brother, you see, would like to know."

Karl rose to his feet. There was no expression on his face. "Gone? Did you go to see her at the cardinal's, then? That was dangerous. Too dangerous for me, anyway."

"He went to see her twice. She was locked in her little kennel, like a bitch who is carrying a litter of great value. But now she is missing, and all her furniture is gone with her."

The blond's lips moved soundlessly. Then he said, "If Rocault had got her locked up, then she probably ran away."

"With her featherbed under her arm? No, Jan. She refused to run away, although I offered to help her do so. She was staying where you put her, like a good girl, and her only fear was that you had been killed by the wolfhound, who by the by is waiting for me outside your door this minute, or that you had forgotten her and would not return with the glass copies of her jewelry you had promised to deliver."

While Damiano spoke Jan Karl had turned away and was staring blankly out the single, viewless window. The Italian prodded him with a boot. "Heh? Did you make copies of her jewelry, at least? Mother of God, Jan! That sweet, stupid little girl loves you!"

Jan Karl shuddered fastidiously. "You exaggerate, Delstrego. How like an Italian you are." He paced across his square box of a room, his hands folded at the front of his long black robe. Jan Karl, with his pale skin and dry face, looked quite spectral in black. "We were friends once, certainly. But she is the sort of woman who does not remember things for long. Her senses are earthy and her feelings very low. I am confident that she no more expects me to . . . to visit her in her confinement than I . . . than I expect . . ."

"Than you expect what, Jan?" inquired Damiano, who was feeling a slow heat of anger spread from his chest out toward his hands and head.

Suddenly the Dutchman turned at bay, his hands pressed upon the edge of the writing table. "I expect nothing from her. I am being ordained, Delstrego. The affairs of the flesh I have put behind me."

Damiano said, "How noble of you. What a sacrifice." He sighed, willing his anger into control. "I didn't really come here to talk about all that, Jan. I think Evienne is better off without you, myself.

"I need you only to tell me where she is gone. Is it likely Rocault himself took her out of the city before his discovery, to keep her from the plague?"

There was a noise in the distance, along the hall, of someone weeping: a man, giving way to deep, hopeless sobs. The cleric was distracted for a moment, and his brow creased. He sank back into his chair.

Damiano also listened, and his lips pulled back from his teeth. "Perhaps you may expect another promotion today," he said with a touch of bitterness.

Jan Karl ignored him. He sat biting his lip. "It was Friday midday that Father Lemaître, the officer of the refectory, confessed that he had agreed to offer poison to Innocent in the Easter dinner. He may have been the very first in Avignon to die. He thought the disease was a judgment upon him."

"Indeed? And for what is the rest of the city being judged?" asked Damiano in a low murmur.

"Within an hour the cardinal had been brought into the palace, and no more has been heard of him since. So I don't think it would have been he who gave the order to remove Evienne."

"Then it must have been the Pope himself who took the girl away," whispered Damiano, only half believing his own words.

Jan Karl cleared his throat. "More likely Commander Sforza, if anyone. But I think, rather, she ran away by herself, Delstrego, once she got wind of what had happened."

Damiano shook his head. "No, for then she would have come to you. She has not tried to see you, has she?"

Karl shook his head.

"I thought not. Tell me, where would the Holy Father have taken her—assuming he took her anywhere?"

The Dutchman raised his hands in complete mystification. "He has thousands of troops in hundreds of barracks and dozens of secret cells beneath them."

Damiano slapped his thigh like a man making a decision. "I will ask him," he announced. "That is the only course."

"You will *what?*" yelped Jan Karl, rising once more. "You will ask . . . the Pope himself . . . what he has done with his enemy's mistress?"

Damiano stood also. "Yes. After all, I have met him, and he seemed very approachable. I will tell him Evienne's complete story, and I'm sure . . ."

"You cannot!" Jan Karl's wail echoed through the room, competing with the cries of the unknown sufferer in the distant reaches of the building. "You can't tell him without revealing my part in . . ." He grabbed at Damiano's gold-chased sleeve. "You mustn't reveal my name!"

Damiano pulled away. "One can't go about telling half-truths to the Holy Father," he said.

Jan Karl put his two remaining left-hand fingers in his mouth and bit down on them. "Wait. Wait, Delstrego, before you try anything as desperate as that. I think I know where they might have taken her."

For some minutes after the witch had left, Jan Karl sat beside his writing table, pouring sand from one hand to the other, his fear and his ambition warring with the memory of Evienne's red hair. His eyes gazed unseeingly at the parchment he had been filling, which began: "I have reason to believe that the following men have been involved in the recent and disgraceful attempt . . ." At last he put that sheet aside in favor of one of those which had come to him that morning, took his fingernail and began to worry at a beribboned blob of wax.

Chapter Thirteen

It was a strange little procession that wound its way through the rabbit-warren of halls and chambers which was the Papal Palace at Avignon. It was led by Damiano (for only he had been told the way), elegantly dressed in scarlet and gold, his black boots striking the tiles soundly. Saara followed: a sweet-faced and barefoot peasant in a dress bright as some child's painting. Her steps made no noise. After her came Gaspare in finery grown quickly shabby with ill-use. His soft city shoes scuffed a nervous and uncertain rhythm, and his shoulders had crawled up his neck. Gaspare wished they would hurry.

In front and in back, stitching the group together, came Couchicou, the cardinal's wolfhound, who did not know where they were going, but had come along for the company.

The oddest part about this small assembly was the sound emanating from it, for Damiano and Saara together sang a song. They were throwing it about between them, from one throat to the other, as one ran out of inspiration or the other desired to speak. It was not, of course, the same song for Damiano as it was for the Fenwoman, as Saara had her traditions, whereas Damiano tended toward vers libre. But the two interpretations fit nicely, and the main theme of it was to the effect that no one should see them marching toward the palace infirmary, down corridors by torchlight, and through enormous halls whose windows overlooked the Rhone.

Damiano took a breath and let his mistress take over the burden of melody. To encourage her effort, he put his arm around her shoulders. "Jan says that people who show cause to be detained—people of a certain status, that is, such as the cardinal, or cause of a delicate nature, such as

227

that of Evienne—are often put into a suite of chambers
behind the infirmary. It is a comfortable situation, he tells
me, except for the lock on the door."

Gaspare looked left and spat right. "I wouldn't want
to be locked in any rooms, however comfortable, near sick
people today."

Damiano's face, which had displayed all the compla-
cent happiness of his amatory good fortune, as well as a
good share of the drowsiness which often accompanies
such good fortune, grew on the instant grave. He stopped
in mid-stride, pulling Saara to a halt with him. "It is as I
said before, Gaspare. You should not be here. It is dangerous for you."

"If you catch the plague, child," added Saara, "we
cannot help you."

Gaspare balled fists at his sides and advanced upon
Damiano. "Stop trying to get rid of me."

The wolfhound, sensing tension in his little pack,
weaseled in between the two humans and, with a
wiggle and lean, knocked Gaspare against the wall. The
boy cursed but did not dare a kick at Couchicou's
slablike side.

Damiano turned away. "To get rid of you? I have
given that up, Gaspare," he muttered to himself. "Two
nations, endless mountains and a plague town were not
sufficient for the purpose."

They needed neither directions nor second sight to
tell them when they approached the palace infirmary. The
stench of sickness informed them of their approach, along
with the sight of piles of straw along both sides of the
corridor wall, on which the afflicted were placed in long
rows.

Damiano had seen plague victims before, and told
himself that he ought to be hardened to the sight. Saying
that did no good, however, for on the green faces before
him, and in their suppurating lesions, pain had been
translated into pure ugliness, and death into an uncon-
querable despair.

"And these are all men dedicated to Christ's service,"
he whispered, dropping his arm from Saara's shoulders.
"It does not seem . . . allowable."

Glassy gray eyes met his, shining from a face made

hideous by swelling. They asked no questions, these eyes.

"He can see me," whispered Damiano. "Despite the spell, he can see me. Is that because he is dying?"

Saara took her lover gently by the arm. "Come, Dami."

Gaspare stared straight ahead. His pinched face had gone slick with fear-sweat. Couchicou, too, walked stiffly, pressing his side against that of the boy, and his rough fur bristled along his back.

Moving quietly among the dying were women in white, whose eyes were weary beyond expression, and whose lips moved constantly, without sound. Benedictines, these were. Damiano watched the nuns and wondered, remembering a girl with flaxen hair who once sat in a high loggia, doing needlework under the white north light of the Alps. Carla Denezzi, postulant of the order of Saint Clare: if fortune did not take him again to the high mountains of his birth, he would never see her again.

It might be she was dead now.

Soon they passed the infirmary hall itself, where the stench was overpowering, and the dead lay in stacks covered by sheets. They came to a turn in the corridor where there were no more piles of hay and no more gentle Benedictines, but far off along a tunnellike corridor could be escried a pair of Papal guards, complete with sword and halberd, like those that stood by the main gate of the enclosure. But these pikes did not point to heaven in parallel. They swayed through the torchlight like fir trees in the wind, for the guards were talking animatedly to another, less impressive figure that pointed repeatedly into the darkness along the corridor.

"What?" whispered Gaspare in Damiano's ear. "What's that happening ahead?"

The witch's ears rather than his eyes gave him that information. For a moment his face went blank with surprise and he grabbed each of his companions by the arm. "By all saints: it's the Dutchman. How did he get here before us?"

Saara said nothing. In the midst of her spell-song, it is doubtful she even understood what Damiano was saying, nor why he pulled them to a rough stop in the middle of an empty corridor. Couchicou prodded them all with his nose, impatient to be going, and then he scented a person he had encountered before now in dubious circumstances. A person of no importance, a person he did not like. The war-dog rumbled like a disturbance of the earth.

Carefully Damiano quieted the dog before he allowed his party to proceed. He suffered a great curiosity to know what was Jan Karl's business.

"It is the seal of the Holy Father himself," the blond cleric was saying. "How dare you impede me in my duty, having seen it?"

It was unfortunately the effect of Karl's Teutonic accent upon the Latin languages that his words came out sounding peremptory at best of times, and when he was excited, quite rude. This effect colored many people's reactions to the Dutchman. Perhaps it was in some measure responsible for the fact that Damiano, whose nature was generally social, could not bear the man's company. Surely it was having that effect at this moment upon the pikemen, who had been already strung to a high tension by the near-presence of plague.

The guard beneath the single wall lamp slapped at the parchment Karl was waving about. He shifted his halberd over one shoulder. "You must give to me the authorization you speak of, Father," he said sullenly, "instead of using it to kill flies this way."

"Father?" hissed Damiano. "Is he a priest already? How could that be, if he was not one a half-hour ago? And if this fellow has no more interest in Evienne, then what is he doing here—getting recipes for poison from the cardinal? . . . I fear there is more going on here than I had thought." And he led Gaspare even closer to the light.

Jan Karl rattled long fingers against the parchment. "What do you want with a page of script, fellow? Could you read it if I gave it to you?" The Dutchman held his breath until the pikeman replied, "No, I cannot read more than a few words. But I know one man's writing from another. I am well acquainted with the signature of the Holy Father."

Jan relinquished the parchment. The guard slouching

against the far wall spoke then for the first time. "What does it matter whether the signature is the Pope's, when it is by order of Commander Sforza that no one can approach Cardinal Rocault?"

Jan's pale eyes widened for a moment like moons. "I know it is Commander Sforza who has this ordered, but it is from the Holy Father the commander's orders come," he stated, his langue d'oc slipping in his anxiety.

Saara herself added her small pushes to those of the dog. "She wants us to squeeze through," whispered Gaspare, as though Damiano was incapable of telling that for himself. The dark witch planted his feet. "Not yet. There are steps in the hall behind us. Can you hear them approaching? Something is going on here I think we ought to understand. Let's hug the wall and wait."

The first guard—the one with an eye for penmanship— smiled widely. "I believe you are right, Father. The Holy Father is the master of us all. Yet there is a certain method in this mastery.

"It is like this: God does not tell the crops to grow with an edict and a seal, but rather He tells the rain to fall and the sun to shine and therefore it is done naturally. In a like manner we soldiers offer our service to the church only through Commander Sforza, who being also a soldier governs us as naturally as the rain and the sun. Do you see?

"And the commander has said that the cardinal is not to leave his apartments in the infirmary except under the commander's eyes, and he has also said that no one at all is to see the cardinal. No one *has* seen the cardinal, in fact, since he was brought here."

"I have no orders concerning the Cardinal Rocault," said Jan Karl hurriedly. "It is only the little Italian girl I need for the information she possesses, naturally. I was told she is being kept somewhere down here."

"She certainly is," agreed the guard. "That is if you mean the little redheaded belle. They are together, for lack of space. So you see, Father, it would be difficult for you to see the girl without also seeing the cardinal, and that is exactly what you may not do." And then the soldier lifted his head as his less sensitive ears also picked up the tread of booted feet. "Perhaps here is the commander himself for you, and your problem can be quickly solved."

But apparently Jan did not want to talk to Commander Sforza. He shied like a horse and snatched at the parchment still held by the poetically minded guard. The guard, acting by reflex, hid the document behind his back and put one hand to his sword hilt. Seeing this, the Dutchman reconsidered his action and jerked away from sword and swordsman. In consequence he nearly blundered into the invisible Damiano, who made his own little dance to the rear.

Couchicou, the great hound, was not one to appreciate complex interactions. Neither was he aware that the group he shepherded through the Papal halls was invisible and so, unassailable. He interpreted the *pas de deux* as an attack upon one of his favorite people by one he did not particularly like. With a bass bellow he sprang, flattening the unhappy Dutchman and knocking Damiano into Saara and Saara into Gaspare until all fell down like gamepins.

She hit her head on stone, knocking herself dizzy. The endless chant was cut off short, and in that moment the ill-lit corridor became a sudden welter of frightened, struggling, highly visible figures, not the least perturbed of whom were the Pope's pikemen.

But a terrified cleric being mauled by a dog, and a man-at-arms with the hair straight up on his head are two different frightened beings and they behave differently. Jan Karl curled himself into a ball and rolled, slightly lacerated, between the wall and the nearest pikeman, who was in self-preservation holding the wolfhound off with his halberd. The other guard stared openmouthed at the three people who had erupted out of the floor, and he drew his sword.

At that moment came a booming hello from down the hall and a matching pair of warriors sprinted full tilt from the direction of the infirmary, their studded leather armor slapping against their legs.

Perhaps because the linguistic complexities of the situation were lost on her, Saara was first to take command. She sat sprawled on the flagstones on the infirmary end of the corridor. The dog's rush had sent both Gaspare and Damiano sprawling forward, past the guard's station,

into the unknown hall. "Run, Dami!" she cried. "Take
your Gaspare to his sister. Flee with her. I will follow
when I can."

Damiano got his feet under him. He had other ideas.
Stealth was a lost cause, certainly, but he still had re-
sources. With a word he summoned flame to each hand
and stepped toward the panicked guardsmen, seeking to
draw their attention away from his mistress.

But the task he had set himself was hopeless, for
nothing as common as a man aflame could pull the men's
attention away from the phalanx of monstrous bears, white
of fur and white of tooth, which stood shoulder to shoulder
and nose to rump, filling the hall between the infirmary
and themselves. All four soldiers gasped in synchrony,
while the air in the corridor grew very, very cold. The
single oil lamp on the wall flickered wildly.

Damiano himself stood in amazement, until all the
bears opened their mouths together and said quite clearly,
"Don't wait, my dear. Your boy has run ahead. I am in no
danger, but Gaspare is."

It was true. The boy was gone. Damiano's quick ears
could barely hear his light dancer's steps fading away into
the unknown corridor. Cursing Jan Karl and the hound
impartially, Damiano followed. Bestial roaring filled the
air, along with the *"yip, yip, kiyip"* of an outmatched dog.

He found the boy picking himself off the flagstone
floor, wiping a bloody lip. "Can't see a damn thing,"
whined Gaspare. Damiano gave him five fingers of light,
and together they loped on, encountering nothing more
except the end of the corridor and a heavily secured
wooden door. Behind this door someone was weeping.
The witch grimaced at the sound, for he had heard too
much weeping lately, and pathos had grown cheap. He
shoved open the bar, while the iron locks undid themselves. Damiano smiled thinly, for he took a certain pride
from his skill at opening things.

They found themselves in a plush, comfortably equipped
chamber that was lit by many wax candles but lacked all
sign of a window. There was a table spread for two people's
dinner: meat, cheese, wine and bread, none of which had
been touched except the wine. There was an ewer for
washing and a pot for pissing, both of which had been

touched. There was a divan, topped with a familiar shapeless featherbed, and upon that there was a form wrapped in blankets.

But that form was not Evienne, for she herself sat on a hard chair beside the table, with a brocade about her, and she shook with her sobs.

The place stank.

"Gaspare!" she cried tremulously. "Oh, I'm *so* glad to see you. Herbert is sick."

Damiano strode directly to the divan and flipped back the cover. Herbert Cardinal Rocault gazed up at him and whether the feverish eyes recognized in Damiano a lute player he had seen once only in the private chambers of the Pope, there was no telling. After a moment Damiano replaced the blanket more gently than he had pulled it back.

"No one came to take care of him," Evienne was explaining with difficulty. "They just shoved food under the door. There was only me. So much work.

"And now," she concluded, with a whistling sigh, "I don't feel well either. It is so depressing."

Gaspare held his sister's hand in a bone-crushing grasp. He looked at Evienne, recognized that she was tired, and saw no more. Partly this was because Gaspare was simple: that is to say, he had no second sight, and partly this was because he was not a very perceptive person where others were concerned. Mostly, of course, it was because he was Evienne's brother and between them was all the family and all the love either of them had ever known, and he was not able to imagine that his sister might be lost to him.

Damiano was different. He looked down upon Evienne and saw the rosy cheeks of pregnancy mottled with a grayish green, and her smooth throat swollen out of shape. "Oh, dear God," he whispered to the air.

Gaspare may not have been able to understand by looking but he could not escape the meaning of his friend's words. His hand slipped to the floor at Evienne's feet. He shook his head fiercely at Damiano. "No," he said. "No."

Once more he touched Evienne's hand and then turned again to the motionless Damiano. "You. If she's sick you have to *do* something!" he cried.

Damiano flinched. "Wh—what? What can I do, Gaspare? Saara and I—we've both told you already that there is nothing..."

Evienne stuffed her whitened knuckles in her mouth and bit down upon them. Then she sniffed. "Are you trying to tell me," she began with a certain rude energy, "that Herbert—that I—have got..." and then this spirit failed her. "Is it the plague?" Her frightened breath wheezed in and out, and then she squeezed her eyes shut. "Oh, no, I don't feel *that* bad—just kind of muzzy. And I ache, and it's so hot in here...." Her words trailed off. "I'm going to die?"

Gaspare screamed, "No! No, no, Evienne, you're not going to die, no, never!" And in a single motion he flung himself at Damiano and wrapped himself around the witch's knees, in terrible parody of his actions only a few weeks earlier when he had pleaded with Saara for Damiano. "Don't let her die," he cried shrilly. "Please, please, Damiano, don't let her die!"

It was as though he were praying to God.

With clumsy gestures Damiano freed himself and stepped over to this girl who had been so pretty. His large hands were shaking. "Signorina, I don't...I don't have any power over this thing. I'm only a man." Awkwardly he touched her hair.

Evienne's eyes were still beautiful, even through fear and disease. Shyly she took hold of Damiano's shirt and whispered, "I am not ready to die. Please understand. I know I must die but not now, for I am young, and this finds me in the middle of my sin. Who will absolve me, if I die here? Herbert? By Mary and all the saints, he's not the one to forgive sins he made happen himself, and he's in no shape to do it anyway. And then...and then I have a baby in me. How can I die now?"

"You see?" seconded Gaspare, as though Evienne's words had proven something. Then he hit his sister a weak blow upon the thigh. "Slutty bitch. What have you done to us now?"

In the distance the ursine roarings continued, along with the panicked cries of men. Damiano sank down upon the carpet and hid his face behind his hands.

Why did they both believe this impossible thing—

that he could cure the plague? Why did it hurt so badly within him that they should believe this? Saara, who knew so much about healing, knew there was no hope.

His course was clear to him. There was no sense in suffering the witnessing of this evil he could not help. Saara had discovered as much a generation ago. It would only drag down the healthy with it, to madness or suicide. The only recourse was flight.

Within a week he could be in Lombardy, upon the clean high hill where springtime reigned all the seasons, alone among the small high-meadow flowers with an elegant, barefoot mistress. Within a week, between Saara's magic and his own.

But Damiano did not move. Wonderingly he watched himself not moving. His resolution was formed, but he seemed to lack the power to carry it through.

Was it because Gaspare's red-fingered grip on his wrist could not be broken? Was it because Evienne was kissing his hand?

"I am not God!" Damiano shouted suddenly. "I . . . am not even one of his saints!"

"Not a saint, no, but almost," wheedled Gaspare. "You are such a good sort of person, Damiano. And you have an angel, and that means something. Send for your angel, Damiano, and tell him . . ." And the boy's eyes changed as he spoke, from his characteristic hysteria to something unfamiliar to Damiano: something calm and lucid and cold. "And tell him to send Evienne's plague into me.

"Yes, into me," Gaspare repeated. "Why not? I'm not anything worth saving. Not even much of a dancer, really. The only thing I do well is to judge other people's music, and no one will pay me to do that.

"But it's all the same to the plague, isn't it? Whether it takes a critic or the cardinal's mistress? And it must be possible to trade one to the other, too, for Jesus sent a man's devils into the pigs. Call your angel, Damiano, my good friend. Remind him of that gospel, if he does not remember. Please, Damiano. Do it."

Damiano called Raphael then, and the angel came.

It may have been only Damiano's imagination that

said the sick chamber did not smell so bad with Raphael standing in it, stainless and glimmering. It was certain, though, that with the first sight of the angel, the witch's misery became lighter, even though he knew how Raphael would answer his question.

He asked it anyway. "Seraph. Can you cure the plague?"

"Oh, no," moaned Gaspare, who blinked about owlishly, as though he might discover the tiny form of an angel in some corner of the room. "Ask more gently, Damiano, or he will never agree to help."

Raphael gazed beyond Damiano to the figure of the terrified girl, who rocked back and forth with her brother's arms wrapped around her and who did not seem to be listening. Then Raphael regarded the motionless form on the featherbed. "Damiano," he said quietly. "If I had power over the plague, no man would have ever died so."

"I thought as much," snapped the witch, and sorrow and frustration made him add, "For a spirit of great reputation, you can't do much."

Blue-black eyes returned their gaze to him. "I'm sorry, Dami. I didn't make my own reputation."

Gaspare only heard one side of this conversation, but it told him enough. "Don't accept any excuses, musician. We have managed so many hard things already—over the mountains at the end of winter, and through Provence starving to death—how can we let my pretty little sister just lie down and die? There must be another way!"

"There must be another way." Oh, Christ! the very words Damiano had used with the Devil, and with Saara herself. And the Devil had nearly had him for his arrogance, and how badly he had hurt Saara, who had done him no wrong, searching for that "other way."

It had been his father's obstinacy in him: that bullish Italian obstinacy which had led him along the odd paths of his life. Stealing witchcraft by force and giving it away in a single grand gesture that did no one any good at all. Making war with the flames of hell as a weapon, and using that weapon against Lucifer himself. Now he was a witch without a staff, singing his spells like a Lapplander—like an infant Lapplander, to be exact.

And no help to his friends at all.

Damiano's lips pulled back painfully from his teeth and he looked away from Gaspare. Had he his staff, he thought bleakly, he would at least try. With his staff he had not been a child in the making of spells. He had known that length of black wood better than his lute, at one time. Though he might fail, with his staff he would at least know how to try.

And then, between one moment and the next, he knew not only how to try, but how to succeed in helping Evienne. He remembered how, on the streets of Avignon, not far from the Papal Door, he had grabbed at Gaspare himself, as though to use the boy as a living focus for his magic, and then, sensing the danger involved, had drawn back. And he remembered how he had entered the earth and gathered the water from it, leaving only a song to mark his way home.

But he could not claim he didn't know what happened when power went from one person into another. Out of all the witches on the earth, he (and his lady) knew that best.

A witch did not die of the plague, or so said Saara. Not unless he used himself too hard. When he had been simple, he had been in peril of the plague. Now he was not.

Clear and accurate. But that statement was a knife that could cut both ways. And dear God, how it could cut! "What is he saying now?" whispered Gaspare excitedly, for in truth Damiano's attitude was that of one who was very thoughtfully listening to something. Instead of answering, the dark witch glanced over at his friend, heavy-browed.

Then he sank down on one knee beside Evienne. "Go away, Gaspare," he said. "Don't touch us."

Gaspare pulled back with alacrity. "Save her, Damiano. Please save her," he begged, his voice cracking with tears.

But the face which looked back at Gaspare's was frozen, and oddly pale beneath its strong coloring. "Be quiet," whispered the witch.

He put his right arm around Evienne's waist and she lifted her suffering head. But there was neither comfort nor gentleness in Damiano's eyes as his left hand wrapped her hair and pulled the girl backward, only a great concentration. "Look at me," he grunted at her. "Don't talk."

The stool overbalanced and Evienne lay back in a

tangle of skirts, supported only by Damiano, whose hands clenched and clenched, whose arms were trembling. In the girl's eyes despair had been diluted with a strange admixture of terror and hope.

When Damiano had stolen power from Saara, the staff had shown him how. It had felt very good, like wine and sunshine and victory, all together. When he broke the staff, releasing to her half his own soul—what then? What had it felt like, then?

It was not a good memory; it made his head spin, and his stomach tied itself in a knot. Damiano did not want to be simple again, and he did not want to stand in Evienne's position of helpless fear.

Once he had been reconciled to that life of many blindnesses. Once he had been prepared to die. Now he was not reconciled to any loss or limitation on a life grown rich as the orchards of Provence.

And Evienne was such an inconsequential person. Without either morals or aspirations, possessing only a little quick-fading beauty, she mattered to him less than his dog had mattered. Much less.

But being inconsequential did not make it easier to die. And how much he cared for Evienne, or even for her anguished brother, had nothing to do with it. Damiano sought the memory of his defeat, and when he had it, he used it to make a song: a song of fire and of loss. Silently it rang in his head. His lips pulled back from his teeth.

Evienne screamed, buffeted by a flaming wind. She arched her body and threw back her head. She cried for her brother to save her. Then she swooned.

And the girl was drowned in fire—Damiano's fire, a flame of brilliant, consuming color that covered her sweet body over until she looked like a soul in the pains of hell. Gaspare gasped and dived toward her, to free her from the witch's awful embrace. Slack-jawed, gray-faced, Damiano slapped him across the room.

He sang his fire into Evienne, feeling his strength enter all the wounded provinces of her body. He heard the dumb, smooth, insistent beat of her heart and he felt the ugliness of the damage plague had done to the veins of her body and in her lungs. Without thought his fire fed itself upon that evil. The wild bright flame grew hotter. It went white, then blue and sang with a pure and unwavering note.

But Evienne was not a staff or a cup or a cloud. Not a vessel of any kind which could be filled with magic, containing it. She was a living being and simple besides. Damiano's strength flowed into her and out again, running away over the carpet like a fire of oil on water. Again and again he filled her, forcing magic into flesh and soul not created to take it, until, by the time the flame ran quiet within a body revivified, Damiano was empty. He lay half across Gaspare's sister, voiceless, panting like a dog.

Far away along the long corridor, a bearlike bellow sharpened into a wail, as Saara the Fenwoman sensed her lover's magic flow out and be lost into the air.

Damiano did not hear her crying, for his attention was turned within, to where his new emptiness had found already a thing to fill it, to where within his trembling shell something unwelcome was finding a home. It was a thing like a groping hand, but fine as mist. It was mindless and determined and terribly hungry.

Damiano knew its name, and he had been expecting it.

For a moment he thought he would not be able to rise, and his hands scrabbled on the slates of the floor. But from nearby came a helping hand. "The devils into the swine," mumbled Damiano to Gaspare. "Strangely, I have never before thought of myself as a pig." He stood swaying for a moment and shook his head.

But it was not Gaspare who had helped him to his feet. Gaspare sat hunched over his sister, who slept now peacefully, with only a slight flush of the skin to mark her short visit in the Inferno. It was the fair hand of Raphael who steadied Damiano, and a white wing wrapped around him like a mantle.

He put an arm about the angel's waist, just below where the huge wings sprouted. "One more favor I have to ask you, Seraph," he whispered hoarsely, staring at the floor. "And I promise I will then request nothing else."

Raphael asked for no promises. He listened to

Damiano, folded his wings around him, and led him away.

Jan Karl burst into the room, bleeding from the shoulder, with his black cassock torn. "Evienne, you idiot, get off the floor. I have come to release you!"

Evienne woke up confused. These days she always woke up confused, and usually a little sick to her stomach as well. But this time her stomach felt fine, at least. Indeed, she felt fine all over, and quite ready to endure a little confusion if it meant Jan had come to get her. She flung herself to her feet, only noticing Gaspare as she bowled him over.

"Gaspare! How long have you..." Some part of her memory returned to her then. She turned to the bed where Herbert Cardinal Rocault lay unmoving. A brief glance told her he would never move again, and she jerked her hand back, shuddering. "Take me away now, Jan. Death frightens me so."

But at that moment Saara the Fenwoman entered the door, not with the form of a bear but in natural shape. "We have only a minute," she announced. "One minute before they are after us." Her eyes swept the room, resting only lightly on the girl before her, with her red hair and generous beauty.

"Where is Damiano?" she demanded, taut-voiced. "What has happened to him?"

Evienne took a possessive step nearer Jan Karl. She regarded Saara's delicate features with disfavor. "Who's this woman, Jan? Is she with you?"

"Where is Dami, you litter of fools?" cried Saara, and Gaspare, whom the events of the last few minutes had left speechless, rose from the floor.

"I... don't know, now," he said, his goblin eyes searching the chamber. "He was here a bit ago. He cured my sister of plague and then I turned..."

"He *what?*" gasped Saara, and once more Evienne shuddered wildly and hid her head against her protector's spavined bosom.

"Get me out of here, Jan. I can't take it anymore."

"He cured Evienne of the plague. He set her on fire, and I thought she would burn up, but instead she is better."

Saara stood perfectly still in the middle of the chamber. "I cannot see him," she said. "Nor hear him nor smell him nor feel him. Anywhere."

Through the streets of Avignon walked Damiano Delstrego, with the plague gripping him around the throat. Beside him came an angel who kept his feet from stumbling.

Never had anything ached so badly, nor had he ever been so sick at heart. It was as though there were needles in every joint of his body and hot lead in his lungs. The cheerful sun mocked him with every step.

Prayer behooved him, certainly, but he could think of no appropriate words except ". . . remember us now and at the hour of our death." This phrase repeated itself dreadfully and without comfort in his mind. O God, God, the sick man cried silently, will You remember Damiano, when Damiano has forgotten himself?

"Wouldn't you know," he whispered aloud, "that I would adopt a plague that was already half done with its job? It should take a man a day at least to be feeling this badly."

He walked on, blinking eyes which grew gummier all the time. "It is important," he insisted to Raphael, "that Saara does not find me, for what I have done she could also do, and I am not about to trade my beautiful lady's life for my own—or for that of Gaspare's ridiculous sister."

The archangel did not reply, but his wings contained Damiano in their own corona of light, and his hand rested on the mortal man's shoulder.

Soon they reached the South Gate of the city, which Damiano had never before seen. They passed beneath. "The gates should be locked," commented Damiano. "To keep the disease from spreading. I myself," he added, with a painful and obstructed sigh, "intend not to encounter anyone at all."

Here, close to the muddy banks of the Rhone, the land was broken into small checkers of vine and green wheat soft as velvet. The road ambled down, keeping close to the water. Under an azure sky, even the weeds were all in bloom. "Oh, God, it hurts!" cried Damiano, meaning either the beauty before him or the lancing pain in his body. He broke into sudden violent tears.

Which stopped just as suddenly, and he blundered ahead. "Raphael, you must take care of Saara for me. She has had so little happiness in her life, and she is so kind—do you know that when we were at war and her storm killed Macchiata she took me all unawares, and she might have killed me then, as she thought I had killed her Roman lover, and . . ." He ran out of breath and reeled, but the angel's hand steadied his steps. "Whatever—she could have killed me. She had every chance to do it and she just stood there and watched. I know I said I would never ask another favor, but Saara is a very gentle creature, Raphael, and you must take care of her."

The angel paused a moment before answering. "But she will not let me take care of her, Dami. She doesn't like me very much."

Damiano nodded, and immediately put a hand to his swollen neck. The hand, he saw, was discolored with purplish blotches. He let it drop. "That's true. Well then, you must tell her I said for her to take care of you, Seraph. It will come to the same thing in the end. Will you do that for me?"

"I will."

He found he was no longer walking on the roadway, but through the silky wheat grasses which rustled at the middle of his calf. They tempted him, these soft green mounds. It would be so much easier to lie down here and stare at the afternoon sky—the afternoon sky of Easter Sunday, Damiano realized, marveling. It was only today he had awakened from a bed of grass, drowsy with lovemaking and very near to Saara. . . .

"Oh, Mother of God!" he moaned, as for a moment the sunlight spun in circles through his head. "Saara! How I love her!"

"And I don't know if she will ever understand." He lifted eyes that had gathered pus like sand in the corners. "She will not understand why I chose to go with you in the end. She will think I did not care."

"I will tell her," whispered Raphael.

But it was doubtful Damiano heard. He was staggering now, and but for Raphael's help would have fallen with each step. "And what about my pretty lute? Who will get that—or will it wind up in someone's hearthfire?" He

winced. "No, it is as His Holiness said. I was not the first,
nor will I be the last. The lute will pass to Gaspare, I
guess. He deserves it, since he has always cared more for
the music than his own dancing." The sick man fixed
Raphael with an admonitory glare. "See that he knows
what to do with it, heh? Maybe he will have a nephew or a
niece to support, if I know the worth of a certain Dutchman."

And then Damiano's head spun like mad planets, and
only when the back of his head touched the earth did he
realize he was falling. He lay on his back and gasped like a
fish on the deck of a boat. "I guess . . . this is far enough. It
will have to be."

The sun moved silently and all the birds of springtime
made their pleasant racket. Raphael folded his legs under
him and sat with wings spread, looking (were there any to
see) like a hawk of alabaster over its prey. Damiano lay
almost as quiet as the sun, save for the sound of his breath,
which came like wind through a tunnel. His eyes wandered.

All was bitter, and the pain bit into his body. But he
was glad for the pain, for the moments when it abandoned
him were worse yet.

The sun was low already when he turned his head to
Raphael. "Water?" he asked. The angel went away and
brought some back in his hands. Three times Damiano
drank, tasting blood with the water from his cracked and
bleeding mouth.

He tried to sit up. "Oh, Christ! Why did this have to
be? Not the plague, Seraph. . . ." He then paused, involved with the effort of breathing.

"I mean why did you ask me to live again? I was ready
to die, only a month ago. Wasn't that enough? Hadn't I
done enough, yet—worked enough, sinned enough, been
sorry enough . . . ?

"Saara, too, had to be hurt?"

Gravely Raphael shook his golden head. "I don't know
why so much is asked of one and not another."

"It was you!" Damiano cried feebly. "You—cut my
hair. You told me not to be a saint. . . ."

"I did not," said Raphael, ruffling worriedly.

But Damiano finished the accusation. "You told me to
live."

He glanced down at his hands in the dying light.

Their color was nothing he did not expect, but the deepening sky was better to look at. "I think I would have made a good old man," he panted. "We might have had...children. Despite what Saara said, she doesn't know everything. Abraham's Rachel had a child. We might have had children." It was dark when next he opened his mouth, and that was to cry out in a panic, "My music! Oh, God, my music! Already now there are two changes to songs working in my mind, and I will never have the chance to try them out. I had only begun!"

Raphael was very near. He bent to kiss the misshapen face beside him, for on this point he understood Damiano very well. But the fever was upon the man: a foreign fire he could not master, but that discolored all his senses. He cringed away from the angel's touch. "Don't. Go away. I stink," Damiano growled savagely. "I can smell myself. Go away, you who are so fond of beautiful things. Go away."

Raphael did not go away, and Damiano, in mad rage, hit him three weak blows on the breast, as he hissed, "What a fool's game this month has been, pretending I had a life to live, when everything the Devil said came true— even to this. Probably the ruby, too. Probably I carried my own death into Avignon."

Raphael put his cool hand against Damiano's cheek. "Hush, Dami. Don't worry about my brother; even the truth becomes a lie in his mouth, and with my own eyes I saw you defeat him in the streets of the city."

"Defeat him?" rasped the dying man, shaking with the anger of his feeling. "He fled laughing, if he fled at all. Satan has always toyed with me, cat-and-mouse. I think I have found a way to happiness and he closes the door in my face. Always."

Then his red-rimmed eyes widened and his head dropped back against the flattened wheat. "Oh, Christ, to whom do I say this?"

"To me, Dami," answered Raphael, uncertainly. "To me you may say whatever you wish, for I am your..."

But Damiano only shrank deeper away. "How you have played with me," he hissed. "Pretending there were two brothers with the same face and different souls!"

"Dami!" Wings of pearl sprang stiffly upward. "What are you saying? Do not be confused between Lucifer and me! You know me, and if that isn't enough, you have seen my brother and me together. It is the fever. . . ."

"Yes, I know you at last, after all these years." Swollen lips drew back from Damiano's teeth, revealing a swollen tongue.

"And there is little to choose between you and your brother. Except that you have the greater hypocrisy. You used me, Seraph. Led me with your pretty tunes and your sermonizing—to be the butt of a joke! And what a joke.

"But for you I would not be here now. But for you I'd be a prosperous burgher-witch in Donnaz, or even back home, in Partestrada.

"But for you I'd not be lying here, perishing like a beast. Can you deny that, Raphael?"

The angel said nothing.

"What is it your brother called me, just this week? 'Bladder of blood and scum. Food for worms.' Yes, very accurate, for my blood is rotting, and already I can feel the worms. Is it fun to play with such toys as me, Raphael?"

The sick man's grimace became a snarl of pain. "Aggh! To think I was such a clod, dolt, simpleton—O Christ— that I was glad for your attention." His attempt to swallow sent trickles of blood down his chin.

"Well, now it's over, and I hope it was all to your satisfaction. May God curse you to the remotest stinking depths of hell!" With the strength of madness he raised himself head and shoulders off the ground, and his left hand flung wisps of torn wheat and bindweed at the perfect, agonized face of Raphael. "To hell! To hell! Damn you to hell!" cried Damiano, till his voice broke and he sank back into the green sea of wheat.

The angel cowered, as though these airy missiles had power to hurt. Then Raphael shrouded himself in his wings and covered his face with his two hands. His weeping, like his laughter, was like that of a man. He spoke one word: "Why?"

It was a question not addressed to Damiano.

Silence called him out, to find his friend looking up at him. "I am so very sorry, Seraph," the mortal said weakly. "I must have been mad for a little while. I said such horrible things."

Raphael gazed at the dying man and was not comforted.

"But what you said was true, my friend. If I had not touched you your path would have been different.

"But please believe me, Dami. If I did you harm it was by mistake. A spirit does badly when he makes changes in the lives of men."

Damiano closed his eyes for a moment, gathering strength. When he spoke it was clearly and after thought.

"If you had not touched me, Raphael, I would not now be Damiano—this Damiano—at all. And I'd rather be the Damiano you touched than anyone else.

"You must know that I love you, Raphael. You should never have let raving words hurt you like that. My teacher. My guide. For whatever you say about your role with mankind, you have always been the messenger of God to me, and by you I have tried to rule my life.

"In fact," and the black, swollen mouth actually attempted a little smile, "I probably should have loved the Almighty more and his music less, but then . . . that's the way I was made.

"Not a saint."

He tried to lift his left arm to touch the beautiful clean face so near his own, but his hand was tangled in the bindweed, and there was no strength left.

Carefully Raphael freed the long fingers with their broad, knobbed joints, and he lifted Damiano's hand and kissed it.

This time the smile was a success. "I don't hurt anymore," Damiano said. Then he closed his eyes and turned his head to one side. With his free hand he scraped at his face, as though to ward off the tongue of an affectionate dog. "Not now, little dear," he murmured, and gave a quiet sigh.

After that the breath did not rise again.

Coda

All through the radiant night an owl flew above the city of Avignon, blotting the dust of stars with its passage. It might have been hunting rats, so purposefully did it circle, and so low to the ground. But if it was hunting, then this was a bad night's hunt, for never once did the raptor fold its wings and plummet toward a kill.

But the rats of Avignon were not a wholesome food, anyway.

In the third black hour, her heavy talons clutched to one of the teeth of the spire of the Pope's Chapel. Its dry bird's body panted and quaked beneath its plumpness of feathers and its pinions hung down limp as tassels, for an owl is not an albatross, to take its rest in the air.

Saara, also, had not slept much the night before.

No sight, nor sound, nor smell nor touch of him. . . .

She tried not to think, for it was difficult to think and be an owl at the same time. Besides, she had spent the hours before sunset thinking, and it had done her no good.

He had cured the plague. Gaspare said he had cured the plague (which was an impossible deed). That he had burned it out of the red-haired girl with flame. Saara remembered Damiano's sweet fire, extinguished in her presence that day, and she mourned it, not knowing if she mourned the man as well as the magic.

He was not in the palace, for she had searched the palace, even to the piled dead under sheets in the infirmary. That search would have been interesting, had Saara the time to care, what with the hidden storehouses and hidden women scattered through the rambling work of stone. There were pictures, both beautiful and curious, and at least one of the

Benedictine nuns was born sighted. But she had spent no thought on either the house or its occupants.

No sight of him, no sound. . . .

She had followed the ox wagons, and in the shape of a dog, thrust her nose among the dead. So many. So many.

Too many people here: meaningless, chattering, blind people, whose quotidian deaths meant nothing to her.

The little redhead, too, was a creature that meant nothing. Without brain or bravery, clinging to that wordy bald man who had screamed like a rabbit when the dog bit him. At least they were a pair that matched. Barnyard fowl, the both of them. (She thought, perforce, in owlish images, and opened her beak in what might have been a cruel owlish smile.)

What had Damiano done to himself for the sake of that bit of red fluff? So free with his pity he was, that he might have given anything. She recalled his stricken face when, along the infirmary corridor, one single dying man had seen them pass. She remembered how he had come (a phantom with huge black eyes) to Lombardy, escaping horror and the pain of the lash.

And she saw him as he had been only one night ago, close above her in the dark, soft-eyed, smelling of grass.

The owl's talons slipped against the spire of stone, and her shape wavered, for no owl's body or soul could contain what Saara felt with the image of her young lover filling her mind.

Better not to think. Better, perhaps, to be angry.

At Gaspare's sister? Yes, why not: fat little hen whining, "Death frightens me so, Jan. Take me away from here." Or at Gaspare himself—another squawking chicken, occasionally turning nasty. Had she traveled and studied and suffered and endured and built her art upon experience, for her life to become the plaything of such mannerless infants?

She could kill the bitch. Why not? She had killed before. The blond unborn-looking fellow would give no fight at all, and Gaspare? To strangle him would be a sizable pleasure.

One heavy, scaled foot scraped flecks of stone from the spire, but then Saara shuddered. Bits of white feather sailed away in the spring breeze, starlit.

She wasn't going to kill anyone. That was the owl talking, not Saara herself. Never again would she willingly kill, and especially not the redheaded girl for whom Damiano had . . .

Better not to think.

Mad orange eyes stared upward, like brass platters set to catch the stars. The only things above her *were* the stars, and the strange dead-tree symbol of the Christian religion, which had been set at the very top of the building.

Damiano (like Guillermo, like Ruggerio) was a Christian. Maybe he was even more of a Christian than the others. Perhaps she ought to ask the help of the Christian elementals in finding him.

Saara did not know the proper incantations to address that symbol of crossed logs. She ground her owl-beak and did her best.

Other wings lighted beside her own. "You, Chief of Eagles," she cried in surprise. "Are you a Christian spirit?"

Raphael was slow in answering. "Among other things."

In the gleam of his plumage and the power of his eyes Saara recognized suddenly that force, greater than her own magic, which had hidden Damiano from her. The owl hissed like a snake. "Take me to him."

"It is for that I have come," answered Raphael.

The rising sun turned the back of her head to red gold. Saara sat upon the damp earth with her hands in her lap, hands curled like an owl's talons. "Didn't you care to bury him?"

These were the first words she had spoken since seeing the body in the wheatfield. She did not turn her head to see whether Raphael was still behind her.

"I didn't think of it," the angel replied quietly.

"That's all right," grunted Saara. "I'll do it. I have a lot of experience at burying people." Then she added, quite casually, "Why can't I cry, I wonder?"

A wind blew from the northwest, making Easter Monday much colder than all the previous week. Yet the chill could not muzzle the courting birds, nor take the sparkle from the wax-green leaves of the nearby grapes. In the distance a single horse or mule whinnied his presence, answered at great length by an ass in a field nearby.

Saara felt the bite of the wind and huddled against it. She might have slowed the air, or warmed it, but neither seemed worth the effort. "You knew, did you not, when you led him here, that I could have saved him?"

Raphael sat down beside her. Without interest she noted that the spirit did look more like a man to her than an eagle. She was sure it had not always been so, for her people knew the Four Eagles of old.

"I knew it. He knew that also," Raphael said. "That is why he bade me hide him from you."

"From me?" she asked, and then, out of nowhere, the tears came. "From me especially, he wanted to die hidden?"

The angel bent his wings around her and they hung in the air not touching, for his desire to comfort warred with the knowledge she did not want her comfort to come from him. "He knew that to save him, you would have taken the plague in his stead."

Now her eyes swam over, and the angel dissolved in her vision like a reflection of the moon in disturbed water. "Yes! I would have been happy to die in his place. I am old, and he is—was—young. I have had a life: children, lovers, much travel. It was not pleasant, but it was long and full of things. I would have been happy.

"Can you tell me . . ." and Saara took a ragged breath, "that he was happy to die in the place of that . . . sister of Gaspare's?"

Raphael sat still. There was no softness in his face as he said, "It was very hard for him to die. And part of that was because he feared you would not forgive him."

"Not forgive . . . oh, no." Saara threw herself forward on the earth, so that her head was only a few inches from the abandoned thing in its rich clothing, with its face covered with leaves.

But she lay passive only for a minute, and turned then on Raphael with newly minted anger. "Why did you let him do that for her? Didn't you know what such a deed would cost?"

Raphael nodded his head. "Yes, I knew." His blue eyes met hers evenly.

"He couldn't have done it but for you!" she cried

harshly, pulling away from the compass of his wings. "But for you I would have found him. But for you, Damiano would be alive now!"

Again the angel nodded.

"Why, then?"

"Because he asked it of me."

"You were his friend!"

Raphael's eyes widened. "I still am."

Saara opened her mouth and cursed Raphael to his face.

His great wings sank in discouragement upon the green wheat. Their pinions lay all awry. "Please," whispered the angel, "try to understand. I did not want Damiano to die. I love him, and all he might have become. But what I did was by his choice, for it was his to choose, not mine. You would have done the same, Saara, in my place."

"Oh, would I?" She could think of nothing to say to this, but after a small pause she observed, "Perhaps spring is not a bad time to die, after all. It is warm, at least, and one is spared the worst of the flies.

"Maybe I will try it out."

Raphael straightened. His wings bowed upward in alarm. "No, Saara. Please don't. There is something else Damiano said, when he spoke of his love for you. He said you were to take care of me."

"Of you? *You?*" Her head snapped up, framed in disheveled brown hair. "Chief of Eagles, have you *need* of anyone's care?"

Then Raphael dropped his eyes. His beautiful hands folded and refolded in his lap, and Saara could see stains of blood and other dirt upon the gossamer fabric of his garment. "I might," he admitted, and then he glanced up at her again with something like embarrassment in his face. "I think it's possible that I will, soon. I am not what I once was."

Drying her eyes, she stared the angel out of countenance. "Yes, I see. You are smaller, I think. Your light is more soft. What happened to you?"

"Damiano," replied Raphael without hesitation.

She grunted, and then a little grin forced its way onto her face. "I can believe it. Did he come to you with an Italian head full of sad songs, pestering you to do things you didn't want to do, taking no denial, but talking, talking, and talking always?"

"Something like that." The angel smiled.

Then her glance sharpened. "And are you sorry now, after he is dead and flown away, while here we sit all soiled with dirt and crying?"

There was nothing but peace on Raphael's face as he answered, "Not at all."

Saara was weaving a green shroud from grasses the angel picked for her, when she heard (for the second time in as many days) a commotion of hooves in the distance. She raised her head to discover young Gaspare once more clinging to the neck of the black Barb gelding like a monkey. The horse proceeded by leaps and bounds with a clean disregard for property lines. His elegant black nostrils gulped air and his tiny fox ears swiveled independently. At his side ran a hound the size of a pony. They were heading, more or less, toward Saara.

She rose to greet the boy, who promptly slid off the animal's withers to the ground. The dog trotted past her, as did the tall horse.

"I am so glad," began the redhead, with a painful groan. "I had no idea whether that cursed black jackass was taking me to my friends, or to Cloud-Cuckooland. And that impossible dog!" Gaspare turned his head in irritation at the noise the wolfhound had begun: a deep, resonant, heartbreaking howl. "What *is* the creature doing now?" He took a step toward the animals.

Saara put a restraining hand upon him. "No, Gaspare. Don't look. Don't go near. It is deadly for you."

But the dog had uncovered enough. Gaspare had no need to approach further.

"Dam . . ." He fell to his knees, gasping. "Dead? Is he really dead?"

"Yes." Saara stepped away, feeling that another person's grief—especially the grief of a selfish, hysterical child like Gaspare—would tear her apart.

But the boy surprised her with five minutes of kneeling silence, in which he stared blankly, round-eyed, biting down upon his hand. Then he crawled to his feet. "I . . . have made a very bad bargain," he said in a small voice. "My great musician for my slut of a sister. It was not what I asked of him. Not at all."

"It wasn't?" asked Saara, feeling her dislike of the boy soften slightly.

With a certain dignity he replied, "Of course not. It was me he was supposed to ask that one . . ." and Gaspare pointed toward Raphael (who stood in his slightly soiled robe on the far side of the body, comforting the beasts) "to exchange for Evienne. Me, not him."

And Gaspare's poor silly face grew longer as he added, "I have a sense of values, after all."

He blinked the tears from his big pale eyes. "He—he was . . ." And then he struck his fist into his palm. "I don't think you really know what he was, lady." His glance at Saara was once more arrogant. "To you he was a pleasant fellow to tickle under a sheet, hey? And what was better, he might make a song about you, glorifying your name to everyone in Avignon."

Saara had no time to reply to this unjust accusation, for Gaspare exploded. "But what he was, was the best! The very best in all of Italy and in France besides!

"For one year. One little year," Gaspare concluded in a softer voice. He shrugged. "And that is it, I guess.

"I won't see one like him again." Gaspare gazed down at the blackened and meaningless flesh that had contained his friend, until the lights of pearl which were reflected even over that sunken cheek and dead hand caused him to raise his eyes.

He stalked over to Raphael. "Hey. Raphael. I can see you."

The angel was taller than the boy. Slowly he smiled down at him and gently he extended his hand.

Gaspare took it less gently, in both of his. He did not return the smile. "You were supposed to give the plague to me, not him."

The angel did not correct this version of the story.

"You got it wrong, so you owe me something," Gaspare declared.

Still the angel made no denial, but gazed seriously into the laughable gooseberry eyes. Gaspare said to him, "Teach me the lute."

Volume Three in the Damiano series

RAPHAEL
by R. A. MacAvoy

Weakened by his contact with mortals, the Archangel
Raphael falls prey to his brother Lucifer, who strips him
of his divinity. Sold in the Moorish slave markets,
confused and humbled by his sudden humanity, Raphael
finds his only solace in the friendship of the dark-skinned
Bedouin woman Djoura, and the spiritual guardianship
of his former pupil Damiano Delstrego.

Accompanied by the rakish Gaspare and an ancient black
dragon, Damiano's beloved Saara embarks on a quest to
rescue Raphael. Their odyssey leads them to a shattering
confrontation with the Father of the Lies and a transcen-
dent reckoning with destiny.

0 553 17156 9

TEA WITH THE BLACK DRAGON
by R. A. MacAvoy

TEA WITH THE BLACK DRAGON is the tale of an uncommon woman named Martha Macnamara, zen practitioner and Irish fiddler, and an equally uncommon man named Mayland Long, who has seen a thousand seasons come and go, and once lived as an Imperial Chinese dragon.

Together they find magic, adventure and romance as they search for Martha's missing daughter in the baffling world of computer wizards and electronic crime.

Come, take tea with the Black Dragon. Your world will never be the same.

TEA WITH THE BLACK DRAGON

'A very different fantasy . . . It's a wonderful book, with beautifully drawn characters and a tremendously varied and unexpected background. I wish I'd written it' *Elizabeth A. Lynn*

'A delight from the cover onwards' *Analog*

'MacAvoy offers that bright and treasured rarity, a new fantasy tale. The bizarre mix of middle-aged eccentric heroine Martha Macnamara, a Chinese dragon in a most unlikely form, and a Silicon Valley computer scandal infuses this book with a remarkable new flavour' *Locus*

0 553 23205 3

TWISTING THE ROPE
by R. A. MacAvoy

Re-enter the fantastic world of the Black Dragon . . .

If you were among the many readers who lost their hearts to R. A. MacAvoy's remarkable first novel TEA WITH THE BLACK DRAGON, you are invited to join Mayland Long and Martha Macnamara in an astonishing new adventure filled with music, mystery and magic.

And if, by some chance, you've not yet had the pleasure of their company, prepare yourself for a special sort of treat. But be warned. In the world of the Black Dragon, nothing is quite what it seems . . .

Praise of R. A. MacAvoy's
TEA WITH THE BLACK DRAGON

'A gem of contemporary fantasy'
Chicago Sun-Times

'A deft blend of the oldest of magicks in a dragon, and the newest sorceries in computers . . . I thoroughly enjoyed it'
Anne McCaffrey

MacAvoy serves up a couple of treasures: her characters . . . She's certainly worth watching'
Washington Post Bookworld

0 553 17385 5

THE BOOK OF KELLS
by R. A. MacAvoy

A majestic novel about a young artist who opens a portal in time to the turbulent age of tenth-century Ireland, THE BOOK OF KELLS is a grand tale of rousing adventures and miraculous wonders – a haunting tale of love and faith so strong that it conquers time itself. Here is R. A. MacAvoy's masterwork of fantasy, a story you will never forget.

Acclaimed author of TEA WITH THE BLACK DRAGON and the DAMIANO trilogy, and winner of the John W. Campbell Award for best new writer, R. A. MacAvoy is a major fantasy writer, praised for her vividly rendered settings, rich imagination and profoundly human characters.

0 553 17188 7

DAMIANO
by R. A. MacAvoy

He was called Damiano Delstrego; wizard's son, alchemist, heir to dark magics. Yet he was also an innocent, a young scholar and musician befriended by the Archangel Raphael, who instructed him in the lute.

To save his beloved city from war, Damiano left his cloistered life and set out on a pilgrimage, seeking the aid of the powerful sorceress Saara. But his road was filled with betrayal, disillusionment and death, and Damiano was forced to confront his dark heritage, unleashing the hellish force of his awesome powers to protect those he loved.

'I am greatly impressed with Ms MacAvoy's *Damiano*. Her style is masterly and her sorcerous duels hold one spellbound. I recommend it highly'

André Norton

0 553 17154 2

RIDERS OF THE SIDHE
by Kenneth C. Flint

Out of the mists the Fomor came to enslave the isle of Eire, a dread race of twisted men ruled by an inhuman lord: Balor of the Evil Eye. But a champion came from out of the sea, a youth called Lugh, seeking his destiny, sent to Eire by the seagod Manannan MacLir to fulfil an ancient prophecy.

With Gilla, a jesting rogue, and Aine, a spirited warrior-woman he came to love, Lugh challenged the Fomor to restore the True King to the throne of Tara, and summoned the Silver Warriors of the Sidhe to fight in the realms of men.

The tale of Lugh of the Long Arm is among the greatest of all Celtic myths. Now this mighty legend comes blazing to life in a new retelling filled with all the fire and magic of the ancient bards.

'An excellent fantasy adventure' *Science Fiction Chronicle*

'Enough derring-do for at least one Lucas film' *Locus*

0 553 17250 6

SONG OF SORCERY
by Elizabeth Scarborough

THE WITCHMAID'S QUEST

Maggie Brown was a hearthwitch, good at whipping up banquets and starting fires, not a *true* witch, like her Granny, who could turn men into birds, or her Aunt Sybil, who could see into the present.

But when Maggie's beautiful but empty-headed sister Amberwine ran off with a raggle-taggle gypsy, it was up to unkept, unruly Maggie to track her down.

So she set out with Ching, the talking cat, and Colin Songsmith, a travelling minstrel who was not so bad once you got to know him, to bring back her wayward sister.

On the way they met a gnome, a unicorn, a mermaid, a lovesick dragon and an enchanted bear, braved ambush, flood and abduction by gypsies, and stormed the lair of a particularly evil sorcerer, in a rescue mission fraught with excitement and danger.

0 553 17282 4

A SELECTION OF
SCIENCE FICTION AND FANTASY TITLES
AVAILABLE FROM BANTAM BOOKS

THE PRICES SHOWN BELOW WERE CORRECT AT THE TIME OF GOING
TO PRESS. HOWEVER TRANSWORLD PUBLISHERS RESERVE THE
RIGHT TO SHOW NEW RETAIL PRICES ON COVERS WHICH MAY
DIFFER FROM THOSE PREVIOUSLY ADVERTISED IN THE TEXT OR
ELSEWHERE.